More Advance Praise

"Extraordinary. With her trademark [...] r characters, Amy Hatvany has written [...]
—Melissa Senate, autho [...]

"*Outside the Lines* is a sad, funny, heartbreaking and heartwarming novel that explores the boundaries of love and how we break those boundaries in its name. You'll want to read this book slowly. When you're finished, you'll want to read it again."

—Rebecca Rasmussen, author of *The Bird Sisters*

Praise for *Best Kept Secret*

"I'm telling everyone about *Best Kept Secret*. It's the realistic and ultimately hopeful story of Cadence, whose glass of wine at the end of the day becomes two . . . then . . . three . . . then a bottle. I love that Cadence feels so familiar, she could be my neighbor, my friend, or even my sister."

—Jennifer Weiner, #1 *New York Times* bestselling author

"I was transfixed by Cadence and her heart-wrenching dilemma. The writing is visceral, the problems are real, and there are no clear solutions. You won't want to put it down."

—Emily Giffin, *New York Times* bestselling author of *Something Borrowed*

"Touching, hopeful, and so real . . . Amy Hatvany writes with depth and compassion about a secret many have kept as she offers the miracle chance of starting over. I loved these characters and this novel."

—Luanne Rice, *New York Times* bestselling author of *The Silver Boat*

"Rarely do I find a book that stays with me long after I've finished it, but this is definitely one. The writing is warm, witty, thoughtful, and that ending—I'm still thinking about it."

—Stefanie Wilder-Taylor, author of *Sippy Cups Are Not for Chardonnay*

"One of the most compelling books I've read in years. This heartfelt, heartbreaking, and ultimately uplifting novel will start an important dialogue about the secrets we keep . . . and it could even save lives."

—Sarah Pekkanen, author of *Skipping a Beat*

ALSO BY AMY HATVANY

Best Kept Secret
The Language of Sisters

outside
the lines

A NOVEL

AMY HATVANY

WASHINGTON SQUARE PRESS

New York London Toronto Sydney New Delhi

W

WASHINGTON SQUARE PRESS
A Division of Simon & Schuster, Inc.
1230 Avenue of the Americas
New York, NY 10020

First Washington Square Press trade paperback edition February 2012

WASHINGTON SQUARE PRESS and colophon are registered trademarks of Simon & Schuster, Inc.

For information about special discounts for bulk purchases, please contact Simon & Schuster Special Sales at 1-866-506-1949 or business@simonandschuster.com.

The Simon & Schuster Speakers Bureau can bring authors to your live event. For more information or to book an event contact the Simon & Schuster Speakers Bureau at 1-866-248-3049 or visit our website at www.simonspeakers.com.

Designed by Meredith Ray

Manufactured in the United States of America

10 9 8 7 6 5 4 3 2 1

Library of Congress Cataloging-in-Publication Data
Hatvany, Amy.
    Outside the lines : a novel / Amy Hatvany.—1st Washington Square Press trade pbk. ed.
        p. cm.
1. Mentally ill parents—Fiction. 2. Fathers and daughters—Fiction. 3. Adult children—Family relationships—Fiction. 4. Domestic fiction. I. Title.
    PS3608.A8658O97 2012
    813'.6—dc22

                                                                    2011018727

ISBN 978-1-4516-4054-0
ISBN 978-1-4516-4055-7 (ebook)

For Stephan

A person needs a little madness, or else they never dare cut the rope and be free.

—*Nikos Kazantzakis*

outside
the lines

October 2010
Eden

The call came at three thirty in the morning, a time slot predestined for the arrival of bad news. No one calls to tell you you've won the lottery in the middle of the night. Your boyfriend doesn't call you to propose.

The shrill of my cell phone dug into my dreams and wrenched me from sleep. *This is it,* I thought. *He's dead.* Six months ago, I'd given the morgue at Seattle General my number along with a copy of a twenty-year-old picture of my father. "I don't care what time it is," I told the hospital administrator. "If he turns up, I'll come right away."

The picture was the last one I had of him. In it, his blue eyes were bright and his smile was wide. My father was a tall man, whip thin but sinewy and strong. He had wavy black hair like mine and wore it parted down the middle and to his shoulders, like Jesus. His expression in the photo gave no clue of the chemical anarchy wreaking havoc in his brain. It was invisible, this enemy that attacked his moods. "This is *not* an illness," he said insistently. "This is who I *am*." He pounded his chest with his fist in emphasis, in case my mother and I were confused as to whom he referred. The medications changed him, he said. They brought on such terrible mental inertia that every one of his thoughts became an unwieldy, leaden task. He preferred the wild highs and intolerable lows to a life of not giving a damn. At first, as a child, I didn't blame him. After he disappeared, blaming him was all I did.

I dressed hurriedly in the dark of my tiny bedroom. Jasper lifted his head, wagged his tail two times, then promptly put his head on my pillow and let loose a guttural sigh. He was ten—an old man of a dog. His brindle coat was wisped through with silver; he slept pretty much twenty hours of the day. I happened upon him in the alley of one of my first restaurant jobs, luring him toward me with bits of pancetta. He wiggled his fat little puppy butt in response and I was a goner. I took him home that night.

Before leaving the house, I walked to the kitchen to put food in his bowl, then returned to my room and scratched his head. "Be a good boy, Jasper," I told him. "Make sure to bite any robbers." His tail gave one solid thump against my mattress in response to my voice but otherwise, he didn't move. He wouldn't venture to the kitchen until after six, our normal waking time. I joked with my friends that Jasper was the best and most predictable man I knew. With him, I'd shared my longest and most successful relationship.

It was early October and the chill in the air had taken on a crisp, palpable bite. I sat in my car for a few minutes with my hands tucked between my thighs, waiting for the engine to warm up. My thoughts seesawed between the hope that the man lying on a slab in the morgue was my father and the prayer that he wasn't. I was ten years old the last time I saw him, numbly watching from our front porch as the medics took him away. This was not how I wanted our story to end—my father dead before I had a chance to heal the hurt between us. But at least it would be an ending. At least I could finally let him go.

After backing out of the bumpy gravel driveway on the side of my house, I maneuvered through my quiet Green Lake neighborhood and headed south. The streetlights glowed eerily amber in the early morning fog as I drove toward downtown. The Columbia Center tower loomed in the distance, about ten blocks from my destination. I'd spent enough time on the streets of downtown Seattle to have its geography stitched into the grooves of my mind. Off the Union Street exit, the hospital was to the east, a well-known homeless shelter fourteen blocks west, an illegal tent city three blocks from there. I pictured the cobblestones of Pioneer Square and the railroad tracks beneath the viaduct where so many of Seattle's homeless population dwelled. I wondered where they had found him. I wondered if he had thought of me before he died.

This last question repeated in my mind as I parked in the hospital garage. I quickly found my way to the basement and was escorted into an icy room barely lit by bluish fluorescent bulbs. On my left was a wall that looked like a stainless steel refrigerator with multiple square floor-to-ceiling doors. The air hinted of something black and fungal beneath an intense antiseptic overlay of cleaning products. I imagined that scent was death.

The technician who accompanied me into the room was the antithesis of what I expected a morgue worker to be—all blond hair and surfer-boy good looks instead of brooding, pale-skin goth. He stood next to me, smelling of spearmint gum. I heard the gentle pop in his mouth before he spoke.

"Are you ready, Ms. West?"

"Yes," I said. I was more than ready.

A dark-haired girl dressed in light blue scrubs stood by the refrigerator wall and opened one of the doors, pulling out a body beneath a white sheet. She stood back with her hands linked behind her in an at-ease stance. The blond technician reached and pulled back the sheet, folding it neatly across the dead man's chest. I kept my eyes on the substantial rise of the man's stom-ach. *This is a mistake,* I thought. *My father isn't fat.* He could have gained weight, sure, but that was another one of the side effects that made him forgo his medications.

The technician stepped back from the gurney and turned his head to look at me. "Is it him?"

I forced my gaze upward to the man's swollen, puffy face. His skin possessed a dusty pallor, as though someone had pulled gray cotton batting over every inch of his flesh. He had scraggly black eyebrows and a beard; his long hair was wet and brushed back from his face, falling in a spidery fan beneath the back of his skull. His eyes were closed.

"I'm not sure," I said. "It might be. Maybe. I haven't seen him for twenty years." My heart fluttered in my chest as I spoke. I didn't expect not to know. I thought I'd recognize him right away. Had my mind erased so much of him? "Can I see his wrists?"

"His wrists?" said the technician. The girl didn't speak.

"Yes."

The technician reached under the sheet and pulled out the man's limp, beefy arm, hairy side up.

I swallowed hard. "Can you turn it over, please?"

The tech gave me a sidelong look but he did as I asked. I looked at the underside of the man's wrist, poised and prepared for the sight of angry red and thickly knotted scars. I blinked a few times to make sure I wasn't just seeing what I wanted to see. But the gray flesh was smooth and bare. If the man was my father, it wouldn't have been. That much I knew for sure.

Relief collided messily with disappointment in the back of my throat. "No," I said, releasing a breath it felt like I'd been hold-ing since my cell phone woke me. "It's not him." A few errant tears edged their way down my cheeks.

"Are you sure? He fits the description. Except for the extra weight, but we figured maybe he'd gained it and you wouldn't know."

"I'm sure," I said. "It isn't him. But I can understand why you'd think it was." I wiped my face with the back of my hand. "How did he die?" I asked, gesturing to the man on the gurney. The man who was not my father. I repeated this phrase silently in my mind to make sure I actually registered it. It wasn't him. My father wasn't dead. There was still a chance I could find him.

"Cardiac arrest," the dark-haired girl said. "The medics brought him in from Pioneer Square. He was dead before they got to the ER."

"Well, I hope you find out who he is," I said. *He's somebody's son. Maybe even another person's father.*

"It's not likely," said the technician. He snapped his gum, then looked guilty. "Sorry."

"That's okay." Death was normal to him; he was accustomed to treating it casually. He spent more time with it than life.

"Let me walk you out," the girl said.

"Oh, I'm fine," I said.

"I'm due for a smoke break anyway," she said, walking over to the door leading to the outside hallway and opening it for me. "It can get a little tricky down here with all the weird turns to get to the outside world. I think they make it that way so no one accidentally ends up down here if they don't really need to come."

"Okay." I looked one more time upon the man who was not my father. "Good luck," I whispered to him, and both of the technicians looked at me strangely. Let them look. The poor man obviously had a rough life; he deserved a few well wishes for wherever he ended up.

Moving along the dimly lit corridor with the girl, I noticed our footsteps quickly fell into the same pattern, her white hospital clogs squeaking along the linoleum. We didn't speak.

"Can I ask you something?" she finally said when we turned a corner and arrived at the door to the hospital parking garage.

"Sure," I said, holding the door open for her to step through. We walked a little farther, stopping twenty feet or so from the door. She pulled out a pack of cigarettes from the pocket of her scrubs. She shook one out of the pack and held it, regarding it thoughtfully before she spoke.

"So, I'm curious." Her voice echoed a bit in the almost empty garage. "Why are you trying to find your dad if he's been out of your life so long? I never knew mine and I couldn't give a shit where he is. I mean, it's cool and all that you want to, but don't you think maybe he likes it better this way? Maybe he doesn't want to be found."

"He's sick," I said, shrugging as I scanned the garage for where I'd parked my car. "He doesn't even know he's lost."

After I drove home from the hospital and took Jasper for a quiet, predawn stroll around Green Lake, I called my mother. It was our Friday morning ritual and God forbid I forgot or slept in past eight o'clock. Each week she sat at her kitchen table sipping green tea and tapping her fingers next to the phone, waiting for it to ring. She wouldn't call me; I was the child. It was expected that I call to check in.

Our weekly call had irritated Ryan, my most recent boyfriend, beyond belief. "Can't we have just one Friday morning where you don't have to call your mother?" he pled with me. "You're thirty-one, for Pete's sake."

"Did you just use the phrase 'for Pete's sake'?" I teased him, trying to lighten the air between us. It had become heavy during the last months of our relationship, bristling with unmet expectations. "What are you, fifty?"

"I'm serious, Eden. You're tied way too tightly to your mother's apron strings."

I snorted. "Oh, so I should be like you, then, and talk to my mother only when I need another withdrawal from her bank account?"

If I remember correctly, that was one of the last arguments we had. Six months later my life returned to normal with Jasper in his rightful spot beside me in bed. It was easier that way.

"Good morning, honey," my mother chirped when she answered her phone.

"Hey, Mom," I said. I sat on my couch, a chocolate leather hand-me-down from my mother and stepfather's last redecorating overhaul project. My mother changed her décor almost as often as some people change their bedsheets. She was a relentless bargain hunter and could completely change the look of a room without spending more than five hundred bucks. When they redid their living room, they gave me the couch, a teak coffee table, and a set of three wrought iron lamps. The only off-the-shelf piece of furniture I owned was the television, and that's only because the flat-screen they had offered me was too large for the walls of my tiny box of a house.

"How are you this morning?" she asked. "Did you have to work last night?"

"Yep. A corporate event in Bellevue. I'm wiped." I worked as the head chef for a large catering company while I tried to build up enough capital and connections in the industry to launch my own restaurant. I dreamed of opening a small, classy café with a lengthy wine list, no more than ten tables, and a seasonal, eclectic

menu. Unfortunately, unless I could find a ridiculously rich inves-
tor, this dream wouldn't be realized any time soon.

"How late did you get in?" Mom asked.

"Only eleven, but I got a call from Seattle General around
three thirty so I've been up since then."

"Oh no," said Mom. "What happened?"

I paused. I knew she wasn't going to like what I was about
to share, but I also knew she wouldn't leave it alone until I told
her. I took a deep breath. "They thought they had Dad in their
morgue."

As I suspected she would be, Mom was silent.

I went on. "It wasn't him, though. It looked like him a little
bit. The dark hair and the height were right, but this guy was really heavy and—"

"And what?" she said, interrupting. Her voice was sharp.
She didn't like talking about him. She'd rather have pretended he
never existed—to tell herself the story that I'd simply appeared in
her womb.

"And he didn't have the scars Dad would have. On his wrists."

She sighed. "I don't get why you're doing this to yourself."

"I don't know how to explain it to you. It's just something I
need to do."

She didn't understand. My search wasn't about her—I knew
she was done with him long ago. That last time, the time when
the medics came, was the end for her. A week later she served
him divorce papers in the state hospital and he signed them without dispute. But me, I wasn't done. I wanted my father. When he
didn't come to see me, when he didn't even try to call, I began
conjuring him in the face of every man who crossed my path.
Each of my breaths became a wish that the next corner I turned
would be the one where he'd appear.

It only took a year for me to stop wishing. At eleven years old, I told myself I was done with him, too. *Screw him,* I thought. *He doesn't want me. I don't want him, either.* By that time my mother had married John and I told myself my new stepfather could fill the empty space in my heart. John was a good man, a fireman with a generous soul. But it didn't matter how good he was or how hard he tried. He couldn't fit in a space custom-built for another man.

My father did try to get in touch with me after I graduated high school, but after eight years of no contact from him my hurt had hardened into hatred and I refused to respond. He was staying on his meds, the two letters I received said. He was back in Seattle. He was holding down a job. *Back in Seattle?* I wondered. *Where did he go? Did something happen that kept him from coming to see me?* I told myself I didn't care. *Too bad,* I thought. *Too little, too late.* I threw his letters away.

There were, of course, moments when I missed my dad. My black hair was just like his, as was my pale skin, narrow face, and vivid blue eyes. Looking in the mirror was a frequent, painful reminder that he was gone. Once, in my early twenties, I went to a friend's wedding only to make a quick exit when her father walked her down the aisle. It was too much to stand, knowing my father would never do the same for me. As more time passed, I started to toy with the idea of trying to find him. Then, last fall, I sat by my mother in the hospital, holding her hand and watching poison drip into her veins in an attempt to annihilate the jagged cells that had already stolen her breasts. I suddenly realized how selfish I had been—how little time any of us are given with those we love. I started thinking more and more about my father, wondering where he was and if he was safe. His letters mentioned time he spent living on the streets. I worried that he was driven back to a homeless existence not only by his illness but by my lack of response. I worried I wouldn't find him in time for him to forgive me.

"You need to find him even after everything he put you through?" My mother's voice yanked me back to the present.

"He's been through quite a bit himself, if you think about it," I said. Jasper whimpered at my feet, where he was taking a much-needed nap after our Green Lake excursion. I rubbed his back with the tips of my toes and he quieted.

"That was his *choice*. Or have you forgotten?"

"I haven't forgotten anything." I sighed. "I don't want to argue about this with you, okay? Can we just change the subject, please? How's Bryce? Is his competition this weekend or next?" My twenty-year-old half brother, Bryce, was the reason my mother married John six months after my father disappeared from our lives. A successful high school wrestler, Bryce had opted for a career in personal training and competitive bodybuilding instead of college.

"It's tomorrow at two. Can you make it?"

"Maybe, but it depends on what time I have to work. I think we have a wedding, but I don't remember for sure. I'll check the schedule when I get in today." I paused. "How's John?"

"He's fine. Down at the station on the tail end of a seventy-two-hour shift. He'll be home tonight."

"You're feeling okay? Not overdoing it?"

"Yes, dear. I'm feeling fine. Dr. Freeland says my counts look great. My energy's up. So you can stop mothering me."

"I'll stop if you do," I teased.

"That's impossible. When you have a baby you'll understand."

"I'd like to have a husband first," I said, then wished I could pull the words back. I wasn't up for one of her pep talks around finding a man.

She sighed. "Well, maybe if you went out a little more you'd meet someone."

I stifled my own sigh. "I work weekends and I'm thirty-two years old with a decent IQ. I have zero interest in the club scene. Most of the men there are only interested in hooking up, anyway. They're not looking for a wife."

"What about the Internet? My friend Patty found her husband online. She said it was like shopping for a credenza!"

I laughed. "I don't think so, Mom. I feel like it'll happen if it's supposed to."

"Oh, fine. I just hope for you, sweetie. You have so much to give."

We hung up a few minutes later and I continued to sit on the couch, thinking about my romantic past. Working in the restaurant industry, I'd dated plenty of men for one or two months. Even a year at a time. Only two relationships before my more recent one with Ryan turned into anything serious.

First was Wyatt, a fellow culinary student whose dark brown bedroom eyes and wicked smile never failed to make my heart do backflips in my chest. He had this effect on a lot of women and I counted myself lucky to have landed him. After a year of dating, filled with lots of great sex and what I thought was meaningful conversation about sharing our lives and someday opening a restaurant together, I realized that I wasn't the only item on Wyatt's daily menu. It turned out he had bigger appetites than that. A dishwasher one night, the hostess and then me the next. He dumped me unceremoniously for a line cook at Denny's.

Sixteen celibate months later, Stephen appeared in my life, a man whom I swore I would not fall in love with after the torture of what I had gone through with Wyatt. But Stephen was sensible, a financial planner who started his own firm at twenty-five years old. He was a safe choice, a careful choice, and he bored me out of my skull. I learned that no matter how much I wanted it to, a successful romance couldn't be based on a mutual adoration of organization and Excel spreadsheets. After eighteen months of trying to meld myself into someone he actually could love, I came to my senses and broke up with him.

Not too long after that particular breakup I read somewhere that until a woman resolves the issues she has in her relationship with her father, she isn't capable of having a lasting, intimate connection with a partner. If there's something broken in her primary relationship with a male, the odds of success in any other romantic relationship she forms are pretty slim. I thought about Wyatt, who had been like my father in so many ways— irreverent, fun, and unpredictable. I wondered if I was attracted to him because of that. The idea creeped me out. I began to wonder if it wasn't the men I chose who were dysfunctional, it was me.

Three hours later, after a catnap and another quick trot around the block for Jasper, I drove downtown and entered the enormous hotel-style kitchen where I spent a majority of my days. Emerald City Events was one of the biggest catering companies in Seattle, located in a large brick building overlooking the waterfront. We provided services to any event, from intimate book club get-togethers to the largest wedding receptions imaginable. The company employed about twenty people in the kitchen, not including the waitstaff, and being the head chef was a busy job.

That night we had three cocktail parties to prep for, one on-site, and two five o'clock deliveries. With rush hour that would prove to be a good trick—I'd need the drivers to be out the door no later than three thirty, just to be safe.

All three parties had ordered chicken satay with spicy peanut sauce. Everyone loved the dish, but it was a pain in the ass to get timed correctly, especially so it wouldn't dry out before service. To avoid that particular pitfall, I made sure to soak the cut-up chicken in a flavorful yellow curry marinade for at least eight hours before I cooked it, but if we didn't get them on the grill soon, they wouldn't cool down enough in time for transport. I was elbow-deep in the preparation of the dipping sauce that would accompany the chicken—a mixture of peanut butter, coconut milk, red curry paste, fish sauce, and sugared ginger—trying to find the exact balance between spicy and sweet. I wasn't in a position to get the meat on the grill.

"Can you get those chicken skewers fired, please, Juan?" I hollered from my station in front of the ten-burner Wolf stove. Ten of my other staff members worked diligently at their stations, cutting, slicing, and stirring according to the directions I printed out for them on a spreadsheet at the beginning of their shift. Their tasks were listed next to the exact time they should start and complete each. Cooking was a game of timing, and I loved it. Organization was key.

"Gotcha, boss!" my sous chef, Juan, yelled from across the kitchen. "I'm on it! The grill is hot as a mofo and ready to *go*." He spun around in some bastardization of a Michael Jackson move and pointed both his index fingers at me like they were pistol barrels. "What else you need?"

I laughed, shaking my head as I stirred the concoction in the enormous stockpot in front of me. "I need you to stop dancing and put together all the veggie trays while you cook the chicken. Wilson and Maria did all the prep earlier, I think. Everything should be in the walk-in."

"You got it!" Juan leapt over to the huge, stainless steel walk-in refrigerator and flung open its door. He was the only employee who didn't need a spreadsheet. I'd worked with him for about five years at that point and I knew I could depend on him to get the job done right. He was the tiniest bit crazy, but it was the fun, kooky variety of crazy, not the scary, I-might-stalk-you type, so while we busted our butts in the kitchen, he always entertained me in the process. At twenty-three, he still lived at home with his parents and five younger brothers and sisters, an arrangement I could never have fathomed for myself. But Juan's father was disabled after an accident at work and his mother had to care for him, so outside of a meager monthly allotment from the state, Juan was the family's only source of income. I made sure he took a hefty portion of any servable leftovers home with him at the end of his shifts.

Within minutes the heavenly scent of charred curry wafted through the air, making my empty stomach growl. I was blessed with a ridiculously fast metabolism—a gift from my father, I assumed, since my mother fought against every pound. I, on the other hand, couldn't go more than a couple of hours without some kind of sustenance, and no matter how much I ate I never seemed to gain any weight. My best friend, Georgia, cast evil curses upon me for this particular trait, while I simultaneously envied her naturally voluptuous hips and great rack. I wasn't super skinny by any means and my chest wasn't totally invisible, but my slender frame certainly didn't invite the wolf whistles Georgia earned just swaying down the street.

I finished the sauce and turned off the burner beneath the

pan. On my way to the table in the back of the kitchen that I kept stocked with snacks for the staff, I checked the sausage-stuffed mushroom caps that Natalie, one of my prep cooks, was working on. They were precariously overfull and, once baked, would morph into a greasy, awful mess. "You might want to back down on the amount of filling, Nat," I advised. "Use the mini cookie scoop instead of a spoon. That way you get them proportioned exactly the same. You'll need to redo them."

I heard her sigh quietly. "Is there a problem?" I asked. She was new; I had meant the advice to be helpful, but I knew from experience my sense of efficiency could be interpreted as brusque. Or bitchy. Take your pick.

"No, Chef," she said. "I'll redo them."

"Be quick, please. We're on a tight schedule." I hopped over to the snack table and made myself a quick sandwich of thinly sliced grilled flank steak and Swiss cheese on a small ciabatta roll. Juan strolled down the line from his station; his lanky frame and fluid movements suddenly reminded me of my father's. I'd managed to push Dad out of my mind since the conversation with my mother that morning, but there he was, back again. The image of the dead man on the gurney in the hospital flashed in my mind, and the bite of sandwich I had just swallowed stuck in my throat.

"You okay, boss lady?" Juan inquired as he sidled up next to me and reached for a three-cheese onion roll. He was the only employee I let call me anything other than "Chef."

I swallowed before speaking. "Yeah, fine. Just tired, I think. I had a late night."

"More private detective work?" I'd told Juan the basics of my trying to find my father. How I'd started by simply putting the name "David West" into an online search engine, then checking every major city's online white pages for his name. David West was an incredibly common moniker—over three hundred in the greater Seattle area alone.

"What are you going to say?" Georgia asked me when I informed her of my plan to call each one of the Seattle numbers. "'Excuse me, but do you happen to be the David West who abandoned his daughter and spent much of his adult life in the nuthouse?'"

"No," I had laughed. "I'll just ask to speak with David West. I'll know his voice."

"You think?" Georgia appeared doubtful.

"Yes."

I made the calls. None of them were my father, of course. I had an old address—the Seattle return address on the letters he sent ten years ago—but I soon discovered the last officially known record of his whereabouts was the state mental hospital out past Monroe. They hadn't seen him in three years and wouldn't give me any more information other than that he had left against medical advice. So after my failed phone calls, the next natural place to look for him was the streets, the only other place I knew for sure he had been.

Juan's voice brought me back to the kitchen. "Yoo-hoo? Eden?" He waved a hand in front of my face. "You in there?"

I blinked and smiled at him. "Yeah, I'm here. Sorry."

"So, more detective work?" he asked, prodding.

"Sort of, I guess." I didn't feel like describing my trip to the morgue. "I'm going to a new homeless shelter tonight. The one down on Pine?"

Juan picked up a piece of pineapple and popped it in his mouth. "You want company?" I shook my head and took another bite of my sandwich. "Awright," he said. "But if you ask me, a pretty lady like yourself shouldn't be wandering the streets at night on her own."

"I appreciate your concern," I said, tossing the remainder of my sandwich in the trash. My appetite had left me. Juan meant well, I knew. But I'd made it this far without a man to look out for me. No reason to start needing one now.

"Eden West, *come on down*!" my father shouted from the base of the stairs. We were playing *The Price Is Right* and he was Bob Barker. It was a cold and clear Sunday morning and my mom was in the kitchen making breakfast. The smoky scent of bacon wafted through the hallway where we played. The sun shot a kaleidoscope of color through the beveled stained glass of our front door onto the floor. I sometimes liked to lie in that spot, pretending the patterned hues decorating my skin were a tattoo. At ten years old I fancied myself a rebel.

I raced down the stairs in my nightgown and bare feet, skipping over the last three steps to land with a decided thump next to my father. The wide wooden planks beneath me creaked in protest and the crystal chandelier above the dining room table tinkled.

"Eden!" my mother yelled from the kitchen. "This house is *not* your personal jungle gym. Settle down!"

"Sorry, Mother!" my dad yelled back in a girlish, mocking voice. "Won't happen again!"

I giggled and my father winked at me. My father's winks were our silent language. *It's you and me, kid,* they said. *We're the only ones who get it.*

"Now, tell me, Miss West, just how excited are you to be

here?" He held a wooden spoon like a microphone and moved it toward my chin.

"Very excited, Bob." I lowered my voice to what I thought was a very grown-up, womanly tone. In that moment, the love I felt for my father was a vibrant, sparkling heat. It lifted me out of my fears, carried me above any of the pain I might have had. It made me feel like I could do anything, be anyone. It felt like magic.

"Which door would you like to choose?" He gestured toward the front door.

"Hmm," I said, tapping my index finger against the corner of my mouth. "I think I'll go with door number one, Bob."

"Excellent choice, Miss West. Excellent choice." He made a two-foot jump over to the door and the chandelier tinkled again.

"Eden!" my mother shouted. "Knock! It! Off!"

"Sorry, Mother!" I yelled, and winked at my dad, who laughed.

"That's my girl," he said. He placed his hand on the doorknob and wiggled his thick black eyebrows suggestively. "What could it be? What . . . could . . . it . . . *be*?" He flung the door wide open.

"A brand-new car!" I screamed. Forgetting my mother entirely, I jumped up and down, screaming and clapping my hands, pretending to be excited about an invisible vehicle. My father threw down the spoon and grabbed me. He hugged me tight, lifting me up and twirling me around the room. My legs spun out behind me. He held me so tightly I couldn't breathe.

"Dad, you're squishing me!" I gasped. I felt my ribs clicking against one another beneath the pressure of his embrace.

"David, please!" my mother said as she rushed into the hallway to see what the excitement was all about. She wore a nightgown the same sky blue as her eyes and her thick blond hair was braided down the center of her back. "Put her down! You're going to break something!"

"Never!" said my dad. "She just won a brand-new car, Lydia! We have to celebrate!"

"It's January," said my mother. She inched around us to shut the front door, her braid swinging like a rope. "Our heating bill is already atrocious."

"Then we'll live in her car!" my dad proclaimed. "Right, Eden?"

"Right!" I gasped again, and he finally set me down. My mother gave me one of her pinched, disapproving looks and I dropped my gaze to the floor, gingerly rubbing my sides and breathing hard. My father sidled up to my mother and grabbed her, spinning her around to kiss her soundly on the lips.

"You know you love me, Lydia West," he said with his face less than an inch from hers.

I held my breath, waiting to see how my mother would respond. It was up to her, I thought. She held the power over which direction he'd go, whether or not he'd spin out of control. She could talk him down, touch his face and soothe and distract him like I'd seen her do countless times before. "Let's go to a museum," she would say. "Let's go find a park we've never been to before and you can sketch the trees for me." She could help channel the energy I saw whirling behind my father's eyes. She could push it onto a path where no one would get hurt.

Instead, she stared at him and put her hands on his chest, pushing him away. He stumbled backward, catching himself from falling by throwing his hand against the wall behind him.

"Have you been taking your medication?" she asked. Her voice was flat.

My insides went cold. I hated it when she asked him that

question. Especially when I knew the answer was no. I'd watched him flush the entire contents of his prescription down the toilet a week ago.

"Our secret, right, Bug?" he whispered, and I'd nodded. My father's secrets were a dark and heavy burden in my chest. Sometimes I worried I carried so many of them they might rise up and blossom as a bruise beneath my skin. Then there would be no doubt—I'd be exposed for the liar I was.

"Yes, I've been taking my medication, *Dr. Lydia*," said my father. His smile melted into a sneer. "Would you like me to take a fucking blood test? Or would you just like to have me locked up again?"

No, I silently pled. *No. Please don't send him away.* A jittery panic rose within me. The last time he'd been at the hospital for a month. Our house was quiet as death.

"Don't swear in front of your daughter," my mother said quietly. "Breakfast is ready."

"I'm not hungry," my father said as he grabbed his coat from the rack by the door. "I need to go. I have places to be, people to see. People who *appreciate* me."

"Daddy—" I started to say. But it was too late. He was already gone.

January 1989
David

That bitch, David thought as he got into his car and revved the engine. *That sanctimonious, self-serving, judgmental, boring* bitch. He noticed he wasn't wearing any shoes. Or pants. His Sunday morning outfit consisted of cutoff black sweats and a bright yellow V-neck sweater. He looked like an anorexic bee. "Bzzzz . . ." he murmured as he jammed the gearshift into drive and pulled away from the curb, tires screeching. He was sure Lydia was watching from the living room window. He threw a halfhearted middle finger in her general direction, just in case.

The radio blared AC/DC's "Thunderstruck." The thrumming vibrations soothed him as he thought about where he could go. Cuba? Mexico? Hawaii? They'd love him in Hawaii. They were laid-back there. They wouldn't care if he wanted to run naked in the surf at dawn or howl at the autumn moon. *Hang loose, man,* they'd say. *Mahalo.* He could learn to carve. He could sell his wares to the tourists—men in checkered swim trunks and fat women in bikinis. Or maybe he should head north, to Bellingham. Close to the Canadian border. There were hippies there, he thought. *I could give up painting and weave shit instead. Blankets. Or those things you put hot pans on . . . what are they called? Oh yeah, trivets.* He'd be a trivet maker. He'd bond with the pot-smoking liberals and set up camp with them in the woods.

Pot. Now there was a good idea. He wondered if his friend Rick was up yet, if he'd slept off the buzz from the night before and was now open for business. Rick dealt the best weed on the coast. Gave David a discount, too, since they'd gone to high school together. Used to get stoned out of their minds in the enormous tangle of rhododendron bushes across the street from the school gym. He slammed on his brakes and flipped a U-turn in the middle of the road, ignoring the horns that blared around him. "Fuck you and the horse you rode in on, cowboys!" he yelled. "Go to hell. Go straight to hell. Do not pass go! Do not collect two hundred dollars!"

He was hungry. Starving, actually. A little bit dizzy. He couldn't remember the last time he'd eaten. Friday, maybe? He'd been painting for days, locked in his studio. Lost in swirls of ocher and green, swept up by the glory of blue. This morning, when Eden got up, he promised he'd take her to Shakey's Pizza for lunch. She loved the Laurel and Hardy black-and-white movies the restaurant played. Eden. His sweet Eden. Nothing like her mother. Eden loved him. Eden loved to play, to join in on any idea David conjured up. A lemon stand instead of a lemonade stand. A midnight frolic in the front-yard sprinkler. Waking up to make cookies at two o'clock in the morning. Mmm . . . cookies. Maybe he should stop at a bakery and pick some up. Or maybe he should make them himself. He doubted Rick had any baking supplies. David did his cooking with Eden. She loved it. Loved the mix of ingredients and creativity. She'd be an artist, like him, for sure. Or a lawyer. His little girl knew how to stand her ground in an argument.

God, he couldn't focus. His thoughts pinballed around inside his head. It felt as though someone else was pulling back the plunger, sending random, rapid-fire thoughts shooting through his brain. He wasn't the person playing the game.

Did Eden tell Lydia that he had flushed his meds again? Did his daughter rat him out? Was she a traitor, like all the rest? Like the nurses in the hospital who convinced the doctors to inject his meds when he got caught hiding the pills under his tongue? No, Eden wouldn't do that. Eden understood him. Eden loved him exactly the way he was. He had to go back to her. He had to. But he didn't want to calm down. He liked himself like this. He liked the rush, the energy, the thrill of moving from one moment to the next with nothing tethered to him. If he was going to go home, he'd have to find a way to settle himself, at least to a point where he could get Lydia to forgive him. Yet another reason spending the day at Rick's was a good idea. Weed was the perfect downer. It settled the crazy, brought on the mellow. At least until it wore off.

The curtains were pulled at Rick's house, but that didn't mean his friend wasn't awake. He never let the light in, too paranoid someone would see him dealing and turn him in. David raced up the ice-cold cement walkway. His bare feet screamed in protest as they came in contact with the ground. He pounded on the door. "Rick!" he shouted. "C'mon, buddy. It's David! It's fucking freezing out here!" He danced on the frosty front porch, jumping from foot to foot, his hands tucked into his armpits to keep warm.

Rick's front door opened slowly. David pushed through the entry and a sleepy-eyed Rick stumbled back against the wall. He was in jeans and a torn white T-shirt. "Whoa, dude. Slow down. Where's the fire?"

"I am the fire, man. Got anything that can put it out?"

"Sure, dude. Sure. Hang on." Rick lumbered his thick, stubby frame over to the locked wall safe where he kept his inventory. It was covered over by one of David's paintings—an abstract watercolor of blues and greens littered with splashes of vibrant orange.

Rick gently removed the painting, then hunched in front of the safe, moving through the slow clicks of the combination lock. A naked woman came out of the bedroom, her hair a wild brown nest around her face. She scratched her ass.

"Is there coffee?" she asked, seemingly oblivious to her nudity. David felt a stirring in his groin. She wasn't his type. She didn't look anything like Lydia. Lydia was soft and blond; this woman was skinny and hard with a bad boob job. Her right nipple pointed off in the general direction of her bicep. He could see the puckered scars. He wanted to screw her anyway.

"I'm David," he said. "I'm an artist. The painting that hangs over the safe is mine. Have you seen it?"

The woman looked at him, blinking. "Nope. Sure haven't."

"That's Ashley, man," Rick said as he walked over to hand David a thick joint. David snatched it up and lit it using a match from a book he saw on the table. He took a deep drag and almost immediately his brain cells stopped slam-dancing against each other. "We just met last night."

"It's Angel, actually," the naked woman said.

Rick chuckled. "Oops. Sorry, baby."

"Whatever," Angel said. She sniffed. "Coffee?"

"I'm out," said Rick.

Angel dropped her chin to her bony chest and gave Rick a look, like *Yeah, and . . . ?*

"I'll go grab some." He picked up the keys that sat by the front door and slipped on a pair of Birkenstocks. He looked at David. "Want to come, man?"

David shook his head. "Think I'll stay here." He took another quick hit, held it deep in his lungs. "Keep Angel company."

"All right. Cool. Don't do anything I wouldn't do." He winked at David, then left.

David dropped onto the worn leather sofa and set the burn-ing roach on the edge of an already full ashtray. He stared at Angel. "You make it a practice to screw men who don't know your name?" He opened his legs so she could see the effect she was having on him.

Angel smirked. "Depends."

"On what?"

"What's my name?" She slid across the room and stood in front of him, her hands on her nonexistent hips.

"Fred?"

"Close enough." She straddled his lap. She smelled like sex.

"I'm married," he said. He thought about Lydia, who by now was surely searching through his things for the medication that wasn't there. He thought about Eden, sitting patiently in the liv-ing room waiting for him to take her out for pizza.

"So?" Angel said, and then she kissed him, pushing her tongue into his mouth. Her breath was sour. He didn't care. Eden would understand about missing lunch. In the end, Eden was al-ways ready to welcome him home.

Angel hadn't been worth it. David knew that now, as he drove toward home. But that's how it was for him. Impulses felt, ac-tions taken, regrets endured. He was disgusted with himself. With his lack of self-control. He was weak and stupid. Why couldn't he manage himself? He was an adult. An accomplished artist. Well, "accomplished" might be pushing it. Adequate. When he could get his shit together, the booth he kept at the North Seattle Street Fair during the summer typically sold out of his paintings. He taught classes at the community college and a few galleries had even shown interest in putting on a show of his work. But *how* to get his shit together, that was the challenge. Sometimes he couldn't finish a single thought in his head. One word ricocheted off the other and his world began to spin. He couldn't hold down a normal job. He couldn't support his family. He was a loser. A fucked-up mess.

He sighed heavily as he turned the car toward his street. Toward Lydia and Eden. The sex with Angel had been bad, awkward and unfulfilling, but things improved after she had her coffee, put on some clothes, and left. David sat with Rick for several hours, finishing off joint after joint, shooting the shit. Not having to do anything. Not having to be anyone. The pot turned down the volume on what seemed to be a thousand radios blaring in his head. David hated his brain. How it forced him to seek relief from himself. Lydia didn't understand why he wouldn't stay on his meds if they helped calm the storms that raged inside his mind. He didn't know how else to explain it to her. The meds not only erased his spinning thoughts, they erased an essential part of his soul. The very center of his being became fuzzy and disconnected. Would Lydia like that? Would she enjoy her life if she had to live it trapped inside a vat of wet cement?

It hadn't always been this way between them. They had met and married young—both only eighteen—but blinded by physical passion and youthful optimism, their adoration for each other knew no end. Even with a baby on the way, even with Lydia's conservative family screaming that she was making a mistake marrying David, they couldn't imagine their relationship failing. As a result of her strict upbringing, Lydia was a little reserved, so she was instantly attracted to David's more daring, flamboyant personality. His openness thrilled her. It drew her out of what she called her "tiny soap bubble of a life." Marrying him was her first blatant act of rebellion.

From the moment they began dating, David lived for entertaining Lydia. He loved to make her smile. He thrived on the dramatic, taking his behavior to whatever extreme was necessary in order to hear her laugh—frolicking around their tiny apartment wearing only his underwear, or singing the Beatles' "All You Need Is Love" to her as they shopped for groceries. But he soon learned it was the little things that pleased his wife most. A bunch of wildflowers swiped for her from an open field, or a quick sketch of the parts of her body David worshipped—her hands, her lips, the curve of her back. He would ask her to lie naked on the bed in the late afternoon sun, gently coaxing her limbs into the image he wanted to capture. He untangled her blond braid so her hair fell wild and loose over her shoulders. "Lie still," he'd whisper against the thin skin of her neck.

"How am I supposed to lie still when you do *that*?" she'd groan, exhaling a low, husky breath, looking up at him with her exceptionally clear blue eyes.

"Art is suffering," he'd tease. And then he sat back and drank her in, pulling her beauty out of the real world into the one he could only see in his mind. The world he traced onto the page.

Even with the birth of Eden when they were only nineteen, David and Lydia's early years had a glowing, easy lightness about them. Lydia worked at various office jobs while David stayed home to paint and take care of their daughter. This had been Lydia's idea—she was dizzied in the best way possible by David's creative energies and talents; she wanted nothing more than to support him in his dreams of being a respected artist. While they were in their early twenties, she helped him find galleries that might show his work; she set up the interview that found him his first job teaching a watercolors workshop. Their love appeared unique, impenetrable. And until Eden turned four, it was. That was when the impulses began, at first just a faint, broken echo in the distant corners of his mind. *You're trapped,* they said. *Run.* He could ignore them, then. Gradually, they became louder, irrepressible—a faster and faster beating drum. *Live,* they said. *Escape. Spin. Love. Fuck.* He felt stifled by his simple existence. The drugs Lydia and his doctors wanted him to take muffled the inspired rhythms that danced in his head, snuffed them out until he lost himself completely.

But hadn't today been another kind of loss? Running from his family? Having to apologize to Lydia, to beg for her forgiveness and understanding yet again? As each moment passed, he felt himself slipping down deeper. Blackness pulled at his thoughts, shadowing over any hope that he would escape this life unharmed. He wasn't sure he wanted to be there anymore. He wasn't sure if any of it was worth it.

He pulled up in front of the house and put the car into park but left the engine running. If he didn't have his studio set up in what used to be their garage, he could have just pulled right in and shut the door. Leave the car running and let the fumes overtake him. It would be quick and silent. No one else would have to get hurt. A quick flash of light glimmered in the front window as the curtains opened. Eden. She saw him. He might as well go in. He turned off the car and walked up the steps in the too-small slippers he'd borrowed from Rick.

"Daddy!" Eden squealed as she opened the door and jumped into his arms. "I was so worried about you!"

Still on the front porch, David wrapped his arms around Eden and buried his nose in his daughter's silky black, apple-scented hair. Would Lydia smell Angel, even beneath the earthy funk of the weed smoke he was drenched in? He needed to clean up before they talked. The last time he took off she'd seen the telling purple bruise on his neck when he returned. She knew right away what he'd done. Even though the doctors told her his impulsiveness might spill over into sexual behaviors, she hadn't believed them. David hadn't believed them either. Not until he was naked in a bathroom with Cerina, the manager of Wild Orchid, a gallery that had bought a few of his paintings. He threw up after the first time it happened. And yet later, he went back for more.

"I'm sorry, Bug," he said to his daughter. "I'm so, so sorry."

Eden rubbed her father's back and squeezed him tighter before sliding back down to the floor and looking up to his face with her almost violently blue eyes. "It's okay," she said. "We can always go another day." She smiled bravely, a thin, false happy mask resting over the disappointment David sensed beneath it. His brave, loving girl. He wasn't sure how he could have helped create something as perfect as she seemed to him. None of his paintings even came close to expressing her kind of beauty. It wasn't something he could capture on a canvas. It was something he lived and breathed.

"I'm going to shower," he said. He blinked a few times upon fully entering the house. Rick never had more than a tableside lamp on in his house. Lydia loved her brightly lit chandelier. David felt as though he were a mole emerging from the damp, dark earth. A stranger in a strange land. He didn't belong here. He didn't belong anywhere.

He took the stairs slowly, one at a time, feeling Eden's eyes on him the entire way to the second floor. The door to their bedroom was open. Lydia was sure to be inside, lying on their bed, a cold cloth over her swollen eyes. She cried when he left, though she tried to hide it from him when he returned. Lydia was so strong. Too strong, maybe, for the likes of him.

When he entered the room, he was surprised to see his wife

sitting calmly on the edge of the bed. She eyed him. "Glad to see you're alive. Your daughter was worried."

He dropped his chin to his chest and looked up at her from beneath his eyebrows with a questioning look. "And you⸮ Were you worried⸮"

"I don't know," she said flatly. "I don't know what I am anymore."

"That makes two of us," David said. He ran a nervous hand through his hair. It felt greasy. He didn't want Lydia to know about Angel. He didn't want to hurt her any more than he knew he already had. "I'm going to shower, okay⸮ And then we can talk."

"I'd like to talk now." Lydia shot him a cold stare with the same transparent blue eyes that had drawn him to her eleven years before. She had the kind of radiant beauty men felt compelled to write songs about and a soft, inviting nature that called out to his broken soul. The first time he saw her, he wanted her to be his safe harbor. His home.

"Can I have five minutes, please⸮ Just five minutes⸮ I smell like shit."

"You smell like pot. Do you think Eden doesn't know what it is⸮ With how often you've come home reeking of it⸮" She twisted a strand of her long blond hair around her index finger, then let it unwind.

"Jesus, Lydia," David said as he took the three steps to their bathroom. "I already feel bad."

"Not bad enough, apparently. What was her name this time⸮" Her words dripped with disdain.

David slammed the bathroom door behind him. He looked in the mirror and saw an old man. He was twenty-nine years old and his face was haggard and lined. His dark hair was a wild, matted mess around his head. After four days without sleep, he looked like a corpse.

"David?" Lydia stood outside the bathroom door. Her voice was muffled.

"What." David stated it rather than asked.

"It's getting worse."

"What's getting worse?" he asked her, knowing full well what she meant. He wanted her to say it aloud. Wanted her to tell him to leave. If she did, maybe he'd have the courage to do it.

"The . . . cycles," she said. "How quickly you move up through the highs and slip back down. The doctors said this might happen. They said if you didn't stay on your meds—"

"I know what they fucking said!" David snapped. "Don't you think I know? I'm the one they talk to."

She sighed. "They talk to me, too. When you're strapped down to a bed having sedatives shot into your arm, they're talking to *me*. They told me it's possible this could keep getting worse and worse if you don't control it." Her voice elevated and then caught in her throat. "I don't want Eden to see this. I don't think she'll survive."

David turned around and pressed his forehead against the door, holding on to the handle. He wanted to let her in. He wanted to have her take him in her arms and hold him the way she used to hold him. Back when they first met. Back when his mind was still his own. "What won't she survive?" he said. His voice was very small.

"You, David. I don't think she'll survive you."

January 1989
Eden

I watched my father ascend the steps. *He's too skinny,* I thought. The knots of his spine showed through the back of his shirt. He was becoming that word my science teacher taught us the week before. What was it again? Like a scorpion or a lobster? Next to math, science was my least favorite subject, so I had to rack my brain. *Oh, that's right. Exoskeletal.* Maybe a man like my father needed to grow a hard protective shell. My mother always told me he was just a sensitive artist. He felt things deeper than most people. Maybe if he had a shell he wouldn't hurt so much. I wondered if I could figure out how to grow one of my own.

I stood in the hallway, listening to my parents' raised voices upstairs. I didn't want to hear them arguing so I escaped to the kitchen. *I'll cook for him,* I thought. *I'll make him something to eat and he'll feel better.* When he was sad, when he locked himself in the garage, he could go days without eating, something I just couldn't understand. Even though I was skinny like my dad, I ate enough to feed an army, according to my mother. When money was tight, like I knew it was now, I tried to control how much I asked for, but it was hard. My father hadn't sold a painting in a long time, so my mother's job as the manager for an accountant's office had to support us.

I wished I was old enough to get a job, other than pulling

weeds for our neighbor, old Mrs. Worthington, and taking her dog for a walk. She only gave me a dollar a week and my mom made me put half of that in my bank account for college. I didn't know how to tell her I wasn't going to college. I didn't like school very much to begin with.

"That's okay, Bug," my dad told me with a wink when I confessed to him how I felt. "You're creative, like me. We don't like being told what to do with our time." There were even days that he would let me stay home with him after my mother had left for work. He'd call the school and tell them I was sick, asking for my homework assignments so I wouldn't get too far behind. We cooked together, or took a long walk just to follow a particular cloud in the sky, always sure to get home before my mother did. Dad tried to be careful about not doing this too often, but at my last parent-teacher conference Mom was shocked when Mr. Pitcher told her how many absences I'd had that semester. My parents had a huge fight in the living room when we got home, too angry with each other to bother making me leave the room. I sat quietly, not wanting to make the situation worse by siding with either one of them.

"She needs to learn, David!" my mother yelled. Her usually pale skin was bright red. "She needs an education!"

"I'm *giving* her an education!" Dad bellowed in return. "I'm teaching her about the school of hard knocks. I'm teaching her the names of flowers and how a saffron thread feels as it melts on her tongue!"

"She won't get a high school diploma for being well versed in the art of *saffron*."

"I didn't get a diploma," my father retorted. "And you married me."

"If I recall, that's a little tidbit from your past you didn't tell me about until *after* I married you." She dropped onto the couch and my father towered over her. His eyes were wild.

"Oh, so you regret it now?"

My mother shook her head and sighed in response, but my father continued before she could speak. "Her grades are fine, Lydia. She's not Einstein, but she's passing. Who cares if she's there every day? She's not going to need to be an expert in American history when she's running a kitchen."

My father understood me. He knew I longed to be a chef. I wanted one of those tall, puffy white hats. And a jacket that had buttons marching up the front like soldiers. As soon as I was fifteen, I was going to get a job waiting on tables and have someone teach me how it all worked.

But at ten, the fanciest thing I knew how to make was macaroni and cheese from a box, so I got the water boiling and grated about a cup of extra cheese. The powdered stuff just didn't add enough cheesy flavor, my dad said. He was the one who taught me that using half-and-half instead of the skim milk my mom kept in the refrigerator made all the difference in how creamy my sauce turned out. He was the one who said that as long as I was careful, ten was plenty old enough to learn how to operate the stove.

"Throw in a dash of garlic powder, too," he said the first time he let me make the boxed pasta on my own, watching over me through every step. "And salt and pepper."

"How much should I put in?" I asked him as I stirred the contents of the pot, careful to hold on to the handle firmly so the pot wouldn't wobble off the burner.

"Just a pinch," he said. "Start small, so you can add more if you have to. Taste everything, every step of the way. You can always add more, but if you put in too much right away, it'll be ruined." He tweaked my nose with a playful pinch. "Remember the artist's rule: less is more."

I smiled at him. "Less is more," I repeated solemnly. I trusted him, even though part of me wasn't sure if that was such a good idea anymore. My mother had cried that morning after he left. She went up to her room and shut the door. I knew better than to follow her. Instead, I did my best to clean up the kitchen from her pancake mess, wrapping the cooked ones in plastic and putting them in the freezer to throw in the toaster another morning.

I took a shower and brushed my teeth and hair, got dressed, and then found a good book to curl up with under a blanket. While I didn't like most of my classes at school, I did love to read, always imagining myself as the heroine in a story. I thought being Anne Shirley, the spunky orphan in the *Anne of Green Gables* series, might be less stressful than dealing with my father's moods. I identified with Frances Nolan in *A Tree Grows in Brooklyn* and her loving but turbulent relationship with her head-in-the-clouds father. But my most recent favorite was *Are You There God? It's Me, Margaret.* I was positive I'd get my period any day.

It only took a couple of hours for my mother to emerge from her room. A shorter time than usual. I heard her door open and her footsteps as she walked across the hall to my room. I looked up at her from my spot on my bed and set the book down onto my lap.

"Hi, Momma."

She smiled at me, but it didn't quite reach her puffy, red-rimmed eyes. She looked like I did after Rachel Myers told me she didn't want to be my best friend anymore. I had cried every day for a week. "Hi, baby," my mom said. "You okay? Did you get some breakfast?"

I shrugged. "Not hungry." She gave me a doubtful look. "No,

really," I said. "I wasn't. I cleaned everything up, though. The bacon is in foil in the fridge and the pancakes are in the freezer."

She came over and sat down on the edge of my bed, reaching out to cup my face in her palm. "How did you get to be such a good girl?"

I shrugged again. I didn't think I was that good. If I were, wouldn't my father want to be with me more? Wouldn't he take his pills like he was supposed to so my mom wouldn't get so mad at him?

"You're worried about Daddy," she said, and I nodded slowly.

"He'll be okay," she said, trying to reassure me, dropping her hand from my face and patting my leg. She didn't sound like she believed her own words. I knew she was sad about how my dad was acting. She missed my old daddy—the one who made sure I got to my doctor appointments and sang her mushy love songs when she came home from work. I couldn't remember the last time my mother had kissed him or shown him any other kind of affection. I had foggy memories of when I was a toddler, watching them dance together, hearing the sweet bubbles of her laughter float through the air.

She sighed and stood up. "I think I'm going to watch an old movie. Want to join me?"

I shook my head and held up my book.

"Okay," she said. "Come down in a bit and I'll fix us some lunch. Are sandwiches okay? I know you were supposed to go out for pizza . . ."

"It's fine," I said, not wanting to talk about my father's outburst or the fact that he'd broken yet another promise to me with her. She went downstairs, and despite her offer of lunch, I stayed in my room, subsisting off the candy bar stash I kept in my closet. I couldn't be around her when my father took off like he had. I could feel her anger and disappointment. I sensed it disconnecting her from him in a way that scared me. *Don't make him leave,* I prayed, unsure if anyone or anything was actually listening. *Don't make my daddy go away.* When I finally heard the familiar grumble of his car out front, I threw down my book and raced down the stairs.

Now, as I crumbled up the leftover bacon into the macaroni and cheese, I heard the water running in my parents' bathroom above me. Next, I tore up lettuce over a bamboo salad bowl, poured in pre-shredded carrots, and added plump cherry tomatoes as a finishing touch.

I heard my father's footsteps before I saw him. He had on jeans and a white T-shirt. I gave him a bright smile. "I hope you're hungry!" I said, gesturing to the table I had just finished setting. "I made it just the way you like it. Where's Mom?"

"She's tired. She's in bed." He shuffled over to the table as he spoke. His hair was wet and plastered against his head. His eyes were so empty and sad I couldn't stand to keep my gaze locked on his. I busied myself by scooping him up some salad and pasta onto a plate. He sat down, slowly, like an old person. Like my grandpa who was dead, but who used to give me a quarter to sing him a song when we visited him in the nursing home.

"I made it with extra cheese and bacon this time," I said. "I thought you'd like that."

"Thank you, honey," he said, his voice cracked by tears. "I don't deserve this." He reached for a fork and held it for a moment but was shaking too hard to keep it in his grasp. It dropped to his plate and then the wood floor with a clatter. He let go of a shuddering sob.

I threw my arms around his neck and hugged him. "It's okay, Daddy. I'll get you another one."

"I'm useless," he cried. "Totally useless. I'm a terrible father. I'm a terrible painter. I should just leave . . . you'd be better off without me. Everyone would." He shoved his face in his hands, making it awkward to keep him in my embrace. I could feel his tears drip down on my forearm. His pain bled into me, pushing through my skin. It made my stomach clench. He only used to cry once in a while; now it was happening all the time.

When he got like this he would crawl into bed for days. He wouldn't shower or work or play with me. He wouldn't paint or dance with my mother in the living room. I didn't understand how he could be Bob Barker that morning and turn into this sad, broken man the same night. I didn't understand why he just didn't take his pills like he was supposed to so he wouldn't do this anymore.

I didn't understand why loving me wasn't enough to make him want to stay.

October 2010

Eden

I headed out the kitchen door around ten o'clock that evening with a quick salute to Juan, who was managing the third and final wave of deliveries to the party in the banquet room upstairs. Thankfully, the off-site cocktail parties went smoothly. The food arrived on time and intact and the servers called in to report that all was well. Things got a little crazy when a server dropped a tray of satay skewers on his way up the stairs to the banquet room, but I had made enough extra for it not to matter. I managed my kitchen by the Six-P Plan: Prior Planning Prevents Piss-Poor Performance. In catering, forecasting probable disasters was a lot less work than cleaning up after them.

"Be careful out there, boss," Juan warned me as he wiped the edge of a white serving tray with his apron.

"Yessir." I laughed, and turned my salute into a dismissing wave as I stepped out into the cold, drizzly evening. I threw my hood up to cover my head and tucked my hands into my pockets. The streets were well lit and there were still plenty of cars out, so I decided to walk rather than drive the few blocks over to the shelter. I'd called a few other shelters to inquire whether they had a David West in their system, but this one, Hope House, was the only one that actually invited me to come. My father's name hadn't shown up in their files, but that didn't mean he hadn't been there. I'd spoken to the program manager earlier in the week and she invited me to bring a photograph.

Just as I turned to walk up the hill from the waterfront, my cell phone buzzed in my pocket. I typically set it on vibrate while I was working and had forgotten to turn the ringer back on when I left the kitchen. A glance at the screen told me it was Georgia.

"So . . . what's the loser's name who brought you home so early on a Friday night?" I said with a smile.

"Ha!" Georgia laughed. "You wish. My night is just about to begin, thank you very much. And the loser's name is Simon. Only he's not a loser. He's a defense attorney. A very successful attorney."

"Oh, great. An *egomaniacal* loser." I loved that I could tease Georgia about her revolving-door love life. She made enough snarky comments about the number of jerk-offs she dated that my pitiful romantic history looked positively successful in comparison. As a life coach for many of Seattle's successful tech-savvy CEOs, Georgia seemed to run into a never-ending supply of eligible, if not suitable, men. She went through dates the way I might plow my way through a carton of ice cream—with gusto and little regard for the effect on her heart.

"Pfft," Georgia snorted. "Whatever. I don't think a woman who hasn't been laid in six months has any right to pass judgment on me. Who are you ever going to meet stuck in your hairnet back in that kitchen?"

"I don't wear a hairnet, Georgia. And I just had this conversation with my mother this morning, so I might have to kill you if you push it with me any further." The light changed and I stepped off the curb to cross the street.

"Oh, fine. You'll die alone and stray cats will eat your face, but whatever."

"I'm not alone. I have Jasper. He gives me plenty of lovin'," I said. I stopped as I came to a crosswalk and dug my cell-phone-free hand deeper into my pocket, jumping around a little to try to stay warm as I waited for the signal to turn. The shelter was on the next block, and I wanted to get there before they closed the door for the night. I'd read that most shelters couldn't accommodate the lines of homeless who stood outside each evening, waiting for a bed. With the weather turning cold, the line would be long.

"Ew. *Dog* lovin'? That's disgusting."

I laughed. "Not *that* kind of loving! God!"

"Okay, okay. Calm down." She giggled. "So, what're you up to, sweetie? All done feeding the masses?"

"I just finished a ten-hour shift. I'm headed down to a shelter right now. It's not too far from work, so I thought I'd stop in and drop off my dad's picture." Georgia was supportive of my decision to try to find my father, even if she didn't completely understand the reasoning behind it. She took on a similar mind-set when I decided to go blond a few summers ago, holding fast to the belief that a person has to learn through her own experiences instead of through lecture.

I gave her a quick synopsis of my visit to the morgue, and she gave a short, low whistle. "That had to suck. Are you okay?"

"Sure, why wouldn't I be? It wasn't him." Even as I spoke, the muscles around my heart constricted, thinking of the relief I felt when the beach-boy morgue worker turned over the man's wrist and I knew it wasn't my father. He was still out there. I could still find him.

"Yeah, but you were standing next to a dead body that could have been him. In a *morgue*. Didn't that freak you out?"

"A little, but I was just happy it wasn't him, you know?"

"I suppose so," Georgia said. "I think you should bag the

shelter and come out with me and Simon. We're headed over to Sequins to dance. It'll be a total madhouse." Sequins was Georgia's favorite go-to trendy party spot. It was the kind of place where you had to shout about an inch from your date's ear and he still couldn't understand you. Where drunk young professionals tried to get in the girls' panties through the power of their bullshit charm. With most of the girls, they didn't have to try very hard.

"That is my personal version of hell and you know it, my friend. I'll pass."

"Now who's the loser?"

"Good-bye, Georgia!" I singsonged into the phone.

"Ciao, chica." Georgia only knew a handful of foreign words and tended to mix languages together when she spoke them. If you teased her about it, she dismissed you as being culturally uncreative.

I hung up and slipped my phone back into my pocket, shivering against the chilly night air. I kept my eyes open for the address the program manager had given me, since the facility was fairly new and she told me they hadn't had time to put up a proper sign.

It's safe to say I smelled it before I saw it. A hard wall of body odor assaulted my senses. I buried my nose down into the collar of my jacket as I approached a line of men, some of whom were speaking loudly, either to the men standing next to them or the building; I couldn't know for sure. Others stood quietly, heads down, swaying back and forth a bit on their feet. Some had shopping carts filled with their belongings, and others carried a hiker's backpack stuffed full. I couldn't imagine my father was one of them. I scanned the faces I could see as I moved toward the entrance. He wasn't there.

"Hey, lady! This ain't no YWCA!" one man jeered as I walked past him. My stomach flip-flopped, but I kept moving.

The man continued. "Hey, I'm talkin' to you! Don't pretend like you don't hear me!" I felt his hand on my arm and I jerked away, turning to him with what I hoped was a friendly smile, despite the shakiness I felt.

"I'm not here to sleep," I said. "I'm looking for my dad."

Another man sidled up to me; his imposing stature made my shoulders curl a little in fear. "Who's your daddy?" he asked in a deep-timbred, suggestive tone.

The men around him cracked up and I smiled again, trying to appear more relaxed. They were blocking the door. "Excuse me," I tried again. "I need to get inside. The program manager is expecting me."

"It'll cost you," the man with the deep voice said.

"What?" I asked, afraid to hear what he might demand.

Just then, the front door swung open and a small woman with spiked, white-blond hair stepped outside. She was the approximate size and shape of a twelve-year-old prepubescent girl. I might have mistaken her for exactly that if not for the eyebrow piercings and tribal sleeves tattooed on her exposed forearms. She gave the larger man a small push. "Sam, leave the poor woman alone." She blessed me with a smile that took up most of her tiny, heart-shaped face. "Eden?"

I nodded gratefully, smiling at her snug green T-shirt, which read, NATIONAL SARCASM SOCIETY: LIKE WE NEED YOUR SUPPORT. She gestured for me to follow her. The men stepped aside for me to pass and I murmured the appropriate "excuse mes" as I did. "Thank you," I said to the woman as she led me down a brightly lit hallway. I could hear the low sounds of men laughing and talking through the walls, and the smell of boiled potatoes hung in the air. "You're Rita?"

"Yep. Don't worry about the boys. Most of them are completely harmless. They just like to talk a bunch of smack. It's all part of the survival game."

"I can imagine," I said. "Thank you for inviting me down." We reached the end of the hallway and she opened an office door, sweeping her arm in front of her body, inviting me inside. It was a small space with no windows, piled high with papers, with barely enough room for her desk, a file cabinet, and two chairs. Technically, it could have been a closet.

"Sure," she said, shutting the door behind her. "Though I don't know what help I can really be. Our computer system is anything but reliable when it comes to recording our clients' names. Many of them won't even tell us."

"It's not a requirement?"

"The only requirement we have is their need for a place to sleep and a willingness to be searched for sharp objects that could be used as weapons. We don't allow those on the premises. A lot of them are paranoid about the system, you know, so they don't want to give their names. Lots of schizophrenics." She pushed a family contact form across her desk and asked me to fill it out. "What condition did your father suffer from?"

"Well, he was originally diagnosed as manic-depressive back in the eighties," I explained as I picked up a pen and began writing in my phone number and address. "But then he started to get a little violent and paranoid, which isn't really consistent with that disorder. One doctor said he might have a generalized personality disorder, but he never stayed on his meds long enough to find out which ones worked the best, so we're not really sure what was going on with him, to tell you the truth. We just know his moods and behavior were all over the place and it got progressively worse."

"Mental illness can be tricky to diagnose." She cocked her head toward her shoulder, but her prickly hairstyle didn't move. "And how old were you when you last saw him?"

"Ten." I leaned over her desk and pulled out a copy of the same snapshot I'd given the hospitals from my purse. She took it and I watched her take him in.

"I'm sorry," she said. "I wish I could say I recognized him. Kind of a tall fella, isn't he?" Just as she said this, her office door flew open and a man appeared at the threshold.

"Have the front doors been locked?" he asked Rita, then noticed me sitting in the chair on the other side of her desk. "Oh, sorry. I didn't know you had company." He was on the shorter side with cropped black hair and an average build. He wasn't what I would call handsome—he seemed rougher around the edges than that. His overall slightly rumpled look told me he probably didn't care if he hadn't shaved for a few days.

"No worries," Rita said. "And yes, the doors have been locked. Sam was out there giving poor Eden a bad time." She gestured toward me. "Eden, this is Jack Baker. He's the crazy bastard who runs the joint. Jack, this is Eden West."

Jack nodded in my general direction. "Nice to meet you."

I smiled. "You too."

"Eden's looking for her father," Rita said, handing Jack the picture she still held. "He's been in and out of institutions and living on the streets."

Jack regarded the photo a moment before handing it back to me. "Sorry, I don't recognize him. But we get a lot of faces around here."

"I'm sure you do," I said. I pushed the photo back at him. "Would you mind putting this up somewhere? In case somebody else knows him?"

Jack hesitated before answering. "I'd prefer not to," he finally said.

I sat back in my chair, unable to hide my surprise. "You don't want me to find him?"

"I don't think that's what he meant—" Rita began to say, but Jack held up his hand to cut her off.

"I can explain it to her, Rita. Can you go make sure the lights are out in the bunk room? The natives are getting restless."

Rita gave me a quick apologetic look and then excused herself, shutting the door behind her. Jack took her place behind the desk. "Look," he said. "I didn't mean to offend you."

"I think I'm more confused than offended." I straightened in my chair, tried to look as confident as possible.

"Let me try to explain," he said. "Our population here is very mistrustful. And rightfully so, most of them. The system has screwed them over time and again. So much so that they're hesitant to even give up their real names."

"Rita told me that, but I don't see why—"

He held up a single finger to stop me. "I know you don't, and I'm trying to clear it up for you. Can you give me a minute?"

I pushed out a breath through my nose. I could see that he wasn't that much older than me, but he came off with a surprising air of authority and entitlement. It sort of made me want to hit him. I crossed my legs and started shaking one foot impatiently.

He didn't seem to notice my irritation, which irritated me more. "Okay. So. We're a newer facility. I'm trying to build relationships with my clients so they can learn to trust me. If they start seeing pictures of their friends on the walls, they're going to go off the deep end about my reporting their whereabouts to the government or some such bullshit and I'll lose credibility. What I do here is very important to me. These people deserve their privacy as much as you or I. It's not that I don't sympathize with what you're going through. I do. It's just that I don't want to jeopardize the bigger picture. Does that make sense?"

"I suppose so," I admitted begrudgingly. "My dad hated systems. The institutions, especially. I get it. And I admire what you're trying to do here." I took a deep breath before continuing. "So, since you're way more familiar with this world than I am, do you happen to have any other suggestions for me? What I could do to try to find him? I have his pictures at all the hospitals and I even went and saw a body last night who I thought might be him . . ." To my horror, I choked up as I spoke, and the tears started to fall. "Sorry, sorry," I said, wiping at my cheeks with fluttering fingers. "I don't know where this is coming from."

Most men get a little panicky when a woman begins to cry and Jack was no exception. His eyes darted around the room until he found the box of tissues behind him and set it in front of me. "Those are the worst kind of tears, right? The sneaky bastards." He pulled a few tissues out and handed them to me over the desk.

I sniffed and laughed at the same time, again horrified as I made a chortled, snot-filled sound. "Sorry." I took the tissues. "Thanks."

He made a dismissive motion with his hand and smiled, a slightly crooked expression that was oddly charming. "Don't worry about it. As long as it wasn't me making you cry. I didn't mean to be rude. I just tend to get pretty protective of this place. And the people in it. I can come off a little abrupt."

I thought of my brief interaction with Natalie in the kitchen earlier and suddenly, I wasn't quite as irritated with Jack. I could even relate to the enthusiasm he felt about what he was doing. "I get it," I said with a sweet smile, figuring I'd see if he had a sense of humor. "You're more of an impassioned idealist than a jerk."

Jack threw his head back and laughed. "Definitely an idealist." He chuckled again, then looked at me. "Have you thought about hiring a private detective to help find your dad?"

I nodded. "I have, but it's too expensive. I've looked all over the Internet and tried to get his medical records from the last institution he was in, but all they would tell me is his last time in residence, which was three years ago."

"Where was the last place you know for sure he was, besides there?" Jack asked.

"I have an old address on Capitol Hill. But that was years ago. It says in the white pages that a totally different person lives there now. A woman."

"So you never checked it out?"

"No. I figured there wasn't much point."

"It's a place to start, though, right? You could talk to the neighbors, see if anyone remembers him."

"I suppose I could." I smiled again. "Thanks."

"And you're welcome to come volunteer any time you like. If you spent some time here, you might get to know some of the guys. If your dad is on the streets, he may even stop by, eventually."

"You won't let me put up a picture but you'll let me come talk to your clients?"

"As long as you're willing to help out, I don't see why not. You get information from people by building relationships. To do that, you need to hang out with them. Do you have any special skills?"

"I'm a chef."

"Perfect," Jack said, and clapped his hands together. "Let's say we find out what you can do with a couple hundred pounds of potatoes."

David knew he needed to get out of bed. Five days had passed since he escaped the house to the sanctuary of his studio. Five days spent beneath the covers of the twin mattress he kept on the floor next to his easel. His eyes were gritty. His body ached from lack of movement and the cold. The space heater only ran sporadically, shutting down as soon as the elements burned too hot. Maybe there would be a fire. Maybe he could let the flames lick his skin and welcome black smoke into his lungs. Maybe that would put an end to his misery.

He would crawl out of bed only to use the tiny bathroom in the garage and to drink from one of the many gallon bottles of vodka he kept in the cupboard. The alcohol burned his throat and obliterated his consciousness. Though he hadn't eaten, he wasn't hungry. He felt empty, as though his organs were slowly deflating. If he stayed hidden long enough, perhaps he would simply disappear.

"Dad?" Eden's voice accompanied her knock on the door. He had locked it behind him five days ago when he fled the dinner his daughter had made him. "You need to eat something, Daddy," she said. "I brought you some chicken soup. I made it just the way you like it, with fennel instead of celery. I added a little lemon juice at the end, just like you showed me. With crackers, too." She paused. "I love you. Please. Open the door."

David's heart seized inside his chest. Eden had been out there every day, asking him to come back. Lydia had knocked once, but only to tell him she had picked up his lithium prescription and that it would be waiting for him inside the house when he was ready to rejoin his family. Tough love, like he knew his doctors had told her to use. He parroted their voices in his head: *Don't enable his depression. Set expectations and be a resource for his proactive behavior. Don't rescue him. He needs to learn how to save himself.*

Ha. Easy for them to say.

He wished he could fling open the door. He wished he was the kind of father Eden deserved. But he wasn't. His body felt weighted, pinned against the bed. He couldn't move. His brain screamed, *Get up!* but his limbs didn't listen.

Eden knocked again. "Daddy . . . ¿" Her voice was fragile, fractured by tears. David could imagine them welling in his daughter's perfect blue eyes, tipping up over the rims of her eyelids to roll down her freckled cheeks. He'd painted that picture time and again, attempting to trap the sorrow he caused her on the canvas so she would never have to feel it again. Obviously, he had failed.

David pulled the covers over his head, burrowing deep into the musty pillow. He stank, but he didn't care. His skin felt oily and thick, coated by his own neglect. It was gratifying, somehow, to smell as bad as he felt.

Eden was quiet, but he could feel her still standing outside, waiting for him. She would leave soon, when he didn't answer her call. But even when she returned to the house he knew he would feel her. Her longing was strong enough to push through any barrier. It wrapped its tentacles around his neck, desperate to extract what he feared he would never be able to give.

"He still won't answer the door, Momma," I said when I walked back into the kitchen. My mother was sitting at the table, a stack of bills and her checkbook spread out before her. A pained expression hung on her face, even as she tried to smile at me. Her blond hair was twisted up in a messy bun and the few lines around her eyes seemed to have deepened over the past five days.

"I'm sorry, baby. You know there's nothing I can do. He'll come out when he's ready."

"He's not eating." I set the tray with the soup and crackers I'd brought him down on the counter. The soup had gone cold; a thin skin of fat sat on its surface. I went over to sit by her.

"I know."

We sat in silence for a moment or two, the only noise the shuffling of the paper in her hands and her almost inaudible sighs.

"It's cold outside, too," I said, piping up. "He might freeze to death."

"Eden!" my mother snapped. "I know! I can't make him feel better. It's his choice to hole up like an animal. I can't make him stop. Believe me, I've tried." I knew this was true. I knew my mother had taken him to countless doctors. They'd also been to five different therapists in the last two years, trying to find one whom my father might respect enough to take their advice.

"Quacks," my father told me. "The lot of 'em." My mother had tried sweet, gentle conversations and she had screamed at him. She locked him out of the house, refusing to let him back in until he had taken his pills. Nothing she did seemed to work.

I scuffed the toe of my tennis shoe against the floor, making it squeak against the wood. "But you're his wife," I said. "If you don't help him, who will?"

She sighed and dropped her pen to the table. "It's Saturday, sweetie. Why don't you go find someone to play with? It might help get your mind off him."

"I don't *want* to get my mind off him," I said. "I want to help him get better."

"Eden—" my mother began, but I cut her off.

"You don't love him," I said accusatorily. I kept my eyes down, staring at the bright red ink on an official-looking envelope that read FINAL NOTICE. I knew what that meant. I knew we didn't have enough money to pay our bills again. My dad needed to get up so he could sell one of his paintings. He'd finished a bunch of them the last time he locked himself in the garage; he'd sell one and everything would be okay. He'd be happy and so would Mom. That's how it worked. But first, she had to get him out of the garage.

"Of course I love him," said my mom. "Don't be silly. But love isn't all a relationship needs. Marriages are supposed to be a partnership. Each person doing their share. Supporting each other." She gave me another tired half smile. "Your father and I used to have that, you know. When you were first born. We were always laughing, always hugging. Even though we never had a lot of money, he did so much to make sure all my needs were met." She paused again. "I wasn't always like this, sweetie. I used to be such a happy person . . ." Her voice trailed off and a blank, faraway look appeared in her eyes. It scared me.

"Are you going to divorce him?" I asked as a lump the size of a golf ball rose in my throat. I knew lots of kids whose parents were divorced. My friend Tara White had a key she wore on a silver chain around her neck so she could let herself into her house after school. She only saw her father on the weekends, and I couldn't go over to play unless her mother was home with her, which wasn't very often. She told me she watched television all afternoon until her mom came home. She said being alone was scary and she missed her father every day. I couldn't stand the idea of living without my dad. I didn't understand why my mom wasn't doing everything in her power to help him get better. He was her husband—it was her *job*.

"I don't know if we'll get divorced," my mom said. I looked up at her with wide eyes. "I don't want to," she said, continuing, "but I just don't know what I can do anymore. He's not getting better."

"So what?" I said, challenging her. "Would you leave him if he had cancer and wasn't getting better? If they cut off his legs and he couldn't walk?"

"That's not the same thing. Your dad has a choice. A person with cancer or no legs doesn't." She sighed. "Now, can you please go find someone to play with? Maybe Tina is home."

I slumped back in my seat. Tina Carpenter lived down the street from us, but her mom wouldn't let her play with me anymore. Not since my dad let us hang our heads out the windows of the car to see what dogs thought the big fuss was about. Mrs. Carpenter saw as my dad drove us up and down the street, our hair blowing back in the wind. Or maybe she heard us, since my dad had encouraged us to howl and bark at an invisible moon. Anyway, Tina told me the next day at school that she wasn't allowed to come over to our house again. "My mom thinks your dad is kind of weird," she said. "Sorry."

Now I shoved back my chair and stood up. "You're going to make him leave," I announced to my mother. "I hate you!"

My mother's blue eyes flashed and she threw her pen down to the table. "You hate me? *Me?* I'm the one putting food in your mouth. I keep this roof over your head. Do you think for one minute your dad would take care of you the way I do if I decided to lock myself away for days at a time? No! You'd be on your own, little girl."

"No, I wouldn't!" I said, trying to fight back tears. "He loves me. He'd take care of me just fine. We don't need you. Maybe you're the reason he stays out there. Did you ever think of that? Why don't *you* just go away and leave us alone?"

"Because I can't!" The flash left my mother's eyes just as quickly as it had appeared. Her shoulders fell.

My eyes stung as though she had hit me across the face.

"Honey," she said, seeing my tears. She tried to grab my hand. I took a few steps back, out of her reach, and ran up the stairs to my room.

She probably wishes I was never born, I thought after I threw myself facedown on my bed. She said it herself; she didn't stay because she loved me or my dad. She only stayed because she had to. Time would only tell if she would leave me too.

October 2010
Eden

"This better be good," was Georgia's greeting when I called her the Saturday morning after my first visit to Hope House. "Like, I-need-to-borrow-one-of-your-kidneys-because-I'm-dying good."

"Good morning to you, too, sunshine!" I said, smiling into the phone. I sat on my couch, sipping my way through a huge mug of coffee and staring out at the rain. The drizzle from the night before had morphed into showers; the raindrops pelted the metal roof of my house, making it sound like I was inside a tin can. Jasper lay at my feet, whimpering, because I still needed to take him for a walk.

"Late night?" I asked Georgia.

"Mmphm," she grunted. "What time is it?"

I glanced at the clock on the DVD player on the shelf by the television. "Almost nine o'clock. Want to go get breakfast?"

"Ugh. No."

"C'mon," I cajoled. "I'm buying. And grease is good for a hangover."

Georgia groaned. "I'm not fit for public consumption. Can't you just come over and cook us something?"

"Nope! I feel like letting someone else do the work this morning. And I want to hear about your date."

She groaned again. "Oh, all right, fine. You win. Where do you want to go?"

"Where do you think?"

"Luna Park Café?"

"Yep. I'm dying for some cinnamon roll French toast. We can take Jasper for a walk afterward to burn it all off."

"We'll have to walk to Portland to burn off those carbs."

"Carbs schmarbs. I'll pick you up in twenty minutes."

"You'd better bring me coffee or I might have to shoot you."

"You don't own a gun. So throw on some deodorant and get ready to go."

Georgia and I had met at the same restaurant where I found Jasper. She was working nights as a server to put herself through the last year of her bachelor's degree in business. Having graduated culinary school, I was a line cook searing steaks or whipping up risotto when a table was done with their appetizer. We first spoke on an exceptionally busy night. Georgia was a new employee, so when she told me to start cooking two filets, I peeked through the stainless steel shelf that guarded the cooks from the waitstaff.

"Are you sure your table is ready for them?" I asked her. I'd seen the apps for that ticket go out less than five minutes before she told me to fire the steaks.

"Yes, I'm sure," she said. "The bastards tore through those mussels like a couple of king crabs. It was disgusting. Like the Discovery Channel or something." She dropped her chin to her chest and gave me a pointed but friendly look. "Are *you* sure you can cook fast enough to keep up with them?"

I laughed. "I'll do my best."

"Fabulous." She winked at me and sashayed back out toward the dining room, her plush hips swinging in concert with each step. She was short but had one of those glorious hourglass shapes and the kind of cascading dark auburn waves that gave men Victoria's Secret wet dreams. I could have hated her for this, but her energy was great, easygoing and accessible. I liked her immediately.

Our kitchen manager, Dean, caught our interaction. "That is one hot piece of ass," he commented to me as he leered at her backside.

"One hot piece of ass whose daddy is an employment lawyer!" Georgia cheerfully called out over her shoulder before the door swung shut behind her.

"Uh-oh," I said. "Can you say 'sexual harassment'? She has a witness, too."

"Whatever," Dean huffed at me, and then went to hide in his office.

It was like that for Georgia, I thought as we sat in a booth at the Luna Park Café, breathing in the luscious scent of garlicky home fries and peppery sausage while we waited for our breakfast to be served. Being attracted to her was a side effect of being a male in her presence. Even hungover she looked gorgeous: Her hair was pulled up in a French twist that somehow managed to appear messy but totally put together. Her skin was creamy and her hazel eyes lit up with every smile. Adding in the cleavage and pouty lips, it was no wonder men were constantly hitting on her. What was best, though, was how unimportant all this was to Georgia, how little she let it infect her ego. "Give me a man who notices my soul instead of my cup size," she liked to say, "and I'll introduce you to the man of my dreams."

"So, tell," she said, now fortified by the triple Americano I'd brought to her house. "How was the shelter?" I knew better than to talk too much in the car. It was a good idea to wait until the caffeine ran a steady course through her veins.

I shrugged. "Okay, I guess, except the guy who runs the place was a little rude at first."

She cocked her head. "Aren't those social-worker-type fellas supposed to be all liberal and easygoing?"

"You'd think so. But he wasn't okay with putting a picture of my dad anywhere. He was afraid it would freak out his clients. Like he was reporting them to the government or something. He was kind of snippy about it."

Georgia poured more cream into the huge mug of coffee in front of her and stirred. "Huh. You're *never* snippy with people at your job, right?"

"Shut up."

She grinned. "I guess I get what he was worried about. Don't you?"

"Sure, after he explained it. I think it was just the way he said it that rubbed me the wrong way."

"Did you want him to rub you the *right* way?" Georgia wiggled her eyebrows suggestively.

I laughed, almost spitting out the sip of orange juice I'd just taken. "Georgia! No!"

She sat back and gave me a knowing look. "Ah. So he wasn't cute?"

"No," I said, then reconsidered. "Well, yeah, I guess he was decent. In a short-man, I'm-afraid-he-might-have-a-small-pecker kind of way."

"Oh, come on, now," she said, rolling her eyes. "That's a total myth. I've disproved it several times myself. Height has no more to do with the size of a man's equipment than the size of his feet."

I laughed. "That's right. What was his name again, the one with the size-fifteen shoe?"

Georgia shuddered. "Ugh. Don't remind me. Tiniest pecker I've ever seen." She held up her pinky finger and waggled it at me. "I gave him a couple merciful faked orgasms and was out the door."

"How generous of you." I took another sip of orange juice before setting down my glass. "Why do you care if the guy at the shelter was cute?"

She gave me another wicked grin. "Because he's the first man you've mentioned since the last one. That mama's boy, Ryan." Georgia was well aware of my most recent boyfriend's propensity to live off his mother's income and insisted on celebrating when I finally broke up with him six months ago. She continued. "There had to be something about him," she said, referring to Jack.

"Other than the fact he started off our conversation by irritating me, there wasn't much. Though he did manage to talk me into volunteering there on Tuesday night."

"Really? Doing what?"

"Cooking. He said the best way to find my dad was to get to know the kind of people he spends time with. Build relationships with them. Like maybe they'd keep an eye out for him or something. Or maybe my dad would just show up there."

"Makes sense. You'll have to let me know how it goes."

The waitress arrived with our plates, which really should have been called platters. Mine was overloaded with the cinnamon roll French toast I'd been craving along with a huge mess of scrambled eggs and maple link sausages. Georgia had gone for broke and ordered the strawberry blintzes with eggs and sausages, too. It all smelled heavenly.

"Oh, holy yum," Georgia moaned as she closed her eyes and took the first bite. "My trainer is going to *kill* me for this."

"So don't tell him."

"I don't have to. It's like he *smells* the extra fat cells on my ass."

I snickered, trying not to spit out my food. "Yet another reason I don't have a trainer."

"You don't have a trainer because you have a freak-of-nature metabolism. It's a miracle I put up with you." She winked at me, then looked thoughtful. "So, I think this guy irritating you is a good sign."

"Really?" I mumbled with my mouth full of warm, sweet bread slathered in syrup. I felt my serotonin lifting, but I wasn't sure if it was from the sugar rush or just spending time with Georgia.

"Yep," she said. "It means he pushed your buttons. No buttons pushed means there's no sexual energy going on. It's classic psychology."

I sat back against the padded booth and twirled my fork. "Do tell, Dr. Freud."

"Oh, it's not Freudian. It's experience. My best lovers have been the guys who irritate the shit out of me. Remember Dean?"

I laughed. "Our sexual-harassing kitchen manager? I still can't believe you actually slept with him. Yuck."

"I know. It was sick." She stuck a strawberry in her mouth and chewed, waving her fork in the air as she spoke. "But he was hellishly good in bed. A total asshole. But you know, whatever a girl has to endure to get off."

At Georgia's loud pronouncement, the couple at the table across from us stopped their conversation and turned their heads in our direction.

"Nice!" I said, ducking my head down and shaking it in disbelief. "Have you no shame?"

Georgia ignored my question. "You know who else pushes my buttons, don't you؟"

"Men with big fingers؟"

She ignored me again. "Your hot little brother. That boy is getting *fine*."

"Um, ew؟ He's my brother, Georgia. He's a kid."

"A kid with massively multiplying muscles, my friend. I'm working out at his gym, remember؟ You should see him look at himself in the mirrors. His cocky attitude pisses me off."

"And you find this appealing؟"

"I know, I'm twisted. But can you say 'boy toy'؟" Her eyes sparkled as she took an entire sausage link in her mouth.

The guy at the table across from us hadn't taken his eyes off her. His female companion noticed this and kicked his leg under their table. "What!؟" he exclaimed, and she shot him a dirty look.

"I'm actually going to Bryce's competition today," I said. "I promised my mom if I didn't have to work I'd find a way to fit it in, so I asked Juan to cover the first part of my shift. Want to come؟"

"Can't. I have an appointment." Since many of Georgia's clients ran Fortune 500 companies during the week, she had to make her coaching services available pretty much 24/7. Their schedule was her schedule.

"Who is it this time؟"

"Some start-up geek who wants to learn to be more assertive with his staff. He's practically twelve, so *that* shouldn't be a problem. His balls should drop any day." She rolled her eyes before glancing at her watch. "In fact, I need to get going."

"What about our walk؟"

She motioned to the waitress to bring our check. "I'll have to take a rain check. Call me later؟"

"Sure. We'll dissect your date with the lawyer." I paused to hand the waitress two twenty-dollar bills and told her to keep the change.

Georgia waved her hand at me over the remains of her breakfast, dismissing the idea. "Eh, there's nothing to dissect."

"He didn't irritate you?"

"Not even in the slightest."

"That's too bad," I said, laughing as I stood up to pull on my coat.

"No worries," she said. "Tomorrow's another day."

By the time I had dropped Georgia off, driven home, and walked Jasper, I arrived at the community center where Bryce's competition was being held about ten minutes after the event began. I spotted my mother and John sitting on the bleachers before they saw me, and the sight of my mother's chemo-induced short hair didn't fail to throw me. I had watched it disappear. I cried with her the first time she brushed her thick blond locks in front of the mirror and huge chunks fell to the ground. Now it was layered on her head in a fashionably spiked mess, similar to the style Rita wore. Even with the weight the steroids had packed on her she looked beautiful. Luminous, really. Nothing could disguise the light in her eyes as she looked up and laughed at something John had said. I had no memory of her looking at my father that way. I knew that she must have. I knew their life together wasn't always filled with despair.

I pushed my way through the crowd and climbed up to their seats. "Hi!"

"Hi, honey," my mom said, giving me a quick hug and a kiss. Out of habit, I gauged her temperature with my cheek against hers. She felt cool. Healthy. I sent off a little thanks to the universe for keeping her alive.

"Eden!" John bellowed. "How's my girl?"

As usual, I cringed internally at his claim on me. *I'm not yours,* the child in me said, pouting. *I'm my daddy's girl.* I was well practiced at not letting this feeling show on my face. The few times I had shown it when I was younger, my mother made me regret it.

"You will show your stepfather respect, young lady," she'd said one time. "Do you understand me?" When I didn't respond right away she gave my arm a little shake.

"Fine!" I pouted in a manner only an adolescent girl could pull off. "Okay! I understand!" I liked John, but it bothered me how hard he tried. Everything was over-the-top. His Hawaiian-print shirts were too loud; he was jolly when just happy would do. He insisted on taking me to Mariners games and I didn't even like baseball.

I squashed my irritation now and sat next to my mother in the bleachers. "I'm good, John. How are you?" Since marrying John, my mother was happier than I'd ever seen, so I did my best to be nice to her husband, if only for her sake. She was an entirely different person than she'd been with my dad—serene, relaxed, and cheerful. She still worked, but only part-time, and she wasn't the only person responsible for paying the bills. Worry didn't constantly pull at the muscles in her face; she no longer cried more than she laughed. There had been a fundamental shift inside her.

"Good, good. I'm great. Kickin' ass and takin' names." He grinned at me. John was a bear of a man, well over six feet tall, and packing enough flesh to make me wonder how he could continue to pass the firemen's physical fitness test. Didn't they make him climb a ladder? He was always clean-shaven and I didn't think I had ever seen him without a perfectly sheared crew cut.

From the day my mother told me she was going to marry John, I couldn't help but compare him to my father. And while he was the physically bigger man, in my eyes John always came up short. My father taught me things; John liked to boast about how much he knew. John was loud, but my father had a pizzazz my stepdad could never match.

I searched the stage for Bryce but instead saw four incredibly well-muscled men in Speedo-type bathing suits striking various poses. "Did I miss much?" I asked. "I had to take Jasper for a walk."

"No," John said. "He isn't up yet. We'll see him in the next round."

"How was work last night?" my mom asked.

"It was good."

"Did you go out afterward?" She prodded me, fishing, I was sure, for whether or not I'd changed my mind and gone prowling for a new boyfriend.

"I did go out, but not to a club, if that's what you're asking," I said. I didn't want to bring up my visit to the shelter, since I knew it would only upset her. I watched her pale eyebrows furrow and knew she was going to push the issue.

"Where did you go, then?"

I sighed, then leaned in toward her. "I went to a shelter to see if I could put a picture of Dad up."

My mother averted her gaze from me to the stage. "Um-hmm," she murmured, tilting her head toward John, indicating that she didn't want me to talk about my father in front of him. I knew this, which was why I'd tried to avoid telling her, but honestly, her reluctance to mention my father in John's presence was a little ridiculous, considering John was one of the firefighters on the scene the night the medics took my father away. He sat with my mother and me in our living room, rattling off soothing words and nodding empathetically when she cried about losing her husband to his illness. Six months later she was pregnant and John had a son on the way and a stepdaughter. It's not like the man didn't know what he was getting himself into.

"I met a guy," I said, knowing this, at least, would pique her interest.

"At a *homeless* shelter?" she asked, swinging her face around to look at me. Her eyes widened as she put her hand on top of my leg. "Please, tell me you're joking."

I laughed. "It wasn't a resident, Mom. It was the guy who runs the place. He suggested I volunteer my cooking services so I can get to know the clients better. See if any of them know Dad."

Before my mother had a chance to respond, John stuck his fingers into his mouth and let out an ear-piercing whistle. I looked to the stage and there was Bryce, standing under the lights wearing nothing but a tiny purple spandex bathing suit. His skin was tinted the approximate shade of an Oompa-Loompa's and his light blond hair looked neon in contrast. He began what I supposed was his routine, working his way through poses similar to the ones the men before him had performed.

I giggled, and my mother elbowed me. "Be nice," she said under her breath.

"I'm trying. But he's . . . my *brother*. It's a little weird to be ogling him."

"All right, Bryce!" John yelled above the rest of the crowd's cheers. "Show 'em what you got!"

"Can he not show so *much* of it?" I whispered in my mom's ear, and she chuckled.

"Well, he does take after his father," Mom said.

"Aaahh! TMI, Mom!"

Oblivious to our amusement, John continued to hoot and holler for his son. After Bryce's weight class left the stage, the three of us made our way down the bleachers. John made sure my mother's arm was hooked tight into the crook of his elbow before taking a step; his hand pressed hard on top of hers. I felt an overwhelming sense of tenderness toward him in that moment, grateful for his unfailing strength when my mother needed it so much. John had his faults, but his devotion to my mother was something I would never question.

We waited outside where Bryce had told John he would meet us for about fifteen minutes. Both Mom and John went to the restroom, leaving me alone when Bryce approached. I was happy to see he had changed into a pair of sweats and a T-shirt.

"Sis!" He gave me a hug. "You made it. Mom said she wasn't sure if you would."

"What, and miss my brother in a banana hammock? No way." Even though Bryce wasn't more than a couple of inches taller than me, I felt like a child in his substantial embrace. He'd been a strong but sinewy teenager, all long, gawky arms and too-big feet. Now his obsessive work at the gym was paying off. It was good to see him coming into his own.

He laughed, flashing a set of unnaturally brilliant white teeth. "You are one of the chosen few."

"You're paying for my therapy, you know. That image is forever burned on my retinas." I punched his arm, then pulled back my fist, shaking out the stinging sensation the contact with his muscle had ignited. "Ow!"

He grinned. "I know, right?"

I grabbed his bicep with both hands and didn't even come close to my fingers touching. "You are getting *huge*. How much weight have you gained?"

"About twenty pounds." He flexed under my touch and my hands popped off. "All muscle, baby."

"Wow," I said. "Remind me not to piss you off."

"Ah, I love you, Ed. You never piss me off."

"That's a lie. And don't call me Ed." Bryce couldn't figure out how to say "Eden" when he was learning to talk so I became "Ed" by default. John made it worse by adding a "Mr." before the nickname. I was thirteen and in the midst of a great deal of adolescent angst. Bryce was two and made a habit of toddling around, pointing at me and saying, "Mr. Ed! Mr. Ed!" to anyone who'd listen. I was already struggling with gaining a sibling after ten years of only-child-hood; this did not further endear him to me.

"Okay, *Ed,*" Bryce teased.

I punched him again and the pain in my knuckles reminded me why I shouldn't have. "Ow!"

He cracked up just as John walked over and grabbed Bryce in a bear hug, lifting him off the ground. "My son, the bodybuilder!"

"Pops, knock it off!" Bryce struggled and managed to drop back down to the floor.

Our mother hugged Bryce. "You looked fantastic up there, sweetie. Very good job."

Bryce scowled. I could tell he was not happy John had picked him up, and I didn't blame him. For a man in his early fifties, John could be as exuberant as a Great Dane puppy.

"What's with the tan-in-a-can?" I asked Bryce, trying to lighten his mood. "Did you lose a bet?"

"Ha-ha," Bryce said. "Very funny. I haven't gotten the right formula yet. You have to do it in layers and all the other guys who compete say it's a bitch to get it perfect. You want to help me put it on next time?"

"Me?"

"Yeah, you."

"Tempting . . ." I pretended to ponder this, tapping my finger against the side of my mouth. "But no. Spray-tanning my naked brother just isn't on my bucket list. You might get Georgia to bite, though."

"If I'm lucky." Bryce's eyebrows rose suggestively as he spoke. "I've seen her at the gym. That girl is smokin' hot."

"Bryce!" our mom said, slapping him on the forearm. "I didn't teach you to speak that way about your sister's friends."

"I did," John said with a hearty chuckle. "You want to come out to dinner with us later, son?" John asked him. "We're going to Olive Garden." Olive Garden was John's idea of high-class cuisine. I did my best to keep my chef sensibilities in their proper place and not hold it against him.

Bryce shook his head. "Sorry, Pops. I have to meet a client at the gym."

"On a Saturday night?" John asked.

Bryce shrugged. "I work when it's convenient for them. If I don't, I don't get paid and I have to move back in with you guys."

"We'll see you later then, honey," my mom said. She hugged him again and John shook his hand.

"I'm proud of you, Bryce," my stepfather said.

"Thanks, Pops."

My heart ached a bit watching this exchange. Despite the ways he managed to get under my skin, John meant well. He'd cheered me on at basketball games and cried when I accepted my high school diploma and culinary degree. He'd told me he was proud of me many times over the years. It wasn't that I didn't believe him, but it wasn't his voice I needed to hear saying those words.

After Mom and John left, Bryce walked me out to my car. The rain had dissipated, leaving a sweet, freshly scrubbed scent in the air. I told my brother about my visit to the morgue and Hope House.

"You let me know if you need some muscle to back you up down there," he said.

"Ah, planning to use your powers of tan-orexia for good rather than evil?"

He reached over and gave my side a quick pinch, tickling me. I swatted at his hand. "Hey! Knock it off."

"You knock it off."

"Okay, okay. I'm sorry. You did great today, little bro." I gave him a quick hug. "I love you, shithead."

"I love you, too." He flashed the smile I knew had won him countless high school girlfriends' hearts and broken just as many. "Be careful, okay? You're the only sister I've got."

David began to emerge from the fog the day Eden brought him his second bowl of chicken soup. "Daddy?" she said. "Are you all right? Are you ready for some soup?" She paused when he didn't answer right away. "Can I come in?"

"I'm okay, baby," he said. His voice cracked from lack of use. "Just leave the soup and I'll get it in a bit. I need to rest a little more."

"Okay," she said. "I'll come back for the bowl later."

He could do this. He would get out of bed for his daughter. He would take the pills Lydia brought from the pharmacy and he would be the kind of father and husband his family needed. He waited until he was sure she had gone back to the house and then forced himself to roll over onto the cold floor. The icy cement sent a shock through his body, as though his heart had been jolted by electric paddles. Good. He needed it. He crawled over to the door and unlocked it. Eden had left a tray with an enormous ceramic bowl of soup, a half-eaten sleeve of saltines, and in a slender glass vase, a small lavender crocus from their front-yard flower bed. He'd planted those bulbs with her the previous fall.

"Let's create the Garden of Eden!" he had said. The two of them loaded into his car and headed to the home store, where

Eden spent an hour hand-picking over a hundred individual bulbs she wanted to blossom in their yard the next spring.

"They're kind of ugly," she commented as she turned over the various tubers in her hand.

"Yes," he told her, "but they grow into something fresh and beautiful." It gave him hope that such loveliness could spring forth from something so seemingly deformed.

She appeared doubtful. "Are you sure?"

"Absolutely."

Eden persisted. "When? How long until we see them?"

"Good things come to those who wait," he promised, though he doubted the truth of his words. He had waited for too many things in his life that had never come—success with his painting, a mind that didn't scream at him with black, sinful thoughts. At what point would he completely give up hope?

Now part of him ached to forget the soup and climb back in bed. There was a flash of movement at the kitchen window. He glanced up and saw his daughter's slight frame behind the white gauzy curtain. She'd been watching for him, making sure he did what he said he would do. His bright paintings mocked him, depicting vivid emotions he didn't remember ever having felt. *A flat affect,* his doctors had called it.

"As opposed to what?" he asked one of them when they described his depressed behavior this way. "A bumpy affect?"

The doctor didn't laugh. Neither did Lydia, who was in the meeting, too.

"Do you know what it's like trying to communicate with you when you get that way?" his wife asked him. "When you've totally checked out? Nothing I say or do matters. All that matters is you and the sadness you feel. What about my sadness, David? What about your daughter's?"

David had shrugged. He knew they were hurting, but there wasn't room inside him for their pain. His was too big. It blotted out everything in its path. Maybe, if he was lucky, it would blot him out.

As he picked up the tray, David sighed and locked the garage door again. He forced himself to sit up on the bed and take small sips of the soup his daughter had made him. It was good. Wonderful, really, for a ten-year-old girl. It heartened him to know her creative talent with food came from him. It had to, since Sunday morning pancakes were pretty much the height of Lydia's culinary aspirations.

After eating, he pulled the covers back over his head. The vodka was gone but he managed to sleep anyway. The next thing he knew, Eden was knocking at the door again.

"Are you awake, Daddy? I brought you more soup."

His eyelids still felt weighted, but he managed to get upright and let his daughter inside. She stared at him with enormous, round eyes, then promptly wrinkled her nose. He reeked, he knew. "Come in," he said. "What day is it?"

"Monday." *Really?* David thought. *I could have sworn it was still Sunday.* "Aren't you supposed to be at school?"

"It's a teacher's workday," she said. She came across the threshold, careful not to jostle the tray she held in front of her.

He closed the door behind her. "Isn't their work to teach you?" David realized the irony of his asking this, considering the number of times he had purposely kept Eden out of school. He was selfish, he knew, wishing she weren't home, wishing he could avoid her completely. Another item to add to the long list of his flaws.

She set the tray down onto his workbench. "I guess not today." She stuck her hands in the pockets of her puffy red ski jacket and looked around. "Brr. It's cold in here. You want to go in the house?"

"Not just yet." David took a spoonful of soup. "Mmm."

Eden's face lit up with her smile. "Really? You like it?"

"It's very good, Bug. What's the green stuff?"

"I chopped up some of the fluffy stuff on the end of the fennel stalks and put it in."

"The fronds?"

"I guess so, if that's what it's called. I tasted it first to make sure it wasn't yucky and it sort of had the same licoricey flavor as the bulb, so I thought it might be nice to not waste it."

"Good idea." David finished the soup, ever conscious of his daughter's watchful gaze, how her eyes flitted back and forth from him to the four empty gallon bottles of vodka on the floor.

When he was done eating, he smiled. "Want to snuggle?" he asked her. "It would help us keep warm."

"You mean in here?" Eden glanced at the messy bed and wrinkled her nose again.

David nodded. "I guess it doesn't smell too good, huh?"

Eden pressed her lips together into a thin line and shook her head; he could tell she didn't want to say anything that might hurt his feelings. They never talked about his disappearing acts into the studio, why he shut himself away. He wasn't sure he could find the words.

David sighed. "Well, how about I come into the house and get cleaned up then? We can snuggle after that."

She grinned. "Okay. I made cookies, too, but I left them in the house."

"Sneaky girl. There's incentive if I ever heard it." He chuckled, the first amusement he'd felt in days. He was a little amazed he remembered how to smile.

He slipped on his tennis shoes and went into the house, happy that Lydia was at work. He knew she hated leaving Eden alone with him when he was like this, but with no school and no money to pay a babysitter, she didn't really have a choice. At least, not until he sold a painting. He moved slowly, but at least he was moving. Stepping inside felt foreign to him, like he was returning from a long trip. Everything looked a little unfamiliar.

After his shower, he came downstairs to find Eden in the living room on the couch. There was a plate of cookies on the coffee table, along with a tall glass of milk. She patted the cushion next to her.

"Want to watch TV?" she asked.

"Nah, let's talk instead." He sat down next to her and pulled her into his arms. She snuggled into his chest and he leaned down to breathe her in. He stroked her hair and she released a heavy sigh.

"Tell me the story of how you and Mom met," she said.

David closed his eyes. "You've heard it a thousand times."

"I don't care. I like it. I want to hear it again. Please?" She hugged him with all her might.

"Oomph!" he exclaimed, and his eyes popped back open. "Okay, okay. I give up. I'll do it!" He felt her smile against him.

"Do you want a cookie first?" she asked. "They're chocolate chip."

"With nuts?"

"No nuts."

"Because we're nutty enough already?" he teased.

Eden didn't respond and he felt her stiffen a bit in his arms. He wondered if Eden thought he was crazy. Or maybe someone had told her he was. Or that *she* was, because she was his daughter. The thought of her enduring this made his heart ache.

"I'll have one in a little bit, Bug," he said. "I'm still full." He sighed. "Let's see. Your mom fell in love with me the minute she saw me."

"Daddy! No, she didn't!"

"Oh, right. I forgot. Sorry." He paused, unsure if he felt up to going back in time. But Eden asked for so little. And considering his behavior over the past few weeks, he owed her. He was in the spot he rarely reached anymore: not too high, not too low. He'd better take advantage of the time while he could. They settled in and he told the story the way he knew she loved to hear it.

"I was seventeen the day I first saw her," he said. "I was sketching portraits down on the waterfront trying to make enough money to get my own apartment. I'd been living at my grandmother's house since my parents died and my welcome was wearing thin."

"Your parents died in a car crash," Eden said.

"Yes, they did." *They abandoned me,* David thought, but then immediately redirected his attention to continuing the story. "So I went to live with my grandmother. But she had already raised her children and got sick of me eating her out of house and home pretty quickly."

"Like I do," Eden said, interrupting. "I have the same appetite as you, Mom says."

"Yes, you do. Now, shush. It was a hot day in August and your mother was with a few of her friends. One of them dared her to come over and ask me to sketch her. She was wearing a peasant blouse and cutoff jean shorts and had the most beautiful skin and the longest, thickest blond hair I'd ever seen. I called her

Rapunzel, which made her very angry. She got these two perfect red circles on her cheeks. I thought she was adorable. I couldn't wait to sketch her."

"Why did it make her angry when you called her Rapunzel?"

David took a deep breath and blew it out before answering. He tried not to think about the irony of what he was about to say. "Because she didn't want me to think she needed to be saved."

"Oh."

"So, anyway, I did the sketch, and it turns out she didn't have enough money to pay for the picture and her bus fare home. And what did I tell her?"

"You told her she could have the sketch for free if you could take her out on a date." Eden knew this story by heart. "And she said yes because you had the kindest eyes she'd ever seen. But she didn't tell you that until later."

"Well, yes, that's true. But she also said yes because she knew it would tick her father off." David nudged Eden. "Your mom is a bit of rebel, you know. Her parents were very strict, so dating a hippie artist such as myself was her way of proving the point that she could do whatever she wanted."

"You were a hippie?"

"Well, not an *actual* hippie. But I had long hair and wasn't going to be a lawyer or some other straitlaced professional, so that was enough for your grandpa to take issue with me." David remembered how Lydia told him that their love was strong enough to withstand her father's disapproval. How she said it was strong enough to withstand anything. Neither of them could have imagined him plunging to such depths. That he would cheat on her, yell at her, accuse her of trying to kill his creative genius with tiny white pills. She never considered the possibility she would end up putting him in a mental ward when he couldn't stop talking about wanting to die.

"But he liked you eventually, right? Before he died?"

"No, sweetie. He didn't. But your mom loved me, and that was enough." For a while, it *was* enough. David longed for those days filled with tender looks and touches from his wife. Images flashed in his brain: the two of them dancing in the kitchen while the dinner he'd made her simmered on the stove; brushing the tangles from her long blond hair before bed; the tears sparkling in her eyes when he unveiled the first portrait he'd painted of their infant daughter. Back when Lydia was his muse and he was her rebellious hero.

Now he closed his eyes again. Fatigue rushed over him. The lithium he had taken before his shower coursed through his blood; the world took on a familiar but fuzzy filter. This was the prologue to becoming a stranger to himself. "You know the end of the story, don't you? Why don't you finish it?"

Eden twisted her face up toward his and he willed his eyes open and gave her a smile. "C'mon," he said. "I always tell the ending. It's your turn."

"Well," Eden recited, "you went on a date to the park. You didn't have a lot of money so you walked there with a picnic basket and a blanket. You found a tree big enough for shade and you talked for hours. You fell in love with the way she slapped both of her hands over her mouth when she laughed at your jokes because she was embarrassed that her front teeth were a little crooked. She fell in love with the way you talked with your hands and pulled hers away from her mouth so you could see her smile."

"And then what?" David asked.

"You kissed her," Eden said.

"And what else?"

"You got married and had me." Her voice was quiet. David held his breath, waiting for her to finish the story. When she didn't, he leaned down and rested his head against hers.

"And we lived happily ever after," he whispered, hoping that somehow he could find a way to make those words come true.

My heart fluttered when I arrived at Hope House the Tuesday afternoon after my initial visit. I was more nervous than I thought I'd be to start my volunteer work with the homeless community, a little scared to be so up close and personal with how my father had been living for the majority of the past twenty years. I had to take several deep breaths to calm my pulse before walking into the building. I'd agreed to be there by two o'clock to help cook the evening meal.

Jack had left me a message on Sunday instructing me to dress casually in jeans, a sweatshirt, and comfortable shoes. Working as a chef, I always wore comfortable shoes—much to Georgia's chagrin, of course, since the woman lived in three-inch heels to lengthen what she jokingly referred to as her "stubby legs"—but it had been a while since I'd been in a kitchen without my chef's coat. It felt a little strange to know I wouldn't be wearing it.

I did my best to swallow any apprehension I felt as I walked through the front doors and back to the office I'd been in Friday night. There were a few men in the hallway standing in groups of two or three. A couple of them made eye contact and nodded in acknowledgment as I moved past, but mostly, they ignored me. I searched their faces out of habit—none of them were my father.

"Hey there," Jack said, looking up with a big smile when I

rapped on the open door. He sat at the desk he apparently shared with Rita. "Right on time. I wasn't sure you'd show."

"Why wouldn't I?" I asked. He wore jeans and a long-sleeved thermal shirt the same color green as his eyes.

"I get people volunteering all the time." He shrugged, looking a little sheepish. Maybe he realized his words rubbed me the wrong way again. "'Oh yeah, I'd love to help,' they say. 'Just tell me what you need.' Then the time comes and it doesn't fit into their schedule or whatever. And I never see them again." He smiled and said, "I'm glad that's not you."

"Me too." I shifted my weight from my right foot to the left and stuck my hands in the front pockets of my jeans. "What do you need me to do?"

Jack stood up, came over, and rested his palm lightly on my lower back. "I'll show you. Rita's already in the kitchen."

"What are we serving?" I asked. We left the office and moved into the hallway.

"Scalloped potatoes with diced ham."

"What about a veg?"

Jack stopped and looked puzzled.

"Oh, sorry. Restaurant speak. Vegetables."

"Ah. Well, if we can sneak those in somewhere we will, but for the most part, we're not dealing with salad fans here. They need a hot, filling meal. Sometimes it's the only one they'll get for a few days."

"Okay." I considered my ravenous appetite and how terribly I'd fare on one meal a day, if I was lucky enough to find it. I had no idea how my father managed to survive. Of course, I still didn't know whether he had.

I followed Jack the rest of the way down the hall and through a room about the size of a basketball court. The room was filled with wall-to-wall cots. We walked a narrow path and I tried not to wrinkle my nose at the musty, sweaty odor. I suddenly found myself fighting back the bitter, painful memory of my father sleeping in our old garage. *Oh Dad,* I thought. *Where are you?*

"How many people do you get spending the night?" I asked Jack.

He looked at me over his shoulder. "It depends, but usually we can accommodate around fifty."

"Do you feed dinner to more than that?"

He turned back to look where he was going. "We feed as many as we can until we run out of food."

"How often does that happen?"

"Both nights we serve dinner. Right now we can only afford to do it on Mondays and Tuesdays. But the rest of the time we usually have things on hand like bread and cheese for sandwiches, and eventually I'd like to be providing a hot dinner seven days a week. We only get so many donations, you know?" He sighed, as though he was disappointed that he wasn't doing more.

I nodded, thinking about the absurd amount of waste that went on at my job. Even with the leftovers I sent home with Juan, there was always food thrown away. My budget consistently included a 10 to 15 percent write-off for excess supplies. How much of that could have been used to feed those who really needed it?

We made our way through another doorway into the kitchen, an area about twenty feet square. There was an L-shaped counter running the length of two of the walls, a large stove and refrigerator on the third, and a wall full of cupboards on the fourth. It was about a tenth of the size of the kitchen I worked in at my job. Rita stood at the sink with four enormous sacks of russet potatoes lying next to her on the counter. The radio by the stove played a bass-heavy tune—the Black Eyed Peas, maybe? Rita smiled when she saw me. It lit up her entire pixie face.

"Eden!" she said, continuing to peel the potato she held. "So happy you could make it!"

"I'll leave you in Rita's capable hands," Jack said. "I've got a ton of paperwork to do."

"Oh sure," Rita said. "You just want to get out of potato-peeling duty. *Again*."

Jack laughed and put his hands on his hips with false indignation. "Come on, now. You'll make me look bad to the new recruit."

"Don't let him fool you," Rita said to me. "He's sneaky."

"Have fun, you two," Jack said. He disappeared out the door.

"He'll be back soon," Rita said. "I was just giving him a bad time. He's great about multitasking around here. He cares too much not to be."

"I can tell," I said, thinking of how protective he was about his clients' privacy.

"He's actually a total softy. Just serious about what we do, you know? He put a lot on the line to get this place off the ground. It's his baby." She nodded toward the stove. "Can you make a sauce for the potatoes? There's milk and cheese in the fridge."

"Sure," I said, again noting her attire consisted of jeans and a snug black T-shirt, this one embellished with the phrase RUNS WITH SCISSORS. It felt a little odd to be the one in the kitchen taking orders instead of giving them, but I reminded myself that I didn't go there to be in charge. I pulled one of the aprons off the wall and put it around my neck. "Anything special I need to be aware of in how you like things prepared?"

"We don't put nuts in anything in case someone is allergic,

but other than that, have at it. I have complete faith in you. Jack tells me you're a professional."

"Yeah, cooking is pretty much what I live for."

"Really? I live for sex." She widened her dark brown eyes and gave me a suggestive, sideways grin.

I laughed. "Well, I like to sprinkle a little of that in where I can, too. Though it helps if you have a partner."

"A pretty gal like you doesn't have a boyfriend?"

I shook my head as I tied the apron strings behind my back. "That is very sweet of you to say, but nope. Not at the moment."

"You'll have to let me do your chart. I'll figure out when Mr. Right will show up."

"You do astrology?"

Nodding, Rita set a potato on the cutting board and began to slice it. "What's your sign?"

"Libra."

"Oooh, the scales." Rita set her knife down and rubbed her hands together conspiratorially. "You're all about love, then. And balance."

"Well, I'm rarely balanced," I said, and she laughed. "Where are the pots and pans?"

Rita directed me to the correct cupboard and I began to build the sauce with a roux. They had margarine instead of butter, so I crossed my fingers, hoping the right chemical reaction would take place in order to thicken the sauce. The music filled the silence and we fell into a comfortable pace of my asking for guidance to find what I needed and Rita telling me where to look.

After about half an hour, the sauce was coming together. Just as I was putting in the shredded cheese, a man with dirty blond dreadlocks stuck his head in through the doorway.

"What's for dinner?" he asked. He was gaunt and had black smudges on his face. "Smells good in here."

"None of your beeswax, Saturn," Rita said playfully. She set the bowl of sliced potatoes she'd been carrying onto the counter, then stood on her tiptoes to reach for a bag of pink and white frosted animal cookies. She opened it and handed a few to the man. "Now, this is our little secret, right? Don't go telling everybody or I'll run out and won't be able to give you any more."

"Would I do that to you, Rita? I think not." He jutted his chin over toward me. "Who's she?"

She rubbed the man's arm and smiled. "That's Eden. She's a bona fide chef, my friend."

"Nice to meet you," I said, continuing to stir the sauce on the stove.

He looked wary but nodded in acknowledgment.

"You better not miss what she's cooking up for you," Rita said. "Now, scoot so I can get back to work!" He left, and Rita came over and dipped a spoon into the sauce. "Mmm. Tasty. We need to get the water boiling for the potatoes."

"We can pour the sauce right on the raw slices," I said. "As long as they're thin enough, they'll cook in the oven just fine. How many baking pans are there?"

"We can fit four in the oven at a time. Dinner is served at six, so that gives us about three hours to cook it all. Does that sound doable to you? I usually just boil the potatoes and pour the sauce over them."

"I think they taste better in the oven," I said. "With the edges and top all browned and crisped up?"

"Oh yeah. Just like Mom used to make." Rita patted her flat belly appreciatively.

I laughed. "Not my mom. I get my culinary passion from my father, for sure. He taught me a lot of the basics." My voice quavered. I swallowed hard to keep the muscles in my throat from closing up.

Rita set her spoon down and gave me an unexpected hug. She was surprisingly powerful for her petite frame. When she pulled back, she kept her hands on my arms and looked me straight in the eyes. "You are a wonderful daughter for trying to find him, Eden. All about the love, like I said. Your life feels out of balance without him."

I nodded and the tears rose up and spilled down my cheeks despite my best attempt to keep them at bay. "I miss him," I whispered. "So much."

"Of course you do. And I have no doubt he misses you, too." She gave my forearms a squeeze before letting go, then clapped her hands together once. "Okay then! We need to get our asses moving if we're going to get done!"

I wiped at my eyes with a dish towel. "Right. So if you spray the pans down with nonstick and fill them about three-quarters of the way with sliced potatoes, I'll get the ham diced."

"I can do that," Jack said. I whipped around to see him standing in the doorway. I had no idea how long he'd been there or what he'd witnessed. *Great.* I'd spent maybe a total of half an hour with the guy and I'd already cried twice. I probably seemed as off-kilter as some of his clients.

Jack walked over to the refrigerator and pulled out two good-sized plastic-wrapped hams. Not the kind from a butcher with a bone, like I would use if I were making this dish for a party, but rather the pressed lunch meat variety of ham, factory-injected with water to keep it moist.

"So, tell me what to do, Chef," he said with a sparkle in his eye. "How do I cut this up?"

I sniffed and attempted a smile. "With a knife?"

He laughed and I went to stand next to him. He pulled out a large serrated knife from the drawer and held it up for my appraisal. "Will this do?"

"It's the right size, but the serration will tear the meat up."

"It's the biggest one we've got," Rita said. "Our peeps won't care if the meat is a little torn around the edges. I say go for it."

"Okay," I said, pushing down the professional chef's voice inside my head that was screaming about using the wrong tool. "And I noticed a huge bag of grated carrots in the crisper. Were you planning to use them for anything?"

"No," Jack said. "The produce guy who donated the potatoes threw those in as an extra. I thought maybe we could make carrot cake or something."

"*You're* going to bake?" Rita said, incredulous.

"No, smart-ass," Jack said. "I was hoping I might talk Eden into it."

"I have a better idea," I said. "Since they don't get a ton of vegetables, how about I throw them into the sauce? The cheese will cover up the taste and most of the color. They'll never know we're sneaking in the vitamin A. They could use it, right?"

Jack smiled and nodded. "Absolutely. I say do it."

Rita agreed. "Definitely. But when you're done with that, there's cake mix in the cupboard. You know. If you feel inclined to whip up some dessert."

"I'll see what I can do," I said. The nervous flutter in my chest had disappeared. I put my head down and did what I knew best. I cooked.

As it turned out, I didn't have time to bake a cake since the oven was occupied with scalloped potatoes until it was time to open the doors for dinner. After dicing up the ham, Jack went back to his office for a while, but then returned to the kitchen a few minutes before six. "We should get the food out there," he said. "I'm sure the guys are chomping at the bit to eat."

I helped him carry out the first couple of deep-dish pans to the dining room. Four rows of rectangular tables were set up and another one sat by the door, where Rita stood holding a huge pitcher of bright red Kool-Aid. We took the pans over and set them down, and Jack went over to the double doors and unlocked them. "Ready?" he asked.

"Bring 'em on!" Rita said. She motioned for me to stand next to her. "Why don't you scoop the potatoes into the bowls and I'll get them their drinks. They'll get their own coffee over there."

I looked over to the corner, where three full coffeemakers sat on a small, round table with white paper cups, just as the rush of bodies lined up at the table where the food was set up. The first man in line grabbed a bowl and looked at me with a toothless grin. I grabbed the serving spoon and filled his bowl.

"Hope you enjoy it," I said with a smile.

"Smells great," he said. "Thank you so much."

"You are very welcome. How are you tonight?"

"C'mon down, Mickey," Rita said to the man before he could answer me. "I got some of your favorite fruit punch Kool-Aid here." She held up a paper cup and he took it. "We have to keep the line moving," she whispered. "Otherwise they'll stand there and talk your ear off. We'll leave the socializing for Jack."

"But I thought I was supposed to be building relationships—getting to know them?" I whispered.

"Let's have you sit back a bit tonight and just take it all in. They'll warm up to you better if you don't force it, you know? They can be a little cautious of newcomers."

"Okay," I said.

And so it went over the next hour, me filling up bowls, smiling and sending the clients down the line to Rita. Jack moved around the room, chatting up different people, men and women alike. "So you guys serve dinner to anyone, but only the men can sleep here?" I asked her.

"Yep," she said. "Safer that way, you know? Too many bad things can happen in the dark."

As I worked over the next couple of hours, I watched the clients mingle, sitting together in groups of two or three, a little like the lunchroom in high school. There were those who sat alone, too, but for the most part, people were talking as they would have at one of the dinner parties I catered. The content of the conversations was much different, of course, and as I served them their meal, I found myself listening in with silent fascination.

"Dude, I got ticketed for sleeping in my car!" I heard one man tell another as they sat at a table nearby. By this point, it was toward the end of the evening and we had run out of food. Jack was slowly ushering people into the bunk room or out the door and Rita was already in the kitchen starting to clean up. I couldn't believe how quickly time had passed.

"You can fight that, man," his friend said. "There's a Washington State law that says if you get tired driving, you should pull over and rest. Show up in court and tell 'em that shit and they have to drop the fine. I mean, how they gonna tell if you weren't driving home from your mama's?"

"My mama's dead," the first man said.

"Well, they don't know that, now, do they?" The men laughed together, slapping each other on the back the same way I'd seen Bryce and his friends do. It helped, seeing this sense of community, and a little while later, as I drove home from my first night at Hope House, I pictured my father connecting with other people like the men I'd witnessed—building another family of sorts. A family that stuck with him longer than my mother and I had. One that loved him enough to keep him from running away.

Three weeks after my father emerged from hibernation in his studio, part of me wished he had never come out. His sadness took on an angry edge I hadn't seen before, and though it was directed at my mother and not at me, I still felt it. It took up all the air in the room.

"Are you watching, Lydia?" my father asked each morning, standing in front of the kitchen sink while my mother and I ate breakfast. He placed the pill on his tongue with an exaggerated motion. "Thsee?" he lisped, and then swallowed, chasing it down with an entire glass of milk.

"Yes, David," my mom said. She wasn't looking at him. "I see."

This was pretty much the extent of their daily interaction. They hardly even looked at each other. Mom left for work, I went to school, and Dad did who-knows-what all day while we were gone. As far as I knew, he never left the house. I worried about him as I sat in class, absentmindedly twirling a piece of my hair, wondering if he was safe, unsure if he'd be there when I came home. One day, Mr. Pitcher caught me. He always called on the person he knew was spacing out. This was not the first time it had happened to me.

"Eden, can you come up here and work out the answer to number eight on the board, please?"

Staring at the complicated mess of numbers on the chalk-board, my face immediately flamed. It was a new way to divide, and I had no idea how to do it. I threw a glance over to Tina Carpenter, who still hung out with me while we were at school even though her mom wouldn't let her come over because of my dad. We ate lunch together, and occasionally I even went over to her house to play. It wasn't *her* fault her mom was so mean. She tucked her curly red bob behind one ear and rolled her brown eyes, as if to tell me she didn't understand how to work the problem, either. Of course, she had probably been paying attention.

"Eden?" Mr. Pitcher said.

Slowly, I slid out from behind my desk and took deliberate steps toward the front of the class. As I brushed past Eric Callahan, a chubby boy who regularly picked his nose and stole other kids' lunch money, he put his hand over his mouth, pretended to sneeze, and spat out the words, *"Your dad's a freak."*

I stopped in my tracks and stared at him. "What did you just say?"

He turned his round, freckled face toward me and reached up to brush his mop of blond hair out of his beady blue eyes. "I *said,* 'Your dad's a *freak.'"*

"That's enough, Eric," Mr. Pitcher said. "One more outburst like that and you're going to the office." He sighed. "Eden, let's just work the problem, okay?"

My blood felt hot. My skin crackled with anger and before I could stop it, my arm shot out from my side, fist clenched. Eric's nose erupted.

"Ow, ow, ow!" he cried, rocking back and forth in his seat, cupping both hands over his nose and mouth.

"Eden West!" Mr. Pitcher shouted. He stomped over and pulled me away from Eric's seat. "What were you *thinking?"*

Tears burned in my eyes as I continued to stare at Eric. "I was thinking he's a jerk." Half of the class laughed, the other half was dead silent. I was usually one of the quiet kids.

Mr. Pitcher held my arm and steered me toward the door. "To the office. *Now*." He turned and stepped back toward Eric, who whimpered like a baby while blood dripped down.

An hour later, my mother came to get me. The secretary in the office told me she was going to call my dad, but I stopped her by saying he was sick. The last thing I needed was for him to come to the school and make a scene in front of everyone. He'd done that before, when I didn't get picked for a part in a holiday play. Too shy to get up in front of that many people, I hadn't even auditioned in the first place, but that didn't matter to my dad.

"It's an injustice!" he yelled as he stood in the hallway near my locker, wearing paint-splattered turquoise sweatpants and an orange sweater. "My daughter's a star!"

"Daddy, don't," I pled quietly. My classmates stopped in their tracks and their eyes burned into me. But he didn't listen, pulling at his hair and continuing on his rant about sexual discrimination and social crimes until the vice principal came to escort him out of the building. I stayed home pretending to be sick for three days after that, too embarrassed to show my face.

Now, after a brief meeting with the head principal, who explained that if I had another physical outburst I'd be suspended, Mom drove me home. "I don't understand why you'd react like that," she said. "It's just not like you."

I shrugged, looking out the window and sinking down as far as possible in my seat. I didn't want to talk about what Eric had said. My mother knew—Mr. Pitcher had told her—but I couldn't bring myself to say the words out loud. The shame I felt burned in my belly. I hated that everyone knew about my father's problems. In that moment, more than anything else, I wanted him to be someone else. To wear a suit and a tie and go to a job that he complained about while he watched football on Sunday afternoons with a beer in his hand. A father who mowed the lawn and knew how to work on our car when it broke. I wanted him to be normal.

"Are you working on a painting, Daddy?" I asked him later that afternoon after Mom had gone back to work and I'd spent a few hours in my room, losing myself in a book. I was rereading *A Tree Grows in Brooklyn,* hoping Frances Nolan might give me some kind of help on how to deal with an unstable father whom she couldn't help but adore.

He was sitting on our couch watching Oprah. His fingers rested loosely around the neck of a pint of vodka. He wasn't supposed to drink with his medication. I wondered if he was fooling us in the mornings. If he'd found a way to hide the pill under his tongue without us noticing. He'd done it before.

"No," he said. His eyes rested at half-mast. "I'm finished painting." He lifted the vodka bottle up and waggled it at me. "Between us, right, Bug?"

If I didn't answer him, did I have to keep his secret? Where did he get the alcohol if he wasn't leaving the house? His friend Rick, probably. I'd seen Rick bring my father little baggies full of what looked like lawn clippings, which Tara White had explained to me was actually drugs. I felt sick thinking my dad was lying to us again.

"Do you want me to help you take some of your new paintings to the gallery?" My chin trembled as I spoke. "Maybe someone will want to buy one again." About six months prior, the Wild Orchid Gallery in Bellevue had purchased a series of sunset watercolors my father had done. They talked to him about doing a show, but according to my mom, he got flaky when he went off his meds and they lost interest.

"They don't want any more of my work," he said. "Nobody does. It's pointless. It's all pointless. They're all out to get me, anyway. They hate all the great artists. Why should I be any different?" He took a swig from the bottle.

I went and sat next to him on the couch. "They don't hate you. They can't. Your paintings are too pretty. Can I see the new ones? The ones you did in January?"

"They'll be worth more when I'm gone." He stared at me, but there was nothing of him in his eyes. No liveliness, no knowing wink. Was this the meds, or was he just drunk? I didn't know how to tell.

My stomach flip-flopped at his words. "Don't say that."

"I can't help it if it's true."

I tried a different approach. "Will you come see the tulips in the Garden of Eden? They're all blossoming now. The hyacinths, too. They smell so yummy."

He blinked a couple of times. "What?"

"The garden we planted," I said with a lump rising in my throat. "Remember? You said if we waited, the good part would come and it did. It's out front."

"Oh, right." He sighed and turned his attention back to the TV. "I'm too tired. Maybe another day."

I stayed upstairs until my mom came home later in the evening. She knocked before coming into my room, where I lay on my bed, trying to figure out my math homework without making my brain explode. Multiplication was a language I just didn't know how to speak.

"Hi," I said, taking in her tired eyes and slumped shoulders. "How was your day?"

She gave me a little frown. "Other than picking my daughter up at school for fighting, it was fine. Busy trying to get everything ready for taxes." She sat down on the edge of my bed and circled her hand over my back. "How are you? Any better?"

I shrugged. She was only being nice about what I'd done to Eric because she knew what he had said.

"Uh-oh. Are you still upset about that silly boy? You can't let ignorant people get to you, sweetie. And that's what he is. Ignorant."

I shook my head but didn't answer her. I didn't want her to see me cry. Again.

She sighed and continued to rub my back. "You're worried about Dad, I know. I am too. He won't go see the doctor, sweetie. He needs his meds adjusted so he's not such a zombie."

I didn't know if I should tell her about the vodka. "He's so mad," I said. "He didn't even want to go look at our garden. And he's not painting." I felt the tears squeeze out and drop onto my worksheet. "I know he has new paintings in his studio, Mom. I saw them. Can't we sell them for him? So you don't have to worry so much about the bills?" I wanted to help my mother. I wanted to do anything to make sure she wouldn't want to leave me, too.

"You are very sweet to think of that, but he locked the door and hid the key. I don't want to break it down. He already doesn't trust me after the last time I did that." Last year, after my dad had locked himself in the garage for over a week, threatening to drink paint thinner, my mom had used a crowbar to pop the lock off the garage so the medics could take him to the hospital. He came back a month later, utterly blank and lethargic. All he did was stare into space.

Now my mom leaned down and lifted up my chin so I was

forced to make eye contact with her. "We'll be okay, Eden. I'll do whatever I need to."

"Like put him in the hospital again?" My lower lip quivered as I spoke.

"He might need to be there. It might be better for him . . ."

"Maybe I could ask him to go to the doctor so he can get his medicine fixed. Maybe he'd listen to me."

She pulled her hand away from my chin and wiped my tears across my cheeks with her thumbs. "He doesn't listen to anyone, sweetie. He can't. That's part of what's wrong with his brain when he gets like this. It doesn't let him hear things, even if they're the right things. Does that make sense?"

"No."

"I wish I knew how to explain it better, but I just don't. It's hard for me to understand, too." She straightened and stood up. "Frozen pizza okay for dinner?"

"Can we have it hot instead of frozen?" I asked.

She rewarded me with a laugh. "Oh, you want it fancy to-night, huh?" She ruffled my hair. "You're a smarty-pants. But I love you to pieces."

Later, after we ate in a silence that my mother tried to fill by asking me silly questions about school and the books I was read-ing, I went back upstairs. But instead of going in my room, I sat at the top of the stairway, tucked behind the railing. My parents were talking in the dining room.

"You're scaring her," my mother said. "You have to get it to-gether, David."

"Why is it me who always has to 'get it together'?" my father answered. "Why can't you?"

"You're not making sense. I can't talk to you about this until you get your meds straightened out. If you're actually taking them."

"Oh, first you want me on my meds, and now that I'm on them you're not happy, either? You know what I think? I think it's you who has the mental illness." His words slurred. He was definitely drunk. "Not me. You. You're completely fucked-up."

"I'm not going to do this anymore, David. I can't. Not with you like this. I'm responsible for everything. The bills, the shopping, the house, helping Eden with her homework. I might as well be a single parent."

I heard a chair screech across the wood floor, most likely my dad pushing it back from the table. "Fucking be a single parent, then! What the fuck do I care? Abandon me. That's fine. Just like everyone else. Just like my parents, just like the galleries. No one wants me. I'm not worth a fucking thing."

"Oh, poor David," my mother said. Her tone was soaked in venom. "The tortured artist. What about his tortured wife? Or his child? Does anyone give a shit about them?"

"Not me." I heard my father's lumbering footsteps and I scrambled to hide around the corner to make sure he didn't catch me listening. My heartbeat pounded inside my head.

"No, of course not you!" My mom was yelling now. "It's never you! It's always someone else's fault. Your medication or your doctors. God forbid you actually tell yourself the *truth*."

"And what's that?" my dad yelled back at her. "Tell me, oh great and powerful Lydia! Don't hold back! Give it to me straight!"

"You're out of your fucking mind! That's the truth!"

"Fuck you!" my father screamed. There was a terrible crash, strong enough to make the wall I was leaning against shudder. The sound of breaking glass and clattering metal made me race down the stairs and into the dining room. My father had upended the table. Shards of porcelain and glass lay all around my mother's feet. He'd been aiming for her. She was standing in the doorway between the dining room and kitchen, her right hand pressed flat against her chest. Her face was flushed bright pink and she was breathing hard, her blond hair loose and wild around her head. My father was slumped to his knees on the floor; his head was in his hands. "I'm so sorry," he mumbled. "I'm so sorry."

"Eden, I want you to go back upstairs," my mother said. Her voice trembled. "Now."

"Are you okay, Momma?"

"Yes, I'm fine. I'm not hurt. I just need you to go upstairs."

My father looked up to me with tears in his eyes. "I didn't mean it, Bug. I didn't mean to scare you."

I took a couple of steps toward him. He began to sob.

"Eden!" my mother shouted. "Don't! You'll cut yourself!"

I looked down at my bare feet. She was right. "I love you, Daddy," I said. My throat flooded with tears. "It'll be okay, I promise. Everything will be all right." I recited the words he'd said to me countless times over the years, when I'd fallen and scraped my knee or had a fight with my best friend. In that moment I realized how empty they were. How pointless it was to say them. I couldn't make my father promises any more than he could make them to me.

I ran up to my room and climbed under the covers. My sobs came hard and fast, racking my body until I was too exhausted to stay awake. I fell into a deep sleep and dreamed of chasing after a shadowy figure. Every time it came within my reach, each time I thought I might have caught up, it slipped away.

It was still dark when I felt someone shaking my shoulder. My eyes were so swollen they barely cooperated when I tried to get them to open. I had to blink several times before I saw my father standing over me.

"Daddy? Are you okay?"

"Shh," he said, hushing me. "Yes, I am. I'm so sorry, Bug, for making things so hard for you."

I propped myself up on my elbows and looked at him. The moonlight shone through my window enough for me to see that he was freshly showered, but his eyes were as puffy as mine felt. "It's okay," I said. "It's not your fault."

"Yes, it is. Your mother was right about one thing. I need to take responsibility for myself. I'm a mess, Eden."

"If maybe you'd go to the doctor, he could get your medicine all worked out," I said. "And then you would be okay." I didn't want to point out that I was pretty sure he hadn't been taking it in the first place. At least, not for long.

"I can't take the medicine. It makes me crazier than I am without it. What happened tonight wasn't me. It was the medication. I'm going to find another way to get better. Do you want to come?"

"You're leaving?" A panicky beat pounded in my chest.

"Yes. I'm going to take my paintings on the road. We'll go to galleries all up and down the coast until we have enough money to come back. I've already loaded up the car. What do you say, baby? I need my wingman. Just like selling lemons at our lemonade stand. It'll be you and me."

"But . . . what about Mom?"

"Mom will be fine. She's good at taking care of things, right? So she'll take care of herself. And you can call her. When we have enough money so she doesn't have to worry about working anymore, we'll come back and we can be a family again."

I tried to imagine what that would be like. Enough money for my mom to never have to work. How happy that would make her. My mind shot off rapid-fire thoughts. I was afraid to leave. But I couldn't let my dad go. I didn't know what to do.

"Do we have to go right now?" I asked. "Can't we wait until morning and talk with her?"

"No, it can't wait. She's finally sleeping and I'm leaving." He turned toward the door. "I understand if you don't want to come, baby. I'm used to no one believing in me."

With that pronouncement, he left. I listened for his steps on the stairs, but he must've tiptoed because I didn't hear them. I sat up and swung my legs over the side of the bed. I was a little stunned that with all the crying I'd done the night before more tears were already streaming down my face. I didn't want my father to become like the shadow in my dream. If I let him go now, I might never see him again. I realized I was still in my clothes—I had fallen asleep in them.

Before I knew it, I had slipped on my Keds and was running as quietly but as fast as I could down the stairs and out the door. I grabbed my jacket and my backpack on the way out and raced to my father's car. He sat in the driver's seat, his hands placed squarely at ten and two. The motor was already running. He'd been waiting for me.

I jumped into the front seat and he looked over to smile at me. It was then I noticed his left hand wasn't just holding the steering wheel, but also a prescription bottle. His window was open and he held the bottle outside. The lid was off. He poured the full bottle of tiny white pills onto the street, right where my mother could find them.

"Ready for an adventure?" he asked, and I nodded my head, too afraid of what might happen if I told my daddy no.

After my first successful dinner was served at Hope House, I showed up the following two Tuesdays with plenty of time to make both the meal and a dessert. The catering schedule at work had been too hectic for me to do any other type of searching for my father, so I found myself looking forward to my new volunteer commitment, though it wasn't only because it gave me the opportunity to keep an eye out for him. I had gone home that first night filled with a kind of satisfaction I hadn't experienced before—a little astounded by the level of gratitude the Hope House clients showed for a simple bowl of warm, hearty food. I was accustomed to people paying ridiculous dollar amounts to eat the elaborate dishes I prepared. I realized how much I took for granted when it came to catering customers being able to afford whatever food they wanted. It was a decidedly different dynamic to cook in order to fulfill the very basic need of keeping people from going hungry. I found myself craving that feeling again.

My third Tuesday helping with the evening meal I arrived to discover Jack holed up in his office doing paperwork and Rita already in the kitchen trying to sort through the ingredients in the pantry. Several five-pound packages of raw ground beef sat on the counter. "If I make meatloaf again, there'll be a revolt!" she said, grabbing her blond spikes with exaggerated frustration. Her

T-shirt was black today and read WHAT I REALLY NEED ARE MINIONS in tiny white letters.

"We'll figure something out," I said, laughing. Though I'd only spent a couple of evenings with Rita, I was drawn to her irreverent sense of humor and unmistakable affection for her clients. I stood next to her and let my gaze travel over the shelves. The week before I'd used up the shelter's excess supply of chicken stock, frozen chicken thighs, and flour to make chicken and dumpling stew. Juan had overordered fruit for a corporate event, so I bought a few boxes at cost and served the clients a fruit salad with whipped cream for dessert. Now an industrial-sized container of Mexican seasoning caught my eye.

"What about taco casserole?" I said. I pointed to the multiple boxes of cornbread mix and stacked cans of dark red kidney beans. "I can mix the beans and the meat with some onions and the seasoning, top that with shredded cheese, and cover it all up with the cornbread batter. Bake for an hour and voilà! Dinner."

Rita hugged me. "You're a genius. Seriously." She slapped her hands together. "Okay, if you get started on that, I'll make a boatload of salad. Jack's produce guy came through with romaine, cucumbers, and carrots."

"I thought the clients don't eat veggies," I said, a little confused.

She shrugged. "Jack said we should at least try to get them some better nutrition. They devoured the fruit you brought last week, so he figured even if they drown the salad in dressing, they'll get the vitamins."

We worked for the next couple of hours, me sautéing ingredients and building the casserole, and Rita chopping up heads of lettuce, shredding carrots, and mixing homemade ranch dressing. While she went to set up the dining room and make coffee, I managed to throw together a huge vat of chocolate pudding with some eggs, milk, and chocolate chips. Jack entered the kitchen just as I was mixing the last batch.

"That's amazing," he said, commenting on my ability to crack an egg one-handed to separate the white from the yolk. Our interactions had been minimal during the first two dinner services; he was friendly enough and seemed to be happy with the food I was putting out, but any conversation had been limited by the amount of time he spent with his clients. Which was his job, of course. I couldn't help but find his obvious compassion for them appealing.

My insides warmed with the compliment. "Thanks," I said. "It's nothing, really. Just takes practice. Lots and lots of practice." I put the last bowl of pudding in the fridge to cool.

He grabbed an egg. "Will you show me how?"

"Sure." I put my hand around his to help guide his fingers into the correct position around the egg. His skin was warm but a little rough. "So, the trick is to be gentle. The shell wants to crack, and all you have to do is let it do its job." I pulled my hand back from his.

"Got it," Jack said. He thwacked the egg against the edge of the bowl, obliterating it. "Oops."

I laughed. "Like I said, it takes practice. And we're going to have to work on your definition of 'gentle.'"

"I'm not a Neanderthal, I promise." He went to the sink and washed the goopy mess off his hands, then we headed to the dining room. He pushed the cart loaded down with the finished taco casseroles while I carried one of the enormous bowls of salad. In a few minutes, we were open for business.

While Rita and I kept the food line going, I watched Jack out of the corner of my eye, impressed to see him issue a hug or handshake to the people we served. He sat down for a few minutes at a time, chatting with the clients. Mostly he seemed to listen, his head bent toward the person he was with, giving them his full attention. Occasionally, he would reach out and hold a person's hands in his own. His eyes were always intent upon the person.

"He's great, isn't he?" Rita asked. I whipped my head around to look at her, unaware she'd been watching me watch her boss. She laughed. "Oh yeah, I caught you."

I blushed up to the tips of my ears and suddenly became very interested in stirring the almost empty pan in front of me.

"Don't worry, sweetie. I won't say a word. But you could do a lot worse."

"I'm not looking to *do* anything," I said.

"Uh-huh." She gave me a pointed look.

"I'm going to get the pudding," I said. On the way to the kitchen, I thought about what I'd just said to Rita. *Was* I looking for anything?

Luckily, I had too much to do to give the issue much thought. I had people waiting for dessert. The next client through the door could be my father.

"So, it's been a few weeks," Jack said several hours later as I was putting on my jacket to leave. "What do you think?" Now that dinner and dessert had been served, we stood in his office while Rita was in the bunk room coordinating the clients' sleeping arrangements for the night.

Jack helped my arms into the sleeves. "I think it's great," I said, turning around to face him. "I'm happy I'm here."

"We're happy, too," he said. "Your dinners are a hit. A lot of the clients are asking if we'll see you on a regular basis."

I nodded. "Definitely. I work a lot of nights, but I usually have Tuesdays off. I'm looking forward to talking with everyone more."

"So they can keep an eye out for your father."

I glanced at him a bit quizzically. "Well, yes, but I also feel like I sort of fit in here." I laughed. "Does that sound weird?"

"Not at all. You seem very at ease. And not everyone can relax around this population." He dropped his eyes to his desk, busying himself by shuffling a stack of papers into a neat pile. I took that as my cue to leave, but before I could, he cleared his throat, looked up, and spoke again. "It's a little late. Can I walk you to your car?"

"Sure," I said, grabbing my purse from a brass hook on the wall. I usually tried not to play the damsel in distress but was surprisingly charmed by his chivalrous gesture.

Jack put on his jacket and we walked down the hallway out the front door. The air was chilly and a steady drizzle fell, so I flipped up the hood on my jacket and tucked my hands into my pockets to keep them warm. There was a bar across the street, and a low bass rhythm thumped through the air. Some of our clients stood outside the bar's door, talking to the exiting patrons—asking, I was sure, for a few dollars or spare cigarettes. Part of me wished I could gather them up and bring them home safe with me.

"Who watches over things when you're gone?" I asked Jack as we strolled toward the parking garage two blocks down from the shelter. "Rita?"

"Sometimes." He threw his gaze both ways before we crossed the street, then looked back at me. "I have a couple other people on staff, too, but I don't take many days off. This place is pretty much my world."

"Is this what you've always wanted to do?" I was curious

about what had motivated Jack to feel so passionate about his work. Did he have a homeless family member, too?

A strange look flashed across his face but disappeared too quickly for me to discern what its significance might be. "Not always. I majored in business and got my master's in organizational development."

"Sounds like you were prepping for the corporate set. What made you change your mind?"

"Long story." He smiled, but the words were clipped. *The end,* they said. I knew enough to figure out he didn't want to pursue the subject. At least not now. We entered the garage and I directed us to my car, standing by it a moment in slightly awkward silence.

"Well," I finally said, "thanks for walking me."

"No problem." He looked around at the empty spaces and shuffled his feet. "It's pretty well lit. You probably would have been fine on your own."

I smiled too. "Probably. But it was still nice of you." I opened the driver's-side door and slipped into the front seat. "I'll see you next week. And hey, I was thinking, if you can get your hands on a bunch of tomatoes from your produce guy, I could make spaghetti. I get a great rate on bulk pasta through work. Seriously. Pennies a pound."

"That sounds fantastic," he said. "I can get more ground beef, too." He placed his hand on the door, holding it open for a moment. He seemed hesitant to speak.

"Everything okay?" I asked.

He nodded. "Oh, yeah. Thanks again."

I pulled the door shut and started the engine. Just as I looked down to put the gearshift into reverse, Jack rapped on my window, shooting my heart right into my throat. I rolled down the window.

"Jesus!" I said. "Did I forget something?"

"No, but I did." He took an audible breath. "I meant to ask you earlier, but we were so busy and then . . . well, I felt a little weird about it. But I'm going to ask you anyway. What the heck, right?"

"Um, I'm not sure," I said. My pulse immediately picked up speed. "That depends on what you're going to ask."

He laughed, a staccato noise. "Right. I was just thinking, you know, about what we talked about a few weeks ago? Your father's old apartment building?"

"Uh-huh."

"Well, I was thinking if you wanted, I could go with you to talk with the other tenants. To see if they remember your dad." He looked down to the ground, then back up to me.

I had half expected him to ask me out, and I wasn't sure if going to my father's old apartment qualified. Still, I appreciated his offer to help. "Really?" I said. "You'd do that?"

He shrugged and smiled. "Yeah, really. I was just thinking it might be easier if you had someone with you. I mean, I'm sure you have other friends or family who could help you out, but I thought that since I'm the one who brought it up, it wouldn't hurt to ask if you'd want some company."

"I'd love it. Thank you. When do you want to go?"

"How about I call you tomorrow and we'll figure it out?"

I nodded. "Sure, sounds good. I'm an early riser." I hoped I was keeping my smile to a reasonable size. I wasn't the kind of girl who got asked out a lot, so when a man expressed interest in spending time with me, I couldn't help but be flattered.

"Me too," he said.

As I backed out of the parking space, I was already anxious for morning to come.

*   *   *

"I think I have a date," I told Georgia when I called her the next day at her office. "But I'm not sure. I need an expert's opinion."

"I have exactly three minutes until my first meeting," she said. "So spill, but make it fast."

I gave her the quick summary of my evening at Hope House, including Rita's teasing and my subsequent conversation with Jack while he walked me to my car. "And he called, just like he said he would."

"Already? At what unholy hour?"

"Seven. And it's not unholy, because I told him I'm up early." I leaned forward on the couch to grab my mug from the table. "He gave me just enough time to have a cup of coffee and let Jasper out."

"So, he asked if he could come with you to look at your father's old apartment building?"

"Yep. We're going today, since neither of us has to work. Is that a date? I mean, technically?"

"Sorry to disappoint you, my friend, but I'm thinking not so much. I mean, he wants to spend time with you and all, which is a good thing. But in order for it to count as a date, it can't really be an errand."

"What if we get lunch afterward?"

"Post-errand meal. Sorry." She laughed. "Look, I'm just happy that you're doing something with your social life other than going to work and walking your dog. And it sounds like at least he has some potential, right?"

"Right. I know I said I'm not looking for anything—"

"Pfft," Georgia said, interrupting me. "Whatever. You are so full of crap and you know it. Rita even knew it and she just met you. So stop lying to your best friend and let me get back to work. I expect a full report tonight. Can you do drinks?"

"Sure. I'll call you later," I said.

"Aloha, bella!"

I hung up, smiling to myself. "Okay, Jasper. I have to get dressed." He wagged his tail and looked at me with those loving, soulful brown eyes that suckered me into bringing him home a decade before. "Want to help me pick out what to wear?"

He barked once, which I took as a yes. He followed me into the bedroom, where I chose to keep it simple in jeans and a V-necked royal-purple sweater. Georgia considered me wardrobe disabled since I rarely dressed in anything other than my chef coat and kitchen clogs. I didn't see the point in spending the money when I could save it for opening my restaurant.

After a quick shower and blow-dry, I threw on a little makeup and got dressed. "What do you think?" I asked Jasper. "Meat-flavored perfume?"

He barked again and waggled his rear end.

"Oh, you would say that, you dirty old hound. We wouldn't want to give Jack the wrong idea, now, would we? This is only an errand, you know, so don't get your hopes up."

After I locked up the house and helped Jasper into the backseat of my car, I punched Jack's address into my GPS and followed its instructions to a neighborhood near the Ballard Locks. I pulled in front of the apartment building to see him waiting under the awning. Jasper barked when Jack opened the door and jumped into the passenger side.

"Hey," he said, and then twisted around in his seat. "Who's this?"

"That's Jasper. Jasper, this is Jack. I hope you're a dog person.

Or at least not allergic. I probably should have asked if it was okay to bring him."

"Totally okay. I love dogs." He extended his arm, his fingers curled under to allow Jasper to sniff him. It was good to see he knew proper dog etiquette. Jasper must have thought so, too, because he nudged Jack's hand with his wet nose. Jack obliged by scratching Jasper behind the ears and thus forever etched himself a place in Jasper's heart. He was easy like that.

"I'd have fifty if I had the space," Jack said when he turned back around and pulled his seatbelt on. "But since I'm gone so much, it wouldn't be fair to have one, even, you know?"

"Yeah, I get that." I selected the address of my father's old apartment building on my GPS, then flipped on my indicator to rejoin the flow of traffic. "But Jasper sleeps pretty much every minute he's not eating or pooping, so I don't worry about it too much. He's getting to be an old fella."

"I plan to have the exact same routine when I'm an old fella."

"One can only hope."

Jack laughed, and then we rode in silence for a few minutes. It wasn't the uncomfortable variety of not speaking, which I took to be a good sign. I'd spent time with men with whom sitting in silence felt akin to having bamboo shoots shoved beneath my fingernails.

"Turn right in twenty-five feet," my GPS told me.

"Thank you, Bertha," I said.

"You named your GPS?" Jack asked.

"Sure. It felt too impersonal not to." I patted the display screen. "Bertha and I are very close. She has saved my life on numerous occasions." I lowered my voice to a conspiratorial whisper. "I'm directionally challenged, you know."

Jack laughed. "Don't worry, I won't hold it against you."

"Turn left now," Bertha's computerized voice ordered.

"Bossy little bitch, isn't she?" Jack said.

"Oh, it's fine. I need someone who'll stand up to me."

"I'll keep that in mind."

Keep that in mind for what? I wondered. *Getting to know me better? Or is he considering having more than a friendship with me?* My insides warmed a little at the thought.

"So," I said after I'd turned up Mercer to head toward Capitol Hill. "Who's holding down the fort for you at the shelter?"

"Starr and Paul, my other two employees. They're both social workers, fresh out of college, so they work cheap and they're almost as gung ho about the place as I am."

"Anxious to help, huh?"

"That's what most people think. That we want to 'help' our clients." There it was again, that slightly irritated tone. The same one he used on me in our first conversation. It was easier to stomach knowing he was more impassioned than annoyed, but still.

I flashed him a quizzical look before putting my eyes back on the road. "And you don't want to help them?"

"Not exactly. How would you feel if someone came to you with this attitude of, 'Here, let me *help* you.' The inherent message being that there is something fundamentally *wrong* with you. That you're somehow 'less than' because you live differently than they do. Most of my clients don't want help. They want to be treated like members of the human race. They want camaraderie and friendship and connection. Like we all do."

"Well," I said, wanting to tread carefully around what was obviously an important subject to Jack, "I hadn't thought about it that way."

"Most people don't."

"But—and I hope you don't mind me saying this—aren't a lot of your clients caught up with drugs? And crime?"

"Some of them, yes. And they're just as much in need of connecting as anyone else. Maybe more so." He sighed. "Is that a good way to live? No, of course not. Are they responsible for ending up in whatever situation they're in? Sure. At some level, they already know that. They don't need me to lecture them on it. And it's certainly not up to me to try to make them change. How well do you react when someone tells you how you should be living your life?"

"Not very well *at all,*" I said. "I've been known to bite. Or kick the offender in the leg."

He laughed and I was relieved to see a sparkle in his eyes. "Look," he said in a much friendlier tone. "This is how I see it. I provide a humane environment so any client—no matter what their choices have been—can come in off the streets and feel worthy of love. If I provide them food and general information about what they can do to *help themselves,* then I've done my job. I personally can't help them. The best I can do is create a space where they can build up their own self-esteem and hopefully as a result make healthier, more productive choices for their lives."

"Is that the 'hope' in Hope House?" I asked, silently impressed with how eloquently he stated his beliefs.

"Exactly."

After another left turn, Bertha informed us that we had arrived at our destination. I showed off my parallel parking skills, then glanced at the building we were about to enter. It was redbrick and only four stories high. Jack and I got out of the car. I left the windows cracked for Jasper, who was accustomed to waiting in the car while I ran my errands. And that's what this was, according to Georgia. An errand I just happened to be running with Jack.

Upon closer inspection, I saw that the bricks were crumbling in enough places to make me concerned about the building's structural safety. The windows were leaded and ornate, but as we ascended the broken concrete steps, I noticed the white paint on the sashes was peeling. "This place has seen better days," I remarked.

"It's an old neighborhood," Jack said. He leaned down and scanned the mailboxes.

"What are you doing?" I asked.

"Looking for the manager's apartment." He ran his finger across the names posted on each box until he happened upon the right one. "Got it. W. Reilly. One-A."

"All right, then. Let's go." We approached the first apartment door. Jack rang the bell, a muffled buzz. After a moment, when we didn't hear any footsteps, he rang it again.

"Coming!" a woman's voice cried. "Keep your panties on! Just need a minute to find my hair!"

"Her *hair*?" I whispered, and Jack shrugged. I imagined a bald little old lady rummaging around in her apartment.

A minute later the door creaked open and an older woman with cloudy blue eyes and a crooked black wig smiled at us. It was immediately apparent she had opted to locate her hair instead of her dentures. "How can I help you young people?" she asked. "Looking for an apartment? I'm afraid I don't have any open right now."

"No, actually," Jack said. "We're looking for any information you might have about an old tenant of yours. David West?"

The woman's eyes narrowed. "And who are you?"

"I'm his daughter," I said. "Eden."

"Oh, Eden," she said. Her expression softened as her eyes moved off Jack and searched my face. "You take after your dad, no doubt. I'd know those blue eyes anywhere." She stepped back and motioned us inside. "Come in, come in. Pardon the mess. I wasn't expecting company."

"Thank you," Jack said. "We don't mean to intrude."

We both maneuvered through the stacks of newspapers that lined the hallway leading into a small living room. The air inside the apartment was laced with the stale aroma of recently fried meat. My stomach gurgled at me—in my excitement to pick up Jack, I'd forgotten to eat. We were definitely going to need a post-errand meal.

"You're not intruding." The woman plopped herself into a well-worn tan recliner; the flowered housedress she wore rode up and exposed her knobby knees. "I'm Wanda. Wanda Reilly."

"I'm Jack Baker, and you've met Eden." We sat on the only other reasonable surface in the room, directly across from her on a tiny wooden-backed velvet love seat. I found the solidness of Jack's thigh muscle pressed against mine reassuring.

"How is your father?" Wanda asked. "I've missed him around here."

"Well," I said, "I actually haven't seen him. Not for years. Which is why I'm here. He sent me letters from this address and I was hoping you might have some information about where he might have moved. I'm trying to track him down."

Wanda furrowed her almost nonexistent brows, pulling together the wrinkles on her forehead like a couple of window treatments. "I remember him trying to get in touch with you. He talked about you all the time. I always hoped you'd come see him."

I looked down, unable to meet her gaze. "It was complicated. I don't mean to make excuses—"

"Oh," Wanda said, interrupting, "you don't need to explain.

I understand why it might have been hard for you, honey. What he put you through was just awful." She dropped her chin toward her chest and gave me a pointed look. "He told me, you know."

I felt Jack's eyes on me, but I lifted my gaze and locked it on Wanda. I wasn't ready to tell Jack the messy details of how my relationship with my father had ended. Outside of my family, Georgia was the only person who knew, and even with her I rarely spoke of it.

"What did he tell you about his life after he wasn't with us anymore?" I asked Wanda.

"Well," she said, "as I recall, he spent some years on the streets. Down in California, I think he said. Where it was warmer. David was a good man, but he had his problems, now, didn't he? There were times I had to use my key to get into his apartment just to make sure he hadn't done something stupid."

I nodded. "He definitely struggled with his demons."

"Don't we all." Wanda sighed. "He did good for a while there. Had himself a job at a little diner downtown."

"What did he do there?" Jack asked. "Do you know?"

"He washed dishes during the dinner shift. The place is closed now, but back then, he claimed to like it since it left his days open to paint, but I never quite believed him on that point. He had his good days and his bad. The bad days got worse and then he was gone. Poof. Just like that."

I swallowed before speaking. "How long did he live here?"

"Oh, not long, sweetie. About a year. But I remember that man. He had a way about him. So charming." She tapped the side of her head with a veined and gnarled finger. "Haven't lost all my marbles yet."

"Did he happen to leave anything behind?" Jack asked. "Anything that might help us figure out where else to look?"

"A few things, I think," Wanda said. "We can go check down in storage, if you want. I know I moved his paintings down there. I'm sort of a pack rat that way. Never want to throw anything away. Might be a box of his things there, too. Books and such. Just give me a minute to get my teeth in." Using the arms of the recliner for leverage, she hoisted herself up, shooing Jack away when he stood up and tried to help her. "I can do it myself, son. Been on my own for going on twenty years now. I'll probably carry my own casket." She shuffled down a narrow hallway toward the back of the apartment.

Jack sat back down and took my hand in his. "You doing okay?"

"No," I said. "Not really." My pulse thrummed in my neck. I wasn't sure if it was due to my nerves or the fact that Jack was holding my hand.

Jack squeezed my fingers. "Sounds like he loved to talk about you."

I nodded. "She said there were paintings. I haven't seen any of his work for years. I'm a little freaked out to think about what it might be."

"You'll be fine. If it gets to be too much, we'll just leave, okay? I'll have it picked up and sent to your house or something, and you can go through it a little at a time. Without an audience."

"What do you mean, you'll 'have it picked up'?"

He looked away for only a second before answering. "I have a friend who owns his own moving company. He owes me a favor."

"Oh." I squeezed his hand, grateful for its warmth. "I appreciate that. A lot."

"Not a problem." He pulled his hand away and stood up as Wanda reentered the room.

"Let's go, kids!" she said.

We followed her out of her apartment and down the hall to a padlocked door. She rummaged around in her pocket for a ring of keys and we both shifted back and forth on our feet as she tried at least ten before finding the one that opened the lock. A weak lightbulb illuminated a steep, narrow wooden staircase leading to a cement floor below.

"Why don't you let me go first?" Jack suggested. "I'll catch the cobwebs for you ladies." He carefully edged around Wanda, who took his hand before taking her first step.

"Such the gentleman," she remarked over her shoulder to me. "You better keep your claws in this one, sweetie. They don't make 'em like this anymore."

I caught Jack's eye and gave him a small smile, which he returned with a wink. *Errand, my rosy-red heinie, Georgia. He likes me. Why else would he be here?* I was pleasantly surprised by how much I was starting to like him, too.

We made our way down the steps. At the bottom, Jack let Wanda take the lead again.

"Down this way, on the end," she said. "I keep a unit for abandoned stuff that I can't quite throw out. I covered David's paintings to make sure they didn't get damaged, but after a while I had to toss the paints. They started to dry up. Like me." She cackled at her own joke.

We waited another few minutes for her to sort through the keys and open the cyclone-fence unit. "They're in the back," she said. "Propped up against the wall by the couple of boxes of his, I think. I put his name on them, if I remember right. You don't mind if I let you two get in there and root around? Instead of me?"

"Of course not, Wanda," I said. "I can't tell you how much I appreciate this."

"T'ain't nothin'. I'll just wait right here."

Jack and I made our way back into the unit. I sneezed a few times as the dust rose when he moved a few things out of the way. It didn't take long for us to find the boxes Wanda had mentioned. Behind those, I saw the telltale white edging of canvas. The paintings were stacked in a row, maybe five deep.

"You want to look now?" Jack asked. "Or do you want to wait?"

My chin trembled before I spoke. "Maybe just one. For now. Okay?"

"Sure." He bent over and pulled the boxes out of the way, then picked up the first painting. The light was fairly dim, but when he flipped over the canvas, I knew instantly it was my father's. It was an oil of the last house he'd lived in with us, white and gabled with its small, square front porch. But the house itself wasn't the subject of my father's painting. What caught my eye was the flower bed planted out in front of the house—the glorious ocean of red tulips, sunny daffodils, and purple hyacinths. I had handpicked each one of the ugly brown bulbs that transformed into those blossoms. I would have recognized them anywhere.

"It's the Garden of Eden," I breathed, and my chest heaved and the tears spilled down my cheeks. "He remembered." Jack gently set the painting down and rested a comforting hand on my back.

"Everything okay in there?" Wanda called out. "Is she hurt?"

I nodded as though she might see me do it. Yes, I was hurt, though I didn't know to what extent. And standing in that basement amongst my father's other discarded things, I wasn't sure whether finding him was worth the price I might have to pay to find out.

March 1989
David

David had no idea where he was going, but he drove like hell to get there. For a couple of hours, he headed south for no particular reason. The southbound on-ramp was closer to their house, was all. He could just as easily have been approaching the Canadian border. Instead, he and Eden had just passed through Olympia. If he kept going at this rate, they would be in Portland before lunch. There were lots of artists in Portland. There were grants he could apply for. Art schools where he could teach. He could make a home for his daughter there.

He didn't know why he'd woken Eden and asked her to come with him. All he knew was he couldn't take another minute in that house. He stewed for hours after he flipped over the dining room table. Lydia had asked him calmly to clean up the mess and then she stepped carefully through the broken dishware, going up the stairs and into their bedroom. She refused to talk with him when he came to check on her. She acted like he wasn't even in the room, detouring around him to go to the bathroom before climbing back in bed. *Fine,* he'd thought. *You're going to act like I'm not here, then I just won't be here. Poof! Voilà! No more husband.* After he was sure she was asleep, he packed his bag, then went downstairs to load as many of his paintings as he could into the backseat of his Honda.

He'd never gotten violent around Lydia before. It scared him that he had. Sure, he'd ranted and yelled and said a thousand things he regretted, but he never lost control. His rage was usually directed toward himself and his failings. Always inward. Now that it had escaped and decided its own path, he had to leave. He needed to protect his family.

Eden's soft snoring over in the passenger seat made him think of a purring cat. Her head lolled toward the window and a tiny drip of saliva hung in the corner of her mouth. Trying not to wake her in the process, David reached over and wiped it with the edge of his sleeve. She stirred but didn't open her eyes. He knew he'd never hurt his daughter. Maybe he brought her along to make sure he didn't hurt anyone else. Eden was his inspiration. His reason to be the kind of man he knew he could be if he just could get a handle on the countless spinning tops in his brain. As long as she was with him, he could get himself together.

"Dad?" Eden spoke with her eyes still shut. "Where are we going?"

"Where do you want to go?"

She lifted her head and turned to look at him with sleepy eyes. "I don't know." Her stomach growled and she clapped both her hands over it and smiled. "Breakfast?"

"Sounds good," David said. He had about five hundred bucks in his wallet—money Lydia had stashed in what she thought was her secret hiding spot in the back of their closet. She put it in a box of tampons, thinking he'd never look for it there. How little she understood about desperation.

It was just starting to get light outside. He pulled off at the next exit and drove directly into a Denny's parking lot. Inside, they ordered orange juice and pancake breakfasts.

While they waited for their food, Eden fiddled with the container of sugar packets. She was unusually quiet.

"What're you thinking, Bug?" David asked her. "There's a big cloud hanging over your head. We're supposed to be on an adventure. You can't have rainclouds on an adventure. They aren't allowed." He reached over and chucked her chin playfully, but she only gave him a wan smile.

"Did you take your pills, Dad?" she asked. She dropped her eyes to her lap. "In the mornings, I mean, in front of Momma and me?"

David sat back in the booth and blew out a heavy breath between his lips. "For a little while I did."

"For how long?"

"A week or so." He paused. "Why?"

"Well, if you weren't taking them, it wasn't the pills that made you throw the dining room table. Like you said." Her voice quavered but she lifted her gaze to his. He saw the fear in her eyes, but it was laced with determination.

"I didn't throw the table, Eden."

She shrugged, a minute gesture that screamed she didn't believe him.

"The thing is, the medicine stays in your body a long time, you know?" David explained. He was willing to do anything to take that look off his daughter's face. He was willing to lie. "So when I had that little bit of vodka, it mixed with the medicine and made me lose control like that. You see, honey? That's what I meant when I said it was the medicine and not me."

He could see the debate raging in her mind. *Believe him, don't believe him.* She stared at him for what felt like a full minute before speaking. "You shouldn't drink, then." Her voice was solemn.

"You're right." He nodded vigorously. "You're absolutely

right. I won't. I promise." He thought about the flask he had inside his jacket pocket. He'd been sipping at it as he drove and he suddenly wanted nothing more than to down the entire contents.

He threw his gaze around the dining room. He was jittery and his eyes were wild—he felt it. The itch to escape ran like thousands of ants beneath his skin. He didn't want to be doing this. Any of it. Why had he brought Eden with him? She would only slow him down. He tapped his foot on the ground in a staccato rhythm. The table shook.

"Daddy, are you okay?" Eden asked.

He took a deep breath. "I need to use the bathroom, Bug. You'll be all right if I'm just gone a minute?"

She nodded. Just as he walked away, the server—a portly, grandmotherly type in a too-tight uniform—delivered their food. "Will you keep an eye on her?" David asked, gesturing toward Eden. "I'll be right back. Just have to use the bathroom."

"Sure," the lady said, and sat down with Eden at the table. "It's not busy. And I need to take a load off a minute anyway."

"Thanks," David said, and rushed off to the bathroom. Once he locked himself in the stall, he pulled out the flask, opened it, and let the liquid burn fire down his throat. He swallowed until there was nothing left. He would need to get more. Stepping out to stand in front of the sink, he stared at himself in the mirror. He didn't recognize the reflection. Gaunt and tired. Broken capillaries around his nose and across his cheeks. He leaned forward, peering intently at his eyes. They were empty. His soul seemed to have vanished. Where had he gone, the man he had fooled himself into thinking he could be? He growled at the mirror, snarling and snapping at the enemy who took him away from his daughter. He wanted to smash his head against the wall to dislodge it. He wanted it to die.

"Are you okay in there, sir?" He heard a woman's voice through the door. "Your daughter is finished with her breakfast and yours is getting cold."

It took a moment for him to come back to himself. "I'll be right there," he said. He blinked several times and splashed cold water on his face before heading back out to the dining room. Eden rushed over to hug him.

"I was worried about you, Daddy," she said. "You were gone so long."

"I was?" he asked. "I'm sorry, baby. My stomach's not feeling so hot." He threw a twenty on the table and smiled at the server. "Thanks for watching her. I'm sorry for any inconvenience."

The woman gave him a strange look. "No inconvenience. I'm sorry you're not feeling well. You want me to box up your food for you for later?"

He shook his head. "No, thanks. We need to get on the road."

"Which way you headed?" she asked.

"Portland. Going to visit family." He put his arm around Eden's shoulders. "Come on, honey. We need to get going." He waved at the woman as they walked out the door. He could feel her watching them. Her eyes felt like daggers in his back.

"We have family in Portland?" Eden asked when they got into the car.

"I don't know!" David snapped. "No!"

Eden went silent and turned her head to face out the window. Her shoulders began to shake.

David sighed as he pulled out of the parking lot. "Don't cry, Eden. I'm sorry I snapped at you. I really don't feel good. Don't you get cranky when you don't feel good?"

She didn't answer.

"Eden. Listen to me. That server was giving me a really

strange look. Like she thought I was doing something wrong. I needed to get out of there, okay? That's why I said we have family in Portland. So she'd leave us alone. Do you understand?"

"I want to go home," his daughter whispered.

"What?"

"I want to go home. I want to see Momma." She turned to look at him with tears welling in her eyes.

"But we're having an adventure, honey. Remember?"

"I don't want to have an adventure!" she cried. "I want to go home. I want to see Mom!" She stamped her foot on the floorboard.

"Too bad!" David roared as he turned onto Interstate 5 heading south. "You can't have her! She didn't want you, you know! She never wanted to be a mother!" Even before David said the words, he wished he could take them back.

"That's not true!" Eden screamed. "I don't believe you! You're a liar! You lied about taking your medicine and now you're lying about this, too! I hate you! I wish you weren't my dad!" She flung out her arm and hit him on his shoulder.

David pushed harder on the gas pedal and gripped the steering wheel so tightly his knuckles went white. "Knock it off," he growled. "Knock it off, *now*."

"No!" Eden screamed. She began to pound on the window. "Help! I need help! Somebody help me!"

"Eden! Stop it! Stop it right now!" David swerved into the far left lane. When the speedometer hit eighty, the console began to rattle. "You're going to make me get in an accident, honey." He tried to make his voice remain calm.

She didn't answer again but continued to let loose huge sobs that sent shudders through her entire body with every intake of breath. He drove faster, hating that he was doing this to her. He shouldn't have brought her. He should have taken all those pills instead of dumping them out and been done with it. Then the only person he would have hurt would've been himself.

They had been back on the road about half an hour when the flash of red and blue lights caught David's eye in the rear-view mirror. He was still speeding. The patrol car gained on him quickly and he heard the megaphone instructing him to pull over to the shoulder. He complied, taking deep breaths to try to calm his adrenaline. "Please stop crying, Bug," he implored his daughter. "I'm going to try to talk my way out of this. Let me do the talking, please." She didn't acknowledge him but did take a couple of deep breaths in what he hoped was an effort to slow her tears.

David rolled down his window and smiled at the policeman, a grim-looking man with a thin, black mustache. "What can I help you with, Officer?"

"Please step out of the car, sir."

"Was I going too fast? It's my little girl, here. She's always telling me to make it go faster."

"Sir, I'm not going to ask you again to get out of the car."

"Aren't you even going to ask for my license and registration?"

The policeman put his hand on the door handle and pulled. "I won't ask again. Let's not make a scene in front of your child."

"I don't understand—" David began to say, but the officer yanked the door open and grabbed him by the arm before he could finish his sentence. "Hey!"

"Daddy!" Eden cried. "Don't hurt him! He didn't mean to do anything wrong. He didn't mean it!"

"It's okay, sweetie," David said as the officer guided him to the back of the car. "I'm right here. Everything's going to be okay." He glared at the officer. "You're scaring my little girl."

"According to her, you're the one who's scaring her, sir." The officer pulled out David's wallet and reviewed his license.

"That's ridiculous. Eden's just having a tough time being away from her mother for the first time. She's homesick."

"Did the child's mother know you were taking her daughter?"

"She's not just 'her' daughter," David spat. "She's mine, too. My sperm, my daughter."

The policeman was not impressed. "You didn't answer the question, sir. Did the mother know you were taking your child away?"

"Of course she did! This is unbelievable. I knew they'd come for me. I knew they'd find me and take her from me. Don't you see?" David pled. *Do anything,* his brain told him. *Say anything. You have to get away.* "Don't you see they're after me? I had to protect Eden. She's my daughter. I needed to keep her safe!"

The officer leaned in and sniffed near David's face. "Have you been drinking, sir?"

"It's barely light out! Of course not!"

"I'm going to have to ask you to accompany me to the squad car, Mr. West."

David took a step away. "I will not. My daughter is in the car. I can't leave her alone."

"You left her alone in the restaurant. Didn't you, Mr. West? She was so afraid she told the waitress her mother's phone number. Your wife is frantic. Now, let's get you into the car so Eden doesn't have to be exposed to anything else that's going to hurt her."

David was speechless. She'd turned on him. He thought Eden was his shining star, but she was just like all the rest. Lydia. The doctors. The ones who betrayed him. He stared at his daughter through the rear window. She was turned in her seat, watching him with wide eyes. He looked back to the officer. "What about my paintings? They're in the back of the car."

"Don't worry about that right now. Let's worry about getting Eden back home to her mother." Just then, the officer made the mistake of glancing away from David for a moment as another squad car pulled up. David took the opportunity to swing his arm around and strike the man square in the jaw. The other officer jumped out of the car and ran toward them. David raced around to grab his paintings from the back of the car.

"Daddy, I'm sorry," Eden said when he leaned inside. She was crying again. Her eyes were red and her nose was runny. "I didn't know what to do. I was scared and I just wanted to go home!"

He didn't answer her. Just as he was putting his hands on one of the larger canvases, he felt the gun at the back of his neck. "Back out of the car, now!" It was a female officer, he realized. He wondered if he could hit a woman. But before he could think about it too long, he felt the strong yank of a man's grip pulling him out of the car and throwing him facedown on the ground. The male officer had straddled his back and was putting handcuffs on him.

"You're under arrest for driving while intoxicated and assaulting an officer," he said through gritted teeth. "You have the right to remain silent. Anything you say can and will be used against you in a court of law." He finished telling David his rights as he jerked him upright and led him toward the squad car. The female officer helped Eden get out of the car.

David heard her soothe his daughter. "It's okay. Everything's going to be all right."

Eden kept her eyes locked on David as he climbed inside the patrol car. She clutched her backpack to her chest. "I'm sorry,

Daddy!" she cried before the male officer shut the door to take David away. "Daddy! *Please!*"

David didn't say a word. He stared hard at his child, watching her sob and shake on the side of the road, wondering if, after this, he'd ever want to see her again.

Eight hours after Jack and I left my father's old apartment build-ing, Georgia showed up at my door with a bottle of Pinot Gri-gio and Thai takeout. When she'd called after she was done with work and asked if I'd meet her for drinks at the Dahlia Lounge downtown, I told her I wasn't up to socializing.

"I'll be there in an hour," she said. I didn't argue, knowing she'd come whether or not I wanted her there. Georgia was good like that.

I lit a few vanilla-scented candles in the living room and we curled up on my couch with our pad thai and filled wineglasses well within reach. "Wow," Georgia commented. "I get candles? You trying to seduce me?"

"Hardly." I gave her a tired smile and took a sip of wine. "How was your day?"

"You don't want to know. I, however, am dying to hear what happened with the homeless-shelter guy. I'm thinking nothing good, considering we're in our sweatpants on your couch?"

"Jack was great, actually. We laughed and talked and even flirted a little. I like him. He seems genuine and sweet."

"The height thing didn't bother you?"

"I didn't really notice it as much as I thought I would," I said.

"He's confident, too, which I like. But not in a short-man's-disease kind of way."

"No Napoleon complex, then. That's good."

"None that I could see." I went on to describe the encounter with Wanda and my response at finding my father's belongings in the basement.

"So you started crying in front of him *again*? What is this, three times now?"

"I know." I sighed. "He probably thinks I'm certifiable. But he was very calm and comforting."

"What did you call it again? The painting?"

"*The Garden of Eden.* Planting that garden was sort of the last happy, meaningful thing my father and I did together, so seeing it like that, knowing he remembered and it was important enough for him to paint after that much time had passed, hit me pretty hard."

"Wait. Didn't you tell me that would be the name of your restaurant? The Garden of Eden?" I nodded. "Ah." She continued. "I like it. And now it makes sense." Georgia lifted her wineglass and took a hefty sip. "What happened after your meltdown?"

"When I drove Jack back to the shelter, I explained to him why I freaked out and then I came home. I've been puttering around the house all day trying to figure out if I should keep doing this."

Georgia set her glass down on the coffee table. "Looking for your dad, you mean?"

I nodded again as I picked up a spring roll from one of the white to-go cartons and took a bite. Jasper whimpered and set his chin on my thigh. I tossed the remaining half of the roll in the air and he caught it. Spoiled mutt.

"I think you should," Georgia said. "It's important for you to get some closure around him."

"I thought I *had* closure. I had him written off as someone whom I'd never see again. It was hard after he left, but I sort of got used to it. He'd cross my mind and I'd feel this intense longing in my chest, but I forced it down, you know? I tried to pretend it wasn't there. And then my mom got sick and I just couldn't imagine a world where I didn't have either of them. I felt so guilty for not responding to him when he reached out to me, I felt like I had to find him."

"I remember. So what's changed?"

I shrugged. "Nothing, really. I just . . ."

"Just what?" Georgia asked, urging me on, when I didn't finish my thought.

"I just hate *feeling* all of this old crap. I saw that painting and everything I've felt about him—all the anger and sadness and fear I haven't really thought about for twenty years—just took me over. It completely sucked and I don't know if I want to keep doing it."

Georgia set her food down and reached over to place her hands on my knees. She looked at me intently. "Eden, I'm going to say something that I'd say to a client if she came to me with this same issue, okay?"

"Oh, boy." I set my food down too. "Look out."

"That's right. Free life coaching brought to you by your loving friend Georgia who knows you better than anyone. So listen up." She took a deep breath and let it out. "Have you considered the possibility that you are too filled with all those crappy emotions you just mentioned to have a healthy relationship? It's like you've pushed down the pain you felt over your dad disappearing, shoving it into the nooks and crannies of your heart, and now there's no room for anybody else." She gave me a small smile and pulled her hands back to her own lap. "Honey, if you were a client, I would tell you to keep doing what you're doing. Keep looking for your dad. What you went through today is like picking at the edge of a scab or pushing at an old sore to get the gunk out. It ain't pretty and it hurts like a bitch, but you're not going to heal until you do."

"Um, first of all, ew. Thanks for the visual." She laughed. "And second, I have thought about all of that. Part of me thinks you're right, but another part thinks it's all going to be pointless if I don't find him." Maybe I could figure out my issues with men and relationships without finding my father. Maybe I just hadn't found the right guy yet.

"I don't think it's about whether or not you find him," Georgia said. "I think it's about what you manage to work through while you look. Life's supposed to be about the journey, right? So this should be part of yours. Maybe you'll learn something about yourself."

"Maybe. And hey"—I playfully punched her in the arm— "I have plenty of room in my heart for you. *And* Jasper *and* my family *and* my job. I have successful relationships. You make me sound like an unfeeling bitch. 'Sorry, my heart's all filled with pain and anger. No room at the inn!'"

She frowned. "That's not what I meant and you know it. I know you have healthy relationships. And you're not anti-male or anything like that. I'm talking about falling in love. Letting a man in close enough to build something with him that might last. You're terrified if you do, he'll leave you and tear you to shreds."

"Like my dad." My lower lip trembled. It was the thing I loved most about Georgia. She was unflinchingly honest but somehow managed to keep you from feeling you'd been socked in the jaw with the truth. Instead, she sidled it up behind you and had it tap you gently on the shoulder. It was probably what made her so good at her job. Those CEOs never knew what hit them.

"Yes. Like your dad." She reached for her wine and leaned back into the couch. "Not that I'm one to talk, of course. You know I have my own variety of emotional barriers against falling in love. Mine just take the form of my busy career. Perhaps having to do with emulating my work-addict father?"

"It's such a relief to know I'm not the only one in the room with father issues." I gave her a grateful smile. Georgia and I had discussed our fathers on more than one occasion.

"Hell no. Are you kidding me? Deep down I believe if I prove to be as dedicated and successful as dear Daddy is, perhaps he'll love me the way I need him to and I can finally allow myself to be loved by someone else." She sighed. "I'm a total cliché."

I applauded. "Nicely done. Where'd you figure that out? Therapy?"

"Nah. It's my job to analyze the internal blocks that keep my clients from getting what they want, personally and professionally. Turning that skill inward was bound to happen. Not that I'm ready to *do* anything about it, you understand. I'm much too immature. Plus I adore the guilt gifts Daddy sends for my birthday. In June."

"But your birthday is in August."

"Try to tell him that." She glanced up at the clock on the DVD player. "Hey, isn't *The Bachelor* on tonight?"

"I think so." I reached for the remote. "Shall we lose ourselves in the magic of reality TV?"

"I'm in," Georgia said, reaching up to twist her hair into a messy bun. She secured it with a chopstick. "What did you make us for dessert?"

"I didn't feel much like baking. You'll have to suffer through with ice cream."

"The things I put up with as your friend," she said. "It's a good thing I love you."

"Somebody has to," I said. "And I'm pretty lucky it's you."

The next day, just as I was getting ready to head into work, Jasper barked and I opened the front door to discover a burly but friendly-looking bearded man standing on my porch. His hand was raised, ready to knock. "Eden West?" he asked. I noticed his name, Tom, sewn in swirly red letters on his blue work shirt.

"Yes," I said, peeking over his shoulder at the white van parked in my driveway. "Can I help you?"

"I have a delivery for you from Jack Baker. Where would you like it?"

I lost my breath for a moment, realizing that Jack had done what he promised once again by having my father's things delivered to my house. *How did he get my address? Did I give it to him?*

"Ms. West?" Tom said, prodding me.

"Oh," I said, startled. "I guess you can just bring it inside. I'll go make sure there's enough space in my spare room. Unless you need some help?"

He shook his head and smiled. "Nope, that's why I get paid the big bucks. Can I leave the door open or will your dog get out?"

Jasper sat next to me, eyeing this stranger on my porch. "He's not an escape artist, are you, Jasper?" I said. "Come on, get out of the nice man's way." I directed Jasper to the floor in front of the couch and told him to lie down and stay.

It only took a few minutes for the paintings and box to be transferred. I thanked Tom and tried to give him a tip, but he wouldn't hear of it. "Mr. Baker takes good care of me. But I appreciate the gesture. Have a nice day, miss." He tipped the ball cap he wore and left.

I looked at Jasper. "What do you think, buddy? Should I go take another look at Dad's stuff?"

He wagged his tail and panted. He was so agreeable—why couldn't more men be like Jasper? I'd feed them and scratch their asses and in turn, they'd curl up in my bed and keep me warm at night. Seemed like a reasonable deal to me.

"Okay, I guess I should. C'mon." I patted my hip and Jasper trotted behind me to the spare room, where Tom had set the box and paintings on the bed. There weren't as many of Dad's paintings as I had initially thought. I ran my finger along the stacked edges and counted six in total. His depiction of the Garden of Eden lay on top. My stomach churned a bit looking at it, but the initial shock at seeing my dad's familiar style and brushstrokes had worn off. In its place was a sense of longing for the man who had planted that garden with me. The man who got down on his knees and dug in the dirt, carefully showing me how to set the fat end of the bulb in its hole, how to press the soil down with the palm of my hand.

"Should I put the daffodils all in the same spot, Daddy?" I had asked him. It was my first garden; I wanted to be sure I did everything right.

"You can put them wherever you want, Bug," he responded. "Mix them up or put them all together. It's your garden. You get to decide."

I was overwhelmed with pleasure at the prospect of being in charge and proceeded to lump a few yellow daffodils next to a couple of bloodred tulips. Next, I threw in a single pink hyacinth for good measure. I continued this random mix over and over until all the bulbs were planted. What resulted the next spring was a colorful but unorganized wild mess and my father had captured it perfectly in his work. Whatever imbalance his brain endured did not seem to have affected his memory.

I wanted to spend more time looking through his things, but a glance at my watch told me I needed to get to work. It was probably better to go through the box slowly. No need to rip the scab off all at once.

I called Jack on the way, happy when he picked up on the third ring. He sounded pleased to hear from me. "How're you doing?" he asked.

"I'm okay, thanks. I received an unexpected delivery."

"Oh, it got there? Great. I wasn't sure if it was too soon to send it over, but I figured you could just put it all in a closet and look at it or not look at it at your leisure."

"I appreciate that. How did you arrange it so quickly?"

Jack paused. "My friend owed me a favor, remember?"

"I remember, but the guy said something about Mr. Baker 'taking good care' of him. I was curious what he meant."

Jack laughed. "Oh, that's just Tommy being an idiot. He's my friend. End of story. Are you on your way to work?" I wondered why he seemed a little weird around this issue again but decided not to push it.

"Yeah, I have a huge menu to get organized for a wedding this weekend."

"So you're really feeling okay? I was a little worried."

A pleasant sensation burned in my belly, knowing he had been thinking of me. "Thank you, but I'm fine. My best friend came over and talked me down off the emotional ledge. I promise I'm not a girl who typically cries all the time. I'm actually sort of a badass."

Jack chuckled. "Oh, yeah?"

"Definitely. If anyone at work found out their chef was such a crybaby, there'd be immediate anarchy. You do realize I'm going to have to swear you to secrecy."

"And what do I get for my cooperation in this little pact?"

"Wow, we've known each other less than a month and you're already blackmailing me?"

"I feel your constant waterworks have brought us close enough together for that kind of intimacy."

I smiled. "Hmm. I don't know. You might be moving a little too fast for me, Mr. Baker."

"I'll go at whatever speed you're comfortable with, Ms. West."

I laughed, enjoying our banter. Was it just banter? Did he talk with all women like this? "So, Jack," I said. "How did you get my address?"

"Rita had it in the family contact paperwork you gave her for if your dad shows up. I hope it was okay I asked her for it."

"Of course. I was just curious." I pulled into the parking garage beneath the Emerald City Events building. I turned off my car and thought about how much I'd rather sit and keep talking to Jack instead of going inside to work. I hung up with a huge smile on my face, one that Juan noticed immediately when I walked into the kitchen.

"Hey there, boss lady! You look like you won the lottery or something."

I laughed as I pulled on my apron and sat down at my desk. "You think I'd be here if I'd won the lottery?"

"Sure you would. If only to bring me a bonus check. For being the best guy in the world."

I shook my head, still smiling. "What have we got on the books?" I asked.

"The Chandler wedding this weekend is pretty much it, besides a couple of small dinner parties tonight and tomorrow. I've already got the ball rolling on those, but we await your spreadsheet before we can get started on the wedding." He slumped down into the chair across from me and pressed the heels of his palms into his eyes.

"You're not working too much, are you?" Since Juan was an hourly employee and qualified for overtime, I typically gave him free rein to work past forty hours as often as he liked. Especially considering his family situation. "Everything okay at home?"

Juan dropped his hands to his lap and sighed. "Pop's having a rough time of it lately. The doctors don't know what to do other than give him more pain meds, you know? I'm trying to give my mom a break at night so she can get some sleep."

"You need to take care of yourself, too, Juan."

He gave me a wry smile. "Coming from the boss lady, who works on high speed and then spends all her spare time combing the streets of Seattle for her father?"

I laughed. "Touché. Just don't overdo it, my friend. Let me know if you need to back off on your hours some."

"Can't afford it!" He popped up and clapped his hands. "Oh, hey. Doug from corporate stopped by with a huge new set of pots and pans yesterday."

"Oh yeah? How are they?"

"They're sweet. All shiny stainless steel with aluminum centers. I had Maria run them through the washer a few times to make sure they were free of all factory chemicals and are good to go."

"Thank you. That's great." I turned on my laptop and got

ready to work, but Juan didn't leave. I gave him a questioning glance. "Is there something else?"

"What should I do with the old and busted ones?"

"Oh, right. Not a lot of room around here for both sets, huh?"

"No, ma'am."

I sat back in my chair, considering the possibilities. An idea struck me. "How about we donate them to a worthy cause? That shelter I volunteered at the other night could use a better class of kitchen tools. Anything left over employees can divvy up and take home."

"Great idea, boss."

"Let me shoot an e-mail off to corporate and make sure it's okay before you tell anyone. I'll let you know."

Juan headed out to the kitchen and I quickly sent an e-mail to Doug, Emerald City Events' VP. After receiving the okay from him to dispose of the used kitchenware however I pleased, I picked up my cell and called Jack, who once again answered before the third ring.

"You again?" he said. I could hear the smile in his voice. "I'm trying to get some work done around here."

"Yeah, yeah. It's me. I was wondering, does your friend with the moving business have anything else on the books today, or would he be available to help me with something?"

"I don't know. Is there a catering emergency? If there was food involved, I could probably convince him to help you out."

I laughed. "Not an emergency, exactly. More like a surprise. For you."

"Me? Now I'm really curious."

"Well, it's technically not *only* for you, but I think you'll appreciate it. Can you give him my number and I'll tell him what I have in mind? Tell him I'll feed him, too."

"He's going to think you developed the hots for him this morning when he dropped your dad's stuff off at your house."

"Maybe I did," I teased. "Maybe this is just a ploy to get that bearded sexy beast to call and ask me out."

"I think he might have to fight me for that privilege," Jack said, and I almost dropped the phone.

"Oh," I said. My heart launched itself against my rib cage.

"'Oh'?" Jack repeated. "I set myself out there like that and all you have to say is 'oh'?" It was his turn to tease me. I could hear it in his voice.

"Sorry, you just caught me by surprise. I'm very flattered."

"As in, 'I'm very flattered, what time can you pick me up?' Or 'I'm very flattered, now get the hell away from me'?"

I laughed. "I'd have to go with option number one. When were you thinking?"

"How about tonight? I know we're both working late, but we could grab a drink afterward. If that would work for you, that is."

"That works for me. Are you familiar with Studio Zen? I know the chef there and the midnight snacks he does are amazing."

"Sounds great. Can I pick you up from work around eleven?"

"Sure. Do you know where it is?"

"I can find it. I'll call you if I get lost. And yes, I'll pass your number along to Tom, but I'm going to tell him he's out of luck if he was planning to ask you out."

"Thanks, I appreciate it. And I'm pretty sure you'll like the surprise. I'll talk with you later, then?"

"It's a date. Bye, Eden."

I hung up just as Juan strolled back into my office. He stopped short when he saw me. "Whoa there, *chica*. Another shit-eatin' grin? You organize an exceptionally pretty spreadsheet already? Or find yourself an online deal on a new outfit?"

Laughing, I chucked a nearby pack of mini Post-it notes at him. Then it hit me—I had a date. And I was at work with absolutely nothing else to wear and no time to go home. The spreadsheet was going to have to wait.

I rode home in the front seat of a police car. My father hadn't looked at me from the backseat of the other car, even after I screamed over and over how sorry I was. I didn't want to get him in trouble, I only wanted to go back home. I never should have followed him out of the house or gotten into the car. I should have woken up my mother and told her he was running away. But it was too late to change it. No matter how much I wanted to, I couldn't take it back.

"Has your dad done anything like this before?" the police-woman who was driving me home asked. OFFICER PHILLIPS, her name tag read. "Taken you?"

"He didn't take me," I said. My forehead was pressed against the passenger-side window and as I spoke, my breath fogged up the glass. I used my index finger to draw a smiley face in the condensation and then immediately wiped it away.

"He didn't?"

I turned to look at her. "No. He told me he was leaving and I went with him."

"But then you got scared and asked the waitress to call your mom, right?"

"Right." I wondered what my mom would do when she saw me. What she might do to my dad for letting me go with him. "Is my dad going to jail?"

"For a little while, yes. He had alcohol on his breath and he hit the other policeman."

"Will he get in trouble for letting me go with him when he left?"

Officer Phillips glanced over at me and smiled before turning her eyes back to the road in front of us. "I don't know, honey. That depends on what your mom decides to do."

"Well, it's not his fault. He asked if I wanted to go and I said yes. It's not like he did anything wrong. It was me." I wanted to make sure that point was clear.

"The problem is, in the eyes of the law, you're not old enough to make that kind of decision for yourself."

"That's dumb."

She laughed and flipped on the turn signal to change lanes. "Maybe, but it's the law. Grown-ups are supposed to make better decisions than the kind your dad made last night. And this morning."

"But it was me who decided to go with him. So I should be in trouble, not him."

"Eden, you can argue with me about this all you want, but your dad is the one who let you leave with him in the middle of the night without telling your mom he was going or that he was taking you with him. And you were scared enough to tell that waitress to call your mom. So you know that something wasn't right about what your dad did, right?"

"Well, maybe not *how* he did it."

"I understand you want to protect your father, but it's kind of past that point now. He's going to be in trouble for drinking and driving and for hitting Officer Peterson. I'm sorry, sweetie, but that's just the way it is."

"Can we listen to the radio?" I asked, turning to look out the window again. I didn't want to talk about my dad anymore. It was making my stomach hurt.

"Sure," she said, and reached over to push the button. "Anything in particular?"

"I don't care."

We didn't speak for the rest of the ride back to my house. When we finally got there, Officer Phillips asked me to stay in the car while she went inside and talked to my mom for a few minutes. I was tempted to argue, wishing I could be the first one to explain what had happened to my mom, but I was pretty sure picking a fight with a police officer wouldn't get me anywhere but in more trouble. I made sure to stay sunk down in my seat, hopeful the neighbors wouldn't see it was me being brought home by the police. After about ten minutes, my mom came racing down the front steps and I jumped out of the car. She wore black stretch pants and a too-tight red T-shirt, and her blond hair was matted. She grabbed me and squeezed me hard.

"Oh god, Eden! I was so worried!" She pulled back and pressed her palms against the sides of my head, searching my face with her eyes. "Are you okay? Did he hurt you?"

"No, Mom! He would never hurt me. I just wanted to come home. I knew you'd be worried."

She hugged me close again and I breathed in the warm, slightly yeasty scent she always had when she didn't shower every day. I tried to make myself believe she wouldn't be this happy to see me if she never wanted me. She wouldn't have cared that I left with my dad. She would have been happy to see me go.

"Let's go inside," she said into my hair, and then looked over to Officer Phillips. "Thank you so much for bringing her home."

"It was my pleasure. Bye, Eden." She waved at me.

"Bye," I said.

Once inside, my mother and I sat down in the living room on the couch. I thought about what my father had said and didn't know whether or not I could ask her if it was true. I wasn't sure if I wanted to hear her answer.

"What happened, baby?" she asked. She took my hands in hers and held them tight. The skin around her eyes crinkled as she peered at me, waiting for a response.

I shrugged. I didn't want her to be any more mad at my father than she already was but I didn't want to lie, either. "Dad came into my room last night after you fell asleep and he told me he was leaving. He said it was his medicine that made him throw the table last night and he was going away to sell his paintings up and down the coast and make us a lot of money so you didn't have to work anymore."

"You know that's not true, baby, right? That it was the medicine that made him do that? I don't think he has been taking it."

"Yeah, I know."

"And then what?" my mother asked, prompting me. "Why did you go with him?"

I shrugged. "I dunno."

"Come on, Eden." She dropped her chin toward her chest. "That's not good enough and you know it. Tell me."

I sighed. "I guess because I was afraid if I didn't, I'd never see him again. And also because I didn't think he could take care of himself. He needed me."

"Oh, Eden." My mother's hand curled into a fist and she pressed it against her mouth.

"I was worried that he'd hurt himself and I thought if I was with him, he wouldn't. But then we stopped for breakfast and he was acting kind of weird and went into the bathroom and didn't come out for a long time. I knew you'd be worried about me and

so I asked the waitress to call you and let you know I was okay."
I looked at her. "So I guess it was you who called the police? Because Daddy thinks it was me."

She dropped her hand back to her lap, where she folded her fingers together as though in prayer. "Yes, I did. The woman at the restaurant said you were okay but that you seemed scared, and I figured the quickest way I could get you back was to get the police involved." She paused. "Did your dad do anything to you, honey? That made you afraid?"

"Not really," I said, picking at a loose thread on my jeans. "He was kind of nervous and didn't really look me in the eye very much. And when he went into the bathroom and didn't come back for such a long time, I thought maybe he'd changed his mind and left me there alone." My eyes filled. "He yelled. A lot. And he hit the policeman, Mom, when we got pulled over. He was kind of drunk."

She leaned over and hugged me again. "I know, baby. The officer told me. It's okay, though. You did the right thing."

"You're not mad at me?"

She leaned back and stared at me. "Why on earth would I be mad at you?"

"Because I went with him," I said, keeping my voice quiet.

"Baby, none of this is your fault. Your dad is sick and needs help. It's not the kind of help I know how to give. We've been trying and trying and nothing seems to work. He just gets worse."

"What are you going to do?"

She sighed and took my hand. "I don't know yet. Right now, at least, he's safe. They'll keep him in jail until his hearing for the drunk driving and assault charges. That gives me a month to figure things out. I'm very angry with him right now."

"I went because I wanted to, Momma. But then I just changed my mind."

"Okay, baby. I understand." She let go of my hand and stood up from the couch. "Why don't you go upstairs and take a shower? I'll fix you something to eat."

"Don't you have to go to work?"

"I took the day off. There's no way I could concentrate when I was so worried about you." She smiled. "I'll go back tomorrow. And you'll go back to school. Today, we play hooky. We deserve it."

As I went upstairs, I thought about my father sitting alone in a jail cell. I imagined a black-striped uniform and the people in charge making him shave his head. I pictured him standing in line waiting for horrible, maggot-ridden food. I wondered if he hated me, and the thought made my stomach ache. I had always kept my father's secrets and now I was sure he'd never trust me again. I was the one who got him in trouble. Now he was gone and this time it wasn't because my mother had sent him away. This time it was my fault. I had no one else to blame.

David sat inside a nine-foot-square cinder-block room he had to share with a three-hundred-pound tattooed drug dealer named Rico. Rico was in on a nine-month stretch for selling cocaine, and the powers that be stuck David in with him because it was the only available bunk.

As his cell mate lay on the bottom bunk, David paced, but there was barely enough room to turn around. Back and forth, and back and forth. He couldn't move fast enough. His thoughts spun. No alcohol or pot to calm the whirling tornados. Lydia could bail him out. Of course she could. She just didn't want to. This was cheaper than paying for the hospital. Let the taxpayers foot the bill for straightening him out this time. Bitch. He was married to a bitch. She'd been out to get him from the beginning. She never really loved him. Getting pregnant was just a ploy to get him to marry her and help her get away from her parents. He couldn't believe what he'd said to Eden, telling her that her mother never wanted her. He imagined the words bouncing around inside his child, their sharp edges slicing her tender flesh to shreds.

"No," he muttered under his breath. "No, no, no." He couldn't do this here. He had to find a way to get his spinning thoughts to stop. He grabbed the sides of his head with both hands, yanking on his hair until his scalp stung. Maybe he would bleed. He would bleed and have to go to the infirmary and they'd look away and he could escape.

"Dude," Rico said from the bottom bunk, interrupting David's thoughts, "who you sayin' no to? And quit fucking pacing."

He couldn't be here. He couldn't do this for another minute. He spun around, his fingers still gripping his hair, and ran toward the wall. The top of his head hit the cement first.

"Holy *shit*!" Rico exclaimed, struggling to lift his enormous frame out from his bed. "What the hell you doin'?"

I'm silencing the demons, David thought. *It's the only way to stop them.* He lifted his eyes and stared at the wall as his forehead rammed into the cement. Lights went off inside his head and he stumbled toward the bunk bed.

"Stop it, man!" Rico yelled. "You're freaking me out!" He stood and tried to grab David, but David jerked away and this time threw his entire body into the wall. The impact jarred something in his arm; he felt it crack. A loud howl erupted in the cell. *Who was that?*

"Guard!" Rico hollered. "Dude's goin' crazy in here, dog! He's screaming! You need to get him, now!"

There's a crazy dog? Where? In the cell? Or is it chasing Eden? He needed to protect them. Or maybe he needed to figure out how to put them out of their misery. He had to come up with a way to bring this giant nightmare to an end.

In the end, Georgia saved me, like I knew she would. When I called and told her I had a real and true date with Jack directly following a ten-hour shift at work, she rescheduled her late afternoon appointments for another day and headed to my house. After feeding and walking Jasper, she declared everything in my closet totally unworthy and texted me to say she'd decided to go shopping. Five hours later, around ten o'clock, she arrived at Emerald City Events just as I was putting the final touches on the fire-roasted tomatoes I would later blend into a savory jam for the Chandler wedding's goat cheese tartlets. Georgia wore boot-cut jeans that showed off every inch of her curves and a teal sweater that made her pale skin appear as if it was lit from the inside.

Juan, the only one left in the kitchen, gave her a generous whistle when she blew in through the doors. "Mmm, *mamacita.* You are one lovely lady."

"Gracias," Georgia said graciously, bowing her head. She had two huge Nordstrom shopping bags in her hands.

"Oh man," I said, eyeing the bags. "What did you do?"

"I picked up three outfits that could work, but I have to see them on you before I can decide. I got shoes, too."

"Before *you* can decide? It's my date, right? I'm not remembering that wrong?"

She pushed me back toward my office. "Yes, it's *your* date. But I'm your personal shopper and I need you to trust me on this." She waved at Juan. *"Adios, monsieur!"*

He gave Georgia a strange look. I'd have to explain about her foreign-language quirk another time.

"Good night, Juan," I said. "Thanks for all your hard work tonight. You're taking tomorrow off, right?" I'd pushed the issue with him earlier, insisting that he let me make up the time he'd covered for me the Saturday when I'd come in late after Bryce's competition.

"Yes, ma'am!" He saluted me. "Good night, ladies."

Once inside my office, Georgia hugged me, then pulled back to gaze at me with bright eyes. "I'm so excited for you!"

"Oh, Lord. It's only a date, Georgia. I have been known to go on them before." I dropped into my chair and gave her a dreamy smile.

She pointed at me, shaking her arm a couple of times. "Ha! Not just a date. Look at your face." She sniffed the air and wrinkled her nose in distaste. "But you smell like food."

"Gee, I wonder how that happened?" I reached up and took my hair down from the messy twist I'd put it in that morning.

"Oh, perfect!" she exclaimed. "Don't move a strand. That I-just-got-laid look really works for you."

I laughed. "I look like I just got laid?"

"Well, no, not exactly. More like you just got out of bed. But it works, and that's what counts." She clapped her hands together. "Okay, you need to take a whore bath, and then we'll try on some clothes."

"Excuse me. A *whore* bath?"

"Yep. Pits and privates."

"Nice." I shook my head and smiled. The phrasing was pure Georgia.

She reached into one of the bags and pulled out a container of mandarin-scented body wash. "Here, this will go with your 'I smell like food' theme."

"Thanks." I stood up and grabbed it from her, then stepped into the small bathroom connected to my office. I quickly stripped, then wet a washcloth with warm water and a touch of the body wash. "I hope you didn't go overboard on the outfits," I called out as I cleaned up. "Studio Zen is pretty casual."

"You're talking to the dating queen, my friend. Just trust me. I know what will work at Studio Zen." She stood just outside the door, waiting for me to scrub up. I dried off and then swiped on some of the deodorant I kept in the medicine cabinet.

"Are you nervous?" she asked when I exited the bathroom in my underwear.

I shrugged and grinned at the same time. "Not really. A little excited maybe. There's just something about him."

"Buttons, I'm telling you. He pushes your buttons."

I followed her back into the office, where she had laid out two separate outfits. My eyes went immediately to a scarlet V-necked blouse trimmed with delicate black embroidery. She had paired it with dark denim jeans and three-inch open-toed strappy black sandals. I sighed. "There is no way in hell I'm wearing those shoes, Georgia. Not only would I tower over him, I'd twist my ankle and end up in tears again."

Georgia rolled her eyes. "Oh, please. You can't go in those clodhoppers." She nodded her head toward my discarded brown kitchen clogs. She grabbed a pair of suede black ankle boots from one of the bags. "How about these?"

I inspected the more practical two-inch wedge heel while I carefully picked up the scarlet blouse. "I like them. They'd put me about even with him height-wise, I think. And this blouse." I started to pull it on, but Georgia stopped me.

"Wait!" She reached into the bag and handed me a matching scarlet bra-and-panty set. "Ta-da!"

"He's not going to see my underwear."

"How do you know?"

"Because I'm not going to get naked with him on our first date."

"Oh, because *that* has never happened before. How long did you know Ryan? Three hours?"

"That was different." I crossed my arms over my chest.

"Hardly." She shook the undergarments at me impatiently. "Put them on. Even if he won't see them. It's not just an outfit, it's an attitude."

I snatched them from her. "Fine!" In the privacy of the bathroom again, I took off my ratty white bra and underwear and slipped into those she had purchased. They fit like a glove, as did the blouse and jeans. I suddenly went from chef to chic.

Georgia looked me over, smiling triumphantly. "I knew it. I bought the other things as backup, but I knew this was the one. You look amazing."

I twirled, looking down at myself, trying to get a better view. "Really? Are you sure?"

She nodded her head vigorously. "Yes. Now let me do your makeup and you'll be ready to go."

I acquiesced, knowing resistance was futile. I trusted Georgia not to make me look like a streetwalker; her own makeup was almost always flawless.

"So, do I get to meet Mr. Wonderful?" she asked. She used the edge of her pinky finger to smudge the charcoal liner beneath my eyes.

"Sure, if you want to." I glanced at the clock. Jack was due to arrive any moment. There was always a small part of me that was hesitant to introduce a man I was interested in to Georgia. Not that I questioned her loyalty; it was more that I couldn't imagine a man meeting her and not wanting to take their chances with her instead of me.

She pulled back after smudging a little red stain on my lips. "Nah, I think I'll pass. I'll meet him the next time."

"You think there'll be a next time?" I was afraid to get my hopes up. I didn't want to wish for something I wasn't going to get.

She winked at me. "I have no doubt."

I walked Georgia to the parking lot. After a quick hug and a wish for good luck, she drove off. Moments later, Jack pulled up. "You look great," were the first words out of his mouth.

"Thanks," I said, smiling. "So do you." He was wearing jeans and a black sweater, both cut to flatter his leaner build. It struck me that he looked a little like Tom Cruise without the slightly crazed look in his eyes.

"Shall we go?" he asked, and I nodded. He opened the passenger-side door for me and I climbed inside. The formality of this felt a little awkward after our casual errand just the day before, so I was happy the bar was only a five-minute drive.

We were lucky enough to find a parking spot right out front. The lounge wasn't very full, so we were seated right away and ordered a bottle of Merlot along with a tasting menu of the chef's select midnight snacks.

"This is nice," Jack remarked, moving his gaze around the dimly lit dining room. The walls were hung with pearl-gray velvet curtains accented by deep plum cloths on the tables. Whip-thin potted bamboo rose up in unexpected places, creating a sense of privacy between the diners, and low votives flickered all around us.

"It is," I said. "I'd love to own a place like this someday. Not too big. Warm and intimate."

He smiled. "I didn't know you wanted to run your own restaurant."

"Oh, definitely. It's sort of every chef's dream, you know? I just haven't built up enough capital yet. And investors are keeping their purse strings closed right now, with the recession."

"I can imagine." Jack fiddled with his water glass. "So, Tom called you, I take it? Despite his disappointment that I asked you out first?"

I nodded. "He did. But he said he couldn't stop by until tomorrow, so I guess you'll just have to wait for your surprise."

"A little anticipation won't kill me." He grinned wickedly. "I actually kind of enjoy it."

"Really? Not me. Give me instant gratification any day of the week."

He laughed. "You were the kind of kid who peeked at her Christmas presents, weren't you?"

"Maybe *one* year." I paused to sip my wine and Jack gave me a doubting look. "Okay, every year. The uncertainty drove me crazy. I couldn't handle the pressure."

"I knew it," he said as our server brought us the first course of buttery Cajun popcorn tossed with sweet and spicy pistachios. We both took a couple of pieces and moaned appreciatively. "Wow," he said. "That's pretty great."

"Not like Mom used to make, huh?" I threw another bite in my mouth.

"Is that where you learned to love cooking? Your mother?"

I shook my head, realizing that it was Rita, not Jack, whom

I'd told about my father teaching me to cook. I hoped I wouldn't cry again. "My father was the cook in the family. He had me standing on a chair whisking eggs for breakfast by the time I was three years old." I took another bite of popcorn, chewed it quickly, and swallowed. "Plus my appetite has always been a little out of bounds, so my dad said if I wanted to eat, I'd better learn to cook. How about you?"

"Me, what?" He smiled and my stomach did a backflip.

"Your family. Are you close to them? Did you grow up in Seattle?"

His smile melted away. "I did grow up here, but no, I'm not close with my family. I'm the black sheep, I suppose."

"Really? How come?"

He sat back and took a long sip of wine, not speaking until he set it back down on the table. "I refused to follow in my father's footsteps. He wanted me to take over his company. I've been groomed for it my entire life."

"Ah," I said. His discarded business degrees suddenly made sense. "And I imagine it didn't go over well when you decided you wanted to work in social services instead?"

He shook his head. "Not very well at all. We don't speak unless there's some kind of family emergency my mother dreams up that demands my presence. She's constantly trying to get my father and me to reconcile, which is really pretty pointless."

I nodded but then fell quiet. Jack finished off a couple of more bites of popcorn, then lifted the bowl to offer me the rest. "No, thanks," I said, holding up my hand. "I'm good."

He looked concerned. "Did I say something wrong?" The server came to the table and took the bowl, replacing it with a tray full of bacon-wrapped shrimp.

"No, no. I guess I was just thinking how ironic it is that

I'm pretty desperate to find my father and you've written yours off."

"I haven't written him off, exactly," Jack said. "We're both just so stubborn about the whole thing, I can't see a way out of it. He won't accept the path I've chosen and I can't walk the one he thinks I should. I'm not sure what either of us can do about that."

"Why *did* you decide to open the shelter?" I asked. "It's a pretty far stretch from the corporate world."

He nodded. "You're right. It is." He looked away from me for a moment, then brought his gaze back to mine. "I guess you could say my work began as sort of a penance."

"A penance? For what?"

"For previous wrongs." He took a deep breath and released it in a short hiss. "I don't tell too many people the details. Are you sure you want to hear this?"

"Of course," I said, wondering what awful act Jack could have committed to make him so uncomfortable talking about it. It was a story he hadn't wanted to tell me the first night I volunteered at Hope House; I was glad he felt comfortable enough to open up a little now.

"Okay," he said. "It happened when I was in high school. I hung around with a big bunch of guys—jocks, mostly. I was on the martial arts team."

"You were a tough guy, then," I said.

Jack gave a short laugh. "Yeah, we thought we were tough. Strutting around like idiots trying to impress the girls. All that predictable, adolescent crap."

"Sounds fairly innocent so far," I said, a little baffled by the apparent conflict in Jack's expression. Whatever he was about to say, he was not proud of it. He could barely make eye contact with me.

"It was innocent, for the most part. We raised a little hell at parties, but nothing too bad until one night, we went driving around downtown and one of the guys, Dennis, came up with the idea to head into Pioneer Square and see if we could pick up any drunk college girls coming out of the bars. Like that was going to happen, right? Hot college girls are always into boys in their high school letterman jackets."

I smiled but didn't say anything, waiting for him to continue.

"So, anyway, we were walking along and this homeless guy came over and asked if we had any spare change. My buddies sort of waved him off and we kept going, but this guy was determined to get something from us, I guess, because he tried to keep up with us, saying, 'Come on, give a vet a break.' Shit like that." Jack took another breath. "So Dennis pulled out his wallet like he was going to give the guy some money, and when the guy reached out for it, Dennis yanked the money back like a game of keep-away, you know?" Jack dropped his eyes to the table and took a big sip of his wine.

I nodded, my stomach turning a bit at what I was afraid Jack might tell me next.

"The guy kept grabbing for the money and Dennis was laughing—we were all laughing until Dennis looked away for a minute and the guy actually nabbed Dennis's wallet and started running. We chased him and finally cornered him in an alley about two blocks away." Jack looked up at me, the pain he felt over this memory evident in his eyes. "A couple of the other guys pinned him down and took all the money he had in his pockets, which was only like fifteen bucks or something like that, and then they took turns punching and kicking him. I screamed at them to knock it off, but they wouldn't listen. When I tried to pull them off of him, they started to come at me, too." He looked up at me, his green eyes clouded with regret. "Watching it happen and not being able to stop them was pretty much the most horrible moment of my life."

"I can imagine," I said, picturing the scene and feeling my stomach twist even further at the images flashing through my mind. Had something like this happened to my father? If it had, did anyone try to help him?

Jack blew a long breath out and sat back in his chair. "I had nightmares about the guy dying in an alley. The guilt was pretty overwhelming."

"Did you ever talk to anyone about it?"

"A few people. I tried to talk to a couple of the guys who were there, too, but they laughed at me, you know? Like it was just a stupid prank and I should just forget about it." His eyes held mine. "But I couldn't. I pushed it down and tried not to let it bother me most of the time, but it always worked its way back up. The look on the guy's face, pleading for me to help him, kept me up at night. It's definitely part of why I couldn't stay working for my dad. I knew I needed to do something to balance out what I'd done."

"Most people would just write a check to the United Way and call it good," I said. "You've gone a little above and beyond, starting a shelter."

He smiled. "I'm an overachiever, I guess. I tried doing volunteer work with the homeless during college and it only fueled the idea of the shelter. I thought about waiting until after I retired or something like that, but I didn't want to put it off. It was just something I knew I needed to do." He leaned forward and reached across the table to take my hand in his. "Have you thought about what you want to do once you find your dad?"

I gave him a half smile. "Not really, to tell you the truth. I've been so focused on the search."

"What made you decide to start looking for him?"

"I've always worried about what happened to him to some extent, but I was pretty angry with him too, for leaving and never coming back to see me."

"But what about the letters he sent when he was living in the apartment? He at least tried to reach out, right?"

I sighed. "Yes. But by that time I was pretty bitter about not hearing from him for so long. All my adolescent angst went in one direction—toward him. I still worried about him, especially after I realized he'd ended up on the streets, but the real catalyst to start looking for him came about a year ago when my mother was diagnosed with breast cancer. She had a double mastectomy and went through chemo. The thought of losing her brought it home pretty hard that if she died, I'd be an orphan."

"That must have been really rough. How is she now?" Jack picked up a shrimp with his free hand and popped it in his mouth. I liked that he didn't let go of mine.

"She's doing well. I still worry, of course. And she wants grandchildren something fierce."

"Did she remarry?"

"She did, but I don't really think of John as my father. I mean, I like him, and he's been great for my mother, but I was so close to my dad before his illness started to get the better of him. Not having him around was a pretty big hole in my life. And then my mom got sick and I just felt this overwhelming need to make sure he's okay, you know? And also apologize for not answering him when he tried to contact me. I know it's a cliché, but life really is so short. I didn't want to look back and regret not at least trying to mend what was broken between us."

"I can understand that," Jack said. "And I'd like to say I'm ready to follow in your footsteps with my dad, but I just don't think I'm there yet."

I understood what he meant. It took me a long time to work up the courage to start looking for my father; I was sure Jack would reach out to his when the time was right. We ate a little more, and our conversation shifted to our siblings—Jack had a younger sister who worked in residency as a plastic surgeon in Los Angeles, so I joked about setting her up with my bodybuilding brother and the two of them raising a brood of physically perfect children. He told me stories about trying to build up enough capital to open Hope House and we discussed the idea of putting on a fund-raiser. I discovered he loved movies but hated TV. He promised he could tolerate my addiction to reality television if I could tolerate his to playing Xbox games online. Before I knew it, we had sipped our way through a bottle of wine and the lights flashed for last call.

"I probably shouldn't drive yet," Jack said. "Want to take a walk? I don't think it's raining." There was no way he was drunk; we'd both only had two glasses of wine. I suspected his offer of a walk was made so we could spend more time together. I wasn't about to argue with that.

"Sure," I said, happy I'd insisted on the boots instead of the towering stiletto sandals Georgia would have had me wear.

Jack paid the bill and we set out on our stroll along the fairly deserted downtown streets. I had a happy, skipping feeling in my belly that only intensified when Jack stopped walking and reached over to lace his fingers through mine. We made eye contact as we touched and I gave him a big smile. I stood very still, my heart thwapping like a helicopter in my chest as he turned toward me.

"I like you, Eden. Very much." His shorter stature suddenly seemed like an enormous advantage with his face at the exact level of mine. If he kissed me, there would be no craning of my neck or standing on tippytoes.

"I like you too," I said a little breathlessly.

He leaned in slowly, his eyes never leaving mine. I closed my eyes as he drew in closer. His lips were soft and the kiss was gentle but insistent. When he reached his free hand up to brush my cheek with the tips of his fingers, it sent sparks off throughout my body. It had been a long while since someone touched me with such tenderness. I couldn't help but emit a low groan.

His eyes snapped open at the sound and he pulled back, though still less than two inches from my face. Illuminated by the streetlight, I saw that he had slivers of gold sewn through the green of his irises.

"That good, huh?" he asked with a small grin.

I gave his arm a playful squeeze and smiled. "No, it was horrible, actually. I think you'd better do it again immediately to make up for that pitiful excuse for a kiss."

He gave a low chuckle and unwound his fingers from mine, bringing both his hands to my face, cupping it before he kissed me again. This time he didn't hold back. I felt his tongue flick against mine, just the tip, questioning. I opened and pressed my body against him. His arms encircled me and as his hands roamed lightly over my back, an unfamiliar sensation rose up in me. Right there, in the middle of the night on a downtown street corner, Jack held me in his arms and for the first time in as long as I could remember, I felt safe.

I didn't sleep much the month my father was in jail. Worry kept me awake—I worried he wasn't getting enough to eat or taking the kind of medicine he needed to get well. I worried the anger in his eyes when the officer took him away would be the last expression I ever saw on his face. I worried there was nothing I could do to make him forgive me.

My mother didn't want to talk about him. If she was worried, it didn't show. She went to work and I went to school and when we were at home, we both pretended it had always been this way. Just she and I, sitting at the dinner table. She and I, watching *Mork and Mindy* reruns. My mother and I, just trying to get by on our own. The problem was I didn't want her to be okay with just getting by. I didn't want her to get comfortable with my father being gone. I also didn't want her to get upset, as she always did, when my father came home. I felt protective of and angry at them both, but mostly, I felt scared.

At night, after my mom had gone to bed, I allowed thoughts of my father to come to me. I remembered the time I was seven years old and my mom was gone for the week at an accounting conference. My dad kept me out of school and drove us four hours to Ocean Shores just so he could teach me to find the Big Dipper in the night sky.

"The stars are clearer at the ocean," he said. "You can't see them as well in the city because of all the lights." We were huddled on the sand beneath a thin blanket he had stuffed beneath the backseat of his car. I was still in my pajamas—he hadn't thought about dressing me in something warmer.

"What's that one, Daddy?" I asked him, pointing up at the biggest, brightest star I saw. It flashed and I imagined it was winking at me.

He peered up, leaning over to see where I was pointing. "Ah, the North Star. Sailors used it to guide them on their voyages, honey. It was the map they used to find their way home."

"Oh." I believed my father, not having any reason to doubt he knew the name of every star in the sky. I couldn't fathom his not having the answer to any question I had.

Could he see the stars in jail? I wondered. Did they have a place outside where my father could stand and breathe fresh air and look up at the night sky? Or was he always trapped in a cell, caged in like the animals at the zoo? I imagined him pacing like a tiger, tight and lean, his blue eyes like lasers, targeting his prey. Were there doctors in jail? I wondered. I had no way to find out. If only he would come home, Mom would forgive him like she always forgave him and I would find a way to make him understand why I'd done what I did.

As the days passed, I fed the idea that when he got out, my father just needed to find the right doctor. Someone who would help him figure out how he could get well. He'd always complained the doctors in the hospital didn't listen to him, so after school one afternoon I walked to the public clinic my mother sometimes took me to when I was sick. The doctors there were nice, so I figured if I just got in to see one, I could find out if they'd be able to help my dad get better.

Having something to do after school was better than going home and spending the afternoon alone, as I had been doing while my father was gone. My mother couldn't afford a sitter and old Mrs. Worthington across the street said she'd keep an eye out for intruders but she didn't have the energy to watch me. The silence in the house was paralyzing; every creak of the floor or bird flapping against the window shot anxiety through my bones. There weren't enough locks in the world to make me feel safe.

"Hi," I said to the receptionist when I arrived at the clinic. "I need to see a doctor. A nice one."

The receptionist, a skinny girl with carrot-colored curls and a turned-up freckled nose, looked up from her computer and snapped her gum. "All our doctors are nice. Have you been here before?"

"Yes. With my mom. My name is Eden West."

"Where's your mom now, sweetie?" She peeked over my shoulder and scanned the waiting area, which only had a couple of other people in it.

"She's still at work." It suddenly hit me that they might not let me talk to a doctor without my mother there. "She's on her way, though. She told me to go ahead and get in for the appointment and she would meet me here."

"What's wrong with you?"

I could tell she was suspicious and I wasn't used to handling all these questions from grown-ups. Usually my mom took care of this kind of thing. "I've been having stomachaches. Bad ones." I lowered my voice to a whisper. "Lots of diarrhea. And gas." It was a little alarming how easily the lies slid off my tongue.

The receptionist managed to keep her composure, but I saw her nose twitch with distaste. She looked back at her computer screen, typed a little, and then smiled at me with closed lips before speaking. "Dr. Adams isn't in today, but Dr. Vick can see you in a few minutes. I assume you have the same insurance company?"

"Yes." I had no idea if this was true, but I figured I'd find a way to sort it out later if it became an issue.

"Go ahead and have a seat and I'll call your name when it's time."

"Thank you," I said primly. "And where's the bathroom?" I dropped my chin to my chest. "You know. Just in case?"

"Through the door on your right." She turned back to her work, happy to be rid of me, I supposed.

I sat in a peach-colored plastic chair and set my backpack on the linoleum floor. The old man sitting across from me had his arm bent at the elbow and held his head in one hand. His eyes were closed. A chubby blond woman was curled up on the only couch in the room. She was pale and breathing fast. I wondered if I might catch something while I sat there. Maybe if I got sick, they'd let my dad out of jail early and he'd come home. If I was sick, he couldn't be mad at me. He would sit at my bedside and read to me, like he'd done when I was seven and had strep throat. He made me homemade Popsicles out of a mixture of orange juice and 7-UP and fed me chocolate milkshakes for breakfast. Getting sick was a brilliant idea. Why hadn't I thought of it before? And where better to pick up germs than at the doctor's?

I glanced around the room, careful that no one was watching me as I rubbed my hands on the seat next to me. Someone sick had to have sat there today. Maybe they sneezed and left me their germs. I licked my fingers.

"Eden West?" A door had opened and a nurse called out my name. The receptionist stood up and whispered something in the nurse's ear. The nurse nodded slowly, both of them looking at me with a concerned expression. Good. She thought I was really sick.

"Right here," I said, and I stood up, grabbed my backpack, and followed her through the doorway and down the hall into an examination room.

"Climb on up." She motioned for me to get on the exam table. I dropped my bag down and did as she asked. "You know what, Eden? I forgot I need to make a quick phone call. Can you excuse me a minute? I'll be right back."

I nodded. "Okay." She left the room and was gone just a couple of minutes. Was she calling my mom? Was I going to get in trouble?

When she came back, she shut the door behind her, smiled, and stood right next to me. If she had called my mom, wouldn't she have said so? Instead, she put her hand on the top of my thigh and something about the tenderness in her touch made me want to cry.

"So, tell me what's been going on with you, Eden."

"I have stomachaches." I hoped the tremor in my voice made the lie sound more convincing.

"I see. When do you get them?"

"All day. All the time. But after I eat, especially." I tried to think of all the times in my life I'd suffered from stomach pains and what had caused them.

"After you eat anything in particular?"

I shook my head. "Not really."

"Do you vomit?"

I made a face. "No."

"Diarrhea?"

I nodded. "Yes. Lots." I figured lots of diarrhea was a significant enough symptom to convince her I had something wrong with me. "And gas," I added helpfully.

"Okay, well, let's take your temperature and blood pressure, and Dr. Vick will be in to talk with you." She set the glass thermometer underneath my tongue and wrapped the blood pressure sleeve around my arm. I swung my legs back and forth, as though I were on a swing, anxious for this part to be over with so I could talk with the doctor about my dad.

"All done!" the nurse announced. "I'll go check to see if your mom has made it yet, and Dr. Vick will be right in, okay, sweetie?"

"Okay. Thank you." She closed the door behind her and I let my eyes wander over the tiny room. There were posters on the wall instructing you on how to cover your mouth with the inside of your elbow when you coughed instead of with your hand. I thought about how many sick people might have been in this room that day, so I hopped off the exam table and went to the sink and rubbed my fingers over the faucet, then licked them again. The sooner I got sick, the sooner my dad would come home.

There was a sharp rap on the door and the doctor entered. I tucked my hands into the front pockets of my jeans and ducked my head down. Dr. Vick was a heavy man with wide-set brown eyes and enormous black eyebrows. His scalp shone beneath the fluorescent lights.

"Eden?" he inquired.

I nodded and hopped back onto the exam table. The white paper crinkled beneath my butt. He sat down on a cushioned stool with wheels and pushed himself over next to me. It felt strange to be looking down on a grown-up. And a doctor, to boot.

"I'm Dr. Vick," he said. "I know you usually see Dr. Adams, but he isn't working today." He smiled. "I hear you're having stomachaches."

"And diarrhea."

He nodded, a serious expression on his face. "Why don't you lie down and I'll see if I can find out what's going on?"

I complied and found myself staring up at a poster on the ceiling with a picture of a kitten hanging precariously from a branch with the words HANG IN THERE, BABY! emblazoned across the bottom. I wondered if the photographer had pushed the kitten off the branch in order to snap the picture. How else would he have captured that moment, unless he was the one who made it happen?

Dr. Vick pushed himself up off the stool and stood next to the exam table. "Can you take a deep breath for me?" he asked. "And hold it for a minute?"

I inhaled and my stomach rose up like a balloon was trapped inside it. Dr. Vick pressed gently with his fingers, wiggling and moving them around my abdomen. I convulsed and blew the air out when he pushed a particularly sensitive spot next to my ribs.

"Uh-oh," he said, pulling his hands back. "Did that hurt?"

"No. It tickled."

He smiled. "Oops. Sorry. You can sit up now."

I did, and he sat back down on his stool. He made a few notes in his chart before speaking again. "So, I don't feel anything wrong right off the bat," he said. "Is there a time of day that it gets worse?"

I hesitated a minute, unsure how much longer I should be pretending I had something wrong with me when I was really here to talk about what Dr. Vick might be able to do to help my dad. I needed to get home before my mom got off work and I was wasting valuable time.

"It sometimes gets bad at night. But I think that might just be because I miss my dad."

Dr. Vick tilted his head and gave a little frown. "And where is your dad?"

"Well, he got in trouble. And so now he's in jail." I didn't like the look on Dr. Vick's face so I rushed to explain. "But it's only for a month and it isn't his fault. He has something wrong in his brain that makes him do wrong things sometimes. He doesn't mean it."

The doctor looked concerned. "What kind of wrong things are we talking about, Eden? Does he hurt you?"

"No!" I didn't like where this conversation was going, so I tried to start it over. "My dad is wonderful. He's an artist and just feels things a lot more deeply than most people. At least, that's what my mom says. He just gets either really good or really bad moods."

Dr. Vick nodded. "I see. Does he go to the doctor for this issue? Does he have medicine?"

I took a deep breath and let it out slowly. "Well, that's why I'm here, actually."

Understanding blossomed on the doctor's face. "You aren't having stomachaches?"

I dropped my eyes to the floor and shook my head. "No. I'm sorry. I just needed to talk to a doctor who can help my dad get better. If you could just give him a medicine that doesn't make him feel so awful and change his personality like the one he usually takes, he would take it and everything would be okay." I paused and looked back up at Dr. Vick. "Do you have that kind of medicine?"

He sighed, a quiet sound. "I'm not a psychiatrist, Eden. And even if I were, I couldn't give you medicine to give to your dad. You should know your mother will be here any minute."

"What?" I asked, a panicky feeling in my stomach.

"Yes." He stood up. "The nurse called her when you first got here. She asked that we keep you occupied until she arrived."

"No, please!" I jumped down and grabbed his arm. "I just

want you to tell me what I can do to help my dad get better. When he gets home. Please? I need you to help me."

Dr. Vick reached over with his free hand and placed it on top of mine. His eyes were kind. "Eden, I understand how hard it must be to have your dad struggle with his moods like this. But there's nothing you can do to fix him. Sometimes people get sick and there's nothing anyone can do to make them get well."

"I don't believe you." My bottom lip trembled. "You're a doctor. It's your job to make people get better."

"That is my job. But I can't fix what's wrong with your dad. I don't know if anyone can."

"Please help me," I said, the tears rolling down my cheeks. "I don't know what else to do. If he doesn't get well, my mom might make him go away."

Dr. Vick carefully extricated himself from my grasp and handed me a few tissues from the box on the counter. I took them and blew my nose hard, probably sending all the germs I'd worked so hard to ingest right back out of my body. I'd never get sick now. My daddy wouldn't come home.

"You can stay in here for a few minutes," he said.

I didn't answer him, instead kept my eyes to the floor. This was pointless. *Doctors are supposed to help people and all he's going to do is get me in trouble.* The nurse came in a moment later with a glass of water I didn't want to drink.

"Your mom is on her way," she said. She put her arm around my shoulders. "Let's have you sit in the waiting room until she gets here, okay?"

I shrugged. I didn't care. I let her lead me wherever she wanted me to go.

My mom showed up in less than fifteen minutes, rushing into the waiting room like she was being chased. She threw her eyes around the room until she found me. "Eden! What were you thinking?"

I didn't answer. I stood up and grabbed my backpack. "Can we just go home?"

She sighed and hugged me. I stood straight and motionless in her arms. She kissed the top of my head. "You can't save him, honey. You know that, right? There's nothing either one of us can do."

I looked up at her. "You're giving up."

"Maybe," she said. "But only because he gave up first."

In the end, David pled guilty for the DUI and assaulting the officer, but since they were his first criminal offenses, his attorney was able to file a plea with the court to have the charges reduced. He was released after only a month in jail. He would have to pay a fine for the assault against the police officer and be on probation for driving under the influence, but considering the circumstances, things could have been much worse.

After he melted down in his cell with Rico, David was transferred to the jail's mental ward, where the doctors loaded him up on meds and David nursed the shoulder he dislocated slamming it into the wall. The bruise on his forehead went away fairly quick, and now, medicated, the turmoil brewing inside him settled into a low simmer. The dosage they gave him wasn't a high one, but it was enough to take the edge off, enough for David to try to figure out his next move.

The morning he left the jail, David stood on the front steps of the courthouse, unsure whether he should call Lydia to come pick him up. She hadn't taken any of his calls during the month he was incarcerated and never came to visit, so he could only assume she was still royally pissed about what he'd done. After fuming with self-justification, he became plagued by the familiar stench of regret. He knew the only way to be washed clean of it would be for Lydia and Eden to welcome him home. It wasn't like he had anywhere else to go.

The money he had taken from Lydia's secret stash was returned to him when he left the jail, so he thought about taking a taxi home but then realized it might look indulgent to his wife. He wanted to impress upon her that he knew he'd made a grievous error but he had changed. For the most part, he was in control of his thoughts and his behavior, and when they threatened to spin off, he steeled his resolve against it. He chanted "I will get well" over and over in his head, and for some reason that seemed to help. Maybe it was the medication, or maybe it was because he hadn't had a drink in thirty days. Now all he had to do was go home and convince Lydia to listen to him.

The officer who had released him gave him a bus schedule, so he consulted it to find one that would drop him near his house. It was midday and both Lydia and Eden would be gone. He thought he might surprise them by being there when they got home. He tried not to think about how poorly that might go over, but he knew they'd always found a way to forgive him before so he had little reason to doubt they would do it again.

It took two bus transfers to travel from downtown to their North Seattle neighborhood. David felt strange being out in the world again, as he did when he was released from a hospital stay. He felt vulnerable and raw, terrified others would point their finger at the crazy man who had shamed his family. *Well, that's going to change now,* David thought. *I'll do whatever it takes.*

When he got home, he noticed Mrs. Worthington, the woman Eden sometimes pulled weeds for, peeking out her living room window from across the street. He waved and gave her a big smile. Let her think he was returning from a vacation or a business trip. He knew Lydia didn't advertise his illness or his resulting escapades. She was too embarrassed by them. He pulled out his keys and hoped Lydia hadn't changed the locks. With her emergency stash of money gone, he doubted she could have afforded it. The key slid in and the tumbler turned effortlessly. David stepped inside and this house he had picked out with Lydia looked foreign to him. The walls seemed closer together. Could they have shrunk? He locked the door behind him and immediately set out to the garage in search of a painting he could sell. Money wouldn't solve all of his problems with Lydia, but he knew it couldn't hurt.

Like the swirling beginnings of a sandstorm in the desert, panicky thoughts rose in his brain. What if Lydia didn't forgive him? What if no matter what he did or said she still wanted him gone? Where would he go? What would he do? Would he ever see Eden again? He needed to tell his daughter he understood why she had asked that waitress to call her mother. He needed to take away the hurt he had caused.

David began to breathe heavily and the sight of the empty vodka bottles on the garage floor roused a craving in him so strong it felt like it might carry him away. *I will get well, I will get well,* he chanted inside his head. It was the barest form of white-knuckled resistance against a growing tide of compulsion. He didn't know how much longer he could keep it up.

"Please," he whispered, not knowing exactly whom he was speaking to. He'd long ago given up any hope there was a God. If there was, He obviously wanted nothing to do with David. When he prayed, he did so to the unseen force that controlled his moods. "Please don't let me spiral down again."

Quickly, as a distraction, David dug through the stack of paintings he hadn't taken with him the night he left with Eden.

There was a trio-study of his daughter sleeping that might sell for a decent amount. The perfect bow of her lips, the careless fling of her arm above her head, a pale blanket rumpled all around her in the late afternoon light. He took the paintings inside and picked up the phone to call the Wild Orchid Gallery. They had loved his work there, once. He could make them love it again.

"Yes," he said when the receptionist answered. "Is Cerina in today?"

"She is. May I tell her who's calling?"

"David West." He listened to the soothing piano music while he sat on hold, drumming his fingers on the kitchen counter. It only took a minute for Cerina to get on the line. He pictured her, lithe as a panther, dressed head to toe in black. He'd slept with her a few times, a year ago. He wondered if that was the only reason she offered to show his work.

"David," she purred. "Long time no talk."

"I know, I know," he said nervously. "I've been struggling a bit. Painter's block."

"Terrible thing, isn't it?" Cerina said sympathetically. "We thought we'd be doing a show for you, but when you didn't return my calls, your wife said you were taking a sabbatical?"

"That's right," David said. *Bless Lydia for that little white lie.* "I have a few great portraits of my daughter I'd like to show you, if you're interested. A trio of a child sleeping."

"Oh? When were you thinking?"

"I could come right now." David realized he didn't have a car. He would have to call Rick and see if he could hitch a ride over to Bellevue, where the gallery was located. His paintings had always done well with the affluent Eastside types.

"I'm not free this afternoon." Cerina made a clicking sound with her tongue. "Too bad."

"Later this week, then?" David gritted his teeth. This was not what he had planned. He wanted to have a handful of cash to give Lydia the moment she came home. But he didn't want to blow it with Cerina. If he worked her the right way, he might even talk her into doing a show. He wondered if he'd have to sleep with her again and was aroused at the thought.

"How about I call you?" Cerina said distractedly. "I'm pretty swamped at the moment, but as soon as something opens up, you'll be on my list."

David recognized the brush-off when it happened. He'd been through it enough times to know. "That'd be great. I'll wait to hear from you then."

"Thanks for calling, David," she said. "Take care."

David heard the phone click in his ear and he hung it up on his end. He stared at the paintings of Eden and tried to think of anyone else who might want to buy them. There was no one. His erratic behavior had burned so many bridges with the galleries in Seattle, he couldn't imagine any of them welcoming him back. He'd have to find another way. Another city, maybe, where he could sell his work. He'd sit on the street corner with it, if he had to, peddling it to passersby.

For now, he decided the best thing to do was clean the house. This seemed like a reasonable activity. After all, he was going to be a new man. He figured he'd better start behaving like one. Do the unexpected. He'd dazzle his wife with his new and improved self, erasing any evidence of the unreliable man he used to be. He started in the kitchen and scrubbed every inch. He vacuumed and dusted, saving the bathrooms for last so he could shower before starting dinner. All the while he repeated in his head, *I will get well, I will get well.* The power of positive thinking had made some men millionaires. He figured if that was true, it could also make him sane.

It was about three o'clock when the front door opened and Eden entered. Her eyes went wide and she froze when she saw him standing in the dining room. He moved toward her with a big smile on his face.

"Hiya, Bug," he said. "I'm home."

She nodded, a stilted movement. Her lips were pressed into a thin line. She looked frightened.

"They let me out," he told her. "I'm so sorry for scaring you the way I did. I'm so, so sorry and I promise I'll never do anything like that again. I understand why you asked the waitress to call your mom, honey. It's okay. I'm not mad anymore."

Eden dropped her backpack to the floor and looked around the entryway. She wiped a finger along the edge of the wainscotting and stared at it. "Did you *clean*?" she asked incredulously.

David nodded. "I did. Your mom works so hard. It was the least I could do." He pushed back his hair from his face. It was still damp from the shower he had taken. "I'm making enchilada casserole for dinner. Want to help?"

Eden took off her coat and hung it up on the rack by the front door. "Okay," she said. The word was hesitant, but David took it as a good sign. He and Eden could always connect in the kitchen. He'd take it slow, he decided. Let her come to him. The last thing he wanted to do was to alarm her again. *I will get well, I will get well.*

They moved into the kitchen and David set himself back to the task of seasoning the chicken breasts he'd found in the freezer with cumin and chili powder. "Why don't you find the shredded cheese while I finish this?" he asked Eden.

She nodded but averted her eyes, walking a wide circle around him to open the fridge. "How do you feel, Daddy?"

"I'm good, Bug. Much, much better." He gave her what he hoped was a strong, convincing smile. "I had lots of time to think over the last month, and I am never going to get to that place again. I swear. I'll do whatever I need to."

"Even take your medicine?" Eden asked as she carefully opened the bag of shredded jack cheese.

"I hope I don't need to, but yes," David said. "I will. I promise."

Eden looked over and smiled, though her eyes were shiny. She ran over and threw her arms around him. He hugged her tightly and tried to hold off the terror he felt pulsing through his veins after promising his daughter he would not fail. Why did he do that? How could he say those kinds of things when he'd never been able to keep his promises before? And worst of all, why did she keep on believing him?

They spent an hour putting the casserole together. David let Eden lay the tortillas in the dish and spread out the sautéed chicken over those. He drizzled a sauce he'd made from canned green chilies and garlic over the chicken, added the cheese and sliced black olives.

"What did you eat in jail?" Eden asked him as she sprinkled more onions over the next layer of chicken. "Was it awful? Did it have bugs in it?"

David laughed. "No, honey. It was bland, but no bugs. Just lots of oatmeal and mystery meat."

Eden made a face. "What's mystery meat?"

"It's when you can't tell what animal it came from. They grind it up and serve it like hamburger patties and call it steak. Only it's not like any steak I've ever eaten." He shuddered. "I'm glad to be home so I can have you cook for me again. I had dreams about your chicken soup."

Eden looked at him with surprise. "You did?"

David nodded and opened another can of chopped olives. "And your cookies. I kept dreaming I was eating them with you. Only I couldn't taste anything."

"That would be kind of scary," Eden said. She put the last layer of tortillas over the top of the chicken and sauce. "There! Is it ready for the oven?"

"Sure looks like it. We'll add the tomatoes for some color when it's done." He picked up the dish and slid it in the oven. "Do you have homework?"

Eden nodded, reluctantly, and made another face. "Math."

"What kind of math?"

"Long division. It gives me a headache." She pressed her fingers against her temples and rubbed.

"Me too. But maybe we can figure it out together. Come on."

They sat at the dining room table for the next hour, trying to wade their way through Eden's homework. David wasn't sure he was showing her the right way to do the work, but it felt so good to sit next to her. He tried to keep his thoughts focused on her. This is how Lydia found them when she walked in the front door around five o'clock.

"David." This was the only thing his wife said. Her expression was hard, almost as though she was wearing a mask. He'd seen it before. She was protecting herself.

David stood up and placed one of his hands on Eden's shoulder. "Hello, Lydia." He knew better than to act like nothing had happened. He did his best to sound contrite.

"Daddy cleaned the whole house, Momma!" Eden announced. "And we made dinner."

Lydia gave Eden a smile. "I can smell it. What did you make?"

"Chicken enchilada casserole," Eden said. "With green chilies. And lots of cheese."

Lydia closed the door behind her and set her purse on the dining room table. "Sounds wonderful, sweetie." She looked at David and her smile disappeared. "I thought you would have the courtesy to call first."

David shrugged. "I was afraid you wouldn't answer."

"I might not have."

"Which is why I'm here," he said.

Eden stood up, and David's hand slid off her shoulder. "Daddy's been helping me with my homework, too, Mom. I'm almost done."

"That's great," Lydia said. "Why don't you go upstairs and I'll call you when dinner is ready?"

"I'm not done yet," Eden said. "I still have two more pages."

"We'll finish it after we eat, okay?" Lydia said. She kept her eyes on David. He couldn't tell what she was thinking.

"Go on," David said to Eden. "Your mom and I need to talk." *I will get well, I will get well.* He suddenly wished he had gotten his hands on some vodka before Lydia came home. He'd be able to calm himself down that way. He knew he could keep a handle on it. He'd done it before.

Eden headed upstairs, looking back over her shoulder as she left. Her eyebrows knit together and she was frowning. David gave her a little wave and a smile. His daughter wasn't stupid. She knew how fragile this all was.

When David heard her bedroom door shut, he looked at Lydia. "She's worried I'll flip the table again."

"She should be." Lydia's voice was cold. Her arms were crossed over her chest.

"I know 'sorry' doesn't cut it, but I am so, so sorry for what I did. I don't know what came over me."

"You know exactly what came over you. Don't lie to me. I'm sick of it."

David's shoulders slumped and he nodded, dropping his eyes to the floor. "You're right. I stopped taking my pills. I drank. I asked Eden to come with me in the middle of the night without telling you. It was wrong. And I paid the price."

"I'm not sure you've paid anything," Lydia said.

David reached into his coat pocket and put the cash he had taken from Lydia's secret stash on the table. "It's all there, except what I used to pay for Eden's breakfast that morning. You can count it."

Lydia looked at the money and then back to David. Her eyes narrowed. "I don't want to count it. I want a husband who doesn't steal from me in the first place."

David sighed. "I know, Lydia. If I could take it back, I would." He hated how this felt. He wasn't a child. He didn't want to be scolded like one. He felt tendrils of rebellion winding through his thoughts. He didn't know how to stop them.

"You can't take it back. You took my *child* from me. Do you have any idea how scared I was? The terror that tore through me when I woke up and you both were gone? With no note? No nothing? I could strangle you for putting me through that, David. But I could *kill* you for putting our *daughter* through it."

"I know. I deserve that."

"Oh, you know?" Lydia laughed. "How can I ever trust you again? And how dare you just show up back at this house like nothing happened?"

"I didn't. And I'm not pretending about anything. I'm telling you I know what I did was wrong. I had a lot of time to think over the last month, Lydia. This is it. I'm done. I'll be seeing a new doctor as soon as I can get in for an appointment. I'll work with them, I promise. I'll do whatever I need to do to make up for what I've done to both of you." He wanted to mean this. He had meant it when he got home only a few hours before. But his determination had already begun to crumble. He felt it breaking away.

"And why should I believe you this time?" Lydia demanded. "You've said the same things a thousand times before."

"I never went to jail before. I never saw that kind of consequence. I realized how much I have to lose. Honestly. I did." David's head began to pound. He felt like he was standing on the edge of a great precipice. All it would take to send him spinning was a light wind. "I called the Wild Orchid. Cerina said she'd call me to take a look at my latest series. I'll be making money soon."

"It's not about the money!" Lydia spat. "It's about knowing you are a safe person for our child to be around. I couldn't give a shit about the money as long as Eden doesn't get hurt. Do you understand me?"

She was wavering. David could sense it. There was a softening in the muscles around her eyes. No matter how angry she got with him, David knew at her core Lydia loved him. It's the reason she put up with so much for so long. He just needed her to do it one more time. Give him one more chance to make everything up to her. To make it up to Eden.

"I understand you." David kept his voice quiet. Compliant. He acted like he always did when he wanted out of the hospital. *Here, I'll be a good little boy if you just let me go home. I'll take my pills and do whatever you tell me to do.* "I promise, she won't get hurt."

"She'd better not." Lydia slumped into a chair and sighed. "Okay. You can stay. But you have to be good."

"I will," he said, and in that moment, he meant it. He *wanted* to be good. He truly did. He wished he was a normal man with a normal mind. *I will get well, I will get well.* The words pounded in his brain, useless ammunition against the fiendish thoughts he already felt swelling inside him. He would drink soon. He wouldn't take his pills. He had no idea how long this resolve of his might last.

November 2010
Eden

When I wasn't working during the two weeks after my first date with Jack, I was busy fighting off daydreams about him. How he kissed me. How he called the next morning to tell me he couldn't stop thinking about me. I hadn't fallen for anyone so quickly in a long time, so part of me held on to the small fear that he might be too good to be true, but as the days passed, I grew more and more comfortable with the idea that I might have met my match.

We talked on the phone almost every night when I got home from work and saw each other almost every day, sneaking in a quick lunch or drink around our work schedules. At each date's end, he took me in his arms and we kissed so passionately my lips were sore the next morning. I kept wondering if he'd invite me back to his apartment and what I'd say if he did. I was sort of an old-fashioned girl in that sense—I waited for the guy to make that move and usually followed my personal no-sex-before-four-dates rule. (Yes, Ryan had been an exception, but tequila shooters were involved the night I met him so I pled not guilty by reason of intoxication.)

Georgia was appalled at this rule, but no matter how much I might've wanted to climb in bed with Jack, I was going to wait for him to suggest it.

"You just don't want to get rejected," Georgia said accusatorily.

"Damn right I don't," I told her. Since my failed romances in my early and midtwenties with Wyatt and Stephen, I'd created all sorts of guidelines around my relationships to minimize my chances of getting hurt. I didn't date artists. I broke it off immediately with anyone who made a promise and didn't keep it or any man whom I caught lying. I didn't expect perfection, but I did expect honesty and follow-through. So far, Jack was hitting the mark.

My mother was thrilled, of course, that I was dating again. "When do we meet him?" she asked during one of our Friday morning check-in phone calls. "Can you come for dinner next week?"

"It's a little early for that," I said. "Let's make sure I don't scare him off first."

"Now, why would you say that? You're wonderful."

"You're my mom. You have to say that."

"I do not. If you were horrible, I'd tell you."

I laughed. "Gee, Mom. How comforting."

She sighed. "I want to meet this man."

"How about we wait to see if we last until Thanksgiving? If we do, I'll bring him to dinner." The holiday was only three weeks away, and with how well things seemed to be going with Jack, I was almost positive he'd agree to have a holiday meal with my family.

"Perfect!" She was immediately appeased, and I hoped Jack didn't mind my making that kind of promise. We hadn't discussed where our relationship was going or how serious it was, but if how he kissed me was any indication, we were definitely on the same page.

The Tuesday following my conversation with my mother, Bryce called me and asked if I'd come over to his apartment and help him make dinner for a girl he wanted to impress. I said yes right away.

When I called to tell him where I was going before dinner at the shelter, Jack said, "You're very sweet. And your brother's sneaky."

I laughed. "He's not sneaky. He's just nervous and doesn't know where to start in the kitchen. The boy lives off protein shakes and egg whites. I started the pork for tonight's dinner at the shelter yesterday while I was at work, so all I have to do is reheat it, sauce it up, and make the coleslaw and brownies." The meals I'd served at Hope House so far had been hugely popular and this week, pulled pork sandwiches and coleslaw were on the menu.

"You are a culinary wizard. I don't know what we ever did without you. I'll see you later, then?"

"Absolutely."

"Can't wait."

I arrived at Bryce's apartment around eleven o'clock in the morning, which left me plenty of time to put together a great meal for his date. I texted him from his building's parking garage and told him to come down and help me carry up what I'd brought.

"Ed!" he exclaimed, grabbing me for a bear hug when he arrived at my car. "You're the best sister anyone could ask for, you know that?"

"Yes, I know." I opened the trunk and pointed to the laundry basket full of food I'd brought. "There you go, big guy. Let's get started."

We headed up the elevator and into his tiny apartment. It

was clean, at least, which was more than I could say for my own house. Pretty impressive for a bachelor pad. Our mom must have passed on her neat gene to him instead of me. I entered his galley-style kitchen and he set the basket down on the dining room table right outside the linoleum. I clapped my hands together.

"Okay! I need you to slice onions. Like this." I gave him a quick demonstration of how I wanted the onions cut.

"What am I making?"

"Mini caramelized-onion-and-goat-cheese pizzas with balsamic reduction and cilantro to start. Lemon chicken and grilled asparagus for dinner, and coconut-pineapple sorbet for dessert." I grabbed the container of sorbet from the basket. "Speaking of, I need to get this in the freezer."

Bryce grinned and ran a hand through his blond buzz cut. "Lisa's going to flip. She probably thinks I'm a muscle-headed idiot who can't cook."

"You are," I teased. I set the dessert in the freezer and pulled the chicken breasts out of their packaging to pound into thin cutlets.

"Yeah, but she doesn't need to know that." Bryce took the Walla Walla sweets and started peeling away their papery skins.

"Why not? Take it from me. Lying to her is not the best way to start off a relationship. Maybe she'll think it's adorable you asked your big sister for help."

"Who says I want a relationship?" Bryce said. He started cutting the onions in half and into quarter-inch slices, as I'd directed. "Maybe I just want to get laid."

"Nice."

"I'm kidding, Ed. I like Lisa. She's a total hottie."

"Do you know anything else about her, besides that? Or is her being hot all that matters?" I didn't often play the wise big sister to Bryce, but in the flush of my new feelings for Jack, I felt the urge to impart some of my hard-earned relationship knowledge to him. I suspected that his raging hormones might make my efforts pointless, but I felt I could at least make an attempt.

"Of course that's not all that matters." He grinned again. "She likes to work out, too. So we have that in common."

"Oh, well then. Clearly, you should be married immediately."

He wadded up a piece of onion skin and threw it at me. It missed but landed in the sink.

"I'll tell you someone who's more than just hot," he said. "Your friend Georgia. I've seen her at the gym a lot lately. She's hilarious."

"You guys talk?" I asked. Georgia had mentioned that she was working out at the same gym where Bryce was a trainer, but she hadn't said anything past that.

Bryce nodded. "She asks me for advice on her workouts, mostly. She dropped her trainer. He was a dick."

"Yeah, I think she got tired of him telling her to exercise. Is she paying you?"

"Not yet. I haven't really asked her to be a client. It's more just a friendly thing. I do check out her rack when we talk, so I guess in a *way* she's paying me."

I swatted him with a dish towel. "You be nice to her or I'll kick your ass."

He held up his beefy hands in mock surrender. "Okay, okay. I'll be nice. I was just kidding. Sort of."

"Yeah, sort of." I went back to pounding out the chicken breast between two pieces of plastic wrap. "She's a little curvy for you, anyway, isn't she? Don't you like the hard-bodied gym bunnies?"

"She's bigger than most girls I've dated, yeah," Bryce said

thoughtfully. "But she's healthy and takes care of herself, you know? That's all that really matters. Plus," he added, "there's something appealing about what those fleshy curves might feel like against my rock-hard abs." He pounded both his fists against his stomach in emphasis.

"Oh, please!" I rolled my eyes.

"You find your dad yet?" Bryce reached into the refrigerator and took out a handful of cooked shrimp and shoved them in his mouth. "Sorry," he said with his mouth full. "Hungry."

"Apparently." I gave the onions a stir and set them on low to gradually caramelize. "Don't you think I'd tell you if I'd found him?"

He shrugged. "I dunno."

"Well, I would." I paused, setting the spatula on the counter. "I did find some of his old paintings, though, and a box of his things."

"Really? What was in it?" Bryce took another handful of shrimp and chomped down on them.

"I don't know." I looked away and focused on organizing the supplies I'd brought for dinner.

"You haven't looked?" I shook my head and Bryce raised his eyebrows at me. "Why not? That's nuts."

"It's not nuts," I said defensively. "I'm just not sure if I'm ready to see what might be in there. It was hard enough seeing his paintings." I told him about the Garden of Eden and finding my father's depiction of it.

"Huh. I'd still want to go through it."

"I will. It just might take me some time to work up the courage."

"Mom's not too happy about your doing all this."

I sighed and started using a biscuit cutter to create flatbread rounds for the pizza appetizer. "I know. She's made that very clear."

"Then why keep doing it?" Bryce dropped into one of his dining room chairs and watched me work.

"Because I need to. Whether I find him or not, I need to feel like I did everything I could. It's complicated, Bryce. He's my dad and he's sick."

"It's hurting my dad's feelings, too, you know."

I stopped cutting and looked at him. "What?"

His eyes met mine. "He feels like he wasn't good enough or something so you want to find your real dad to make up for it. That's what's getting to Mom the most, I think. That it's hurting him."

"She never said anything to me about that," I said, slightly taken aback. John was always so jovial around me. I never thought about his being upset by what I was doing and immediately felt bad for it. "Maybe I'll talk to him and try to explain."

"I don't know how much good it will do. He'll just pretend he's not hurt. The big bad fireman can't show any weakness." There was more than just a little scorn in Bryce's tone. "'Toughen up, son!'" he said, mimicking his father. "'You want those other boys to think you're a pussy?'"

"Bryce . . ." I started to say, but he waved his hand, dismissing me.

"You don't have to say it, Ed. I know he loves me. But he's never going to see me as anything other than a skinny little boy."

"But look at you," I said. "How can you say that when you've gotten so big? And brown?" Bryce's Oompa-Loompa look had morphed into more of a dark tan since I saw him at his competition. It was still a little extreme, but at least he no longer appeared like he would glow in the dark.

He flipped me off and I laughed.

"Come on," I said. "Get off your ass. I need you to get the asparagus ready and squeeze the lemons. Think you can do that, muscle man?"

"Anything for you," my brother said, and I knew he meant it. Besides seeing my mother so happy, the best thing that came out of her second marriage was definitely Bryce.

With all our jabbering and goofing around, it took about two hours for us to finish prepping and cooking the dinner. I left him around one o'clock with written, step-by-step instructions on how to reheat the meal. I ran back home to let Jasper out, then over to my work to pick up the forty pounds of slow-cooked pork I'd made the night before. I'd gotten the meat at cost from my supplier and within the Hope House dinner budget. Juan helped me load the two enormous plastic tubs of meat into the back of my car and wished me well for the evening.

"I've got everything under control, boss," he said. "I'll see you on Thursday."

"Thanks, Juan. You're the best." I gave him a quick, impromptu hug and was on my way. Anticipation danced in my belly as I drove to the shelter, knowing I'd get to spend the next ten hours with Jack. I drove around the back of the building to drop off the plastic tubs at the kitchen door. Rita answered when I knocked.

"Eden! Good to see you." She was wearing capri jeans and a tight pink T-shirt emblazoned with the phrase WAG MORE, BARK LESS.

"Good to see you, too," I said. "I come bearing meat. Lots and lots of meat."

"Jack's right there." She nodded toward an empty, dirt-filled lot on the other side of the alley. "Hey, buddy!" she hollered with her hands cupped around her mouth. "Your lady has arrived with dinner!"

Feeling ridiculously pleased at being called Jack's "lady," I stood on my tiptoes to see over the top of my car. He strode toward us with a smile. "Hi," I said with a wave. "What're you up to?"

He came around my car and stood next to me. "Just checking out the lot, trying to figure out what in the hell to do with it."

"It's yours?" I asked.

"Yep," Rita said. "It was part of the property deal when you bought this place, right?"

Jack shot her a hard look and a flash of guilt lit Rita's face. "I'm going to get the coleslaw started," she said. "I'll see you inside, Eden."

"Okay," I said. "What was that about?" I asked Jack after she'd gone back into the kitchen.

"Oh, nothing." He turned to face me and leaned in for a kiss. I felt butterflies all the way down to my toes. He pulled back and smiled, touching the tip of his nose to mine. "Hi."

I grinned, feeling giddy. "Hi."

"I want to do something with the lot, so I was just hanging out in it a bit, waiting for inspiration."

"Any luck?" I asked, placing my hands on either side of his waist. I could feel the warmth of his skin through his shirt.

Jack sighed. "Not really. I was thinking maybe an outdoor sleeping area, but I'm not sure about the zoning. I'll have to check it out with the city." He peered into the backseat of my Honda. "What's in the tubs?"

"A crap-ton of pork. I need a burly young man to help me get it in the kitchen and into some pots so I can sauce it up. Know of anyone?"

"Well, I've got the young part down, but I don't know about the burly. I might have to call Tom in to pinch-hit for me."

I punched his arm playfully and he let me go to open the door and carry the containers inside. I went to park my car and came back to the kitchen to find Jack and Rita in an intense discussion. Jack's face was close to hers and Rita was nodding but frowning too.

"I'm not interrupting, am I?" I asked.

Both Jack and Rita looked up and immediately rearranged their expressions into smiles. "Oh no," Rita said. "Just business stuff." She brightened her smile further. "Want to get started? Word's gotten out on the street about your mad cooking skills. I think we'll be busy tonight."

"Really?" I said. "I'm glad." I looked at Jack. "Are you staying to help?"

He shook his head, still smiling. "No, I've got a ton of paperwork to do. Come get me if you need any more heavy lifting."

"You know I will," I said. I was disappointed he wouldn't be hanging out in the kitchen with me for the afternoon, but I smiled and waved him off. It was a fine line between showing him how interested I was and sending him running from my rampant need to be with him every minute. Nothing drove a man off more quickly than a clingy woman.

"He's a goner," Rita commented after he'd left.

"What do you mean?" I asked as I reached to tie an apron around my waist.

"All week long it's been 'Eden says this' or 'I want to take Eden there.'" She grinned. "He's toast."

I blushed and she laughed. "Oh, boy," she said. "You're toast, too. He's an Aquarius, so it's a good match for you. I don't even have to do your chart. I knew it the minute I saw you two together that night in the office."

"You did, huh?"

"Oh, yeah. Sparks flew. I was lucky to escape when I did."

Rita and I spent the next few hours getting the meal ready. I put together a homemade barbecue sauce while she chopped up about fifty heads of green and purple cabbage for the slaw. We pulled the massive amounts of pork apart and heated it up slowly on the stove, stirring in the sauce to help keep it moist. A local bakery had donated about ten racks of hamburger buns and I made five cookie sheets full of espresso-laced brownies. When it was all ready, Rita buzzed Jack to come help us set up, and we opened the doors for dinner.

"The line's down the block," Jack remarked before he let the first rush in. "I hope we have enough."

I helped Rita serve for the first hour, putting together sandwiches and scooping up good-sized portions of coleslaw onto paper plates. One of Jack's other employees, who introduced herself as Starr, showed up, so when the line calmed down to a dull roar, I was able to go back to the kitchen to fetch the first tray of brownies and take it around the dining room, serving each individual. Every tall, skinny man with long, dark hair sent my heart skipping a beat, but none so far was my father. Jack came over to assist me in serving the brownies, introducing me to his regular clients.

"This is Jade and Cheyenne," he said, gesturing toward two older-looking women sitting together at a table. They were painfully thin—skeletal, really—and wore heavy makeup and skintight, peacock-hued T-shirts. "Ladies, I'd like you to meet Eden."

"Hi," I said with a smile. "Would you like a brownie?"

"Only if you sit down and eat one with us," one of the women said. She had black stringy hair pulled up into a ponytail on the top of her head. "I'm Jade."

I looked at Jack and handed him the tray of brownies, snagging three in the process. He obliged with a smile and walked away to finish handing out dessert on his own. I sat down at the table across from Jade and Cheyenne and gave them each a brownie. "Thanks," I said. "I'm wiped out."

"You work today?" asked the other woman, whom Jack had introduced as Cheyenne. She was blond with thin, greasy braids and no teeth. Like Jade's, her face was pitted with angry acne scars that her elaborate makeup did nothing to hide.

"Sort of. I helped my brother cook a meal to impress a girl and then I came here to cook all afternoon. I think I need to find a career that doesn't have me on my feet so much."

"You should give sex work a try," Jade said. "You're definitely on your back more than your feet!"

Cheyenne cackled and popped a bite of brownie in her mouth. "Oh yeah, I'm sure this pretty girl wants to come be a hooker."

"Sex worker," Jade said, correcting her. "And why not? We make a living."

"And we shoot it right up our arms," Cheyenne said. She reached over and patted me on the arm. "Don't worry, honey. We're just jokin'."

"I figured." I smiled. "How long have you been coming to Hope House?"

Jade looked at Cheyenne and tilted her head. "What, since it opened?" she said. Cheyenne nodded. Jade went on. "We heard Jack was a good guy and he brought the nurse in for free HIV and hepatitis tests. Then he started doing dinner and we was hooked." She moved her gaze back to me. "The food's been hella better since you got here, though."

"Well, thanks." I felt oddly privileged to have been asked to sit down with these women. I knew from both Rita and Jack that their clientele didn't open up very easily to strangers. I imagined what it must be like to be them, to live in their world, and I shuddered a bit internally. What did it feel like, I wondered, to have people on the street avert their eyes from you to avoid interaction? Was this how my father lived now? Alone and unacknowledged?

"What time's your next job, Jade?" Cheyenne asked with her mouth full of brownie. Her question jolted me out of my thoughts about my dad.

"Seven o'clock," Jade answered. "I got a regular for a half-'n-half in the alley behind his office. Get this. Dude wears *pink lace panties*." She snorted. "How 'bout you?"

"I got nothing. It's the corner for me tonight, see what I can dig up."

"You need to lower your rates," Jade advised.

"Fuck that. I don't got any teeth, so I can charge more!" She opened her mouth wide to reveal slightly frightening pink and empty gums.

Jade reached in her mouth and pulled out a set of dentures. "No, *I* can charge more. I provide options!"

Though a little horrified at the content of their conversation, I burst out laughing. They looked at me, confounded by my amusement. "I'm sorry," I gasped. "I can't help it. 'I provide options!'" They still stared at me like I was out of my mind so I explained further, trying to catch my breath. "As a chef I provide options for soup or salad and you provide teeth or no teeth. Different profession, similar business model." I cracked up again.

Both ladies smiled and started to laugh, too. It struck me how surreal this conversation was. Like any other talk I might have with Georgia—a simple exchange of information about our respective lives. The subject matter might be entirely different, but the sense of connection was the same.

Jack came back over when he saw us laughing. "What's so funny?" he asked.

"Options," Jade said, and all three of us giggled while Jack appeared baffled.

He sat down next to me, pressing his leg against mine. "Did Eden tell you about her father?"

"No," I said. "I didn't." It hadn't crossed my mind to bring it up. Did my dad utilize a sex worker's services? I cringed to consider it.

"What about your dad, honey?" Cheyenne asked.

Jack looked at me expectantly, so I took a deep breath and explained to the ladies what had brought me to Hope House in the first place. They listened intently to my description and took a long, hard look at the snapshot of him I kept in my purse.

Jade ran her finger along the edge of the photo and smiled softly. "It's nice," she said, "that you're looking for him. My family wrote me off a long time ago. They think I'm a piece of shit. Which I am."

"No," I said, standing up to hug her. "You're not." She clung to me for a moment and I pressed as much feeling as I could muster into my embrace before she pulled away. I hugged Cheyenne, too.

"We'll keep our eyes open for your dad, sweetie," Jade said. "If we see him, we'll let him know where to find you."

"Thanks," I said sincerely. "That means a lot."

"Oooh! I got a date," Jade said, noticing the time. "See you next week, Eden?"

I nodded. "I'll be here."

"Bring some more of those brownies, too," Cheyenne said. "They were *bangin'*."

After they left, Jack took my hand under the table and traced the outline of my fingers with the tip of one of his. My breath shuddered. He glanced at me sidelong with a wicked half smile. "Problems?" he asked in a mock-innocent tone.

"No," I breathed. "No problems." Holy crap, this man knew what he was doing. I tried not to think about where he might have learned it.

"That was great of you, you know," he said, pulling my hand up to kiss the inside of my palm.

I smiled at this gesture. "What was great?"

"Hugging them like that. They don't get a lot of physical affection. Some from each other, maybe, but not nearly enough. Outside of the men who pay them for sex, they're basically touch-starved."

I shrugged. "I'm an affectionate girl."

"Lucky me." He traced the sensitive nerves of my hand again and then continued up the underside of my forearm.

"What are you doing after your shift tonight?" I asked. Excitement skittered along my skin.

He locked his eyes on mine. "I don't know. Did you have any wild ideas?"

"Well, I was thinking you might come over to my place," I said, attempting to keep my breathing pattern normal.

"Won't Jasper be jealous?" he asked.

"He'll live."

He leaned over and brushed his lips against mine. "I'd love to," he whispered.

What the hell, I thought. Rules were made to be broken. *Georgia will be so proud.*

May 1989
Eden

My daddy tried.

He tried like he had always tried after he did something horrible. Except this time he tried harder, because taking me with him in the middle of the night and ending up in jail was, according to my mother, the most horrible thing he'd ever done. He cleaned the house and grocery-shopped and made my mother and me delicious dinners out of simple ingredients. He brought his easel into the house and painted every room, reasoning that if we ever had to move, we could rebuild our memories from his canvases. He went to the doctor with my mom without arguing and came home with a bag full of pill bottles that sounded like a baby's rattle when he walked by. As far as we knew, he took them.

I wanted to believe he was doing better. I wanted to believe the smiles he showed me were real. But his hands shook and his eyes were dark. The flickering joy I usually saw in them was nowhere to be found, no matter how hard I tried to make him laugh. The mask he wore was so thin—as transparent and fragile as tissue paper. I was certain it would crumple and blow away in the next stiff wind.

"Daddy?" I said one afternoon when I got home from school. It was a warm spring day and we were sitting in the sun on the front porch, sipping from cans of root beer and eating celery smeared with peanut butter. He was staring off into space and didn't respond, so I nudged him. "Daddy?"

He rolled his head slowly around to look at me. "What, Bug? Everything all right?" He wasn't drunk, but his words were labored. They sounded the way I felt when I had to drag myself out of bed to go to school.

I nodded. "Yes. Everything's fine. I was just wondering . . ." I didn't know how to ask all I wanted to know. *Is your brain okay? Is the medicine working? Are you drinking and I just don't know it? Do you still want to leave me? Are you ever going to get well?*

"Wondering what?" he asked.

I started again, trying to compress my inquiries into one. "Well, how are you feeling?"

"How am I feeling?" he repeated. He dropped his eyes to the can he held, running his index finger along the rim of its mouth. Mom always yelled at me when I did that; she said I'd slice myself on the can's sharp edge.

"Yes. You seem kind of sad."

He sighed. "How could I be sad when I'm sitting next to the prettiest, smartest girl in all the world?"

I smiled. "Daddy. Seriously."

"I am being serious. That's an honest question. How is it possible for me to be sad when I have you?" He reached over and swung his arm around my shoulders, hugging me to him. He was so skinny. He cooked, but he barely ate. I was worried. When he took his meds, he usually ate more, not less.

"Look at your garden, Eden," he said. "It's still so beautiful."

I glanced down on the side of the stairs at the Garden of Eden. The tulips and daffodils had faded away, only to be replaced by clusters of vibrant bluebells and towering shocks of orange tiger lilies.

"Should we take Mrs. Worthington a bouquet?" he asked, releasing me from his embrace. "She's watching us. Maybe she'd like one."

I looked across the street just in time to see Mrs. Worthington's curtains swing closed. "No," I said. "She's not very nice."

He bumped me gently with his knee. "Maybe she's not nice because no one brings her flowers."

"You told me before she's not nice because she has a stick up her wrinkly old butt," I reminded him.

He laughed, but it was a forced sound. "I hope you didn't tell your mother I said that. She'd have my hide."

"No," I said quietly. "I didn't tell her." All my father's secrets felt like stones in my belly. I was sure if I fell over the side of a ship, I'd sink.

"Good." He patted my leg and stared off into space again. "I'm going to try and sell a painting," he said after a few minutes. "Maybe two."

"You are? That's great, Daddy! Which ones?"

"The ones of you sleeping on the couch."

"Who are you going to sell them to?"

"The Wild Orchid Gallery."

"Do you think they'll want to do a show?" I asked excitedly. A show meant my dad would be working. A show meant he'd be making money.

"No." His voice was flat.

"Why not?"

"The gallery owner wants something I don't want to give her."

"Oh," I said, and crunched on another celery stick. "Daddy?"

"What, Bug?"

"Are you happy?" I thought this maybe was a better question

than asking if he was sad. I thought maybe he'd answer me with something other than another question. I wished he'd just tell me the truth.

My father turned suddenly and took me in his arms, hugging me with such strength I thought I might break. "I don't know," he whispered in my ear. "Are *you?*"

I buried my face into his neck. He smelled of sweat and Old Spice. "I think so," I said. "I think I might be happy."

"Okay then," he answered. "Then I'll be happy, too."

May 1989
David

The demons were winning. No matter what he did or how hard he tried, David felt them writhing around inside his head, gnawing at his resolve to stay well like a dog on a bone. He went through the motions of being normal but could not combat the feeling that at any moment he might crack wide open and be revealed as the imposter he was. Still, he forced himself to do what he knew was expected of him. The impulses were there, of course. They throbbed in his body like a second heartbeat. They snipped and snapped at his heels, trying to get him to trip up. He knew it was only a matter of time before he stumbled. So he kept quiet. He kept his movements small and measured so they wouldn't spin him out of control. He helped around the house and spent time with his daughter. He kept the angst he felt a secret from his family, just like the pills he pretended to take. He was smarter about that this time, making sure to flush them instead of stockpiling them away as he had done before.

"How's the new dosage?" Lydia asked one Saturday morning when Eden was still in bed.

"Fine," he said. He knew the chemically induced lethargy the meds usually brought on so well it was easy to mimic. He made sure to speak slowly, as though his tongue was too thick for his mouth. He hated lying to his family but he hated what the pills did to him more. It was worth it to pretend.

"The car insurance is due," she said.

David looked at her, this woman he'd promised to love, honor, and cherish for the rest of his days. How could he have made such a promise at eighteen? How could he have known what would happen to him? She was so beautiful. Too beautiful for the likes of him. She'd made it exceptionally clear since he got home from jail that there would be no physical affection between them. Not that there had been much of that in the past few years, but they would at least come together on occasion out of need for sheer physical release. But this morning, when he tried to caress one of her breasts after she got out of the shower, she slapped his hand away and blasted him with a look so cold he felt it inside his bones.

"I was planning on visiting Cerina today," he said. "Maybe things have changed and she'll want to buy a painting."

"That would be great." Lydia smiled, a tentative thing. She still didn't trust him. David didn't blame her. He didn't deserve it. He didn't even trust himself.

"How much do we need?"

"Eight hundred."

"I'll have to sell more than one to get that."

"Maybe you could get a job," Lydia said.

"Doing what?" David didn't want a job. He wanted to be free of this aching pressure in his head.

"Teaching, maybe? At the community college? Or private lessons? Any extra income would help."

David nodded, but he knew he was in no shape to be out in the world. He could barely hold it together at home. How would he pull it off in front of a classroom? Broken thoughts twisted and howled in his head, desperate to be let out. He willed them to be silent and for a moment, they obeyed.

Lydia busied herself at the sink, scrubbing dishes from dinner the night before. David had made pepperoni lasagna with three kinds of cheese and Eden immediately claimed it as her new favorite meal.

Eden. She sensed all was not well with him. He was not that good an actor. He felt himself being pulled down again, spiraling into a darkness he knew better than the light. He was exhausted from all this. He couldn't stand the thought of maintaining this charade another moment.

"What's Eden doing today?" he asked Lydia.

She looked over her shoulder at him as she continued to scrub. "She has Tina Carpenter's sleepover party."

"What about you? What are your plans for the day?" David tried to sound bright and interested. He wanted nothing more than to be left alone. To wallow in the black mood hanging over him. He wanted to sleep, to escape. But first, he knew he would have to try to sell Cerina the painting. He'd promised himself and his family that he would be a different man. He had to maintain his front.

"I'm going in to work to catch up on the monthly billing. I need the overtime." Lydia turned off the faucet and reached for a dish towel to dry her hands. "So you'll go talk to Cerina while I'm gone?"

"I said I would, didn't I?" David snapped.

Lydia tensed, her hands gripping the striped yellow towel. "Don't do that," she said in a low voice. "Don't you even *start* to do that."

"Sorry." David sighed. He was hanging on by a thread. But just barely. At any moment, he might just decide to let go.

*   *   *

The Wild Orchid Gallery was two blocks south of Bellevue Square Mall. David parked next to the small stucco building and took a deep breath before going inside. He needed to do this. He needed to sell the painting—maybe even all three in the study—and be on his way. That's it. Nothing more. Then he could go home, find the bottle of vodka he'd stashed in the attic, and get on with his day. Eden wasn't home and Lydia said she'd be working. He had enough time to drink and sober back up so neither of them would suspect what he'd done. He had earned this temporary reprieve. He planned to take it.

The bell above the door tinkled when he swung it open. Cerina stood at the reception desk, her black shiny hair cut in a reverse bob that exposed the tender nape of her neck. David had bitten that spot more than once when they had sex; Cerina liked to be handled a little roughly. She looked up and her mouth curled into a knowing smile.

"David," she said. "How nice to see you. To what do I owe the pleasure?"

"I thought I'd show you the work we discussed last month," David said. "Just in case."

Cerina raised an impeccably plucked eyebrow. "In case of what?"

"In case you've come to your senses and want to buy the series."

Cerina threw her head back and laughed. "Cocky," she said. "I love it." She slithered around the desk and came over to embrace him. He felt himself stir at her touch. He wouldn't. He couldn't do it to Lydia. Not again. He was going to be a better man than this. He would fight his dysfunction and he would win.

"I'm happy to see you," Cerina said breathily with her lips pressed against his ear. Shivers ran through his body and he fought the urge to bend her over right there. *No,* he told himself. *You will not do this.* He forced himself to pull away. She looked up at him in surprise. "No?"

"No," David said shakily.

Cerina ran her hand up his thigh, brushing over his erection. "I don't believe you."

He stepped back, out of her reach. "Let me get the paintings." His body was betraying him, just like his mind. He couldn't control either of them. He couldn't control a thing.

She shrugged. "Suit yourself, Romeo. I'll take a look, but I can't make any promises." She gestured toward the walls, which displayed a collection of bright abstract murals. "As you can see, I'm all full up. He's a fabulous artist. Willing to give me anything I want." She looked at him pointedly.

So this is what she wanted. And probably why she wouldn't see him the last time he called, the day he got out of jail. She felt slighted by him—how he didn't pursue her after their first few encounters. He had spun off his meds and she thought his disappearance was about her. She had no idea what was wrong with him. "Trust me," he said. "You'll want these."

David went back out to his car to retrieve the paintings. He was proud of this series he'd done of Eden sleeping. He'd managed to capture the innocence and vulnerability of the moment, illuminated by the warm glow of the sun streaming through the front window. He carried them back into the gallery, where Cerina looked them over.

"They're excellent," she said. "I love how her arm is flung over her face in this one, then off the couch in the next. I can almost see the movement in between the two poses."

David smiled. "That's because she wasn't posing. I sketched her for a few hours while she napped, then retreated to my studio to paint." He paused, daring to reach out and put his hand on Cerina's lower back. He couldn't help it. He wanted her. "So, you like them?"

Cerina arched her spine in response to his touch. "Yes." She looked at him questioningly. "Can you give me what I want?"

Lydia wouldn't have to know, David reasoned. It would be over quickly and he would bring home the money and Lydia would have no idea. He would make both of the women happy. He leaned down and kissed Cerina's bloodred lips. They tasted like cigarettes. He could lose himself here, in the touch and taste of another woman. She pressed herself against him and he knew he would give in. He was too tired to fight. He was done pretending, done holding on to the hope he'd ever be the kind of man his family deserved. There was no turning back now.

Three hours later, David could not take a hot enough shower. His skin was red and pulsing and his heart jackhammered in his chest. The water rained down and down and down and still did nothing to cleanse him. He was done. There was nothing more he could do to save himself or his family. The voices roared in his head. He slammed back the vodka in order to drown them out but this time, the alcohol only seemed to fuel their determination to be heard. The shame rose in hard, angry waves inside him. Cerina had taken him into the back room and locked the door, telling her assistant to watch the front while she brokered the deal for his paintings. David left an hour later with cash in hand and any remaining self-worth shattered around his feet.

He *was* worthless, he decided as he turned off the shower,

then stood naked and dripping in the bathroom. Totally and utterly worthless. He wasn't meant for this life with a wife and a child. He couldn't handle the responsibilities. He wasn't built for it. Maybe he wasn't built for any kind of life. Maybe the world would just be better off without him.

It wasn't like the thought hadn't crossed his mind before. The inviting pull of permanent oblivion had danced along the edges of his thoughts for years. When he first began to lose himself. When Lydia had him committed for the first time. And now, when he was so disgusted with his own behavior he couldn't stand to look in the mirror. He knew when he was in jail that he needed to find a way to end his family's misery. He thought he could white-knuckle his way through to normalcy. He thought he could do it without the meds. He couldn't decide which was worse—life on the meds or life off of them. He concluded it was just *life* he couldn't stand. The simple act of breathing had become too much to bear.

He was so tired. Tired of the struggle, tired of the lies. "I'm tired," he said aloud to the empty room. "I don't want to do this anymore." His words echoed back at him. How much easier it would be to succumb to the darkness. He'd tried to do the right thing and he'd failed, just like every time before. His life was a pointless mess. There was really no reason to continue it.

There was Eden, he thought as he stumbled down the hall toward her room. He pushed open the door and looked inside at the ruffled lime-green bedspread she'd picked out because "pink is for sissies." He smiled as he remembered her saying those words. His opinionated yet fragile young daughter standing in the aisle at Sears with her arms crossed over her tiny chest. Who would protect her if he left? And perhaps more relevant, who would protect her if he stayed? What was it that Lydia had said a few months ago? That she was worried Eden wouldn't survive him? Well, there was only one thing to do then. But he'd have to be good and drunk to do it.

The bottle of vodka was still in the bathroom. He staggered back down the hall. Stepping onto the tiled floor, he caught a glance of himself in the mirror. Who was that devil? It scared him to not recognize himself. Was he possessed? Had the evil spirits in his head taken him over so thoroughly that his outside appearance was forever changed? He had to end this. He had to end this now.

As he scrambled toward the bottle he'd left on the edge of the tub, David's stomach bent in on itself and he feared he might vomit. He dropped to his knees, breathing hard. He couldn't remember the last time he ate. His hip bones stuck out in frightful knobs. He was disappearing anyway. His body was erasing itself. Why not speed up the process?

The air in the bathroom was muggy and thick. He outstretched his arm to reach the bottle, fumbling to get his fingers around its slippery neck. He stood back up, bracing himself with one hand against the wall. Putting the bottle to his lips, he let the hot liquid burn the back of his throat. When he finished swallowing, he opened his eyes and saw his reflection again. This time it was him. David West, failure as a man. Failure as a father and husband. A pitiful excuse for a human being, standing with a towel draped around his waist in the bathroom his wife worked to pay for. The two thousand dollars he'd earned today wouldn't last long. Now she could use it to pay for his funeral.

With an angry howl, he launched the bottle he held at the mirror. Both shattered instantly and sprayed shards of glass all over the room. They sparkled in the light and for a moment, David had the urge to paint this. To capture the moment so it would not be forgotten. But who would want to remember it? Not his daughter. Not his wife. Once he was gone they would forget him and both would be the better for it.

He stooped down to pick up the largest shard of mirror by his feet. It was shaped like a diamond, jagged on one edge, smooth and clean on the other. Which would be better to use? It didn't matter, he supposed. As long as it got the job done. This would all be over soon. He could feel the ache to escape inflating inside him. How sweet a relief it would be.

He put the shard to his left wrist, staring at the swollen river of blue veins beneath his pale skin. How long would it take? He didn't know, nor did he care. All he wanted was for the end to come. He pressed the jagged edge into the base of his palm and pulled downward, releasing an animalistic screech as the pain seared through his body.

A huge rush of blood poured from the wound. He had opened the vein. Did he have it in him to finish this? He shook with pain, tears rushing out of his eyes, the sobs tearing at his lungs. "It'll be over soon," he cried. "It'll all be over soon."

He had just managed to shift the shard into his now injured hand and was pushing it into the flesh of his right wrist when the sound of the front door slamming burst through his concentration.

"Daddy?" he heard Eden call out. "Where are you?"

Eden. Jesus Christ, what was she doing home? She wasn't supposed to see this. David swooned from the blood loss and stopped the second incision. The two inches he'd managed to slice downward bled anyway, though not as bad as his other wrist. Oh god, he was dizzy. He dug deep into himself to call out to his daughter. "Eden!" he tried to yell, but his voice was weak. "Don't come up. Do you understand me? Do not come up those stairs!"

He fell to his knees again and then over onto his side. He curled fetal on the cold bathroom floor. His eyes closed. He felt numb, disconnected. He tasted metal in the back of his throat. This was the end, he thought. He could finally let everything go.

The door swung open and David's eyes fluttered. There was his daughter, standing in the doorway. Her mouth was open like she was screaming but he couldn't hear a sound. He blinked heavily, slowly, and there was his daughter rushing toward him, slipping in a puddle of his blood. His eyes closed again and the last thing he felt before everything went dark was his daughter's arms around him, cradling his head, sobs racking her body as she began to watch him die.

November 2010
Eden

Waking up naked with Jack curled around me was surprising to say the least. I rarely slept well with another person in my bed—something my past boyfriends had complained about when they found me on the couch the mornings after they stayed over. I didn't readily share my sleeping space with a man and when I did, I knew I'd be in for a long, uncomfortable night.

But the morning after I invited him home, there Jack and I lay, on our sides with him tucked snugly behind me. His left arm was slung over my waist with his hand resting on one of my breasts. Jasper lay splayed on the floor, snoring peacefully. I sucked in my stomach, self-conscious about the small belly roll Jack's forearm rested upon. He shifted when I moved and nuzzled his nose into my neck.

"Good morning," he murmured.

I scooted a few inches away from him and shifted over onto my back, looking at him. His dark hair was mussed and the olive-toned skin of his face was creased from sleep.

It was still fairly dark outside, probably no later than seven o'clock. I didn't know for sure; the alarm clock had landed on the floor sometime last night. I smiled and tried not to exhale what I was afraid might be my fiendish morning breath at him. "Good morning."

He leaned over and kissed me, apparently unconcerned with the breath issue. I let myself be taken in by his touch, his fingers trailing along my sides as they had the night before. Images of our bodies pressed together flashed in my mind and I felt a pulling, aching sensation between my legs. *Oh god. Am I remembering correctly? Did we really do all of that?* I pushed him gently away.

"You'll be late for work," I said with a smile.

He propped himself up on one elbow and grinned, showing off his slightly crooked front teeth. "I'm the boss. I can be late if I want." His eyes traveled the length of my body. "I might even take the day off. You're not working, right?"

"No, I'm not." I did my best to resist the urge to yank the blanket up and cover myself. If he wanted to look, let him look. If there was something he didn't like, better I know it now so we could both be on our merry ways.

"Damn, you're beautiful," he said, and I felt myself blush to the tips of my toes. I wasn't used to this kind of adoration. I had a hard time taking it in.

"Thank you," I said, trying to breathe normally. "You're very kind."

"Just honest," he said, and he kissed me again.

"I don't normally invite boys over for sleepovers, you know."

He chuckled. "Oh, really? I should consider myself lucky, then?"

"No. I just didn't want you to think this is something I do all the time." I did reach for the covers then, pulling the sheet up to cover my breasts.

"Eden," he said gently, "I didn't think that."

"What did you think, then?" I asked, unsure if I really wanted to hear his answer.

He leaned over with his face less than an inch from my own. His breath was warm on my skin. "Wow," he breathed.

"Wow?" I repeated.

He nodded. "That's what I thought. Last week, last night. That was the word that came to mind whenever I got to spend time with you."

To my horror, my eyes filled and I fought not to cry in front of this man yet again. What amazed me wasn't that he said it; what amazed me was the fact that I believed he meant every word. I had a pretty decent bullshit detector and there was not an ounce of insincerity in his voice, no falter in his gaze. I swallowed back the tears and gave him a big smile. "Well," I said, more than a little flustered, "that might be the sweetest thing anyone has ever said to me."

If he saw the tears, he decided not to say anything. All the more reason to like him. He sat up and patted my hip. "Can I make you some coffee?"

"Are you kidding?" I asked, spinning to sit on the edge of the bed. I reached for my sweats and pulled them on. "It's my house, I'll make you coffee. And breakfast, too. I need to feed Jasper anyway." At the sound of his name, Jasper lifted his head and stood, wagging his tail expectantly.

"Can I hop in the shower?" Jack asked.

"Of course. There should be fresh towels on the shelf."

"Thanks." He came around the bed and put his arms around me, kissing me again.

I groaned. "I'll never get breakfast made if we keep this up."

"It's already up," he half growled, pushing himself against me.

I laughed. "I can see that. Or feel it, as the case may be." Jasper whimpered by the door. "I need to feed the pup. I'll take care of you later, sir."

"Oooh. Bossy." He wiggled his eyebrows at me suggestively. "I like it."

He let me go and went into the bathroom while I put on a bra and a T-shirt and practically skipped out to the kitchen. After Jasper returned from his morning trip to the backyard, I gave him his scoop of dry food with a capsule of fish oil drizzled on it for his aging joints. While he ate, I started the coffee and pulled out the eggs to make a quick veggie-and-cheese frittata. I didn't have to work that day, but I knew it was a rare thing for Jack to take time off.

"You don't have to spend the day here," I said when he crossed the threshold into the kitchen after his shower. "If you don't want to." He had put on his jeans from the night before but nothing else. I resisted the urge to run my fingers across his bare chest. He wasn't in perfect shape, but the lines of his body were definitely appealing. I wanted to memorize them.

He dropped into one of my kitchen chairs, picked up the mug of coffee, and eyed the slice of frittata I'd set out for him. "Now, why would you say something like that?" he asked. "Like you assume I feel obligated to hang out with you."

I shrugged and felt a twinge of regret in my gut. Not that he was here, not that I'd invited him home with me, but that I hadn't revealed how truly twisted I was when it came to relationships. I'd joked about it, sure, but he had no idea just how deep my fears went. I had no idea how to make it clear without his running from the room like I'd lit him on fire.

He took a sip of the coffee and stared at me with clear green eyes. They seemed to pierce right through to the most vulnerable space inside me.

"What?" I said. I busied myself with putting dirty dishes in the sink. "You're making me nervous."

"You're not used to having someone love you, is that it?" He didn't look away.

Love? Did he just use the word "love"? Panic ignited in my chest.

He sighed and set his mug down on the table. "Repeat after me," he said. "I, Eden West, do solemnly swear to let Jack Baker get to know me." He waited. "G'head. Repeat it."

I smiled at his silliness. "Okay, okay," I said, holding my hands up in mock surrender. "I get it. I'm sorry." I went over to stand next to him and he pulled me to him. I kissed the top of his head. "You're right, you know."

He squeezed me around my waist, pressing his face into my stomach. "Right about what?" His words vibrated against my flesh.

"I'm not used to having someone love me," I said, making my voice as small and quiet as possible. This small revelation felt huge to me. I didn't normally share that kind of truth.

"Why not?" he asked. He looked up as he spoke, setting his chin against me. I had to look away.

"Too scared, I guess. I don't let them." I held my breath and looked back at him, wanting to see what Jack would do with my confessed vulnerability.

"I can relate to that," he said. "What else are you scared to do?"

I hesitated, wondering just how willing I was to open up to him. He waited, his gaze never leaving my face. "I'm scared to go through my dad's things," I finally said. "I'm afraid of what I might find."

"I'll help, if you want," he said. His hands rubbed my back in a soothing circular motion. "Unless it's something you need to do alone."

I shook my head. "I do too many things alone."

"Me too." A strange look passed over his face, an expression I might have called grief had it not disappeared so quickly.

I leaned down to kiss him, my hands cupped on his cheeks. "C'mon," I said. "Your breakfast is getting cold."

We both ate and after that he threw on a shirt and very graciously offered to take Jasper for a walk while I took a shower. When they returned, I was in the spare bedroom staring at my father's belongings. Jasper trotted over to me and circled three times before lying down next to the bed. He let out a guttural sigh as he rested his chin on his front paws and closed his eyes. Jack followed him into the room and stood next to me, taking my hand in his.

"What do you want to look through first?" he asked. "The paintings or the box?"

I took a deep breath and let it out before responding. "The box, I think. It's more of the unknown." I really didn't know what I expected to find. A map leading me to where he might have gone, where he lived the past ten years? A phone number? I realized what scared me most was the possibility I wouldn't find answers, only more questions.

"Okay," Jack said, letting my hand go and stepping over to the bed. He carefully rested the stack of paintings against the wall, which left plenty of room for the two of us to sit down. I opened the box and reached inside. I pulled out a couple of old crewneck sweaters with horrid geometric shapes and held them up for Jack's appraisal.

He cringed. "Um, 1984 called and wants its sweaters back."

I laughed. "So he wasn't a fashion plate. He didn't need to be. He was an artist."

"Aren't artists supposed to have an eye for what looks good?"

"He subscribed to the philosophy that beauty is in the eye of the beholder."

"It sure is." He reached over and caressed my cheek with the tips of his fingers, staring at me intently.

I flushed pink with pleasure. "Flattery will get you everywhere, my friend." I pulled out a couple of books, *Moby Dick* and *The Catcher in the Rye*. There were a few pairs of paint-splattered jeans and some CDs: Talking Heads, Nirvana, Etta James. My dad always did have eclectic musical taste. I looked inside the box and beneath another sweater, I saw the edges of some paper. I pushed the sweater out of the way and found a small stack of letters, yellowed with age and tied with a silky brown ribbon. I pulled at the ribbon and squinted at the print on the first envelope. My mouth dropped open.

"What?" Jack asked, seeing the expression on my face. "What is it?"

"They're addressed to me." I pointed to the envelope. "And look at the postmark. July 1989." I flipped through the next few letters in the stack. "August 1989. September, October, and November." I looked over at Jack, whose eyebrows were pulled together, creating a deep furrow in his forehead. "Five letters."

"Sorry, am I missing something?"

"I didn't hear from my dad until after I was out of high school," I explained, my heart rate rising. "He found my address when I moved out of my mom's house and sent me two letters when I was twenty. Which I never responded to. These," I said, holding up the stack and shaking them in the air, "were all addressed to me at our old house, right after he left when I was ten. The one I lived in with him."

Jack stared at the envelopes again. "They're marked 'Return to Sender.'" Understanding crept across his face. "Your mom didn't give them to you."

"Apparently not." I felt the anger mount in my body, blossoming across my cheeks in a bright red flood. She lied to me. She told me he never wrote. That he never called. I asked her over and over again if he wanted to see me and she told me no. I cried night after night and she just let me suffer. I tore the first letter from the stack, opened it, and read it quickly to myself.

July 8, 1989

> *Dear Eden,*
> *I know you don't want to see me. I don't want to see me either, after what I've done to you. To your mother, too. I can't say I'm sorry enough times to make clear just how disgusted I am for letting myself get to that point. What you saw that night is something I can't take back, no matter how many times I wish I could. The doctors here tell me you might someday find a way to forgive me, but first, I need to forgive myself. Well, I'm nowhere near being able to do that, so I guess you've got a long time to go, too. Don't worry, baby. I understand. I've made you so many promises I didn't keep. I'm so ashamed of myself. Please know that I love you and I'll never stop trying to make up to you what I've done. You are my treasure, my one gem in the world. I miss you so much.*
>
> *Love, Daddy*

I dropped the letter onto the bed and wiped away the tears that rolled down my cheeks. "I can't believe my mother lied to me. Why would she *do* that?"

"I don't know," Jack said gently. "Maybe she thought she was protecting you."

"From what? Knowing my father loved me? That he didn't

actually abandon me for all those years? That he tried to stay in contact with me?" My breath was tight in my chest. I was trying hard not to lose it completely.

"She must have thought she was doing the right thing at the time," Jack said. He reached over and stroked my hair.

"Well, she was wrong." I pulled away from his touch and he looked hurt. I took a deep breath. "Sorry. I'm just kind of overwhelmed right now." *And pissed off. Really, really pissed off. How dare my mother not tell me about these letters? What else is she hiding? Did she know where he was all this time? Does she know where he is now?*

Jack dropped his hand to his side. "I understand. Do you want me to leave?"

I paused for a moment, torn between the desire to be with him and the need to deal with this on my own.

Seeing my hesitance, he stood up. "It's okay, Eden. I get it. I'll head out and let you do what you need to do."

"It's not that I don't want to spend time with you," I said quickly, wanting to reassure him. I reached up and touched his arm. "I do. And I also know I said I shouldn't go through my father's things alone, but I wasn't expecting this. I really need to go talk to my mom." I paused. "Are you mad?"

"Of course not," he said.

I gripped the letter in my hands. "Thank you for understanding."

"You'll call me later?"

"Absolutely." I set the letter down and walked him to the front door, where he had left his car keys and wallet the night before. We kissed and he left, leaving me no choice but to turn and face the memory of what I found that night on the bathroom floor.

May 1989

Eden

I'd never seen so much blood. I held my father's head in my arms and watched helplessly as his wrists oozed red onto the white tiled floor. It looked like he'd spilled a can of paint. I remembered my mother telling me the best thing to do with a cut was to put pressure on it, so I grabbed the nearest towels and wrapped them around my father's wrists as tightly as I could. I heard a person screaming in a guttural, anguished pitch. It took a moment to realize that person was me.

My daddy was limp and heavy in my arms. His eyes were closed. "Wake up!" I screamed. I shook him. "Don't do this, Daddy! Don't do this to me, *please!*" I glanced wildly around the room, desperate to call for help and not leave him. But there was no way. No phone anywhere closer than the hallway. "I'll be right back," I told him. "Don't die, Daddy. Please don't die!"

I raced out the door over to the phone and dialed 911. "My daddy's hurt!" I wailed. "There's blood everywhere! Please, you have to help him!"

"Okay, honey," the operator said calmly. "I'm sending the ambulance right away. I need you to stay on the line with me."

"No! I have to go back to my daddy. I have to be with him!" I sobbed, my chest heaving and swelling with every breath.

"I understand, sweetie, but I want you to stay on the phone

with me until the medics get there. They'll be quick, I promise. You just hang in there."

"I can't! I have to go be with him!" I picked up the phone and carried it with me back toward the bathroom. It just reached the doorway but I couldn't step inside. Staring at my father's motionless body, I wished desperately my mother had agreed to buy the cordless phone I'd wanted for my birthday last year.

"How old are you, sweetie?" the operator asked.

"Almost eleven," I said, my breath hitched on the words.

"Where is your dad bleeding?"

"His wrists."

"Did he cut himself on something?"

"The bathroom mirror is broken all over the floor. He's holding one of the pieces. A big one. The tip has blood on it." *Oh no. He did this to himself. He's trying to die, just like he said he always would. He's going to leave me.*

"Okay, sweetie. I understand. What's your name?"

"Eden."

"Like the garden of Eden?" she asked, and I started wailing again, thinking of the flower bed in front of our house. "Shh, shh," the operator said. "It's okay, Eden. Everything's going to be all right."

I couldn't answer. I was crying too hard. I stared at my father, but he didn't move. Was he dead? Did I get home too late? The party at Tina's had been stupid, and I was bored, so I pretended I had a stomachache and decided to leave. *Why didn't I come home earlier? I could have saved him. He never would have done this if I had been with him.*

"Eden? Are you still there?" the operator asked.

"Yes," I whimpered. "Tell them to hurry, please. I think he might be dead."

"They're almost there, sweetie. Just hang on. Where's your mother?"

"At work."

"Where does she work?" I heard the sound of a keyboard clicking. "Can you give me the phone number?"

I took a deep breath and recited it. As I was speaking, I heard the whine of the siren coming down our street. "They're coming!" I said. "I can hear them."

"Okay, Eden. That's good." The operator's voice was low and soothing. "But stay with me until the medics are inside, okay?"

"There's so much blood," I blubbered. My face dripped with snot and tears. "How can he be alive if there's so much blood?"

"Eden, I want you to go downstairs and let the medics in, okay?"

"I don't want to leave him," I said, sniffling. He still wasn't moving.

"I know, but they don't want to break down the front door unless they have to. Please, just go let them in and then you can show them where your dad is. I'll call your mom and she'll be there soon, okay? Is there a neighbor you can go to while you wait?"

I thought about Mrs. Worthington and realized I'd rather die than go to her house. "No." The sirens got louder and then they stopped. The red lights flashed outside, spinning through the front windows. "They're here. I need to put the phone down to let them in."

"Okay. You're a very brave girl, Eden. You did exactly the right thing."

I hung up and raced down the stairs. I flung the door open just as the medics ascended the front steps. "He's upstairs!" I said. "Hurry, please! He's bleeding!" *Oh god, please don't let him die.*

One of the medics, a tall man with a trim blond beard, smiled at me. "Okay, honey. We're here. Everything's going to be okay." He pushed past me with another man, carrying a wheeled stretcher between them. "You stay here, okay? We'll take care of your dad."

I glanced over his shoulder and saw a fire truck pull up next to the ambulance, and then my mother's car behind it. She must have left work earlier than she thought she would. She leapt from her car and tore up the front lawn.

"Eden!" she screamed. "What happened?" She rushed up the front steps and took me in her arms, squeezing me tighter than she ever had before.

A fresh round of sobs took me over and I couldn't answer her. She pulled back a little and grabbed my hands, turning my arms over, touching me everywhere she could see. "Are you hurt? Are you bleeding? What happened?"

I looked down and realized I was covered in my father's blood. It coated my skin, stuck to my clothes—there was even some in my hair. I smelled like a handful of pennies. "It's Daddy," I said, crying. My jaw jittered and shook as I spoke. "He cut his wrists."

My mother's expression went from frightened to horrified. "Oh my god," she said. "Oh my god, oh my god!" She hugged me to her again. "Are you sure you're not hurt?"

"Yes!" I cried. "But there's so much blood, Momma! What if he dies?" *Would it be my fault for not coming home sooner? Did I put enough pressure on his cuts to save him?*

She didn't answer but instead held me tighter, rocking me back and forth on the front porch. Many of our neighbors were now outside, watching. Mrs. Worthington had even crossed the street to stand on the sidewalk in front of our house.

"Go away!" I screamed through my tears. "Stop staring at us! Go home!" I hated their prying eyes. I hated knowing people talked about my family like it was broken.

"Shh, shh," my mother said, trying to soothe me, running her hand over and over down the back of my head.

A fireman approached us, a tall, broad-shouldered man with a kind smile. He set a large hand on my mother's shoulder. "Mrs. West?"

She turned her head to look up at him. Tears were streaming down her cheeks, too. "Yes?"

"Why don't we go inside, so we'll be out of the medics' way when they bring your husband out?"

My mother looked at the front door, then back to the fireman. She looked dazed. He gently urged us into the house and to the living room, where we sat down on the edge of the couch just in time to see the medics bring the stretcher with my father on it down the stairs. Covered up to his chest with a blanket and black straps to keep him from falling, he was ghostly pale, his shoulders crusted with crimson stains of his blood. His eyes were closed.

"Momma?" I said. I looked at her, then back to the fireman.

"Is he alive?" my mother whispered, and the fireman touched her hand.

"Let me go find out." He stood and followed the medics down our front steps and out into the yard.

"I want to see him," I said, trying to pull away from my mother's grasp.

"No, Eden. Stay with me. The fireman will be back in a minute to let us know how he is." Her face was whiter than I'd ever seen it before. Her lips were pressed into a thin, pale line and her makeup was smeared down her cheeks in black and blue smudges. She looked like she'd been beaten.

"No!" I yelled, and yanked away from her embrace.

"Eden!" she screamed. "Come back!"

I ran down the front steps, ignoring her command. The big fireman grabbed me before I got to the ambulance. I wrestled against his hold, but he was too strong.

"It's okay, honey," he said. "Your dad is alive. They'll take him to the hospital and the doctors will take good care of him. I promise. Everything's going to be all right."

He meant well, I knew, but there was no way for him to understand how many times I had heard my father say those exact same words only to find my world crumbling around me. I stopped struggling against his grip and the fireman let me go. I ran back inside the house and straight to my mother, who, unlike my father, I knew would tell me the truth.

May 1989
David

All David knew was blackness. Drifting in and out of varying shades of gray. Heat seared up his arms, voices shrieked inside his head. *Is this hell? Have I finally ended up where I belong?*

Days passed. Or maybe it was weeks. It could have been only hours. David didn't know, nor did he care. Violent images sprang forth in his dreams: vicious, rabid monsters bared their teeth and ravaged his flesh. Every breath felt like glass had shattered inside his chest. Occasional soothing tones combated the screeching noise between his ears, along with gentle touches urging him to open his eyes.

David didn't listen. He replayed the last thing he saw over and over in his mind—his daughter standing in the doorway, about to watch him die. He punished himself with that vision, the angst on her face, the terror shining in her eyes. This is what it came to. This is how it all came to an end.

"Open your eyes, David," a voice said. The sound was muffled and echoed as though it traveled underwater to reach him. "My name is Sue, and I'll be your nurse today." There was a pause, and she touched his arm. "It's time to wake up, David. Can you open your eyes?"

A nurse. He wasn't in hell, then. Or was he? A nurse meant

the hospital, which meant he had survived. This was a whole other version of hell. He had done the unthinkable and his daughter witnessed it all. He'd never be able to undo that kind of damage. He never wanted to open his eyes again.

There was nothing left in this world he wanted to see.

November 2010

Eden

The rest of my father's letters were much like the first. They told me little of where he was living or how he survived during those first six months after his attempt to end his life, only that he was sorry for the pain he caused and longed for the day when he could see me again. The last letter was the shortest and left me no clue where he'd gone for the next ten years when I didn't hear from him.

It read,

> *Dear Eden,*
> *You don't want to see me, that much is clear. And while I can't blame you, I'll continue to wish for a change in your heart.*
>
> *I'm thinking of leaving Seattle. Leaving the rain and darkness and green. But don't think for a minute I'm leaving you. I AM you. In your blood and thoughts, inside every breath you take. As long as you are alive, so will I be.*
>
> *Love, Daddy*

Wanda, the apartment manager, mentioned California as a possible place he had lived, but where would I even begin to look in that state? Especially if he was homeless there. The two letters

I received from him when I was twenty were similar in tone but also spoke of the time he'd spent living on the streets. I was so angry with him back then, I didn't keep them.

After I read the letters twice through, I only debated a moment over calling my mother versus going to see her. It was the kind of conversation we needed to have face-to-face. I needed to see her reaction when I told her I knew that she had lied to me for almost twenty years. I needed to look her in the eye so she could see the damage she'd done.

I called to make sure she was home and asked if I could come over.

"Of course, honey," she said. "I'm just rearranging the living room. Is everything all right?"

"Not really," I answered. "I'll be there in a little bit." I hung up and immediately called Georgia to fill her in on the letters my mother had hidden from me.

"Holy crap," she said. "That sucks. Do you think it's a good idea to go talk to her now?"

I grabbed my purse and snapped my fingers for Jasper to follow me outside to my car. "Waiting won't change what she did."

"No, but you're pretty pissed off, which doesn't always make for the most productive conversations."

"I don't see myself getting any less pissed if I put it off." I shut the back door behind me and locked it, tucking my cell phone between my shoulder and ear.

"Okay. It was just a suggestion."

"I know, Georgia. But I've needed answers my whole life." *Why did my dad get sick? What was really wrong with him? Why didn't he take his medication long enough to get well? Why did he leave me? Did he ever really love me at all? Where is he?* I felt my jaw tremble and I gritted my teeth to keep from crying. Why the hell did I always seem to cry when I got angry? I was irate, not sad. I wanted to hit something, not sob like a baby. "I need to understand why she did this."

We said good-bye and I hung up before I realized I hadn't told her about Jack spending the night. Jasper whimpered in the backseat as I drove, picking up, I was sure, on the stress I felt. "It's okay, buddy," I said, trying to soothe him. "Momma's fine. I just need to take care of something."

I let Jasper loose in my mother and John's fenced backyard, then entered their house through the back door. "Mom?" I called out from the kitchen. "Where are you?"

"In the living room, honey!" she called in response.

I walked through their kitchen and down the long, narrow hallway. Pictures of my family hung all over the walls. My mother and John, Bryce as a baby, me feeding my brother a bottle. My graduation, then Bryce's, then John's award ceremony for bravery during an especially dangerous factory explosion. There was no evidence I ever had a father before 1990. My mother preferred it that way.

"Hi," I said when I saw her sitting on the couch. Her legs were propped up on the coffee table and she wore a bright blue handkerchief over her head with a matching velour sweat suit. Her cheeks were flushed, and despite my anger, I was hit with an immediate fear the cancer had come back. "Are you feeling okay? You don't have a fever, do you?"

She smiled and her eyes lit up. "I'm fine, baby. Just moving furniture around again while John's at work. Are you okay? You sounded upset on the phone."

"I am."

"Well, come sit down." She patted the cushion next to her on the sofa. "Tell me all about it."

I stood in the doorway, unable to do as she asked. The rage I felt tensed my muscles, gluing me to one spot.

She tilted her head and furrowed her forehead. "What's wrong? Did something happen with the new guy you're seeing?"

I shook my head. "No. We're fine. It's about Dad."

Her shoulders slumped, visibly disappointed. "Oh, Eden. I thought you might give that up."

"Why would you think that?" I asked angrily.

"I don't know. I thought maybe since you found a boyfriend and had something positive to focus on you'd let it go."

"Well, I haven't." I crossed my arms over my chest and glared at her. "In fact, I went to dad's old apartment building with Jack and we found some of his paintings. And a box of his things."

The muscles in her face seemed to freeze beneath her skin; panic flashed in her eyes and she began to blink rapidly. "What kind of things?"

"Letters, mostly. They were addressed to me in 1989. And then returned to sender. By you, I assume."

Her blue eyes widened and filled with tears. "Oh."

"Oh?" I said, feeling the tightness in my chest begin to shatter into more of my own tears. "That's all you're going to say? 'Oh'?" I took a deep breath and blew it out through my nose, trying to calm my pulse. "You lied to me, Mom. You said he never wrote. That he didn't want to see me."

She lifted her chin and it trembled. "I did what I thought was right." She paused. "Maybe it wasn't the best decision—"

"Maybe?" I said, cutting her off. "More like it was a completely fucked-up decision. How could you do that to me? I cried every night, missing him. You knew that. You *watched* that. You knew I wanted to see him and talk to him and make sure he was okay and you kept him from me. How could you possibly have seen that as the right thing to do?"

"He was a train wreck, Eden. Being around him tore you apart. You were always so busy rearranging yourself trying to make him happy. I didn't want you to spend your life doing that, honey. I wanted you to be free of him. I wanted us both to be free." Her voice shook with emotion but I had no sympathy. She brought this on herself.

"Free of knowing my father loved me? That despite everything wrong with him, he still thought about me? Yeah, I definitely should have been freed of that. Good choice, Mom."

"I struggled with this, Eden. I swear I did."

"You didn't struggle half as much as I did not knowing it!" I shouted. I'd never yelled at my mother like this. But the anger was bigger than me, bigger than anything I'd ever felt. It took me over. My whole life could have been different. I could have seen my father, spent time with him. Maybe even convinced him to get help. But no, instead my mother let him rot on the streets. She let me believe he didn't give a shit about me.

She cringed. "I just wanted to protect you. After what he did, after all you saw that night. No child should experience that kind of trauma. I just couldn't stand the idea of him putting you through it again. I thought it was better this way, I really did." She sighed. "Then when you got those letters from him at your house after you moved out and you didn't want to see him, it confirmed for me that I'd made the right choice."

"I didn't want to see him because I thought he'd abandoned me, Mom!" I tried not to scream, but I felt my tone escalating toward hysteria with every word. "I spent the first ten years he was gone thinking he forgot about me completely and I was pissed as hell. *That's* why I didn't write him back. Now I find out he tried to keep in contact and you just let me believe he didn't care. You let me cry and suffer and think he was a piece of shit. If I'd have known he'd written me, I wouldn't have ignored him the way I did. He was *homeless,* Mom. He probably still is. And now I can't find him and he'll never know I love him and it's *your fault*!"

She started to cry in earnest. Her shoulders quaked and she put her hand over her mouth to muffle the sounds. She looked small and vulnerable sitting on the couch. Regret sat like a block of cement on my chest, but I was too angry to apologize. She was the one who needed to apologize. She was the liar in this room, not me.

"Were there more letters? Ones that you didn't send back to him?"

"No. He only sent those few."

"Did he write to you? Did he say anything that might help me find him now?"

"No, Eden. He didn't. I swear."

"Does John know about this?" I asked, continuing my interrogation. "Does he know what you've been keeping from me?"

She shook her head and dropped her hand back down to her lap after wiping her tears away. "No. I didn't tell him."

"Because Bryce told me John's upset that I'm looking for Dad. I thought this might have something to do with it. That he didn't want me to find out you lied. That his perfect wife maybe isn't so perfect." I was hitting below the belt but I couldn't stop. "Are you sure he doesn't know?"

She nodded and sniffed. "He thinks you're looking because he wasn't a good enough father to you."

"It has nothing to do with him." My eyes darted around the room, taking in all my mother's fine things. The picture-perfect world she'd built after the one she'd lived in with my father. She hadn't wanted to be Rapunzel when she met my father, but she ended up letting John rescue her after all. And she was happier for it. At least she seemed to be. I suddenly understood her constant need to redecorate; always rearranging her outer world was a way to try to maintain a sense of inner calm. But she couldn't. Not with the lies she'd told.

"Do you know where he is?" I demanded.

"No, Eden. I don't."

"Did he ever call? Did you talk with him?"

"He only called once, from the hospital, to tell me he'd sign the divorce papers. Never after that."

"What else haven't you told me?"

"Nothing. You know everything. He wrote those letters and I sent them back. That's it."

"That's more than enough," I said. My bitterness barbed each word.

"I'm ashamed I stayed with him as long as I did," she said quietly. She wouldn't look at me; instead, she kept her eyes on the floor. "I let you be exposed to so much of his illness that you never should have seen. I was so young. So stupid. I should have left long before he slit his wrists, Eden. I should have left the first time he refused to take his meds or after he slept with a stranger. Taking him back after he went to jail was the biggest mistake of my life. I spent a long time feeling guilty for that. Protecting you from getting hurt by him again was the only way I knew how to deal with it. I thought a clean break was the best thing. I honestly believed that." She lifted her gaze to me, her eyes pleading for understanding.

I dropped my arms to my sides and glared at her. "You believed wrong, Mom," I said, and for the first time in my life, I turned my back on my mother and marched out the door.

*   *   *

I didn't know where to go. After leaving my mother's house, I drove aimlessly with Jasper in the backseat. I ended up heading downtown, taking the Union Street exit and going west toward the waterfront. Where my parents first met. Where my father might still be. I found a parking spot beneath the viaduct and hitched Jasper to his leash. I didn't have a plan. I only knew I had to look for my dad. He had to be down there somewhere.

It was a typically drizzly, gray Northwest autumn day and walking along the waterfront, I had to steer around the tourists who were crazy enough to come to Seattle in November. I watched businessmen and women on their lunch hour stopping at Ivar's Seafood Bar for some of the city's best clam chowder. I scanned the face of every homeless man tucked into a corner beneath an awning. I showed my father's picture to several of them.

"Have you seen him?" I asked. "This picture is old, but I thought you might recognize him anyway."

"Don't know him," was the answer, if I was lucky enough to get a response at all. Many of the people stared off into space, dazed or drunk or some combination of the two. I wanted to shake them. Didn't they understand how important this was? What if someone in their own family was looking for them? Wouldn't they hope someone else would offer to help? I felt desperate for this search to end but couldn't fathom giving it up. Especially not now, knowing what my mother did. How hurt my father must have been when those letters came back to him. How deep did that hurt go? Did it lead him to attempt suicide again? Did he succeed? Is that why I couldn't find him? Was I looking for a man who no longer existed? Was I chasing a ghost?

What bothered me most was not the fact that my mother

didn't give me the letters when my father's suicide attempt was so fresh. I supposed I could even understand her reasoning, though I wasn't sure I was ready to acknowledge this out loud. What bothered me was that she continued to lie about it, even after she had the chance to tell me the truth. To tell me about the letters when my father wrote me again. She was the parent I trusted. The one I turned to for security and support. When my father said she never wanted to have me in the first place, the very core of me didn't believe him. Even at ten years old, I knew not to trust it. I understood that he lied. I'd seen it time and time again.

My concept of my mother had been the complete opposite. She was someone I could always rely on to give me the facts, no matter the consequences. Would I need to revisit everything she'd ever told me? Would I always question her version of the truth, never knowing if she was being honest or just trying to protect me?

As I stopped to let Jasper sniff at one of the artwork pigs on the pier, my cell phone rang in my pocket, interrupting my jumbled thoughts. I fumbled to answer, catching the call on the last ring, too late to see the caller ID.

"Hello?" I said loudly. My reception was always lousy close to the water.

"Hey, it's me." Jack's voice came over the line and I was so happy to hear it, my breath caught in my chest.

"Hi, Me." I scanned the pier for an empty spot on one of the benches to sit down. There wasn't one.

"Are you okay? Did you see your mom?"

"I did see her, but I'm not sure if I'm okay, really. I'm not sobbing, though, so I guess that's a good thing." I took a deep breath. "How are you?"

"I'm glad you're not sobbing." He paused. "Are you busy? I have something I need to talk to you about."

Oh no. He's already regretting sleeping with me. I opened up too much too soon and he didn't mean any of the wonderful things he said. I've got too much craziness going on with my family and now he's going to tell me he doesn't want me to come around anymore. I never should have let him in. I never should have believed something as good as this would last.

"I'll be right there," I said, figuring I might as well get the conversation over with. First the fight with my mom and now this. It was turning out to be one hell of a day. "I'm not too far away, actually. Down at the waterfront."

"You didn't go in to work, did you?"

"No, I'm where my parents first met. I come here sometimes, thinking my dad might come back."

"And has he?"

"Not today." I kept my voice hard, steeling myself against the disappointment already flowing through my veins.

"I'll see you soon, then."

"I have Jasper with me. Is it okay if I bring him?"

"Of course. Will you come around back, though, through the alley entrance?"

"Sure." I decided that instead of trying to find another parking spot near Hope House, I would just walk the ten or so blocks over to get there. Maybe the exercise would do me good. I tried not to think too much about what Jack might have to say.

When Jasper and I turned the corner into the alley behind the shelter, I saw Jack and Rita standing by the back door. They waved and I picked up my pace to reach them. I really wanted to get this over with.

"Hi," I said. "What're you doing out here?" Though the drizzle had dissipated, they were both a little muddy and wet and wearing garden gloves. Why would Rita be with him if he was planning on breaking it off? Was he looking for a way to cushion the blow? If he broke up with me with Rita standing next to him, I was going to scream.

Rita tilted her head toward the deserted lot across the alley. "We've been working."

I turned my head and saw that the lot had been completely cleared of any and all trash. The soil had been overturned and was now dark, not just from the rain. It looked as though it had been mixed with some kind of fertilizer. It smelled like it, too; the earthy scent of manure hung in the air.

"Working on what?" I asked, swinging my gaze back to look at Jack.

He reached over and took my hand. "Come look."

"Here," Rita said, taking Jasper's leash from my grasp. She grinned from ear to ear. "I'll hold on to this fella."

Jack led me over to the lot and pointed to a stack of weathered railroad ties over by the brick wall. "See? We'll be able to build raised beds with those. A friend of mine over at the train station gave them to me for free."

"Okay," I said, drawing the word out. I looked at the railroad ties and then back at him. "I still don't get it."

He grabbed my shoulders and turned me around to face the corner off to our left, which was taken up by an enormous pile of yellow-netted bags filled with flower bulbs. "It's the new Garden of Eden," he said. "I checked with the nursery and since we haven't had our first freeze, it's not too late to get the bulbs in the ground. I'm going to leave a few of the beds empty so the clients can help plant some vegetables next spring. Maybe some tomatoes and corn." He squeezed my hand. "It gets great sun back here and I'll have to put up a fence with a lock so people don't just come in and steal from it, but I think it's a great use of the space, don't you?"

For a minute, I couldn't speak. He wasn't breaking up with me. He was giving me a gift. One more meaningful than anything else I'd ever received.

Jack leaned over and kissed my cheek. "Don't you like it?" he asked.

I pressed my lips together and nodded briskly. I looked at him, hoping my eyes conveyed the emotion I felt. My heart ached, but I couldn't tell whether it was more from the pain of the argument with my mother or the happiness I felt seeing the garden. I threw my arms around his neck and pushed my mouth against his ear. "I love it," I whispered. "Thank you."

He pulled back and kissed me. "My pleasure."

"You did all of this this morning?"

"I've been thinking about doing it since we found your dad's painting in the basement and you told me the story of how you two planted your garden. But I had some help getting it started." He shifted and nodded his head toward Rita, who was crouching down and scratching Jasper's belly. She looked up and gave me a thumbs-up sign and another huge grin. I waved and smiled back, then gave Jack a playful smack on his shoulder.

"So," I said, "when I was here yesterday you already knew what you were going to do with the lot and you didn't tell me?"

He shrugged innocently. "I wanted to get the beds in first, but after the morning you had with the letters from your dad and having to talk with your mom, I thought you could use something positive. A few clients volunteered to clear out the rest of the garbage and Tom brought in the topsoil from the nursery. It still needs a lot of work, but I thought maybe we could get the bulbs in this afternoon." He smiled. "But we do have one problem."

I looked at him quizzically. "Oh yeah? What's that?" At that point, I wasn't sure I could handle another problem.

"I've never planted a garden before. I'm excited to see how it turns out."

"Well," I said, hearing my father's low-timbred voice as I repeated the same lesson he'd taught me so long ago, "good things come to those who wait. I'll show you how to start."

When my mother first told me she was pregnant, I didn't believe her. I understood the basics of how babies got made, but I couldn't imagine she'd actually allowed John to do that to her. Really, I couldn't imagine anyone doing anything so completely gross, but picturing John doing it to my mother was especially disturbing. I also didn't believe that she loved him and he had asked her to marry him, which was what she told me after she said she had a little brother or sister for me growing in her belly.

"He's a wonderful man, Eden," she said. We were sitting in the dining room, eating the grilled cheese and tomato soup I'd made us for dinner, when she got home from work. "He's been there for me so much over the past few months. I don't know what I'd do without him."

I didn't look at her, instead used my spoon to toy with the bright red liquid in my bowl. "What if Dad comes back?" I said in a low voice. I lifted my gaze and stared at her defiantly. "What if he comes home and you're with someone else?"

Her expression fell and she sighed. "Your dad and I are divorced, honey. He's not coming back."

"How do you know?" I asked, challenging her. "You don't know. He could just be stuck in the hospital. He could be really sick and you wouldn't even know because you divorced him."

"We divorced each other, Eden. I know it's hard for you to understand, but it's really much better this way. Your father and I weren't good for each other. He wasn't good for you, either. You saw that. No one who was good for you would do what he did."

"Yes, he *was* good for me," I said stubbornly. My daddy was sick, that was all. He didn't mean what he'd done. He was just very, very sick. I didn't blame him for cutting his wrists. I couldn't dream of the kind of pain he must have suffered that pushed him to that point. I told myself that the doctors were still making him well. That he'd get out of the hospital and come take me away.

"John adores you, you know," my mother said, interrupting my thoughts.

I was silent. I hated John. I hated him with his big feet and his loud laugh and his stupid jokes about how many firemen it took to put in a lightbulb.

"Don't you like him?" my mother asked.

I still didn't answer. I stared at my soup, thinking how closely it matched the shade of my father's blood, spilled on the bathroom floor. My eyes filled. "I don't want you to have a baby," I cried.

My mother reached over and rested her hand on my arm. "I understand it might be difficult for you at first, sweetie, but I think if you give the idea of being a big sister a chance, you'll grow to love it."

"Will the baby live with John instead of us?" I asked hopefully. I saw this as a possible compromise.

"No, it won't. I'm going to marry John and we're all going to live with him."

I swung my gaze up to her face. "I don't want to leave our house!"

She sighed again, pulling her hand back to rake back her

blond hair from her face. "There are too many bad memories for us here. It'll be a fresh start for all of us. You, me, John, and the baby. I promise, everything's going to be better than ever."

I didn't believe her. I didn't want to leave my memories in this house. I wanted to take them with me, leaving a trail of them for my father to find when he finally came back to save me.

After just over six months in the locked ward, David left the state hospital with fifty bucks, thirty days' worth of meds, and the clothes on his back. He meandered down the long driveway toward the road, unsure exactly where he should go. The divorce papers made it clear his marriage was over, and the only other place he knew he might be welcome was Rick's house. After an hour-long bus ride, David was there.

"Sure, man," Rick said. "You can stay here awhile."

David nodded his thanks and offered to cook all of Rick's meals and promised to keep the house cleaned up. The life-skills class he had been forced to sit through at the hospital for the last month emphasized the importance of cleanliness—for his body and his surroundings. Back in July, after he'd already spent almost two months in the hospital, David wrote Eden the first of five letters, telling her how sorry he was for what he put her through. He told her how much he loved her. When the letters came back marked "Return to Sender," David shoved them into the one small box he kept with him, full of Salvation Army clothes and a few books. She didn't want to see him. That much was clear. And at his core, David didn't blame her.

Rick's pot customers weren't always comfortable with David sitting in the house all day, as a possible witness to their drug deals, so after making breakfast each morning for a few months, David headed downtown to Pioneer Square. He found he liked the noise of downtown Seattle, the constant distraction it provided. Especially since he had stopped taking his medication and the fiends had taken up residence in his head again. He found himself muttering as he sat in Pioneer Park, pacing back and forth on the small patch of grass where other men often sat and wasted the day away.

"You got a home, man?" one of them asked David one late fall day. The man was tall and thin like David, but with shaggy blond hair and sunken blue eyes. He wore a black trench coat and ratty cargo-style jeans.

David shook his head briskly and continued to pace. A voice in his head spoke to him. *Don't talk to him. He'll try to kill you.*

"You can crash with me," the man said. "If you'll give me your shoes."

David walked away. He saw a little girl with long, black hair standing on the corner and he took off after her. "Eden!" he cried. "It's Daddy!" The little girl didn't turn her head. Eden was ignoring him, just like she had with the letters he'd sent. He needed to talk to her. To tell her the reason he stayed away. That he was only protecting her. She didn't answer his letters, but now she was here, looking for him.

The man with the little girl whipped around when David's hand landed on the little girl's shoulders. There was fury in the man's dark eyes, and he grabbed David's hand and pulled it away from where it lay.

"What the *hell* do you think you're doing?" the man said through gritted teeth. "Get your hands off my daughter!"

David shook his head. This man was obviously confused. "She's mine. My daughter. You *took* her from me." The little girl cowered, curling into the man's side. "Eden? Bug?" The little girl began to cry, and David backed away. Now he was hurting her again. He couldn't keep doing this. *Oh god. What is wrong with me?*

His blood began to race in his veins, pumping hot and furious. He grabbed his long, dark hair, pulling at his scalp until he felt tufts beginning to yank free. The pain didn't work anymore. It didn't soothe the screaming in his head; it didn't snap him back to reality. *I can't do this. I can't. I need to get well again so Eden will want me back.* David took off running again down the street, across three lanes of traffic, all cars blaring their horns at him as they were forced to slam on their brakes to keep from smashing into him. He thought maybe he should let them.

David ran. He ran toward the waterfront, beneath the viaduct. Night began to fall, the air a fluttery purple around him. He ran until his lungs burned like fire in his chest, until his leg muscles were rubbery and loose. He didn't know what he was running from. Himself, maybe? The wildness starting to ache in his flesh again?

Turning into an alleyway, David slowed down enough to see a cardboard box the size of a washing machine next to a dirty green Dumpster. It was cold and starting to rain. All David wanted was to feel warmth. To sleep, to escape the churning thoughts that blared in his head. He crawled inside the box and curled up fetal, tucking his hands beneath his cheek as a pillow. He closed his eyes and rocked back and forth, back and forth, until sleep came and rescued him from the cold, dark night.

A week later, David went back to Rick's to grab the letters he'd written to Eden. He tucked them, along with a change of clothes and the five hundred dollars Rick gave him when David told his friend he was leaving, into a green backpack he'd found in a downtown alley. The last letter that had come back to David informed Eden he was thinking of leaving Seattle, and maybe he would. He was finally in charge of what he would do.

It was terrifying at first, not having a house to return to each night. But during the days, on the streets, he talked to people who didn't seem to care about his rambling speeches or his dark, villainous moods. He found out about the soup kitchens where he could get a hot meal and the shelters where if he got there early enough, he could have a bed for the night. He learned where he could take a shower and where it wasn't safe to hang out. He watched the way other men and women panhandled on the street corners but couldn't bring himself to do the same. Instead, he used some of the cash Rick had given him and purchased a used easel and a sketch pad. Going back to his roots, he charged to sketch portraits, and some days he even made enough to pay for a cheap hotel room. He always made enough for a bottle of booze, which, for the most part, kept the fiends in his head at bay.

The lack of rules and boundaries appealed to David. No one to tell him what medicines to take or ways he shouldn't behave. He danced if he felt like it or climbed beneath a blanket for days. David got the idea in his head he should head to California, where it was always sunny. He didn't have to ask permission. He didn't have to do anything other than bag up his things and stand by the side of the road with a sign that said SAN FRANCISCO. Eventually, a car came along that gave him a ride to Portland, then one to Ashland, and finally, he arrived in the City by the Bay.

Day by day, gradually, he kept himself busy enough doing nothing that he didn't feel the gaping hole in his chest that missed his daughter. He filled it with vodka or cheap wine, with meaningless banter with other men who knew what it was to have their minds betray them. He ran his fingers over the angry red raised scars on his wrists, the left one much worse than the right, and forced himself to blank out the memories of the daughter he left behind.

He stopped resisting the twisted thoughts that rose inside him, allowing them to come and go as they pleased. He felt no pressure to be someone other than exactly who he was in each moment. For the first time in his life, David felt free.

"You can't miss Thanksgiving, sis," Bryce said two weeks after my fight with my mother. My brother and I were standing in my living room; he had come over to pick up another dinner for a date, though I doubted it was for the same girl. I'd made up this meal in advance and put it in a picnic basket complete with a bottle of sparkling cider and wineglasses. Though Bryce looked at least twenty-one, and I'm sure could have gotten a bottle of wine if he wanted it, I wasn't going to encourage the behavior.

"I won't miss it," I said. "I'll be spending it at Hope House, serving turkey dinner to people who really appreciate it."

He sighed. "Mom's real upset, Ed."

"She should be." I dug around in the basket to make sure I'd remembered to put in the *dulce de leche* brownies for the dessert. "I'm upset, too."

Bryce grabbed my hand. "Will you look at me, please?" he asked.

I lifted my eyes and saw the pain in his. My heart ached. "I'm sorry, Bryce. I'm just having a really hard time with all of this. She lied to me." I'd already filled him in on the details of the letters I'd found in my father's things.

"For all the right reasons, yes, she did lie. C'mon. You know that, right?"

I hesitated. Of course I knew she meant well. Intellectually, I knew she was human, that as a parent she was bound to make a few mistakes. But emotionally, I still felt like a ten-year-old child crying in my bed, wishing with all my might my daddy wanted to see me. I didn't know how to make those feelings go away. Especially not in time for Thanksgiving, which was only six days away.

"I understand why she thinks she did the right thing. I'm just so hurt by it I can't see straight. And until I can, I don't feel like I can be around her. It's not the end of the world if I don't show up for the holiday, Bryce. I've worked them before and it's never bothered her."

He took the picnic basket from me and frowned. "It's not the same and you know it." He gave me a kiss on my cheek. "But I love you anyway. Thanks for the eats."

"You're welcome," I said, and shut the door behind him. He was right. I was overreacting. But I couldn't figure out a way to stop. I called Jack and asked him for the umpteenth time for his thoughts about what I should do.

"I'm not the person to ask," he said. "I'm not exactly the poster child for healthy family relationships."

"But I care about what you think," I said. "Am I being totally unreasonable?"

"I refuse to answer that question on the grounds that it might prevent me from getting naked with you."

I laughed. "Okay, okay. I get it. You're not going to give me any answers."

"Right. Unless the question is if I'll come take advantage of you later; then my answer is yes."

"I've got a late shift tonight. Big corporate event at work."

"I don't care how late it is. Rita's staying overnight with the troops, so I'm free. Call me when you're on your way home and I'll meet you there."

I told him I would, then hung up to promptly dial a person less willing to enable my bad behavior.

"Georgia Mills's office," Georgia said when she answered her cell.

"You're not at the office yet?" Georgia only answered her cell phone that way when she was in her car.

"Nope. I'm stuck on freaking 405. Traffic sucks."

"Yes, it does." I gave her a quick recap of my brother's scolding words. "Do you think he's right?"

"God, Eden. You *know* he's right. I've already told you I think you should make peace with your mom. Life is too short for this kind of bullshit. Isn't that why you started looking for your dad, because life was too short to not have at least tried to find him? So she fucked up. So what? We all do. Put your big-girl panties on and deal with it."

I was quiet. Maybe I shouldn't have called her.

"I don't mean to be harsh," she said in more gentle tones. "But you did ask."

"Yes, I did. I'll work on figuring out what I should do." After we hung up, I looked at Jasper. "So do you think I need to put on my big-girl panties?" I asked. He whimpered and began to pant. "Oh, you think I should wait a while, too, huh? That's my boy." I scratched his chest and his back leg went haywire in response. "Maybe I'll call her after Thanksgiving, what do you think?" He barked and wagged his tail. There was affirmation if I'd ever seen it. I'd take it even if it did come from a dog. Jasper hadn't failed me yet.

*   *   *

The week before the holiday flew by in a flurry of shopping for Hope House and prep for the two hundred private turkey dinners Emerald City was catering. Things like pies could be done well in advance, and the turkeys were prepped and sitting in the walk-in, waiting patiently for Juan's capable hands to roast them. I'd talked Doug in the corporate office into donating twenty-five turkeys and fifty hams to the shelter, promising him the PR would not go unnoticed. Jack and Rita set up a food drive in front of the Safeway near his apartment and managed to procure enough instant mashed potatoes, canned yams, and green beans to feed an army.

In order to be sure we could fulfill all of our catering orders and cook the turkeys for Hope House, Juan and I stumbled into the Emerald City kitchen at three o'clock in the morning on Thanksgiving Day. We fortified ourselves with caffeine, and as soon as Juan pulled the last turkey out of the ovens to wrap up for our catering orders, I had the shelter's turkeys ready to put in. The plan was to have Rita warm up the ham in the shelter's kitchen, and thankfully, Jack had secured Tom to help me transport the turkeys. He showed up around eleven to load up his delivery van and I followed him in my car, which was loaded down with pies and an arsenal of canned whipped cream. Juan had offered to run the kitchen for the double-time holiday pay it would bring, so I happily handed over the responsibility of making sure all the parties received their custom orders. It was a crazy dance of timing and coordination and somehow, we managed to pull it off.

I had gotten to the point where I almost preferred working in the shelter's kitchen than the one at Emerald City Events. There was something more homey about the smaller space and rickety stove, something that brought more satisfaction to me than whipping up seared foie gras and pancetta-wrapped figs for a cocktail party of Seattle's social mavens. I wasn't sure exactly what that meant—whether I was so enthralled with Jack that I wanted to be near him or whether something deeper was going on with me related to my career. But the holiday was not the day to figure it out. I pulled up to the back door by the kitchen and helped Rita and Jack unload my car.

"The turkeys look amazing," Jack said. "Tom brought them and the hams about an hour ago."

"They smell amazing, too," Rita added. She wore capri jeans and a snug, chocolate-brown T-shirt that had a picture of a cartoon turkey above the words GET STUFFED. "Were those sage leaves pushed under the skin?"

I nodded, setting my tenth apple pie onto the tiny amount of counter space that was left. "Herbs and melted butter rubbed under the skin makes all the difference in the flavor of the meat. I hope they stay moist enough."

"I've kept them in the cooking bags like you said," Jack said as he shoved the last can of whipped cream in the refrigerator. "But the mashed potatoes still need to get done. And the green beans. And the rolls."

"Slow down, cowboy," I said, laughing. "We've got plenty of time. I'll take care of the potatoes if you'll go park my car." I dangled the keys at him. "Please?" He kissed me as he took the keys from my fingers.

"Get a room," Rita commented with a smile. "Dinner's served at three. We need to get a move on."

Jack left and Rita and I set to getting huge stockpots of water, milk, and butter boiling for the mashed potatoes. "Are Starr and Paul coming to help?"

"Nope, they took the day off to spend with their families."

"What about you?"

"This is my family," she said simply. "Since I came out a few years ago, my parents don't want anything to do with me."

I stopped stirring. "I'm so sorry, Rita. That's awful. Are you dating anyone?"

"Not currently," she said with a grin. "But I'm working on it. You're out of the running since Jack nabbed you."

I laughed. "I never knew I was *in* the running!"

"Oh yeah. Absolutely. I'm tired of all those scary old butch women hitting on me. I need to find myself a nice lipstick lesbian."

"But you knew I was straight, right?"

"Of course. The way you drooled over my boss sort of gave it away."

"I didn't drool!"

"Uh-huh." She laughed. "Did you know I was gay?"

"I had no idea until you just said it."

She rolled her eyes and gave a weary sigh. "I need to work on sending out a stronger vibe."

Jack bounded back into the kitchen, his eyes glittery with energy. "What can I do to help?" he asked, rubbing his hands together.

"Cut down on the caffeine, I'm thinking?" Rita suggested.

He jumped over to her and pretended to strangle her from behind. She laughed. "You can start slicing up the hams and turkeys. We need them in the foil casserole dishes and set up out on the tables. Think you can manage that?"

He performed a mock salute. "Yes, ma'am!"

The three of us handling the entire Thanksgiving meal on our own was a little daunting, but I figured I'd dealt with wedding receptions and a few dinner parties without any help, so we could find a way to make it work. Jack spent about an hour cutting up the meat and taking it out to the dining room. When Rita went out to check on the setup, Jack came over and hugged me.

"I'm so happy you're here," he whispered in my ear. He smelled like turkey and sage. It made me want to lick him.

"I'm happy I'm here, too," I said, putting the finishing touch of roasted garlic into the pots of potatoes.

"No regrets about not being with your family?"

"None." This wasn't entirely true. My mother had left me another long, apologetic message earlier in the week, asking me to please come to her house for the holiday dinner. We'd always cooked it together—well, truth be told I cooked while she set the table—even if I had to work and we had to have dinner on another day. I called her back and told her I was committed to working at the shelter.

"The whole day? You couldn't stop by later for dessert?" she asked. Her voice was both hopeful and sad.

"No," I said. "I can't. I'll call you this weekend, okay? We can talk then." I didn't want to hold a grudge against my mom, but I truly didn't feel like I was at a point where I could forgive her completely.

Now Jack pressed his forehead against mine. "I don't believe you."

I smiled. He already knew me too well. It was a little bit scary. "What about you? When was the last time you spent a holiday with your family?"

He sighed. "It's been a while."

"How long is a while?"

"Three years."

"Well, how about I make you a deal?"

"Oh man," Jack said, stepping back from me. "I'm not sure I like the sound of that."

"How about if I make up with my mother, you at least have to try to talk with your dad?"

He stared at me long enough to make me avert my eyes. "You drive a hard bargain, Ms. West."

I looked back at him and smiled sweetly. "Yes, I do."

"I'll think about it, okay? For you."

"Oh no," I protested. "You're not doing it for anyone but yourself. I'm just giving you a push in the right direction."

"I'll show you a push," Jack growled, and he grabbed for me. I jumped out of the way and took off toward the other end of the kitchen. "Mmm," he said. "You want me to chase you around the campfire, like a caveman?"

"Unk, mumba," I grunted, and winked at him.

At that moment, Rita reentered the kitchen. "Look who I found knocking at the front door," she said. For a moment, I felt my heart stop, thinking perhaps my father had heard from other Hope House clients where he could find me. Instead, behind Rita followed Georgia, Bryce, John, and my mother. My jaw dropped.

"Hey, lady!" Georgia said, coming toward me. "Happy Thanksgiving!"

I let her hug me, squeezing her a little harder than I probably should have. "Are you behind this?" I asked softly next to her ear.

She pulled away and grinned. "Yep! I sure am." She waved at Jack. "Hi! I'm the best friend."

"Georgia," Jack said. "Nice to finally meet you."

Bryce came over to me after her. "Hey, Ed. We figured if you wouldn't come to us, we'd come to you. See what we could do to help." He looked over to Jack. "You must be Jack. My sister can't stop talking about you."

I swatted his shoulder. "Bryce!"

My brother chuckled and shook Jack's hand. "Nice to meet

you," Jack said. He winked at me. "I've heard a lot about you, too." Jack walked over to where my mother and John stood, both of them looking a little uncomfortable. He extended his hand to shake John's. "I'm Jack Baker."

"John Morrow," my stepfather said. "And this is Eden's mother, Lydia."

Jack smiled warmly at my mother and gave her a hug. "You have an amazing daughter, Mrs. Morrow."

"Thank you. I certainly think so." My mother smiled, though her eyes were still nervous. "And please, call me Lydia."

"And call me John," my stepfather said. "Just don't call me late for dinner!" He guffawed at his own joke.

Georgia nudged me with her elbow. "Go talk to your mother," she hissed through her teeth. "It's Thanksgiving. Be nice."

I glared at my best friend but did as she said. Jack moved aside and I stood in front of my mother as she looked at me with wide, glassy eyes. "Hi, Mom," I said. "Happy Thanksgiving."

"Thanks, sweetie," she said. "It's good to see you."

"You too." I swallowed the lump in my throat and gave in to the urge to hug her. She clung to me tightly, her fingers digging into my back.

"I'm so sorry," she whispered. "I never meant—"

"I know, Mom. I get it. I was just so mad at you."

"Are you done yet?" she asked.

"Not quite."

She laughed, a quiet thing, and pulled back from me, wiping her eyes. "I hope it's okay we came to help. You know I'm not much in the kitchen, but I can serve or clean or whatever else you might need."

Jack touched my mother's arm. "I think Eden has the food portion of our meal under control. But I could sure use some help in the dining room with decorations. I'm a little centerpiece-deficient."

"We'll both come!" John bellowed. "Lydia can point to where she wants things and we'll do the grunt work!"

"Sounds good to me, sir," Jack said.

John looked at me and raised his eyebrows. "'Sir'? I like this boy already, Eden."

Jack led them out of the kitchen and I was left with Rita, Georgia, and Bryce. "Thanks a lot, you two," I said to my best friend and brother. "Way to ambush me."

"Well," Bryce said, "we got talking and decided you were being way too stubborn for your own good."

"That's right," Georgia said in agreement. "So we intervened. Anyway, you've been talking about this place for almost two months. I wanted to see it."

I pulled out the stuffing from the oven and set it on the counter, then turned with my hands on my hips to face my best friend.

"Here," Bryce said. "I'll take that out to the dining room and see if I can help. Don't want Pops to pull a muscle." He and Georgia held each other's gaze a little longer than was comfortable, but I waited for him to leave before saying anything.

"What was *that* about?"

She gave me wide, innocent eyes. "What was what about?"

"That look between you and my brother."

"Oh, that." She averted her eyes from me and moved them to Rita. "What can I do to help?"

"Georgia Leighton Mills!" I exclaimed.

Both she and Rita looked surprised but then laughed.

"They walked in together, if that tells you anything," Rita said as she grabbed a huge basket of rolls and escaped to the dining room, leaving me alone with my best friend.

"Traitor!" Georgia called out after her, but Rita only laughed, apparently enjoying the role of instigator.

I grabbed Georgia's arm. "Are you sleeping with my brother?"

"Not currently, no." She yanked her arm away and took a deep breath, tiny lines of worry stitched across her forehead. "Look. I meant to tell you, but the fight with your mom blew up at, like, the *exact same time*. I didn't want to upset you even more when it happened."

I dropped onto a stool by the counter with my shoulders slumped. "When *what* happened, exactly?"

"Well . . ." Georgia said, shifting her gaze away from mine, then back again. "You know he and I have been talking and flirting at the gym. It was totally innocent until he asked if he could make me dinner."

"And you said *yes?*"

Her chin fell toward her chest as she nervously ran her fingers through her loose amber curls, shaking them out. "I did." She threw her hands up in a gesture of surrender. "It was a total moment of weakness. I've been dating all these jerks and I'm starting to wonder what's wrong with me. I'm so tired of being single." She took a deep breath. "Then suddenly, a sweet, gorgeous young man wanted to spend time with me? I think my ego said yes more than me."

I nodded slowly. Georgia talked a tough game about being fine on her own, but I knew she ached to be appreciated—to fall in love. And as much as I hated to admit it, I could see being flattered the same way if a younger man asked me out. Before meeting Jack, I might have even said yes. But still, it was my *brother*. The idea made me queasy.

"So, we ate and talked and it just sort of . . . happened." She shrugged. "Listen. He and I both agree it was a mistake. A one-night kind of thing. We talked about it the next morning and he was remarkably mature about just staying friends." She paused and looked up at me with her huge, round hazel eyes, about ready to cry. "Are you going to be mad at me now, too? I'm really sorry I didn't say something sooner, but it's not exactly an easy subject to bring up, and with everything else you have going on . . ."

I sighed. "I don't think I'm mad, exactly. More like a little creeped out. It's so Mrs. Robinson." A thought struck me. "Wait. Were you the picnic dinner?"

She nodded, her lips in a tight smile. "Those caramel brownies were amazing."

"Oh god." I shook my head. "This is crazy."

She laughed, throwing her head back. "It *was* crazy. It's fine, we're friends. No hard feelings."

"Okay," I said, smiling weakly. "But please don't tell anyone else."

"Deal," she said solemnly. "Now, let's talk turkey!"

With four extra sets of hands to help serve the meal and make runs to the kitchen for refills, Thanksgiving dinner went off as planned. Georgia and Bryce took the meat station, and John and Mom took care of mashed potatoes, stuffing, and yams, while Jack and I made sure people got some green beans and fresh, hot yeast rolls slathered in butter. The clients helped themselves to dessert.

"This gravy is awesome, Eden!" Jade said when she came back for a second helping. "Thank you so much."

I smiled. "You're very welcome, Jade. Make sure you save some room for dessert!"

She groaned. "I have to work later. I don't want to hurl all over a customer."

I laughed and went around to give her a hug. "Where's Cheyenne?"

A sad look passed over Jade's face. "She's in jail. Sixty days. I'm not sure she's gonna make it."

"Why not?"

"She gets dope-sick pretty bad. Not a lot of sympathy for us junkies in there."

I hugged her again. "I'm sorry. Maybe I can go see her next week. Take her some brownies."

"Only if you can fit a file in them," Jade said with a wink. Then she went over to sit down at the table with her other friends.

"Your mom has been watching you," Jack said when I got back behind the table.

I looked over to my mom, who was smiling at a short man in a dirty black trench coat as she filled his plate with ham. "Huh," I said.

"It's pretty great they all came down here."

I nodded. "Yeah, I guess."

"You guess?" he said. "My family wouldn't be caught dead near this place. You have one fight with your mother and she's here to volunteer. Maybe you should give her a little credit."

I scooped out a serving of green beans to the next person in line. "I do. I still just have a hard time with the lying thing. I've always been able to trust what she says."

"The world doesn't judge us by what we say, Eden. It judges us by what we do. And I think what your mom is doing by being here is pretty fucking cool."

I looked at him sideways, cautious of his tone. "Are you mad at me?"

He shook his head. "I'm not mad. I just don't want you to

throw away a relationship because of one mistake. That doesn't bode well for our future."

My stomach churned at his words, at the thought of losing him over something as stupid as my pride. I set down my spoon. "Okay," I said.

"Okay, what?" he said.

"Okay, I'm going to talk to her. Really work things out. I don't want to throw anything away. Not with my mother and not with you."

Jack smiled and his eyes lit up. He leaned over and kissed my cheek. "I've got a handle on things here. Go."

I squeezed his hand before I walked over to the table where she and John stood. "How's it going, Mom?" I asked. "Do you need a break?"

She smiled at me with tired eyes. "I am getting a little wiped out."

"Come on. We'll go sit in Jack's office for a bit and let you put your feet up." I looked at John. "Is that okay?"

"Of course it is," John said. "I'll just keep feeding the masses." He gave me a hearty grin and I spontaneously reached out and hugged him, hard.

"Oomph!" he said. "What was that for?"

"For being a great stepfather," I said.

His chin lifted and he smiled with his bottom lip trembling. "Only because I have a great stepdaughter. She brings it out in me."

My mom followed me through the bunk room and into Jack's office, where I let her sit on the chair and pulled the other one around for her to put her feet up. I rested against the door I had closed behind us. "So, what do you think of all this?" I asked her.

"It's smaller than I pictured," she said. "I guess I imagined a warehouse of sorts. This is more like a remodeled office building."

I nodded. "I think Jack chose it for the location. It's in pretty close proximity to the hospital and the viaduct, where a lot of the clients hang out."

"He's doing a good thing here. You too, honey. It's nice to see you put your cooking skills to such good use. I'm glad I came." She sat very still.

"I'm glad, too." I took a deep breath. "I need to apologize for getting so angry, Mom."

"You had every right to be angry. I shouldn't have lied to you."

"Well, maybe so, but I still shouldn't have yelled at you like that. I could have listened to your reasoning a little bit more. Or tried to understand it better. I hurt you, and I'm sorry for it."

She gave me a tender look and I suddenly felt four years old. I wanted to climb into her lap and let her hold me. "I'm sorry, too," she said. She reached into the front pockets of her jeans and pulled out a piece of paper and unfolded it, spreading it flat across her lap. "So I've done a little digging."

I tilted my head toward my shoulder. "Digging?"

"Yes. About your father. I remembered you told me the last place he was hospitalized for sure was out in Monroe. They wouldn't give you any details because you weren't the emergency contact."

I nodded, the muscles in my throat convulsing. I was a little terrified to hear what she might have to tell me.

"Well, I am." She looked up at me. "He always listed my name, I guess even after I married John. The nurse I spoke to told me your dad was there because of a psychotic episode. He committed himself about three years ago. They took as much of a history as they could get out of him."

"Oh, Mom." I couldn't believe she had done this. Not after

how much she fought against my looking for him. Not after all the dead ends I'd faced.

"Now, don't get too excited." She held up her hand, palm facing me, then dropped it back to her lap. "All I found out is that he did live in California for several years. San Francisco, to be exact. He came back up here and lived in that apartment building you found. That's when he tried to get in touch with you again. He told them he tried to stay on his meds and get a job so he could get his life together for his daughter. He was very proud that you had become a chef."

"How did he know?" I whispered, still in shock.

"They weren't sure about that. I asked them the same question. But he went off his meds again and went back to the streets. It sounds like he stayed in Seattle for the most part. He did visit a shelter down in Portland, though. A sort of halfway house that runs a special program for artists with mental illness. He told them he'd go back there after he got out of the locked ward." She looked up at me and held out the piece of paper. "That's all I could find out. I haven't called the place in Portland. I thought you might want to do that."

I stumbled over to her and fell to my knees, wrapping my arms around her waist. I rested my head on the soft flesh of her belly and let the tears come.

"Shh," she said, trying to soothe me. "Don't cry. I'm sorry I didn't do this sooner. I should have."

"You're doing it now," I said, looking up to her through blurry eyes. "That's the only thing that counts."

September 1994
Eden

I still had dreams about that night. I still saw my father bleeding out in the bathroom, but in my dreams, instead of being unconscious, he reached out while his wounds dripped onto the floor. I could not hear his voice but saw him mouth the words "Save me" time and time again. I willed myself to go to him, but I could not. I was immobile, paralyzed by fear. I couldn't save him. There was nothing I could do to help. I woke with a start each time the dream visited me, my breath caught in my throat, my cheeks wet with tears. At fifteen, I'd given up hope my father would return, but a part of me just couldn't let him go.

Most of the time I was a well-adjusted teenager. I fought with my mom and John about how late I could stay out on Friday nights and when I could go on a date alone with a boy who drove. I babysat Bryce, who at four years old had finally become something more than just annoying. He liked me to read to him and dig with him in his sandbox; I liked him to ask me in his cute toddler voice for "avamacados" or tell me a farm smelled like "cow madure." I spent time with my friends and still hated anything to do with math. I was an average student in my other classes, determined to follow my dreams of becoming a chef. At sixteen, I pestered the owner of the café near our house for a job in the kitchen until he finally gave in and let me wash dishes a few nights a week. I was promoted to prep cook in less than a year. I learned to julienne and chiffonade, and how to debone a trout without tearing up its delicate flesh. John gave me his old Ford Explorer so neither he nor my mom would have to cart me around. For all intents and purposes, my life was full.

Since we had moved in with John five years before, my mother had made it clear my father was not to be discussed. She didn't tell me this outright, but I learned it soon enough from how she carefully avoided any reference to him when she talked about our past.

"Eden's a wonderful cook," John said one night when I made spaghetti for dinner. "She must have had a wonderful teacher."

"She certainly is," my mom said, acknowledging John's first statement but not the latter.

I sat at the table, spinning the noodles around and around on my fork. I could feel her eyes on me, knowing she didn't want me to bring my father up. It was as though she thought my memory of him would fade away if we didn't say his name out loud. And to some extent, I suppose she was right. He wasn't in my thoughts as often as he was after he first disappeared. My longing for him had aged into something less tangible—an occasional craving instead of a constant sense of starvation.

There were moments when I missed him profoundly—I was a junior when my high school sponsored a father-daughter breakfast.

"You could take John," my mother suggested when she read about the event in the quarterly newsletter the school sent out to parents. We were sitting in the living room, where I was trying to watch TV while my mother pretended to be cleaning. "Dusting with an agenda," I liked to call it.

"He's not my father," I said, leaning to peek around her so

I wouldn't miss a moment of MTV's *Real World*. Despite my issues with John, the change in my mother since my dad left our lives was for the better, I knew. After he was gone, she rarely got stressed out or angry, and even when she did—if I refused to pick up my clothes or Bryce accidentally broke her favorite coffee mug—her response was stern but never enraged. It was as though all her fury was used up on my father and what was left in its place was tolerance and a newfound sense of peace. I felt a little guilty for liking my mother more the way she was with John, as though I were somehow betraying my dad.

My mother sighed and set down her feather duster. "Can you at least pretend to respect him?" she asked wearily.

"I do respect him. I'm just not going to take him to the breakfast."

My mother didn't push the issue further and I didn't attend the event. I had fantasies about it, though—visions of my father showing up on our front steps, dressed and ready to escort me. And then my heart would crumple in on itself, shattered by reality. Feeling his gaping absence from my life all over again.

"Your dad is nice," my friends would say of John when they came to spend the night.

"He's not my dad," I'd tell them. "My dad is an artist. A painter."

"What happened to him?" they'd ask, and I'd make up some story of how he lived in New York and traveled the globe, looking for inspiration. It wasn't like he would come back to prove me wrong. And after all, considering the ugliness of the truth, it wasn't like anyone could blame me for wanting to lie.

The sunshine in San Francisco was not as plentiful as David thought it would be. Still, during the six years he lived there most days it was warmer than Seattle and definitely easier to find patrons who wanted their portrait done. He'd set up a stool and easel at the wharf a few mornings each week, displaying some of his work to catch a customer's eye. Tourists from all over the world asked him to capture their image on the page, etching in charcoal the outlines of their faces, the telling wrinkles around their eyes. He kept his rate low and only worked until he had enough for a bottle and a bed, which usually didn't take very long. He set the easel and folding stool in a locker at the bus station and got on with his day. Food was easy enough to find most days. People threw away so much.

When he wasn't at the wharf, David made his way to Golden Gate Park, either by foot or bus. He still stayed awake for days at a time, especially when his fractured, twisted thoughts had their way with him. But it was easier now that he didn't fight to quiet them so much. The alcohol he drank merely kept them sleepy. Some days, there was nothing he could do to keep them silent. When that happened, he just let them come. He let the thoughts whirl inside his head and make him dizzy. He paced the sidewalks and muttered beneath his breath. He didn't have to pretend he was normal. There were crazier people than him on the street. He felt at home with them, like he'd finally found a place where he fit. He napped when he was tired, and on better days, he talked to people he passed by. Sometimes, they even had a conversation with him.

One afternoon a man sat down next to David on a park bench. He looked like he might be about David's age and wore a blue pin-striped business suit. He had a brown paper sack that carried his lunch and the first thing he did was offer David half of a ham and cheese sandwich, which David accepted gratefully. They sat back against the bench and stared out at the vibrant blue water. The fog had lifted early that day and the air was clean enough to see for miles.

"Beautiful out there," the man commented.

David agreed. "Yes, it is."

"Where're you from?" the man asked.

"Seattle," David said, munching on the sandwich. He lifted it up a bit, so the man would see. "This is good. Thank you."

The man nodded in acknowledgment and took a bite of his own half. "Do you have family up there?"

"A daughter." David's heart skipped a beat thinking of Eden. How old would she be now? Twenty? A woman. Older than he was when he married Lydia. Had she forgotten him completely? Did her mother make sure of that?

"Do you talk with her?" the man asked.

David shook his head and popped the last bite of sandwich into his mouth. The man handed him a bottle of water, which David accepted with gratitude, as he had the sandwich. People's generosity never failed to surprise him. Especially to someone like him.

"My wife and I can't have children," the man said. "She's heartbroken."

"That's terrible," David said. "My daughter is the best thing I ever did."

The man looked at him sideways. "So why don't you go see her?"

"Look at me," David said, gesturing down his body with a wide sweep of his arm. He wore holey jeans and a torn-up T-shirt. His shoes were good, but only because the shelter he'd stayed at the week before had a rack of used clothing that happened to have a pair of old hiking boots that fit his feet. He was clean, for the most part, thanks to the shower in the motel room he paid for a few nights before, but both his hair and beard were long and unkempt. Anyone looking at him with his ratty stuffed backpack would guess he didn't have a home.

"So?" the man said. "Can't you clean up and go see her?"

He said it like it was the easiest thing in the world. He didn't understand what David had done. He didn't know about the blood. He didn't know about the monsters that screamed in his head. David knew how to quiet them. He knew the shelters would send him to the hospital if he wanted to go. He could get back on his meds. He could go back to Seattle and find his daughter. He wouldn't just send a letter; he would track her down and make her listen to his apologies. If she was still there.

"You know," David said to the man, "I might just do exactly that."

The wait to get into the psych ward for treatment was long in San Francisco. David asked the social workers at the shelter if there was anywhere up in Seattle he could go and they found a bed at a facility in Tacoma. A Greyhound bus ride later, David was back in the cool white halls of a hospital. The demons screeched at him for his heresy. Hadn't they lived in peace together for the most part over the past decade? Hadn't they worked out a deal?

David silenced them as best he could, welcoming the first shots of sedatives that flowed through his veins. Once they started him on lithium again, he knew he'd be numb, but wouldn't having Eden in his life again make it all worth it? He was determined to be well enough to be welcomed back into her life. He knew how to play the game. He talked with the doctors about life plans and therapy. They promised him if he stayed on the mood stabilizer, he could have a happy and productive life. More than anything, David wanted to believe them.

Two months later, he was stable enough to move into a studio apartment on Capitol Hill. The social workers at the hospital helped him get a dishwashing position at a downtown café and his landlady, Wanda, was a sweet old soul whom David bonded with immediately.

"You're the grandmother I never had," David told her. He had a grandmother, but she was nothing like Wanda.

"Oh, hush now," Wanda said, blushing. "Go on."

David told her stories about Eden, and Wanda let him use her computer to search for information about his daughter. The Internet was a new concept for him, so Wanda helped him figure out how it all worked. All he found was an address for her apartment in North Seattle and an announcement from a culinary school. Eden West was listed at the top of her graduating class. There was a picture of the students in their tall, white chef hats—the kind that Eden always proclaimed she'd wear. And there, standing in the middle of the photo, was his daughter. She was taller, of course, but it was without a doubt her narrow face, her vibrant blue eyes and dark, long hair. She was smiling ear to ear and holding her diploma up like a trophy, above the heads of the other students. She had become what she always knew she would. She was a chef.

"Look," he said to Wanda. "That's her."

Wanda leaned over his shoulder and peered at the screen. "She's a lovely girl. You should call the school."

"She's already graduated. I found her address, though."

"Then go see her!" Wanda said. "What are you waiting for?"

Hesitation played at the edges of his cloudy thoughts. He was numb again. He had nothing to offer her. Her life was already bigger than his had ever been. Would she even want to see him? Was she ashamed?

"I think I'll write her a letter first," he told Wanda, who shrugged her shoulders and told him to suit himself.

That night, David sat down to write. He told Eden how sorry he was to be out of touch for so long. He told her about living on the streets, but that he was back on his meds and was even holding down a job. He asked whether he could see her. He told her how much he missed her every day.

Weeks passed before he sent another letter. He never heard back from his daughter and the second letter was the last one he sent. It had been too long; too much damage had been done. Gradually, David fell off his meds. He picked up his painting again, furiously trying to capture as much as he could remember about his life with his daughter. He worked long and hard on a series of the Garden of Eden. His thoughts spun; his drinking began again. The days grew darker and the splintered, raging voices in his head grew loud until finally, a year after coming back to Seattle, David abandoned his job and his apartment and went to the streets. He kept his eyes forward, leaving all hopes for a new life behind him. This time, he didn't look back.

December 2010
Eden

I had to work several long days in a row after Thanksgiving to make up for taking the actual holiday off. I also wanted Juan to have some time at home with his family, so I was swamped with organizing the heavy load of upcoming Christmas party orders on my own. I waited until the Tuesday morning after the holiday to call Common Ground, the halfway house in Portland my mother had told me about. The place where my father might be. I wasn't sure why I waited, exactly. Maybe it was the fear that it wouldn't be open anymore and the one meaningful clue I'd found in my search for him would lead nowhere. When I finally picked up the phone, I was relieved to discover that they were still in business and they'd be happy to let me come show them a picture of my father. The program manager, a man named Matthew Shockley, wouldn't give out information about client files over the phone, but if I came in person, he'd talk with me. He, like Jack, took his clients' privacy very seriously.

I told as much to Jack, who came over that night after we got done with the dinner at Hope House. It had been my first day off from work since the holiday, but I didn't even consider not showing up to cook the clients their meal.

Now it was late, about two A.M., and Jack and I were lying in bed after making love. The candles I'd lit when he arrived at midnight flickered, on the verge of going out. The man had stamina.

Jack rolled over on top of me after I relayed everything the program manager at Common Ground had said. He used his arms to prop himself up so he didn't squish me. "So, when's your next day off?"

"Um, I think I get Monday and Tuesday next week." I loved the feeling of him on me. The sheer weight of him was reassuring.

"Not until then, huh?" Jack said.

"Nope. The holidays are my busy season. Our calendar is booked with at least four major Christmas parties every night." I tilted my head and shifted a bit beneath him. "Why?"

Jack felt me move and fell off to the side, pressing his body up against me. He bent his right arm and set his head in his hand. "I was thinking we could take a road trip."

"What kind of road trip?"

"I hear Portland is lovely this time of year."

I smiled. "Are you serious?"

"I'll make the reservations for us in the morning."

"You are the sweetest man on the planet, you know that?"

"I know." He winked and gave me a slight smile. "Would you like to invite Bryce and Georgia to come with?"

I grabbed my pillow and walloped him over the head with it. "No, I would not." Even though I'd talked with Bryce over the weekend and he really did seem okay just being friends with Georgia, I still felt a little strange about the idea of spending time with them together.

"Too bad. I already invited them."

"Excuse me?" I held the pillow in midair and stared at him. "When?"

He grinned. "On Thanksgiving, after you told me about your

mom giving you the name of the shelter in Portland. I'd like to get to know them better and they want to help find your dad. They both offered to come if we ended up taking a trip down there."

I sighed and dropped the pillow behind me. I had to admit their offer was a generous one, considering that no matter what they said, it probably wasn't totally comfortable for them to spend a prolonged amount of time together right now. "Did you invite my mom and John, too? Are we making this a family affair?"

He laughed. "No. Though John did ask if he and some of his guys from the station could help build the fence for the garden. I wasn't about to turn away free labor."

"Well, that's nice of him," I said. John really was a great person.

"Yes, it is. You've got a good family."

"Don't think I've forgotten about our little deal, either, Mr. Baker."

"What deal was that?"

I poked his arm. "Don't play dumb with me. You said you'd try to talk to your dad if I made up with my mom."

"Well, you had it kind of easy, don't you think? She showed up on Thanksgiving and you didn't have to make much of an effort."

"I had to swallow my pride and apologize. Believe me, that took *plenty* of effort."

"Hmm," he said, staring at me through narrowed eyes. "If I remember correctly, I said I'd *think* about talking to him."

"What's the big deal with you two? There's got to be more to the story than you just not wanting to take over his company."

"Nope, that's pretty much the story." Jack rolled away from me and over onto his back. He laced his fingers together and put them behind his head, staring at the ceiling.

"Jack," I said, not wanting to rock the boat too much, "I feel like you know so much about me. I want to know you better."

"You know I'm falling for you." He turned his head to look at me and I scooted over to curl up next to him. He pulled one of his hands free from behind his head and wrapped an arm around me. I snuggled in and rested my cheek on his chest. I felt like a puzzle piece, clicking into place.

"Yes, I know. I'm falling for you, too." I paused. "But I want to know more about the man I'm falling for. All your nooks and crannies."

"Sounds kinky."

"Jack."

"I'm not very good at opening up," he said.

"You can trust me," I said.

"I know I can," he said quietly. "It's not you I'm worried about."

I was silent, waiting for him to continue. I'd told him so much about my life, my father's illness and suicide attempt. My emotions had been spilled out all over the floor pretty much since the day we met. I was ready for him to offer me a little more of the same. He'd told me the story of what he witnessed his group of friends do to the homeless man, how it had spurred him to open the shelter. But I wanted to understand other parts of him. I wanted to know where he came from.

"What do you want to know?" he asked after a few minutes of neither of us speaking a word.

His words startled me; I'd half thought he'd fallen asleep. "When was your last serious girlfriend?" I asked, fairly drowsy myself.

"Five years ago. Her name was Darcy." He said her name like it was something sour in his mouth.

I snapped awake, instantly hating her, whoever she was. I pictured her glistening and perfect, with long, flat-ironed blond hair and a cute turned-up nose. It made me feel ill to think about his kissing another woman the same way he kissed me. "How long were you two together?"

"Since we were twenty."

I did some quick math in my head. He was thirty-one and it ended when they were twenty-six. That meant they'd dated for six years. *Six years?* That was longer than the relationships I had with some of my appliances. I was suddenly very intimidated.

"Who ended it?" I asked in what I hoped was an interested but lighthearted voice.

"I did." He was still staring at the ceiling. "Both of our parents thought we'd get engaged. She thought we'd get engaged. She hinted about it often enough."

"But you didn't love her?" *Please, please, tell me you didn't love her.*

"I cared about her, I guess. We'd known each other almost our entire lives. It was sort of expected we'd end up together."

"Like how it was expected you'd take over your dad's company?"

"Exactly like that."

"What does your dad's company do?"

Jack laughed, a short, barking sound. "The question is, what doesn't it do? Baker Industries has its fingers in pretty much every pot. Mergers and acquisitions, imports, exports, technologies. You name it, the Baker name is probably stamped somewhere on the paperwork."

"You're one of *those* Bakers?" I was stunned. Baker Industries was one of the largest multinational corporations based in Seattle. Emerald City Events had catered more banquets and dinners for them than all of our other clients combined. It was such a common last name, I never thought to link Jack with the company.

"Yes, I'm one of 'those' Bakers." I felt him move his head, so I adjusted enough so I could pull back and look at him. "You've heard of us, I guess?"

"I've done a lot of catering for the company's events." Questions began shooting through my mind. Was Jack a trust-fund baby? Or did his father disinherit him when he didn't follow the path expected of him? Was that why they didn't speak, because Jack didn't get the money he was expecting?

"I'm sure you have. Dad's fond of high-end parties."

I was silent for a moment before a thought struck me. "Does Tom actually work for you, then? I remember he said, 'Mr. Baker takes good care of me,' but you said it was a joke."

Jack shook his head. "No, Tom's just a friend. He does work for my dad, though. That's how we met."

"Aha. Now it makes sense." I went back to the ex-girlfriend. "So, why did you end it with Darcy?"

He sighed. "It's complicated."

"Isn't it always?" I said, attempting to keep my tone light.

"I made it more so by leaving my position as VP for my dad's company. I told Darce I wanted to live a more simple life and do something to make up for what I'd done to that man back in high school. I also wanted to build something of my own instead of riding on my father's coattails. I wanted to create my own success instead of just inheriting his."

"And she didn't understand that?" *Please don't call her "Darce,"* I thought.

"Oh, she understood it. She even supported me in it the first year or so after I quit working for my dad. She helped with some of the initial fund-raising and grant applications. She's a lawyer, so she was good at that kind of thing. But then the novelty of the situation wore off, I guess, and she started having a hard time with the idea of not living the lifestyle she was accustomed to." His words were bitter. "Once reality set in, it turned out what she really wanted was all the money and prestige that came along with marrying Jack Baker, not Jack Baker himself. I felt like an idiot for ever believing anything different. So I broke up with her."

"That sucks," I said sympathetically. Jack didn't strike me as someone who'd fall easily for a disingenuous woman. It could be that she thought she could leave the wealthier lifestyle but after living it awhile discovered she wasn't cut out for a simpler life. I wasn't sure that made her a bad person, exactly, but I was happy the result of her decision was my ending up with a man like Jack.

"Did she come from money, too?" I asked.

"Not really. I mean, her mother was successful in my dad's company, which was how we got introduced in the first place. We dated and our families cooked up the idea we'd get married and I'd head up the company with her as the trophy on my arm."

I cringed, shifting my prior vision of her to statuesque Brazilian supermodel. "Trophy, huh? She must be very pretty."

"Some might think so," he said. "Not when I finally saw her true colors. I wanted to build something meaningful with my life, you know? And she just trashed it. When I broke up with her, she called me an idiot and a loser who'd never amount to anything. My father pretty much followed suit."

"Oh, Jack, I'm sorry." I hugged him and kissed his chest.

He shrugged, mindlessly rubbing my back with his open palm. "It happened a long time ago. The sting has worn off. But you can understand why I'm hesitant to go see him. I don't think his opinion of what I've chosen to do with my life has changed any. I don't know how I'd explain to him how so much of what

I'd been given in my privileged life were things I didn't need or really even like."

"Like what?"

"Like country club memberships and summer houses. That kind of thing. My dad is all about accumulating more and more stuff. More money, especially. I wanted a simpler life. Less encumbered by things, more enriched by people." He rolled over to look at me. "I tried to make him happy for a few years. I worked with him, schmoozed over business dinners and Saturday golf. All that crap. And I was good at it. But I hated it. I literally had to force myself out of bed in the morning to go to work. I felt like I was living someone else's life. Like I wasn't being the person I was meant to be."

"Did your dad disinherit you when you told him how you felt?"

"Does that matter?" There was an instant edge to his voice— a guard thrown up. Money was obviously a touchy subject for him. I'd need to be careful how we talked about it.

I sat up and pressed both my hands flat against his chest, pushing him from his side over onto his back. I stared him down, unblinking. "It absolutely does *not* matter to me. I fell in love with an idealistic, underpaid social worker, okay? I couldn't give a shit about your bank account."

He smiled. "You fell in love?"

My cheeks suddenly burned and I had to avert my eyes from his. "Did I say that? I think I said, 'I'm falling *for*.'"

He nodded. "You did. But that was earlier." He reached up and touched my cheek with the tips of his fingers, gently turning my face back toward him. "I'm pretty sure you said you fell in love with me."

My heart pounded. This wasn't good. I wasn't supposed to

say it first. How could I be in love with him in such a short time? It was only infatuation. A crush. Lust, even. I made myself look at him. His expression was kind; his gaze was softened by the warm light the candles created.

"I'm falling in love with you, too, Eden," he said. "It's scaring the shit out of me."

I laughed and threw myself on top of him, shoving my mouth against his neck to kiss it. "We'll be scared shitless together, then."

"Sounds like a plan." He paused. "And, Eden?"

"Yes?" I asked a little dreamily, basking in the glow of being told he was falling in love with me, too. It was better than any drug, any success I could ever reach.

"I didn't mean to make you feel bad about asking about my inheritance. It's just an old button of mine. So many women I've dated, as soon as they found out about my family, they became all about what I could do for them. What I could buy them or what kind of trips I'd pay for. It's why I pretty much stopped dating altogether."

"And then I came along," I said, still pressing my lips against his neck.

"Yes, you did. And I'm happier for it." He squeezed me, then rolled me off the top of him. "And just so you know, my father didn't disown me financially. But I haven't touched my inheritance since I quit my job with him. The only thing I did was use it for collateral to buy the building and land around the shelter. The down payment, the mortgage, that all comes from my own personal savings and the funding and donations I've drummed up on my own. That's why it took almost four years to raise enough capital to open the doors. I live in my crappy one-bedroom apartment and love it. I don't see myself ever going back to the kind of existence my family wants me to have. You should know that up front."

"I don't care where you live, Jack. I really don't. I'd hang out in a cardboard box with you."

"Well, at least we'd know some of our neighbors."

We both laughed, and he tucked my back against him, spooning our bodies together. "Now, get your nook in my cranny, woman."

I giggled and snuggled up to him, making sure every inch of my skin was pressed up against his. Our breathing fell into a slow, synchronized pattern, and within minutes the last remaining candle flickered and then went out.

Since Georgia's Mercedes was too compact to fit all of us and our bags, we ended up setting out for our road trip to Portland in Jack's SUV. We dropped Jasper off with my mom, then drove to pick up Bryce at his apartment, and then Georgia at her house.

"You want the front seat for the leg room?" I asked Bryce as Jack helped Georgia fit her suitcase into the back of the vehicle. Despite my brother's apparent nonchalance about their one-night stand, I thought he might be uncomfortable sitting next to Georgia for the entire trip.

"No, thanks," Bryce said, surprising me. He had completely backed off on the tanning; his skin was almost a natural shade again.

Georgia came around the corner of the car. "I'm okay in the backseat," she said, though not quite looking at Bryce as she spoke. There was only the tiniest bit of tension between them—perhaps it was embarrassment more than anything else. Rather than draw attention to the situation, I decided to ignore it and act as if nothing had ever happened, taking them at their word that they were fine.

"We should get going," I said. Everyone climbed into the car and we hit the freeway headed south. No one spoke much as the miles and hours passed, but anticipation wiggled in my belly as we got closer to the Washington/Oregon border. What if my father *was* actually living at Common Ground? What if he was living peacefully in a place that encouraged his art and helped keep him on his meds? I tried not to get too excited about the possibility, as Jack had advised, but I couldn't help it. Something about this felt right to me.

Georgia spoke up as we crossed over the Columbia River and into Portland. "Are we there yet?" she asked sleepily. Lost in my own thoughts, I hadn't realized she had been asleep.

"Almost," Bryce said.

"Do you want to check in at the hotel or go straight to the house?" Jack asked me, turning his head only for a moment so he could smile at me.

"I'd like to go straight there," I said. "If you guys don't mind."

"I don't mind," Georgia said. "That's why we're here, right?"

"Right," Bryce said. He reached his thick fingers through the headrest and briefly massaged my shoulder. "You doing okay, sis?"

I nodded. "Yep. Just a little nervous. Sort of how I felt when I first arrived at Hope House."

"You were nervous?" Jack punched a few buttons on the GPS to look up the address he'd programmed in for Common Ground. "I never would have guessed."

I looked at him. "Really? I was a wreck inside. And you were such a jerk."

"And now you love me." He flashed me a quick wink.

"I know, I know," I said. "What's *wrong* with me?"

"Hey," Georgia interjected, "you guys are dropping the L-word up there?" She leaned forward and poked Jack's arm. "She's pretty great, isn't she, Jack? How could you *not* love her?"

"Georgia . . ." I moaned.

Jack laughed. "It's okay, Eden. You're right, Georgia. You obviously have excellent taste in friends."

"Damn straight," Georgia said. "Just remember, if you hurt her, I'll kick your ass."

"Duly noted," Jack said solemnly. He followed the GPS's digital directions, took the exit marked "Downtown/City Center," and then turned right.

"I'd be careful, dude," Bryce warned Jack. "Georgia's kind of a badass. And I'm Eden's brother, so I'll be next in line if you screw her over."

"Oh my god," I said. "You guys, please."

Jack laughed again, pulling into the parking lot across the street from where the GPS told us our destination was. "You've got a posse, baby. I'd better be careful not to break your heart."

I rolled my eyes and shook my head a few times, secretly pleased Georgia and Bryce were putting on such a protective show. Then my eyes wandered over to the house, a two-story colonial with a small front yard and a wraparound front porch.

"You want us to go in with you?" Georgia asked. "Or wait here?"

I looked at Jack. "I don't know. What do you think?"

"I think you and I should go in first. Then grab your bodyguards for backup, if we need them."

Georgia laughed. "Sounds good to me. Let us know if you need us."

Jack and I went up the front steps of the house and knocked at the front door. A moment later, it was opened by a portly bald man with three chins and squinty small eyes. When he smiled, the apples of his cheeks pushed up so high, his eyes disappeared completely.

"Hi," I said. "I'm Eden West. I'm looking for Matthew Shockley? He's expecting me."

"You found him!" the man said, reaching out to vigorously shake Jack's and my hands. "But call me Matt, okay? It's nice to meet you! How was your drive down?"

"Uneventful," Jack said. "Thanks for letting us come."

"Of course, of course!" Matt exclaimed. "Happy to help. Come on back and we'll talk a bit." He turned around and hitched up his sagging white painter's jeans by the belt loops, but not before we caught a glance of his butt crack.

Jack swallowed a snicker, but I was too nervous to laugh. We followed Matt down the hall to a small room off the kitchen. The walls were dark and paneled but covered almost floor-to-ceiling with various paintings—oils and watercolors, charcoals and delicate inks. Were any of these my father's? We took a seat on the small couch in the corner of the room while Matt settled into a large padded recliner behind a desk.

"So, after we talked, I took it upon myself to look up your father's name in our system."

"Did you find anything?" I asked, clamping my fingers together tightly as though in prayer.

He bobbed his head. "Yep, sure did." He lifted a yellow manila folder and held it up. "He's right here."

"Here? As in staying here right now?" I asked, unable to keep the excitement out of my voice. Jack reached over and rested his hand flat on the top of my thigh in a soothing touch. My muscles hummed with anxiety.

"No, no," Matt said. "He's not here now. But he was just a

couple of weeks ago. Stayed with us for about a month this time around."

"This time around?" Jack said. "He's been here more than once?"

"Yep, yep," Matt said. "We have to cycle people through. There are only so many beds. They have to get approved through the psych ward at the hospital as good to go, and if there's room and they qualify, they come here. They can stay up to three months."

"But he was only here a month?" I said.

Matt blew a breath out of his thin lips. "David isn't crazy about staying on his meds. The rules are, if you're not following doctor's orders, you're not allowed to stay."

My hopes fell a bit as he spoke. "How does the program work here, exactly?"

"I'd be interested to hear that, too," Jack said. "I run a shelter up in Seattle and I'm always looking for new ideas for programs."

"Hope House, right?" Matt said. "Eden told me that on the phone. I've heard good things about it from some of my clients."

"Really?" Jack said, sitting up a little straighter.

"It's a tight-knit community," Matt said. "A lot of our peeps travel back and forth between Seattle and Portland. We hear about the good and the bad. Hope House has a good rep."

Jack sat back and put his arm around my shoulders. I rubbed his leg a little, acknowledging that I understood how important it was for him to hear about the work he did.

"And your program?" I asked, prodding Matt to continue.

"Oh, right," he said. "Sorry, my Ritalin hasn't kicked in yet today. ADHD makes me nuts. But that's why I'm perfect for this place, I guess. I understand the clientele." He chuckled. "Okay, but enough about me." He took a breath before continuing. "Common Ground was founded about ten years ago by Arthur Rein-hart, a local sculptor who struggled with clinical depression and bipolar disorder. As part of his therapy, he started teaching art classes at a few shelters around town and he realized how many of the people he got to know there suffered from the same kind of illnesses he did. He was just lucky enough to come from a rich family who made sure he didn't end up on the streets. After a year or so, he came up with the idea to buy this house and turn it into a place where homeless artists with mental illness could live after they were hospitalized. Which a lot of them are. They can paint or sculpt as therapy and get settled into a normal routine. Kind of as a transition back into the real world." He threw his hands up in the air in front of him. "That's about it, folks."

"That's amazing," Jack said. "Do you help them with getting a job?"

"We do." Matt nodded. "I'm just one of the six social work-ers we have on staff. There's also a nurse practitioner and a psy-chiatrist who comes two times a week to manage the clients' meds."

"Is Mr. Reinhart still involved?" I asked.

"He died two years ago. Overdose."

My eyes filled for this man I didn't even know. Even after cre-ating such a wonderful place, he still couldn't find a reason to live. His illness wouldn't let him. Jack's hand, which was resting on my shoulder, squeezed in reassurance. "How is the house funded, then, if he's gone?"

"His family has been kind enough to continue to take care of us as a tribute to their son. We host fund-raisers, too, of course, with art for sale and things like that, but the majority of our fi-nancing comes from the Reinharts. They're wonderful people. Real philanthropists."

I took a deep breath before speaking. "Do you know my father?"

Matt nodded. "I do. He's a very talented artist. But like I said, he fights the rest of the program here. He manages to fake it for a while but doesn't do well with expectations and rules. But I'm sure you know that."

I nodded. I knew it all too well. "Do you have any idea where I might find him? Any place he might hang out or stay after he leaves here?"

Matt pulled a sheet of paper out of my father's file. "I thought you might ask me that, so I took the liberty of putting together a list for you. It's not much, but there are a few haunts he's talked about. Where he goes to sketch people for money." In one great huff of breath, he leaned over his desk to hand me the piece of paper.

I jumped up to take it from him. "Thank you so much, Matt. I can't tell you how much this means to me."

Matt stood and smiled, his eyes disappearing again. "It's my pleasure." He nodded toward Jack. "Be safe out there, okay? Some of these aren't the safest places to visit. Not where I'd usually send tourists in our fair city."

Jack reached out and shook his hand again. "Don't worry. She has bodyguards in the car."

Matt gave him a quizzical look.

"Private joke," I said.

"Ah, gotcha," Matt said. "Do you have a minute to come look at something? I won't keep you long."

"Sure," I said, clutching the piece of paper he'd given me to my chest. I was so close. I could almost feel him.

We followed Matt down the hall again and into a large room with a bay window. Two couches flanked a river-stone fireplace and a low table sat between them.

"There," Matt said. "Above the fireplace."

My eyes followed where he directed. Jack grabbed my hand and held it tightly.

"Oh my god," I said breathlessly. "That's me." Just above the mantel was a portrait, an image of my face. I was probably about ten, the last time my father had seen me. He had somehow captured the fragile mask I wore. Hints of a more secretive sadness and fear showed in my eyes and in the small, worried lines of my forehead. It was the portrait of a young girl trying to look at peace when inside she was waging a war.

"It's gorgeous," Jack said. "Eden, it's really, really good."

My bottom lip trembled, but I managed to hold myself together. I could not believe the scope of my father's gift. I couldn't believe how much his illness had taken from him. How much it had taken from me.

"We've had more offers on that painting than any of the others combined when we do our fund-raisers," Matt said. "But David refuses to sell it. He asked if he could leave it here for safekeeping, though. He always tells me he'll be back, that he'll find a way to silence the rumblings in his head." He smiled at me. "That's the thing about your dad, Eden. He has a way of saying it so you believe it might be true."

July 2007
David

Sitting on a bench in downtown Portland, David knew they were after him again. The men who would try to steal his art supplies, the only way David had to make money to live. They'd kicked his ass in Seattle a few months back so he hitched a ride to Portland, thinking they'd never find him there. But they had. He knew they had. He was their prey. He could feel them breathing down his neck. He felt the demons gearing up, spitting fire into his blood, tensing his muscles into angry steel bands. *No, no, no,* David thought. *I can't do this again. I can't fight. I want to run. There isn't anywhere I can hide. I've been to California and back to Seattle and they always find me. They find me in the hospital and on the street. I have to get away.*

David leapt up from the bench and began to pace up and down the street, muttering beneath his breath. "Leave me alone," he begged. He hit himself in the head with the meat of his right palm, trying to knock his whirling thoughts on their asses. If he could dizzy them, maybe they'd leave him alone, too. Booze kept them sleepy, but he was out. No money, no booze. He had to find another way to silence them. He bumped into a woman pushing a stroller, causing her to stumble.

"Hey!" she exclaimed, and David kept walking, throwing an arm out toward her. He only meant to caution her to stay away, but instead he hit her across the face. The woman began to scream. The baby in the stroller screamed, too. David dropped to his knees, clutching the sides of his head.

"No, no, no!" he moaned. He rocked back and forth, banging his head onto the hot cement. He barely felt it. "I didn't mean to hurt her. I didn't. Eden, please, I didn't mean to hurt you."

People began to gather around him, murmuring. Their low tones screeched like sirens in David's ears. "Leave me alone," he cried. "Please. I just want to die. I need to die." He continued to rock with his forehead pressed into the sidewalk, anchoring him in place. Maybe he could push his way through to hell. Maybe he was already there.

A policeman approached. "Sir, I'm going to ask you to come with me now," he said. David shook his head, grinding it into the pavement. The policeman grabbed David's right arm and twisted it behind his back, slapping handcuffs onto his wrist quicker than David could pull away. He stopped struggling and let the officer lead him to the back of the patrol car. The whispers from the people on the street jabbed at him like knives.

He knew what came next. He knew the mental ward at the jail would lead to the mental ward at the hospital. He'd ended up there again after admitting himself to the state hospital in Washington a few months before. Or was it a few years? David wasn't sure. Doctors were a bunch of lying bastards, no matter what year it was. "Here, we want to help," they said. And then, out come the needles and pills and looking at him like he's a piece of shit.

"I am an artist!" David told them. "You have the wrong man!"

"You are an artist who suffers from mental illness," they said.

"No!" he roared. David upended the table in front of him and then came the straps around his wrists and ankles again. The doctors had promised him they wouldn't use these if David cooperated. So he cooperated, and they strapped him down anyway. Liars, the lot of them. It wasn't him they needed to strap down— it was his wild, malevolent thoughts. Find a way to suck them from his head and lock them away.

The only man who wasn't like the doctors was a man named Matt who kept coming back to see David in the Portland jail ward. Matt had seen some of David's sketches on the street and asked the officers to call him the next time David was brought in. But Matt was a part of the system David didn't trust.

"I have a house you can live in and get well," Matt had said. "You can paint and get stabilized on your meds. It's a special program for artists who have the same kind of problems as you."

"The only problems I have are the fiends in my head," David spat back.

Matt, a huge man with tiny, kind eyes, gave David a warm smile. "Your art can help make those go away. But first, we need to get them under control."

The first time he went to Common Ground, David only stayed two days before he was back on the street. The walls around him felt like they were closing in; he needed to see the sky. He couldn't breathe anywhere but outside. The next, he stayed a few weeks and was able to paint. This time, the time he accidentally hit the woman with the stroller, he wasn't sure Matt would let him back in. He slammed his forehead against the patrol car's backseat window.

"Don't," the officer said in a stern voice. The officer didn't understand. David was only doing what he knew would keep the demons dazed long enough to get him to Common Ground.

December 2010
Eden

The rest of our first day in Portland Jack, Georgia, Bryce, and I spent searching the places Matt told us to look. Portland seemed like such a clean, lovely city, it was difficult to believe there were any areas where we might not feel safe. But when we arrived downtown, both Georgia and I were happy we had Bryce and Jack with us. Loud groups of young men stared at us as we walked past, eyeing us with an energy that made me feel like we could very well become their prey. It was no worse than anything we saw in Seattle, but somehow with the streets being so unfamiliar, it felt more threatening. There were plenty of retail stores in the area, but we went directly to the art store where Matt suggested my father might be hanging out. When he wasn't there or anywhere nearby, we walked a twelve-block grid with no luck.

Ever determined, we headed to the next area on Matt's list, a neighborhood just north of downtown Matt had noted was somewhat known for its homeless population. We showed copies of my dad's picture to as many people as would stop to talk with us, but after six hours of driving around and combing the foreign streets, we were all exhausted and decided it was time to check into our hotel. The optimism I had felt at the beginning of the day in Matt's office slowly faded into discouragement.

"Thanks for booking each of us a room, too," Georgia said to

Jack after we grabbed a quick bite to eat in the hotel restaurant. We stood in the lobby next to a fountain where I threw in a few pennies and made a wish, just in case.

"Yeah, man," Bryce said. "That was very cool of you."

Jack shrugged and raked his fingers through his dark hair. "Not a big deal. I'm glad you guys could come with." He put his arm around me and hugged me to him. "Aren't you glad, Eden?"

I nodded, surprised to realize that despite my initial reservations, I was happy my brother and best friend were with us. Any tension I had sensed between them had dissipated completely as we went about our day, so I decided if they could be adult about the situation, so could I. Jack and I both waved at them as they walked away, toward the elevators. I leaned into Jack, resting my head against his shoulder. He kissed my forehead. "Ready for sleep, baby?" he asked.

I nodded again but found the opposite word of what I was feeling pop out of my mouth. "No."

He laughed. I pulled back and smiled at him sweetly. "Can we go look at the train station?" Union Station was the last place Matt had on his list of my father's possible haunts.

Jack looked confused. "I thought we were going to do that tomorrow."

"We were, but I was just thinking, it'll be full of commuters and tourists in the morning. If we go now, he might be easier to spot." I didn't know if this was true. I only knew that despite the aching fatigue in my bones, I wouldn't be able to sleep until we'd checked this final place. My motivation was winding down; I needed to take advantage of the little I had left.

Jack smiled and shook his head. "I'm up for it if you are."

"I am." We walked back out to the garage and as we reached his car, he opened the door for me. I climbed inside and sighed.

I was tired. Exhausted, really, but I couldn't help but feel compelled to finish out this search tonight. I told myself if he wasn't at Union Station, we'd get up in the morning and head home. I voiced this to Jack as he looked up the train station on his GPS and punched it in as our destination.

"You're sure you want to leave? You don't want to check out other shelters while we're here?"

"I'm sure," I said, staring out the window at the city's glittering Christmas lights. "I've been thinking a lot about how I need to start focusing more on what I have in my life instead of what I don't. And I have a lot." I reached across the console and stroked the soft, dark hair on his arm. "I'll still keep feelers out in the hospitals and shelters for his name, but I think I might be done focusing so much on so actively trying to find him."

"There weren't any other clues to where he might be in the box we found at his apartment?"

"Nope. Other than the letters, it was mostly clothes and books. And I think the letters pretty much told me all that I needed to know to begin with."

"And what was that?" Jack pulled into the fairly deserted Union Station parking lot and turned the car into a space. He turned off the engine and looked at me. Even with his messy hair and sleepy eyes, my heart swelled just seeing his face.

"That he tried to see me. That he didn't leave and never looked back. He missed me. He loved me. Everything I thought about the way things happened was wrong. And I feel at peace about it somehow."

Much like the parking lot, the inside of Union Station was pretty empty. A few travelers lugged their large suitcases behind them; others strolled slowly to their gate. A loud voice came over the speaker, announcing that the 9:10 to Seattle was departing in five minutes. Jack and I walked around slowly, taking everything in. There were many obviously homeless people scattered across various benches, some stretched out in sleep and some sitting at attention, looking as though they were waiting for an arrival that might never come.

We walked the length of the station back and forth two times, Jack checking all the men's restrooms and every other corner inside the building. After about an hour, we dropped onto a bench near the doors where we'd come inside.

"It's no use," I said. "This is pointless."

Jack patted my leg. "You want some coffee?" he asked.

I smiled at him gratefully. "That would be wonderful."

"Black, right?" He popped up from the bench.

I nodded, loving that he paid attention to how I took my coffee. It made me feel like part of a settled-in couple, one who knew each other's habits and tastes. According to Jack, he liked his coffee sweet and creamy, "like I like my women," he said.

"You got it," he said. He approached the dreadlocked young man working behind a coffee cart about twenty feet away from the bench where I still sat. I watched him order our coffees, then pull out the picture of my father from his pocket. I stood up and walked over to the cart myself to better hear their conversation.

The man peered at the photo over the counter. "Is he in trouble?"

Jack shook his head. "Not at all. This is his daughter. She's trying to find him."

The man looked me up and down and grinned. "You look like David. He never said he had a daughter. And a pretty one, to boot."

"When did you last see him?" My heart sped up in my chest. *He knows my father's name.*

"Last night, I think. Around closing. He hangs out down at the other exit, the small one by the lockers, trying to catch the tourists. He's really talented."

"Which way?" I asked excitedly, throwing my gaze around the immediate area. We hadn't gone outside to look, thinking he'd be inside for the warmth. But maybe Matt had been right. My father was still in Portland. There was a chance I'd find him here.

"There," the man said, pointing us down the long corridor to the large glass doors. "Beneath the clock outside."

"Thank you!" I said, and grabbed Jack's hand. Forgetting our coffees, we strode quickly in the direction the man had pointed, away from where we had entered the station.

"Slow down, Eden," Jack said, half laughing. "If he's there, he'll just be sitting there, not running away from you."

"I know, I know," I said. "I can't help it. He could be here!"

I pushed past several people standing in line at the ticket booth. "Excuse me, excuse me," I said as they grumbled at us. "Sorry, sorry."

Finally, we reached the doors and stepped outside. It was dark outside, but the area was well lit enough for it to appear like daytime. I glanced wildly around, not seeing him and not seeing him. My heart dropped. "Where is he?" I asked. "Do you see him?"

Jack, not being much taller than I, strained to see over the heads of a group of tourists standing next to us. He jumped up once, letting go of my hand in the process. "There!" he said loudly. "Over there!"

"Where?" I asked frantically. My pulse raced through my veins; my entire body shook, saturated with adrenaline.

"Come on," Jack said, pulling me through the crowd. He elbowed his way past, not stopping to apologize as we stepped on a few toes. When we got to the other side of the group, he pointed toward the corner of the entryway, next to a wall. "There."

My pulse pounded in my ears as I followed his finger with my eyes. I saw an easel with a sketch pad set upon it. On the stool behind it sat a tall, thin man with straggly black hair shot through with gray, which hung to the middle of his back. He had a heavy beard and wore faded jeans and a thick brown jacket with worn-out hiking boots. I could only see his profile, but the aquiline nose was unmistakably my father's. He was there. He was less than ten feet away from me.

My breath left me and I swayed where I stood. If not for Jack grabbing me, I may have fallen over.

I couldn't speak. All this time and there he was. *What if I hadn't wanted to come to the station tonight? What if I'd given in and gone to bed?* I might never have found him. And yet, there he was. My father. The man I loved first and who first loved me.

Jack urged me toward him, giving me a little push. He stood back, letting me take this first moment alone with my father. The tears rose in my throat as I approached him.

"Daddy?" I managed to choke out, and he turned to look for the voice that had spoken the word. His face was so pale and tired. His expression was bruised and battle scarred—he was a mere shadow of the man I used to know. Was he the shadow I'd chased in my dream so many years ago? Did I have some kind of premonition of this pursuit? I couldn't be sure. But then it didn't matter, because his face blossomed into that smile I knew so well, less a few teeth. He knew me. He saw my face and he knew me right away.

"Bug," he said simply. "What're you doing here?"

A sound that was half laugh, half sob strangled in my throat. "Looking for you," I said. "I've been looking for you."

"You have?" He looked surprised. He set down his pencil and stood up, outstretching his skinny arms to hold me. "Well, I'm right here."

I rushed toward him and threw myself into his embrace. He was skin and bones; I could feel the xylophone of his rib cage against my cheek. I sobbed and sobbed and my father soothed me, kissing the top of my head, his familiar touch and murmured words filling a space long empty in my heart.

"Eden, my love, don't cry," he whispered. "It's okay, honey. Daddy's here. Everything's going to be all right."

December 2010
David

At first, David thought it was a dream. He was sitting outside the exit of Union Station, setting up his easel for the late evening travelers. Since leaving Common Ground a few weeks before, he had made enough for a bottle every night, enough to keep the beasts in his head sleepy. That was enough, David thought. That was all he really needed.

But there was her voice. Eden. His daughter, calling him Daddy.

When he looked toward the sound, there was this beautiful woman standing before him. Her dark hair fell to her shoulders, her vivid blue eyes the same as they'd always been. All sound around them seemed to disappear and he smiled. "Bug," he said, calling her the nickname he'd given her when she was a baby. "What are you doing here?"

"Looking for you," she said. She cried as she spoke, but she smiled, too, so David knew she was happy.

He didn't know whether it was all really happening or his mind was playing tricks on him until he was holding her. The smell of her skin, the solid strength of her grasp—these told him she was real. A young man approached and stood next to them. He was on the shorter side, with dark hair, kind green eyes, and a softness around his smile that told David he had a good soul. Eden's husband, perhaps? Was she married? Did she walk down the aisle without him? Not that he could blame her, of course. He was lost to her many years before. He had no one to blame but himself.

"How did you find me?" David asked his daughter, pulling back just far enough to gaze at her pretty face.

"Matt Shockley, at Common Ground," she said, lifting a hand to wipe away her tears.

"Matt?" David was puzzled. Had he been microchipped? Were they tracking him again? What exactly was going on here? "How do you know him?"

"It's a long story," Eden said. She shifted to David's side, keeping an arm wrapped around him. "Dad, this is Jack Baker. He's been helping me look for you. He runs a shelter up in Seattle called Hope House. Have you been there?"

David shook his head, trying to take all this in. "No, don't think I have." He reached his hand out and Jack took it. The man's handshake was firm, a good sign. Not her husband, then. A boyfriend, perhaps? As he rested them upon Eden, Jack's eyes were full of emotion. He loved her. *But she's a little girl. How could she have a boyfriend? Wait. What year is it again?*

David shook his head, trying to straighten the jumbled thoughts in his brain. Eden was here. She'd been looking for him. Why had he stayed away from her so long? Why did he never go back to find her again? He knew why. Because he couldn't keep enough meds in his body to stay well. If she had talked to Matt, Eden already knew this. Then what did she want with him?

"So, what now?" Jack said, practically voicing the question in David's own mind.

Eden looked at Jack, then back to David. "I don't know," she said shakily, but with a smile on her face. "I wasn't expecting to actually find him. Now that I have, I don't know what comes next!" She took David's hands in her own. "What do you want to do, Dad? Do you have a place to stay tonight?" Her eyes were so bright, so happy. He could not refuse her.

David nodded. "I just need to get a few more dollars together for the room."

"Oh, no," Eden said in protest. "You're staying with us." She looked at Jack. "Right?"

Jack hesitated, only for a second, but David saw it. "Of course," Jack said. "David? Do you want to come with us?"

"Of course he does," Eden answered for him. She hugged David again and he couldn't believe the emotion that exploded inside his body. He hadn't felt anything like it for years. He didn't think it was still possible. He suddenly wanted to paint, to throw violent swirls of red and purple on the page, to trap the feelings where they wouldn't overtake him.

"Do you live in Portland?" David asked, still confused a bit as to how she had managed to find him. This was happiness, right, these feelings inside him? He'd been numb for so long, he couldn't know for sure.

"No, we both live in Seattle, Dad." She looked at Jack. "Can you carry his things, baby?" she asked him. *Baby.* Oh, his daughter loved this man, too. There was a tenderness in her voice David recognized as the same Lydia had once had in her own for him.

Jack looked at David. "Is that okay, David?"

"Is what okay?" David took a step back. "What do you want to do to me?"

Jack's expression softened. "I'd just like to pack up your things for you. We'd like to take you to the hotel where we're staying." Jack looked at Eden. "And we'll figure out what we're going to do in the morning?"

"Yes," Eden said in agreement. "We'll get a good night's sleep and talk in the morning." She looked at David. "Okay, Dad?"

"Sure," David said, unsure of exactly what it was they had to talk about. But his daughter wanted him to come, so he would go. He didn't see any other choice he could make. He watched Jack carefully fold up the easel and stool while Eden held on to the sketch pad. She chattered on about how long she'd been looking, and all this time, he'd been so close. David's mind spun, trying to wrap itself around the moment. He was going to the hotel with his daughter and her boyfriend. That was as much as he could grasp.

"Will they let me in the hotel?" he asked when they climbed into a car and started driving toward downtown. He hadn't showered in a few days. Money hadn't been great.

"Of course they will," Eden said. She sat next to David in the backseat. "You're my guest, and you're spending the night. We'll get a roll-away bed. Or another room. I'll pay for another room if they have one near ours, okay?"

"Okay." David stared out the window, not saying much until they got to the hotel.

After he parked, Jack turned around and smiled at him. "Let me go check for another room, okay, David?"

"Sure," David said. He already liked this man, the one who loved Eden. His daughter had chosen well. Jack got out of the car and Eden squeezed David's hand.

"I just can't believe you're here," she said. "I've been looking for so long."

"I tried to get in touch with you," David said.

Eden's face fell. "I know. I'm so sorry, Dad. The first time, when it all first happened, when you left? I didn't know. I didn't know about the letters. Mom sent them back to you, not me."

"She did?" David's head buzzed. Anger suddenly pulsed through his veins; he felt his face turn red. *That bitch. It was her fault all along.*

No, David told himself. *Not now. We can't do this now.*

"She thought it was the right thing to do at the time," Eden told him. "I just found out about them barely a month ago."

"Oh." His blood still wouldn't settle in his flesh; it churned until David wanted to scream. He didn't want to be in this car. He wanted to go back to the train station.

"I got the other two, the ones you sent me about ten years ago?" Eden said, interrupting his thoughts of escape. "But I was so angry, thinking you just left without a word to me, I didn't answer them." She looked at him with tears in her eyes. "I'm so sorry, Daddy. If I had known, it might not have been this way for you. We might have kept in touch and you wouldn't have ended up like this."

"Like what?" David said, instantly set on the defensive. Eden appeared too wrapped up in her excitement to notice.

"Living on the streets," Eden said. "I could have helped more. Been a support to you."

"Huh." David took a couple of deep breaths. "After what I did? What you saw? You still would have supported me?"

"I'd like to think so," she said. "Oh look, there's Jack." She opened the door and jumped out of the car. "Did you get a room?" she called out.

Jack nodded and gave the thumbs-up sign. David slowly climbed out of the car, not sure where he was headed or how long he'd stay.

It didn't take long to get my father settled in a room down the hall from ours. It was just past midnight when I hugged him again and told him I'd see him in the morning.

"You'll be okay?" I asked him.

He gave me a minute smile and nodded. "I'll be fine, Eden. Thank you for the room."

"Okay. I'm just down the hall if you need me. Number 242."

"Good night," he said, moving to close the door.

"Good night, Daddy." I choked on the words, so thrilled after all this time to be able to say them. After he shut the door, part of me wanted to push it right back open, curl up in bed with him, and stay up for hours, telling him every detail of my life from the moment he was taken away in the ambulance twenty years before. I said as much to Jack when we got back to our own room.

"He might be overwhelmed by all of this," Jack said gently. "You might want to take it slow."

"He was happy to see me, though, wasn't he?" I asked.

"Yes," Jack said as he pulled off his shirt and jeans. "But he was quiet, too. I could almost hear the gears turning in his head, trying to take the situation in. He might not be comfortable with full disclosure yet—his or yours."

I sighed and plopped down on the bed, still fully dressed. "Should we tell Georgia and Bryce we found him?"

"Maybe shoot them each a text, so they'll be prepared for it in the morning?"

"Good idea." I grabbed my cell and punched in a quick message to them, knowing they both usually turned their phones off at night. Jack was already in bed when I brushed my teeth and washed off my makeup. I climbed in beside him and curled up against his warm body, resting my cheek against his chest.

"Think you're going to sleep?" he asked.

"It's doubtful." I craned my neck up to smile at him. "Thank you for helping me find him. I'm so excited I can barely stand it."

"Do you have any idea what you want to do next?"

"Bring him home with us."

"What then?"

"I don't know. I'll have him stay with me for a while until I can figure it out. I'll need to find him a doctor and a place to live. A job, too, so he can support himself." I wasn't sure what he'd be capable of doing. Washing dishes at my work, maybe? I could make sure he worked the same hours as I did. I could keep an eye on him.

"Eden," Jack said, "try not to get ahead of yourself with all of this. You don't know what your dad wants to do."

"He'll want to be with me," I said, a little bit annoyed Jack would suggest otherwise.

"You don't know that for sure. Not yet." He shifted upward so his back was resting against the padded headboard. "It's probably not a good idea to steamroll into his life and take it over. He might end up resenting you for it."

"He'll resent me if I find him and then just take off again." I rolled over onto my back and looked at him. "I'm not going to abandon him, Jack. I know all too well how that feels."

Jack reached over and smoothed back the hair from my face. "I know you do. And I'm not trying to bring you down or say you should leave him here. I just want to make sure we take his wants into consideration, too."

"I will," I said. "Of course I will."

"Are you okay? Not freaking out too much?"

"I'm fine," I said, but I could feel the adrenaline shooting through my veins like lit sparklers.

"C'mere," Jack said, and I crawled over to wrap myself around him again. He reached over and snapped off the light, but even in the comfort of his arms, I could not find sleep.

After several hours of tossing and turning, at five o'clock, I finally gave up the fight and got out of bed to shower. I was pulling on my clothes when Jack awoke and smiled at me sleepily. "You get any rest?" he asked.

"Not really," I admitted. "I think I dozed in and out, mostly." I could still feel the excitement in my blood; my body felt like it was bubbling with energy and my skin was itchy with anticipation to see my father again.

"You going to check on your dad?"

I nodded, walked over to kiss him, and left the room. Neither Georgia nor Bryce had texted me back, so I assumed they both were still sleeping. I walked down the hall and knocked softly on my father's door. When he didn't answer right away, a deep panic began to pound in my belly. What if he'd left? What if he couldn't take it and he just walked out the door in the middle of the night? What if all of this was for nothing?

My panic calmed a few seconds later when he opened the door. "Hi, Bug," he said. He had showered and shaved his beard.

He wore jeans but no shirt, and I tried to conceal my shock at the sharp angles of his bones beneath his skin. His shoulder joints looked like doorknobs sticking out at the top of his fleshless arms.

"Hi, Dad," I said. "Can I come in?"

"Of course," he said, opening the door so I could pass through. I went over to sit on the chair by the dresser.

"Did you sleep okay?" I asked. He sat on the bed, and his posture was rigid; his fingers gripped the edge of the mattress until they turned white.

"A little. Not much."

"Me neither," I said, smiling. "I was too excited."

He gave a tight nod, pressing his lips into a thin line.

"Are you okay with all of this, Dad?"

His eyes flashed a slightly wild look. "What do you mean?"

"Nothing, really. You just seem so quiet. I know it's a lot to take in at once." I paused. "Do you want to hear about how I found you?"

"I do," he said, settling down on the edge of the bed; it looked like the covers hadn't even been pulled back.

"Should we order some breakfast first? I can call room service."

"No, I'm not really a breakfast person."

"Oh," I said, for the first time feeling a little uncomfortable. A little scared, even. What did I know about my father, really? Twenty years had changed him physically, for sure, but how much had changed with his illness? Had his violence worsened? His depression? He told Matt he'd be back to Common Ground, which I interpreted as his saying he wanted to get well. Was it possible that he just couldn't? I didn't want to believe that. I wanted to believe that with the right kind of love and support from me, he could find his way back to a better life.

"So, why did you start looking for me?" my father asked. He looked at me with wide, anxious eyes and I realized he was feeling just as uncomfortable with me as I was with him. Jack was right. I would need to take this slow.

So that's what I did. Over the next two hours, I told him how my search had begun with mom's illness, then proceeded to all the Internet searches and phone calls I'd made. I told him about the man I saw in the morgue and how I'd started volunteering at Hope House. I told him again how I found the letters Mom hadn't shown me, how as a way to apologize, Mom reached out and found the one clue that led me to Common Ground, which ultimately led me to him.

He interrupted me every so often, using a stilted, uncomfortable tone, asking for clarification. He had a hard time making eye contact, but I told myself that was a temporary state. This was all too new to expect him to be comfortable. For the most part, he was very quiet, picking at a loose thread on the paisley bedspread.

"Do you want to come back to Seattle with me, Dad?" I asked. I held my breath waiting for his response.

"And do what?" he finally said.

I looked down at my hands to see that they were shaking. I clutched them together to ease my nerves. "I'm not sure, exactly," I said. "I'd like to help get you settled. I want to spend time with you."

He seemed surprised. "You do?"

I went over to sit by him and grabbed his hand. "Of course I do. I've missed you all my life." My throat closed up and I tried to choke back tears. They fell anyway. "I need my father. I can't let you get away from me again."

*   *   *

A little while later, I introduced my father to Bryce and Georgia in the lobby of the hotel. Dad kept his eyes glued to the shiny marble floor and clutched his easel and the worn brown leather backpack that contained all his worldly possessions.

"It's good to meet you," Georgia said warmly. Her auburn tresses hung in perfect ringlets around her face and her expression was open and sweet.

"Mr. West," Bryce said, extending his hand. "We're glad you're okay." Knowing how John felt about my search, my brother's show of respect meant the world to me.

"Hello," Dad said. His gaze was still stuck to the floor and he didn't reach out to shake Bryce's hand. My brother smiled at me and winked. Jack smiled at me, too, then gently took Dad's elbow and led him toward the parking garage. Bryce walked with them, but Georgia grabbed my hand and held me back. Her thin eyebrows were pulled together and she frowned.

"Are you doing okay? Not freaking out?"

"Why does everyone think I might be freaking out?" I sighed as I pulled my hand away from her, crossing my arms over my chest.

"It's a big deal finding him, Eden. Before you got down here, Jack told us that last night you said you were going to give up the search if you didn't find him in Portland. So now suddenly here he is right when you were about ready to be done with the idea. Kind of an emotional about-face, don't you think?"

"I guess," I said. I wanted less hesitance from the people I cared about and more excitement. "Well, rest assured I'm fine. He's a little overwhelmed, I think, but I'm taking it slow and giving him some space."

"You call moving him to another city and into your house 'slow'?" She gave me a doubting look.

"Georgia. I don't need this right now." My blood pressure started to rise. Why did everyone insist on questioning me on my decisions? I was a grown woman. I'd deal with the consequences, whatever they ended up being. "I need you to support me, okay? That's what I need."

"I do support you. I just care about you and don't want either of you to get hurt."

"I'm not planning on it."

"It's not something you can control. What if he freaks out on you? What if he loses it and ends up slitting his wrists again?"

"Georgia!" I'd had enough. "That's not going to happen. I'll talk with you later, okay? I appreciate your concern, I really do. Just let me do this my way. My dad and I will figure it out together."

Georgia and Bryce offered to rent a car and drive back to Seattle on their own, so as not to put my dad in a car with more people than he could manage, so five hours later, Jack pulled up in front of my house to drop my father and me off. The ride home was fairly quiet; I sat up front with Jack in order to not pressure my dad into talking the whole time. He had agreed to come back with us but was still subdued. I didn't want to make too quick a movement and throw him completely off balance. My plan was to get him in to a doctor as soon as possible and get him back on his meds. We'd figure everything else out as we went.

Jack helped us get my father's things into my house. I realized I'd need to get Jasper at some point, but I didn't want to stop by my mom and John's house with Dad in the car. I figured the reunion between my mom and dad would have to be something they both were ready to handle. His first day back was definitely not the day to do it.

"Want me to go get Jasper for you?" Jack asked as we were getting the last of my bags out of the car.

I smiled at him. "You reading my mind or something? I was just trying to figure out how I was going to manage that."

He hugged me. "I'll get him for you. Do you want me to break the news to your mom, too, or do you want to do it?"

"Wow. I hadn't thought about that." My brain still buzzed with excitement at having found him at all. Practicalities and specifics about how I should navigate his return with me were far from my mind. I glanced over at my dad, who was standing on the sidewalk, staring at my house. "Would you mind telling her?"

"I wouldn't have offered if I did." He kissed me, then shook hands with my dad.

"Mr. West? I'm going to pick up Eden's dog for her. It was a pleasure meeting you, and I'll see you in a little bit, okay?"

My father looked at Jack with a slightly dazed expression. "Yes, good. Okay. Nice to meet you too, son. And call me David, please. Only doctors call me Mr. West."

"All right, then, David. I'll be back in an hour or two. That should give you time to get settled in." He came over to kiss me again, then climbed into his car and drove off.

I led Dad inside and showed him the spare room. The bed was still littered with the contents of the box we'd found at his old apartment and his paintings still rested against the wall. His eyes went straight to them—his depiction of the Garden of Eden was on top.

I maneuvered around him and cleared his belongings off the bedspread and back into the box. "These are yours, Dad, from your old apartment building. Wanda gave them to us a few weeks ago." He was silent, so I went over and rubbed his arm. "Everything okay?" I asked.

He nodded, his eyes still glued to the painting. "That's mine."

"I know. That garden was such a great thing we did together. I've always remembered it. When I saw it was important to you too, even after all those years apart, I was pretty overwhelmed. It's a beautiful painting."

"It was a beautiful garden," he said. I told him about the one Jack planted behind the shelter. "I'd like to see that," he said.

"In the spring, you will." I smiled. "Are you hungry? Can I make you something to eat?" We hadn't stopped on the drive home; I was too anxious to get him in my house.

"More tired than hungry. I'd like to lie down."

"Of course," I said. "I'll leave you alone. The bathroom's just down the hall on your left." I reached over and hugged him. His body was stiff, unyielding. I tried not to let that upset me. "I'm happy you're here."

He kissed the top of my head but didn't say anything.

"Just holler if you need me, okay?"

He nodded and I left him alone. I walked into my living room and dropped to the couch, trying to absorb the fact that my father was actually in the other room. I still couldn't quite believe it. I needed to get on the phone and try to find a doctor.

My cell rang just as I was digging around for it in my purse. It was Rita.

"Hey there," I said. "How are you?"

"Not as good as you, it seems."

"Jack called you, I take it?"

"Yep, this morning, before you guys left Portland. He asked me to get the name of a few doctors who might be able to get your dad in tomorrow. You got a pen or do you want me to e-mail you?"

I smiled, knowing Jack didn't completely agree with what I was doing with my dad, but that hadn't kept him from using his resources to do what he could to help. "E-mail would be great, actually."

"You got it," Rita said. "You doing okay?"

"It does feel a little surreal, but overall, I'm just really happy. I finally get a chance to get to know him."

"And how is he doing?"

"He's resting right now. I need to call work and take some time off, I think, to deal with all of this." I cringed a little, thinking about what corporate's reaction might be when I told them their head chef needed to take a week off during the holiday rush, but I was sure Juan was more than capable of handling the kitchen on his own.

"Probably a good idea. We missed you guys for dinner here last night. After my lame meal of hot dogs and potato chips, the troops were asking for you."

"They were? That's great to hear." I paused, anxious about the phone calls I needed to make. "Hey, Rita, I hate to cut this short, but I need to make some calls."

"No problem, *chica*. See you soon."

After hanging up, I took a couple of deep breaths to calm down before calling Doug in the Emerald City Events corporate office to ask for the next week off. After I explained that the spreadsheets for all the scheduled events had been done and all Juan would have to do is make sure the kitchen staff followed them to the letter, Doug okayed the vacation. I called Juan and filled him in on the past days' events and thanked him profusely for running the kitchen in my absence.

"No worries, boss lady," he said. "I got it handled. You just spend some time with your poppa and get him all set up."

"Thanks, Juan. I'll have my cell, if anything comes up you need my help with."

As I hung up, Jack knocked on the front door. I opened it, and Jasper came bounding inside, his whole body wiggling in his excitement at seeing me. Jack shut the door behind him while I sat down on the floor to let Jasper love me up.

"I think that dog just French-kissed you," he said.

I smiled, scratching Jasper's chest and letting him continue to lick my face. "He missed me."

"I missed you, too," Jack said. "Do I get to French-kiss you, too?"

I jumped up and wiped my mouth with my sleeve. "Now?"

He held up his hands in mock surrender, smiling at me. "Um, maybe after you brush your teeth?"

I laughed. "So much for unconditional love."

He dropped to the couch and patted the cushion next to him. "Where's your dad?"

"Sleeping, I think. Unless you noisy boys woke him up when you came in." I sat down and leaned on him, and he put his arm around my shoulders. "I talked to Rita. Thank you for having her get those numbers."

"Did you have a chance to call any of the doctors?"

I shook my head. "Not yet. I had to call in to work to get some time off."

"How much did they give you?"

"Just a week, but I should be able to get him settled somewhere by then, don't you think?"

"I don't know," he said. "Does he want to be settled?"

"Jack. Please don't." I pulled away from him and gave him a hard look. "I will talk with him about what he wants to do, okay? You've made your point. I get it. I need to take his wants into consideration. I promise, I will. So lay off it. Please."

"I didn't mean to push."

"Well, you are. I need you to be my boyfriend, not his social worker, okay? That's what I need."

"Okay." He pulled me back to him. "Sorry. I'm out of practice at this whole relationship thing. I do what I know best."

"You're bossy?"

He laughed. "No. I advocate. There's a difference. But your dad hasn't asked me to advocate for him, either, so I'll shut up about it. For now."

"Deal." I was tired and didn't want to argue anymore. "Are you working tonight?"

"Yeah, I need to get going pretty quick. Rita's only staying until eight."

"Oh!" I said, suddenly remembering where he had picked Jasper up from. "How did it go with my mom? Did you tell her that we found him?"

He nodded. "I did. She took it pretty well, I think. But she was definitely shocked. I don't think any of us thought we'd actually find him. She said you should call her tomorrow. I think she's worried about you, too."

"There's nothing to be worried about," I said adamantly. "Everything's going to work out just fine."

The voices chanted in David's head. *Leave now, leave now.* He wasn't drinking to quiet them. Not much, anyway. Eden only kept wine in her house and he couldn't have too much of it without her noticing.

He listened for her to get into the shower, then snuck down the hall into the kitchen. Eden kept her wine on the counter, so David pulled the cork on the bottle and took a few long, hard swallows, waiting for his mind to calm. It was only enough to take the slightest edge off of how he felt. Eden was taking him to the doctor this morning and David wasn't sure he was going to survive this reunion. Trying to white-knuckle his way through had never worked before and he doubted it would work now.

"Are you ready to go, Dad?" Eden called out from the bathroom, and David hastily took another swig of wine, then shoved the cork back into the bottle's open mouth. He needed to tell her. He couldn't stay. He needed to get back out in the world where he belonged.

"Just need my shoes," David said instead. He heard Eden's footsteps in the hallway and when she entered the kitchen, the hopeful look on Eden's face was too much to disappoint. She wanted to help him so much. Couldn't he at least try for her sake, after all she'd done to track him down?

So there he was an hour later, with his daughter, at the doctor's office. They sat in the waiting room, Eden flipping through a magazine, David staring at the pattern in the wallpaper. His right leg bounced up and down in rapid rhythm until Eden reached over and touched it.

"You okay, Dad?" she asked.

He gave a brisk nod and tensed his muscles to keep them still. When the nurse called his name, both of them stood.

"Just Mr. West, please," the nurse said. "The doctor will call you in after a while."

Eden looked shocked but quickly recovered. "Oh. Well. Of course." She sat back down. "I'll see you in a few minutes, Dad."

"Okay," David said, and followed the nurse back to a small exam room with a growing sense of dread in his belly. She took his temperature and blood pressure, then told him the doctor would be right in. She closed the door behind her and David imagined the cell doors in the mental ward. White, heavy, and impenetrable. He would never escape.

David sat on the exam table. His skin crawled being inside the familiar medical surroundings. He didn't want to be here. He shouldn't be here. He was doing this for all the wrong reasons. How could he say this to his daughter? How could he possibly make her understand? His thoughts spun around and around in his head. *Tell her you can't do this,* he thought. *Tell her the truth and be gone. Go back to where you're happy. Go back to where you can be yourself.* But who was that? He didn't know for sure. He did know that the moment the doctor told him he needed to be on meds, he might very well scream.

"David?" A soft female voice spoke his name as the door to the exam room he was in opened.

He cleared his throat. "Yes." *Keep it simple. Don't say too much. Be normal and maybe she won't want to drug you up too much.*

A petite woman with short black hair stepped into the room, shutting the door behind her. "I'm Dr. Shaw. It's nice to meet you."

David nodded. "Nice to meet you, too." He eyed the thick folder she held in the crook of her arm. Damn. She had obviously already gotten her hands on his medical history. How do these doctors do it so fast? His entire life summed up by other peoples' opinions. People who didn't know him. People who didn't live with a brain like his in their heads. Who were they to tell him what he should do? Was it Eden who gave the doctor his file? Or Lydia? He wondered if his ex-wife would want to see him. He wasn't sure if he wanted to see her, even if she did.

Dr. Shaw set the folder down and sat in the chair across from David. "Can we talk for a minute before I speak with your daughter?"

David gave a short, fast nod. He didn't trust this woman.

"Great." Dr. Shaw smiled tightly. "So, I've had a look at your file and it appears that you've never had a diagnosis that sticks. Is that true?"

"Yes, that's true." David kept his answers short. He wanted to appear balanced despite the voices raging at him to bolt out of the room. He gritted his teeth to keep from screaming until they squeaked inside his head.

"Well, without an official diagnosis, we'd have to start you on a low-dose regimen of lithium, the amount you were on most recently, just to get you in balance. If we don't get results with that, there are several other families of drugs we could play with until we find one that works." She gave him a sharp look down her nose. "But you'd have to promise me you're going to stay on them long enough to see which ones are going to work. Your file indicates you've had a lot of trouble around this before."

David swallowed the knot in his throat before speaking. "It's different this time."

"Different how?" the doctor asked.

"I'm not doing it for me. I'm doing it for my daughter." That, at least, was an honest answer.

"I'd prefer you were doing it for yourself."

Damn, David thought. *Wrong answer.* He tried again. "I guess I meant I'm doing it for both of us. To give us a chance. She told you we've been apart twenty years?"

"Yes, she did. The last time you saw her you were bleeding out from a suicide attempt." She looked at him pointedly.

David didn't answer. *Sanctimonious bitch.*

Dr. Shaw looked skeptical but stood up and proceeded with the physical exam. She pushed and prodded, listened to his heart and lungs. "You're malnourished," she said when she was done. "We'll get you on protein supplements and vitamins. I'll want to get some blood work done, too. Your liver's a little distended. You're a drinker, yes?"

David nodded. How did doctors always know this? From his file? He wished he could rip it from her hands and tear it to shreds. He flashed briefly on the idea of tearing *her* to shreds, but thankfully, the thought flew out of his brain as quickly as it had flown in.

"Having any withdrawal?"

"Not much. I've had some wine." *Not enough. Not nearly enough.* Eden would have to go back to work eventually, right? He'd be able to find some cash and get a bottle.

"I'm going to give you a prescription for an anti-seizure med called Neurontin. It was originally used for epileptic patients, but it works well for alcoholics as they detox, too. Don't drink. Have your daughter get you to AA if you have to. I'm putting you on ten milligrams of lithium, twice a day to start. Okay?"

"Okay." David knew it was pointless to discuss anything further. The doctor had already decided how she was going to treat him after reading his chart. She hadn't even waited to meet him. That's what they all did. Not one of them said, "David, do you *want* to be on lithium? Do you *want* to stop drinking?" They all assumed that he would. His daughter assumed the same thing. She was like Lydia that way. Determined to rescue him when he wasn't sure if he didn't just prefer to drown.

Saturday morning, the third day my father was in my house, I woke to the sound of Jasper growling. "What is it?" I asked sleepily, reaching over to pat his warm head. Jack had worked the night shift at the shelter, so it was just my father and me. Jasper growled again, despite my touch. It was early, still dark outside, so I propped myself up and flipped on the lamp by my bed.

"Sorry," my father's voice said, to my surprise, and my hand flew to my chest. I looked up and saw him standing in the doorway, staring at me.

"Holy shit, Dad," I said, breathing fast. "You scared me." I patted Jasper, who apparently still wasn't used to my father's presence. Jasper finally quieted. "What're you doing? Is everything okay?" It struck me just how much I felt like a parent in that moment, how my mother used to grill my dad with the exact same questions.

He nodded. "I didn't mean to scare you."

"It's okay." I sat up and smiled. "Come on in. What time is it?"

"I don't know. Early, I guess." He paused before taking a few steps over and sitting on the edge of my bed. "I was watching you sleep."

I cocked my head and pulled up a corner of my mouth. "You were¿ Why¿"

He shrugged. "I'm not sure. I used to do it all the time when you were little. It calmed me when I got wound the wrong way." His face was still so gaunt. Dark circles bruised the spaces beneath his eyes. I wondered if he was getting any sleep at all.

I reached over and put my hand on his arm. "Are you feeling like that now¿ Hasn't the medicine kicked in yet¿"

He shook his head. "I don't feel it. I've been on it so many times, I think I've built up a resistance. It takes time to start working, anyway."

"You've been taking it, though, right¿" I hated to ask the question, but I had to. Even after twenty years, I feared his patterns hadn't changed. The fact that I had slipped into my mother's old role of policing his behaviors felt wrong somehow, knowing how much he hated it. He shot me a glowering look, one I recalled well from my childhood. It was the exact same look he used to give to my mother. *Back off,* it said. *Stop treating me like a child.*

This was not how I had envisioned our reunion would go. We'd spent the last two days in my house together edging around each other carefully. He was in his room a lot and not eating much. I was cooking like crazy to keep myself busy. Was I wrong about all of this¿ Had he even wanted to be found¿

"Well," I said pointedly, ignoring my discomfort and unwilling to give up on him, "then maybe we need to ask the doctor for something stronger."

"I hate taking anything stronger. You remember that, right¿ You remember how miserable the medication makes me¿" He gritted his teeth; I saw the muscle along his jaw twitch.

"I do," I said, a tight feeling in my chest making it difficult to breathe. "But it's the only thing that works, Dad. At least, that we know of."

"I've managed pretty well on my own." He spoke quietly, in almost a whisper.

"You drink. That's not an effective way to manage a mood disorder." Dr. Shaw had advised me to be direct with my father and not enable his rationalizations about his condition, the same advice other doctors had given my mother for years.

"It's the way I've managed mine." He stared at the floor. His hands were folded in his lap, clasped together so tight his knuckles turned white. "It keeps the voices quiet."

Voices? The doctor hadn't mentioned anything in his file about my father hearing voices. Wasn't that a sign of schizophrenia? I decided it was better to not ask for clarification on this point. "You've managed it so well you ended up in the psych ward again three years ago," I said instead. "It'll get better soon, Dad. I promise. We'll get your meds sorted out and get you a job—"

"A job?" he said, interrupting. "I have a job."

I must have looked confused because he went on to explain without my asking for clarification.

"I sketch people. It's a good job."

"Of course it is, Dad, but you can't really make a living at it."

"I've made a living at it for twenty years. It's kept me alive, hasn't it?"

I nodded. "Yes, but I was thinking you could maybe wash dishes at my work. You could work the same hours I do so we'd get to spend a lot of time together. Eventually, you could even get your own place again. Maybe Wanda would have an open apartment. I'm sure she'd love to see you."

He didn't respond. His right foot tapped a staccato rhythm on the floor, causing my bed to shake.

"Dad?" I said. "Are you okay?" I had asked him this so many times in the past three days, I was tired of saying the words. I knew he must be tired of hearing them, too.

"I don't know," he said. "I think I'll go take a walk."

I swung my legs off the side of the bed. "I'll go with you. Just give me a minute to get dressed."

"I'd like to be alone, Eden." He looked at me with a blank expression. I couldn't tell what was going on inside his head. The little girl in me cried out, *Daddy, don't leave.*

"Oh." I paused, not wanting to tell him I didn't trust him. I wanted to trust him. I had to. I couldn't keep him locked up in my house. "Are you sure? I need to take Jasper, anyway."

"Let me take him," said my father. "He needs to get to know me better so he won't growl so much."

I hesitated, and my dad saw it.

"I can take the dog for a walk, Eden. I've managed to survive twenty years on my own. I think I can handle thirty minutes with your pet."

My stomach knotted at the anger in his words. I suddenly felt ten years old again, afraid of what might happen if I told my father no. "His leash is by the back door," I said, my voice subdued. My father stood up and snapped his fingers, and surprisingly, Jasper followed him out of the room, his ears perked after hearing my father say the magic word, "walk."

I curled back up in my bed, trying to wish away the sinking feeling in my stomach. Would he come back? Would I see him again? Maybe he'd take off and I'd never see my father or my dog again. Then what would I do?

I glanced at the clock. My father had been gone about twenty minutes. I wondered if he'd gotten lost. I leapt out of bed, trying not to worry. I'd shower, make some coffee and breakfast for us when he got back. And he *would* come back. I couldn't let myself believe anything else.

From the moment Dad returned with Jasper from their walk, I took care not to bring up the issue of his getting a job. Over the next couple of days, we continued to spend most of our time in the house, me cooking and him either sleeping or watching TV. I offered to go buy him some art supplies so he could have something to work on, but he refused.

"I'm not feeling very inspired right now," he said. "It's the meds." He was slouched on the couch, staring out the window into the wet, dark night while I stood in the kitchen, stirring a pot of chicken paprikash. Jack was due to come over for dinner with us any minute.

"Oh," I said. "Well, hopefully that will get better as your body adjusts. You did some amazing work at Common Ground. I saw the painting of me they keep above the fireplace. I loved it."

"I did that one when I went off my meds," he said flatly, turning to look at me. "That's the reason I can't stay there, Eden. I can't be creative when I'm weighed down like this. I lose my muse completely."

That's not all you lose, I wanted to say. "Maybe you just haven't found the right combination yet," I suggested instead. "Or the right dosage. Mom always said the problem was you didn't stay on anything long enough to figure what would work." I wanted to remain positive, to focus on the solutions rather than the problem.

He didn't want to let me. "That's right," he spat angrily. "*That* was the problem. Not that she tried to shove the pills down my throat when I didn't want to take them."

My eyes filled at his outburst. I spun around toward the stove, busying myself by stirring the homemade dumplings I'd just coated in butter a few moments before. Why was this happening? We were right back where we were twenty years ago, only now I was a grown woman who could stand up to him. And here I was, playing my mother's part, watching him like a hawk, trying to force him into doing the right things. And it wasn't making any difference. He was still fighting against taking his meds. He still didn't love me enough to want to stay well.

There was a quick knock at the door and Jack appeared. "Hey there," he said, shutting the door behind him. "It's raining like crazy out there. I wouldn't be surprised if we see an ark floating across Green Lake in the morning." He shrugged off his jacket and hung it on the coat tree by the door. "Hi, David. How're you doing tonight?"

My father stood erect and stared at Jack. His blue eyes were lit with anger. "Trying to convince my daughter I'm not a problem that needs to be solved. Or medicated."

Jack swung his gaze over to me and I shook my head slightly, to say, *Don't push the issue.* He seemed to sense the tension in the air between us. "Of course you're not," Jack said. "This is a difficult situation for both of you. But the good news is, the both of you want the same thing."

"And what is that?" my father demanded. I'd forgotten how imposing he could look when he was angry. I felt about three feet tall. I was glad Jack was there.

"You each want to make the other person happy. It's a place to start, right? Having the same goal? You just need to figure out the best way to make that happen without stepping on each other's toes. Which could take some time." He took a step toward my dad and offered his hand. "It's good to see you, David. Will you sit down and eat dinner with us?"

My father threw his eyes to me, then to Jack, then back to me.

"Yes, Dad," I said. "Please. I'm sorry if it seems like I'm pushing you. I don't mean to. I'm really just trying to figure this out as I go."

"There's nothing to figure out!" he bellowed. "I'm not a puzzle. I'm not something that's broken you need to patch back together! I'm just me, Eden. I'm who I was twenty years ago. I figured myself out back then. I figured out I was happier not being married to your mother, not trying to fit myself into the mold of what she needed me to be."

"Did it make you happy to not be my father anymore, either?" I asked, chucking the spoon I held into the sink, where it clattered against a water glass. I looked at him defiantly. "Is that why *you* didn't try harder to find *me*?"

My father looked at me like I'd stabbed him. "I'm going to lie down." He pushed past Jack and strode toward the bedroom where he'd been staying.

Jack looked at me helplessly, as if he were saying, *I did what I could.* I sighed.

"Daddy, I'm sorry!" I called out as he moved down the hall. "Please. Will you come eat with us?"

The bedroom door slamming was his answer. I turned back toward the stove and grabbed the edge of the counter to hold myself up. I was shaking. This is not how this evening was supposed to go.

"Let him calm down," Jack said. "He'll be okay. He just needs a minute to himself." He came up behind me, wrapped his arms around my waist, and kissed the side of my neck.

I started crying when his lips touched me. I tried to wipe away the tears as fast as they fell. "Did I make a mistake, Jack? Maybe I shouldn't have brought him here?"

"I don't know, Eden. I really don't."

"He's not doing well," I said, sniffing. "I thought he'd do better than this. I thought he'd be happy to get to stay with me." I turned around inside Jack's embrace and looked at him. "Tell me the truth. I want to know what you really think. Don't give me the bullshit boyfriend answer. I want to know what you, Jack Baker, think of my decision to bring him home with me."

Jack sighed and leaned forward to rest his forehead against mine. "Are you sure? You might not like it."

"I'm sure." With that intro, I could pretty much guarantee I wouldn't like whatever he wanted to say. But I'd already asked.

He pulled his head back from mine and stared at me. "I think you meant well, Eden. I really do. I just don't think you thought it all through hard enough. Neither of us really expected to find him when we went to Portland. I certainly didn't. I was actually pretty happy when I heard you say you'd be done with any kind of aggressive search for him if he wasn't at the train station. I thought we had a chance of being something pretty amazing together."

I swallowed and pushed him off me, looking at him in disbelief. "And suddenly we don't?"

"I didn't say that. But I do see you getting sucked into this thing with your dad and I can't compete with that. You can't save him, Eden. He doesn't want to be saved."

"So you're telling me to give up? You think I should just say, 'Good luck on the streets, Dad. Drop by and see me sometime'?" I didn't want to hear this. I wanted him to believe I could make a difference in my father's life.

Jack threw his hands up in the air in a frustrated, helpless gesture. "I'm not saying give up, I'm just saying you could change how you're looking at this. Open your mind to the possibility that your father's choice to live outside the lines of society is fine for him. It might not suit you or me or the majority of other people, but it suits *him*. And at the end of the day, that's what matters. He's not a thief. He's not dealing drugs or hurting anyone. He's a mentally unstable man who has found a way to cope with his condition."

"But it's not coping if it's harmful to him. The doctor said his liver is practically shot from all the alcohol."

"It's *his* liver, Eden. His body, his choice, and his life. You asked me what I think, and that's it. I think you need to back off. Stop shoving your idea of who he should be down his throat. Get to know him for who he actually *is*. You don't ask our Hope House clients to be anyone other than exactly who they are. You bear witness to their lives and validate their existence without telling them they're toxic and broken the way the rest of society does. Why can't you do that for your own father?"

I shook my head. He didn't understand. "He's too sick to be able to make rational choices. I think the only thing I can do now is have him committed." I whispered these words to make sure my father didn't hear them. "He needs time to get his meds straight. Maybe a year or more. He's never been institutionalized long enough to get on the right track. They always let him go too early. I've been doing some reading online and I could have him put on a twelve-month mental health hold. His history of hospitalization is more than enough to make it happen."

"That's a stupid idea, Eden."

"Stupid?" I fumed. "Are you kidding me? Did you just tell me I'm stupid?"

"No, I said the idea was stupid. You're fooling yourself if you think locking him up is going to be some kind of magical fix. It'll make him worse. And on top of that, he'll hate you for it."

"I didn't say it'd be a magical fix. I just think it's the only way. I can't quit my job to be with him 24/7 and he needs to be supervised to make sure he does what he's supposed to."

"And who made you God to decide what he's supposed to do?" Jack raked both sets of fingers through his dark hair. "Jesus, you sound like my father."

I staggered back a step. I knew how much Jack despised his father's attempts to control his life, but that he would lump me in the same category for only trying to help my father was unfathomable.

"I think you should leave," I said coldly. "Now." My chest ached with the thought of never seeing him again. But if he wasn't supportive of me, what was the point of being with him? He was just like the rest of the men I'd dated. And now I was through.

Jack stared at me without speaking for a minute, pushing breath after breath out of his nose. "Are you sure about that? You're going to throw away what we have over this?"

"You're the one throwing it away, Jack. Not me."

"*You* asked for my opinion. *You* said you could handle it. So I tell you and you lose it." He shook his head. "You need to grow up, Eden." He turned around, strode toward the door, and grabbed his coat off the rack. "Give me a call when you do."

I jumped when the door slammed behind him. Jasper, who was sleeping by the fireplace during our entire exchange, barked at the noise. I slumped into a dining room chair, my forehead pressed against the palms of my hands. I couldn't believe what had just happened. I felt numb. I wanted to take it back. I wanted to run after him and tell him he was right and I was wrong and ask him if he'd ever be able to forgive me. I wanted to, but I couldn't.

I heard the door to my father's bedroom open; he crept down the hall. "Where's Jack?" he asked, standing in the entryway to the living room.

I rolled my head to look at him. "He's gone," I said, unable to find the courage to speak the reason why.

I didn't sleep that night. I tossed and turned in my bed, plagued by the image of the disappointment on Jack's face before he walked out the door. There was no doubt now that I was the reason for all my relationships ending. I'd lost the man who so obviously loved me, who loved me enough to be honest with me when I asked him to be. Was I testing him by pushing him away? I didn't know. I did know I was wrong, but I didn't know how to admit it.

Jasper whimpered at my side, his own slumber interrupted by my constant movements. It was early still, four A.M., but I heard my father's door open and his footsteps move into the bathroom. We hadn't talked much the night before; I was too upset after Jack left. We ate in silence and then both went to our separate rooms. I thought about calling Georgia and telling her what happened with Jack, but the ache in my chest was too big to find words to describe it. Instead, I climbed beneath the covers and held Jasper to me, crying as softly as I could. I cried because my father didn't love me enough to get well. I cried because I seemed fundamentally incapable of letting a man love me without inevitably pushing him away. I cried because I didn't know how to fix all that was wrong. I thought finding my father would solve all the problems in my life. But as it turned out I was still left with the biggest problem of all. I was still left with me.

The toilet flushed and I turned on my light and got out of bed. Dad stopped when he saw me stick my head out of my doorway.

"You're up?" he asked.

I nodded. "Couldn't sleep."

He gave me a half smile. "Me either."

I grabbed a thick sweatshirt and pulled it over my head. "Want some coffee?"

"I think I'll try to sleep a bit more, if you don't mind."

I stopped in my tracks. "Oh. Okay." Once again, he didn't do as I expected. Why didn't he want to be with me as much as I wanted to be with him? I shut my bedroom door behind me and leaned up against it, trying to hold back the tears.

I suddenly felt a longing for my mother so deep it sank me to the floor. We'd only spoken briefly since I brought my dad to Seattle. After Jack told her we'd found him, she'd called to make sure I was doing all right. I'd told her I was, but that was four days ago, before the doctor appointment and my father's anger and Jack walking out the door. I felt as though I was falling apart. Would she be awake this early? Probably not, but I needed to talk to her. Despite how well I knew the emptiness of the words, I needed my mother to tell me everything was going to be okay. I got back up and grabbed my cell phone, using the voice-activated system to dial her home number. I hoped John didn't answer the phone.

It rang six times before she answered. "Hello?" she said grog-gily. "John?" She must have thought it was her husband calling from the station. I couldn't help but be glad he wasn't lying next to her to hear our conversation.

"Momma, it's me," I said, my voice breaking on the words. "I'm sorry I'm calling so early."

"Eden, honey." Her words were slow and heavy with sleep. "What's wrong?"

"Jack left me," I said, letting the tears flow. "And Dad's so angry. I'm screwing everything up, Mom, and I don't know how to fix it." I dropped to sit on the floor next to my bed and Jasper settled in next to me. "I thought he'd be so happy to see me he'd do everything he needed to stay well. But he doesn't care. He hasn't changed. He's exactly the way he used to be. He doesn't love me."

My mother sighed. "He loves you as best he can, Eden. I know how you feel, baby. I always thought if I just loved him enough, he would want to get well. I thought if I did all the right things, gave him the space he needed to be an artist, then he would take his meds and become the man he was when I met him. But we can't control what another person does, sweetie. Ultimately what kind of life they lead is their choice."

"But Dad's not capable of making those kinds of choices for himself. I think I need to commit him to an institution." Jasper raised his head and gave a low growl; I patted his belly to calm him.

"And when he gets out of the hospital," said my mother, "he'll most likely go back to doing exactly what it is he wants to do." She was quiet for a minute. I heard her breathing low and slow into the receiver before she spoke again. "Eden, I've been down this road with your father a million times. It wasn't until he tried to kill himself that I figured out it wasn't my place to try to turn him into a person he just didn't have the ability to be. It was the most painful realization in my life that he couldn't be my husband or your father. His illness wouldn't let him. It wasn't that he didn't want to. He *couldn't*. As soon as I was able to accept that, I finally gave up the fight. I let him go."

"But I don't *want* to let him go."

"I meant that I had to let go of who I wanted him to be."

I sniffled and wiped at my eyes. "That's what Jack said."

"And it wasn't what you wanted to hear, so you attacked him for it?"

I was silent. That's exactly what I'd done. I released a huge sigh. "I did attack him."

"Do you love him?"

I nodded, then remembered she couldn't see me. "Yes," I said quietly.

"Is this it? Do you think he's the one?" She could hardly keep the excitement out of her voice. Leave it to my mother to be curious about Jack's possibility as marriage material when I was in the middle of an emotional crisis.

"I'm pretty sure he is, yes, Mom." I realized how deeply I meant this and I suddenly felt an urgent need to see him. I didn't want to wait a minute longer.

Realizing what I had to do, I hung up and sighed. Jasper whined and I realized he'd been awake for almost an hour and hadn't been outside to pee. "Sorry, monster dog," I said, and got up to let him out. He trotted down the hall toward the back door, which I suddenly realized was flung wide open, swinging in the wind. The hallway was freezing.

"What the hell?" I said aloud. I glanced down the hall to my father's bedroom. That door was open, too.

"Shit," I said. "Oh, shit." I raced down to his room and looked inside. His backpack wasn't by the bed. The two drawers I'd filled with jeans and sweatshirts for him were empty; the prescription bottles on the dresser were full. He'd taken his sketch pad and his jacket and just like that—just like all the times before—he was gone.

December 2010
David

After sitting in his room a minute, David had gone to tell Eden a cup of coffee was actually a great idea, trying to be cordial after his angry outburst the night before. When he got to her bedroom door, he heard her talking on the phone. She was crying. He knew he shouldn't, but he pressed his ear up against the door.

"I think I need to commit him" were the only words he needed to hear before he spun back around.

Over my dead body, he thought. *I'm not going to get locked up like that again.* Who did she think she was, tracking him down like an animal and then trying to trap him in a cage? He loved his daughter, yes, but he would not stand for this. Not again. He refused to let Eden treat him like her mother had. He'd leave before that happened. He'd leave right now.

David tiptoed back down the hall and grabbed whatever clothes he could stuff into his backpack from the dresser. He left the pills, of course. Let her see that and understand for once and all that she could not force him to swallow them. He was done being medicated. Evil rhythms chanted in his head, urging him on, telling him it was the right thing to leave. They even told him to sneak some money from her purse—just enough to buy a bottle and a room to sleep in. He grabbed his sketch pad and his pencils and out the back door he went.

It was a cold, dark December morning. Sharp little pellets of frozen rain struck him as he moved down the street. He didn't care. He put his head down, tucked his hands into his pockets as deep as they would go. He would find a room, then a liquor store when one opened. That was all he needed to be well and he'd be damned if he'd let anyone tell him anything different.

I pounded on the door to Jack's apartment, hopeful he hadn't gone back to the shelter after leaving my house the night before. It was five thirty and I'd spent an hour driving around my immediate neighborhood, looking for my father, without any luck.

My chest had been tight and aching as I drove to Jack's place, but I knew I needed to see him. I didn't call, too afraid that he wouldn't pick up. This was the kind of apology I needed to make in person.

When he didn't answer right away, I pounded again until I heard his footsteps coming to the door. "All right, all right," I heard him mutter. "Keep your panties on."

I smiled despite myself, remembering how Wanda had said those exact same words when Jack and I went to my father's old apartment building. The door swung open and Jack stood in front of me, a surprised look on his face.

"He's gone, Jack," I said. "I know I was a total bitch to you and I didn't sleep last night at all. And now he's gone." My teeth were chattering and I wasn't making any sense. All the profound, apologetic words I'd planned to say had completely left me.

Jack furrowed his eyebrows and ushered me inside. "Hold on, one thing at a time." He closed the door and led me into his living room and sat me on the couch next to him. He threw a thick down comforter around me and rubbed my upper arms briskly, trying to help me warm up. "Better?" he asked.

I nodded, my teeth still chattering. I'd driven around with my window down, looking for my father, yelling his name out until my throat felt raw.

"You don't look better. Let me get you some coffee." He entered his tiny galley kitchen and poured me a mug. I took it gratefully and let the hot liquid warm me from the inside.

Jack sat back down next to me and pushed my wet hair out of my face. "What happened?"

My bottom lip trembled as I tried to speak. "I was wrong last night, Jack. And you were completely right. I'm so sorry. I don't know what made me be like that. I was just so wrapped up in the idea of saving my dad. I couldn't listen to reason. You were right and I was wrong, okay? Please say you still want to be with me. If you don't, I'll understand, but right now, I really, really want you to say yes."

He chuckled and put his hands on both sides of my face. He leaned in and kissed me. "Yes. Yes, yes, yes. I still want to be with you. I was just pissed. I tend to bluster and run when I get pissed."

"Are you sure?" My eyes filled. "I haven't ruined everything?"

"Of course not. We had a fight. People do that, you know. But only the real grown-ups take the time to apologize. Even if it is at five thirty in the morning."

"Oh god, I'm sorry. Did I wake you up?"

"No, I had already made coffee and was about to take a shower. I didn't sleep last night, either, I felt so bad about how we left things. Now, what's going on with your dad?"

I took another drink of coffee, then leaned back against the couch and filled him in on what I knew.

"I've been driving around for an hour, screaming his name."

I laughed, a sharp, bitter sound. "I realize how stupid that is. He's gone. He didn't want to stay with me. I guess I don't blame him. Not with how I was treating him."

Jack looked thoughtful. "I didn't get the feeling he was going to bolt last night, even though he was angry. Did something else happen?"

I considered his question. "Nothing that I can think of. I was talking to my mom about the possibility of hospitalizing him and she was saying the same things you did about it. She also told me you'd like it if I said I was wrong."

He smiled. "I like it more that you came over to say it." He paused. "Wait, do you think maybe your dad heard you on the phone?"

I sighed and put a hand over my eyes. "Shit. You're probably right. He probably heard me and left. Damn it." I dropped my arm to my side. "I'm an idiot, you know that? What the hell was I thinking, bringing him up here and trying to mold him into this idea of a father I've made up over the last twenty years?"

"You were thinking you were going to help him," Jack said gently. "Maybe he'll come back."

"Maybe he won't," I said glumly. After everything I'd wished for, everything I'd hoped might happen when I found my father, I barely had a week with him and then he was gone. And it was my fault.

"You never know, Eden. He knows where you live now, right? And he knows about Hope House. Give it some time. He might just surprise you."

The rest of December flew by in a rush of work and holiday preparations. I tried to go about my days without thinking too much about where my father might have gone, but the fact that he'd left sat like a boulder in my chest. I kept busy planning meals for Hope House, working out a deal with Doug at corporate that any excess food supplies would be automatically routed to the shelter's kitchen as a charitable donation. Jack's clients were suddenly offered tasty treats like prosciutto-wrapped poached asparagus and black-truffle raviolis in addition to the regular menu of meals I organized. I kept my eyes open on Tuesday nights as I served dinner at the shelter, ever hopeful my dad might appear. I worried about him, especially when Seattle suffered an unusual cold snap right around Christmas. The snow fell and fell and Jack found himself filling the hallways of Hope House with sleeping bags and extra blankets, trying to accommodate as many people overnight as the building's fire code would allow.

Jack and I spent the holidays serving up as many meals as we could. I stewed huge pots of chili and hearty lentil soup that could be heated up when I couldn't be there, stretching our supplies as far as they possibly could go. Even still, we lost a few clients during the cold. Saturn froze in an alleyway down in Pioneer Square. His heart stopped while he huddled beneath the thin blanket he believed would keep him warm throughout the night. We held a small memorial service for him on New Year's Day. I wondered who would come to my father's funeral if he were to be found in an alleyway, too. My heart ached picturing him suffering this fate; my ears perked every time my phone rang, expecting I might hear from the morgue. Expecting to identify the body and tell him good-bye.

"Aren't you going to call Common Ground?" Georgia asked me one early January evening. "Maybe your dad ended up back there."

"I thought about it," I said as I tried to calculate just how many pounds of phyllo dough I'd need to serve mini spanakopita to five hundred people scheduled to attend a banquet the next night at work. "I was even going to write a note for him and leave it there in case he showed up again, but I feel like I had my chance and screwed it up. If he wants to see me, he knows where I am. I really don't think it's a good idea to hunt him down."

"Are you sure?" Georgia asked doubtfully. She picked up her glass of wine and took a sip. "If you found him, you could just explain you made a mistake and apologize. Start fresh with him."

"I can't, Georgia. After what I put him through I really feel like he needs to be the one to initiate contact. It's not that I'm not worried about him, because I am." I looked out the window at the dark night. I imagined him huddled on a street corner, not having enough money to get a room to sleep in. "But if I pursue him now, he'll just see it as me forcing myself on him again. I'm not going to do it. It goes against every instinct I have, but I feel like waiting for him to find me is the only way we'll be able to start over."

She sighed and set down her wineglass. "I'm sorry it worked out this way, sweetie. I really am."

I shrugged and gave her a small smile. "Me too."

"He's so talented," she said. "It's really just so sad." She threw her gaze to my father's painting of the Garden of Eden, which I'd hung above my fireplace. I'd taken the other paintings to Hope House, and with Jack's blessing I hung them in the hallway. The box of my father's things was packed up and put away, all except his letters, which I kept in the nightstand drawer next to my bed.

"A thin line between madness and genius, I guess," I said. I didn't think my father was crazy, per se. Chemically imbalanced, yes. But cognizant enough to decide the kind of life he wanted to live, even if that meant it was a life without me.

Despite my resolve not to look for him, after the holidays I did go see Wanda and asked her to keep an eye out for my dad, just in case he decided to visit her. I also invited her to come help out at the shelter, if she would like to get out of her apartment more.

"I'd love to. Not sure how much I can actually help, but I can talk." She reached over and squeezed my hand in her gnarled grasp. "And I'll let you know if your dad shows up here, honey."

"Thank you," I said.

"How's that handsome man of yours treating you?"

"Jack? How'd you know he was my man?"

She gave me a knowing look. "After you've been alive as long as I have, you know how to recognize these things. I could tell the minute you two sat down in my living room. He ask you to marry him yet?"

I blushed. "It's way too soon for that. We've only been dating a few months."

"You know when you know," she said with a gummy grin.

You know when you know, I thought to myself every time I was around him after that. And I did know. I knew I was in love with Jack. I knew he was the best man I'd ever been with. There was a gentleness about him that amazed me, a level of self-awareness and compassion I'd never seen. He was committed to the work he did but also could be silly and fun. One Tuesday night as I cooked sloppy joes for the Hope House clients, he pretended to be Princess Leia, placing hamburger buns next to his ears and prancing around the kitchen like a fool. "Help me, Eden West!" he cried in a girlish falsetto. "You're my only hope!"

"Carrie Fisher you are *not,*" I said, laughing. There was something cleansing about the easy happiness we shared. My heart was lighter than it had been in years, as if the heavy burden of all my father's secrets had finally been lifted. I felt comfortable and safe with Jack, compelled to tell him every one of my thoughts and feelings, even when it was a terrifying thing to do. He listened when I needed to speak about my father, held me when I needed to be held.

"You're just trying to get lucky," I teased him when he took the initiative to fix a shelf in my bathroom that had been broken for months.

"I got lucky back in October, when I met you," he said. There was not an ounce of insincerity in his words. For the first time in my life, I felt like I could fully trust a man. I felt like he knew everything about me and loved me anyway.

"Is he perfect *all* the time?" Georgia asked when I went on dreamily about some wonderful thing Jack had said or done. "I might have to hurl if he is."

"No," I said. "He's hardheaded and opinionated, too. And he gets pissed off when things don't go his way." Jack had yet to reach out to his own father, but I knew pushing him on the subject would only make him dig in his heels. I had faith he would do it when he was ready, just as I had had to wait to be ready to find my dad.

As the days passed, I tried not to think about where my father had gone. Was he back in San Francisco or Portland? Was he around the next corner I'd turn? I couldn't help but hope despite the disappointment threaded through my veins. I had to come to terms with the fact that I might never see him again.

"I'm sorry your dad isn't here to see you be so happy," Mom said during one of our Friday morning check-in calls. "With Jack, I mean."

The muscles in my throat tightened up. "I find myself looking for him at the shelter all the time," I said. "Ridiculous, I know."

"Not ridiculous," Mom said fondly. "Optimistic. It's one of your better qualities."

After we hung up, I thought about whether or not that was true. Was I an optimist? Or just delusional? I believed I'd find my father and I did. And even though it hadn't worked out the way I'd planned, my search had led me to Jack and to the shelter. I finally felt like I was contributing to something that made a difference in the world. Something that might give another person their own quiet reason to hope.

David missed his daughter, but he knew he couldn't go back. He'd looked too long and too hard to find a way of life that worked for him. If he went back to her, he knew he'd fall victim to trying to please her, to doing the dance he had done with Lydia time and time again. He went back to the life he knew, to sketching strangers for enough money to get by. To sitting on park benches and staring up at the sky.

He wanted to be the father Eden so desperately deserved, but after years of struggling, years of trying to force himself into a role he just couldn't play, he'd learned to settle into the man that he was. He was a man ruled by his demons, a man who didn't fit in. He chose a life on the edges of society instead of in the midst of it. It was the only way he knew, the only way he'd survive.

Still, he missed her. He would see a woman with long, black hair and want to run after her. He stuck close by Seattle in the months after he left her house. He fought against the urge to see her, to give in to her demands for normalcy—to conform. He knew they were both better for his staying away; the voices in his head counseled him against doing anything that would put his freedom in danger of being taken away.

And then the day came when David saw her. Not in person, not on the street, but in a newspaper he pulled from a garbage can. There she was in black and white, just as she had been in her culinary school graduation picture. Only this time, she stood in front of a small window. Her dark hair hung past her shoulders and she was smiling ear to ear in her white chef's coat. The headline read in bold, black letters: LOCAL CHEF OPENS THE GARDEN OF EDEN. David quickly read the story.

Eden West, longtime head chef of Seattle's largest catering company, Emerald City Events, has opened the doors on her lifetime dream: her own restaurant.

"I've been waiting for this day my entire career," West said with a smile as warm and welcoming as her café's elegant yet comfortable décor. The seasonal menu includes robust, spicy butternut squash soups in the fall, heirloom tomato caprese salads in the summer, and a few consistently amazing pasta dishes and seafood plates, like the ones this reporter sampled: smoked tomato risotto with prawns.

West supports a local homeless shelter, Hope House, by offering jobs in her

kitchen to the shelter clients who want to work. She also plans to mentor any of them as fledgling chefs, should they show any interest in the trade. West's fiancé, Jack Baker, is the founder and program manager of Hope House and silent partner in her restaurant. West continues to cook the Tuesday evening meal for Hope House clientele.

When asked why she was inspired to name her business the Garden of Eden, West credits her father, a talented artist who has battled mental illness most of his adult life. "He gave me my love of food and taught me how to plant a garden," she said. "He was the best father he knew how to be."

Choking back his tears, David carefully tore the small clipping from the paper and tucked it into the inside pocket of his coat, next to his heart. Within a few hours, his impulses took him and he made a decision. He hitched a ride to Portland, back to the city where Eden had found him. He thought distance might be the answer, but soon he found himself on the doorstep of Common Ground. He waited until he knew Matt was inside the building, and then he knocked.

"David!" Matt exclaimed when he saw him. "Long time no see."

David nodded, and Matt invited him in. They entered the living room, where David's eyes went straight to the painting of his daughter, the innocence and fear so perfectly captured on her face. It was an expression that had burned into his mind when she was a child, that blend of terror and hope he knew his illness created inside her.

"You haven't been admitted through the hospital," Matt said. "I would have gotten a phone call. What can I do for you?" He looked at David expectantly.

David stared at the painting, then turned his eyes to Matt. "I'd like my painting," he said. "I'd like to take it with me."

"Did you find a buyer?" Matt asked. "I thought you were dead set against selling."

"I was. I mean, I am." He looked at Matt with pleading eyes. "Please. Can I just take it?"

Matt reached above the fireplace and took the painting off its hook. "Of course," he said. "It's yours. Though I'll be sad to see it go." He handed it carefully to David, who held it gingerly in his hands. "You sure you don't want to talk to a doctor while you're here? We can get you all set up on another treatment plan," Matt said. "See if we can make it work for you this time around."

"I'm fine," David said. He was done with meds, done with doctors and their treatment plans. What was he being treated for, anyway? Not adhering to society's rules? He liked only answering to himself. It was the only treatment plan that seemed to work.

Matt wrapped the painting in a couple of thick plastic garbage sacks, taping the edges to protect the canvas from moisture. David thanked him and was soon on his way back north. It took longer than he thought it would to find a ride, but once he was safely ensconced in the backseat of a trucker's rig, he knew without a doubt he was doing the right thing.

It was a cold and sunny spring morning when the driver dropped him off on the Seattle waterfront. It was early yet; a low, white mist rested on the sound. The fishermen were loading up their trucks to take up to the Pike Place market but store owners had yet to unlock their doors.

David stood on a corner, considering making the hike to Eden's house, but he was too afraid she'd be there. He suddenly remembered the shelter Jack mentioned he ran, and quickly David scanned the area for someone he could ask for directions. His eyes landed on a man tucked up beneath a doorway off the side of the pier.

"Good morning," David said. "Do you happen to know where Hope House is? A shelter around here, I think?"

The man opened his eyes sleepily, his right arm curled tightly around a huge bottle of beer. "Over on Pine Street. Around ten blocks from here, near Pioneer Square. Good eats there, but don't think they serve breakfast."

David issued his thanks and walked in the direction of the shelter. The wind off the water was icy and brisk; the sun hadn't risen high enough in the sky to take the edge off the chill in the air. He tucked his coat around his neck and held tight to his belongings—the pack on his back, the painting he'd so carefully transported. As he approached Pine Street, David turned up the alleyway, thinking he'd be less likely to be discovered if he went to the back door. He hoped there was a sign so he could find the right building.

Halfway up the alley, a scent caught David's attention. A sweet aroma lifted on the wind and brushed past him. He quickened his pace, and as he did, the scent grew stronger. It was then that he saw it. A fenced lot filled with a crazy mess of flowers—a wild configuration of hyacinths and daffodils, tulips and pansies. He stood in front of the chain-link fence, the fingers of his left hand looped through the links. He'd never seen anything like this in the middle of a city, nothing so beautiful since he'd lived in the house with Eden and her mother those many years before. There was a sign posted next to the locked gate. THE GARDEN OF EDEN, it read in happy yellow print. FOR DADDY, it said in tiny letters below. David's eyes filled at the sight of his daughter's handwriting. He knew it was hers from the loopy *y* at the end.

He looked at the sky to make sure it was free of clouds; he didn't want the rain to ruin his gift. It was clear and blue as far as his eyes could see. Carefully, he unwrapped the painting he had retrieved. He touched the outline of his daughter's face on the canvas, gazed into her blue eyes one last time. He knew she would find it here. And then, without question, despite all that he had failed to be, she would know the truth. She would see the painting and have no doubt her father loved her still.

Acknowledgments

In the beginning, there was my friend and fellow author Sarah Pekkanen, who read early pages of this manuscript and said, "Yes! Keep going!" I am infinitely grateful for her kind words and encouragement to forge ahead with the story as it attempted to fight its way out.

I was thrilled to connect with Laura Meehan, whose keen insight and remarkable editorial skill saved me from death by overuse of the word "stepped," along with a few other grammatical tics that seem to plague me. Her input helped turn this story into what it is today, and I am so happy to call her not only my colleague but my friend.

For continued support, reassurance, and vast knowledge of the publishing industry, I am indebted to my agent, Victoria Sanders, who never fails to tell me the down-and-dirty truth and always, always makes me laugh. She is a loyal and wicked-smart advocate, and I cannot believe my luck to have her on my side. Thanks also to Victoria's team, Chris Kepner and Bernadette Baker, who provide expert assistance at a moment's notice.

There is little doubt that finding an editor who believes in your work is every writer's dream, and I am thrilled to have the privilege of partnering with Greer Hendricks at Atria Books. Greer is an impossibly kind, positive, and perceptive professional—her gentle guidance and inspired thoughts undoubtedly make my work better.

Many thanks to the other amazing people at Atria who make this writing journey possible. To name only a few: Judith Curr, Chris Lloreda, Paul Olsewski, Lisa Sciambra, Cristina Suarez, Rachel Zugschwert, Sarah Cantin, and Carole Schwindeller. I'm grateful for the entire sales team at Atria, who so graciously welcomed me during my trip to New York.

I spent many hours in the company of some astounding people while researching this book—huge thanks to the staff and volunteers at the AIDS Outreach Project & Snohomish County Clean Needle Exchange, including Cheri Speelman (program director), Matt Standerfer, Carrie Parker, Mike Blackshaw, Patty Hellman-Scherping, and Angel Chovanec, as well as the phenomenal clients who generously shared not only their meals with me but their stories. Cheri's many years of experience working with the homeless community informed much of Jack's viewpoint in the story—I am beyond grateful for her compassionate wisdom.

And finally, my life wouldn't run smoothly without my best friend and husband, Stephan, who joyfully cleans up the messes I make in the kitchen and takes the kids to the movies so I can write. Thank you for believing in me, loving me, and laughing with me every day.

outside
the lines

AMY HATVANY

A Readers Club Guide

Questions and Topics for Discussion

1. It's become a bit of a cliché that great artistry can't exist without some madness. Do you agree with this?

2. Though much is written in women's fiction about relationships between mothers and daughters, there is less emphasis on those bonds between fathers and daughters. In your opinion, how are they different, and how does a girl's relationship with her father impact how she develops as a woman?

3. Eden recalls that for years when friends asked about her father, *"I'd make up some story of how he lived in New York and traveled the globe looking for inspiration. It wasn't like he would come back to prove me wrong. And after all, considering the ugliness of the truth, it wasn't like anyone could blame me for wanting to lie."* Why do you think Eden lies? Is it because of the stigma surrounding mental illness, or is there something else at work? What role does shame play in abandonment?

4. How did the alternating perspectives of Eden and David affect your reading experience? Did knowing more about David's darker thoughts and actions make you feel more or less sympathetic toward him?

5. In one of the David chapters: *"The doctor had already decided how she was going to treat him after reading his chart. . . . Not one of them said, 'David, do you want to be on lithium? Do you want to stop drinking?' They all assumed that he would."* Had it ever

occurred to you that individuals with mental illness may not want to be treated or "cured"?

6. Though David wrote Eden many letters over the years, she never received them, as they were intercepted by her mother. Did you empathize with Lydia's decision? What would you have done in her place?

7. How do you judge David? Is he responsible for his actions?

8. As a young girl, Eden accuses Lydia of "giving up" on David. She responds, *"Maybe . . . [b]ut only because he gave up first."* What do you make of this idea? Is it Lydia's responsibility to try harder than David? Why or why not?

9. *"What did it feel like, I wondered, to have people on the street avert their eyes from you to avoid interaction?"* Did this novel make you think differently about how you interact with and look at homeless people?

10. Jack is careful to refer to the people who come to his facility as "clients." Why do you believe he does this? What do you think about it?

11. *"What was he being treated for, anyway? Not adhering to society's rules? He liked only answering to himself. It was the only treatment plan that seemed to work."* If David isn't committing any crimes, do you see any problems with him living as he chooses?

12. Jack is wary about Eden's eagerness to swoop in and save her father, once she finds him in Portland. As you were reading, did you share his hesitation, or did you empathize with Eden's approach?

Enhance Your Book Club

1. Consider reading *The Glass Castle* by Jeannette Walls as a group. Discuss how being raised by mentally unstable parents, who choose to live life in unconventional ways, impacts both Eden and Jeannette. For these women, do their choices as adults seem to be a reaction to their upbringing?

2. Imagine that you're the casting director working on the film version of *Outside the Lines*. Who would you cast in the roles of Eden, Jack, Lydia, David, and Georgia? What about Bryce and Rita?

3. Visit a local homeless shelter as a group—perhaps when the facility is serving meals to its clients. At your next meeting, discuss whether or not reading *Outside the Lines* affected your experience at the shelter.

A Conversation with Amy Hatvany

Your previous novel, *Best Kept Secret,* was told exclusively through the point of view of your protagonist, Cadence. What was it like to write from two perspectives in *Outside the Lines*? Did one voice come more easily than the other?

I thought jumping back and forth between David's and Eden's perspectives would be disconcerting for me as a writer, and in the end, it actually turned out to be invigorating. It kept my mind focused, and maybe even a little more motivated to keep writing. I'd finish one of David's chapters, and then be excited to find out what Eden's thoughts and feelings were about the same event or time frame. I think the alternate viewpoints worked out so well simply because this is not solely Eden's story, nor is it only David's. It's the story of who they are to each other.

I was honestly surprised how easily David's voice came to me. When I began, I thought writing from his perspective would give me a more rounded vision of him and his world, even if I ended up ditching the multiple perspective idea and writing solely from Eden's point of view. And then he turned out to have such a strong presence in my head, it just sort of took over and I ran with it.

Not only does *Outside the Lines* switch narrators, the novel also moves back and forth in time. Was this a decision you

made before you began writing, or did the story tell itself to you that way?

Moving back and forth in time was another technique I didn't spend a lot of time considering at the beginning; the idea popped into my head and I thought I'd give it a try and see how it worked. I figured if it was clunky or uncomfortable, it would, at the very least, help organize the plot's timeline. And then it turned out to be such a fun way to move through the story. Every time I sat down to write, my brain cells were hopping, pushing me to focus on time and circumstance in addition to which point of view I was writing from.

What kind of research did you do for this novel?

When the idea for the book first came to me, I was lucky enough to already be volunteering for a local program that works with the homeless population. I helped prepare a weekly meal and had the privilege of sitting down and getting to know some lovely people. Many were kind enough to share their stories with me; most just appreciated having a warm, safe place to connect with others in their community. Like Eden, I became the "Brownie Lady," based on the mocha fudge treats I'd bake from scratch each week.

Spending time with this subculture in our society was fascinating, and I learned so much—not only about them, but about myself. I learned that what most people want—no matter where they live—is to be heard, loved, and valued for exactly who they are. Our society spends a lot of time trying to meld us into what it thinks we should be, and I don't know about everyone else, but when I'm told I "should" do something, I tend to bristle and rebel. But when I'm met where I stand, accepted and loved for just being me, I can find motivation for growth.

Best Kept Secret is about a mother recovering from her addiction to alcohol. **Outside the Lines** is about a daughter searching for her father, a mentally ill man who is now living on the street. Can you tell us more about why you're drawn to writing about family dynamics, particularly those in which the parents are flawed?

Hmm . . . maybe that's a question for my therapist? Ha! Actually, the truth is I'm drawn to writing about family dynamics simply because I believe how we grow up shapes so much of who we become. And flaws are what make characters interesting!

I like to play with the concept of it's not what happens to us, it's how we respond to what happens to us that defines who we are. There's a lot of room for dramatic potential in stories where a parent struggles with something to the point that it impacts the family. I was especially drawn to writing about the father-daughter dynamic in this book because I think it often goes unexamined. That relationship has such an influence on who a woman ultimately becomes, and how we relate to our fathers is often the basis of how we relate to all men.

What led you to the epigraph that you chose for this novel? How does one distinguish between a little madness and too much madness? Where do you think David falls in that spectrum?

I love that particular quote about madness, because from my perspective, it encourages creative risk taking, and the sense of freedom that comes as a result of leaping off the ledge into an entirely different world of writing a novel.

As for how you distinguish between a little and too much, I think when a person's "madness" becomes a physical threat to other people or damaging to society in general, that's when it crosses the line. David teeters on the edge of too much, which for me is what made him so interesting to write about. Take away his madness and who is he? Is he the same person, or just a dulled-out, gray version of himself? Only the readers can decide that for themselves.

Some of the most interesting dynamics in this novel are between Eden and her stepfather and Eden and her half brother. What did you draw upon to craft these relationships?

Because I'm remarried, I'm part of a blended family and have witnessed the dynamics of one firsthand. I'm lucky that my daughter adores her stepdad, but I thought a lot about what it would be like if she didn't. I wondered what would happen if a daughter canonized her birth father to some degree and therefore had a difficult time fully connecting with the man who took over that role. Eden has a complicated relationship with her stepdad: on one hand she appreciates the comfort he brought her mother after so many years of strife living with David; on the other she resents that he is in her life because what she really longs for is David.

I loved writing about Eden and Bryce's relationship. I've watched how my son connects with my stepdaughter—they have a sweet, fun sibling relationship (except when he's purposely annoying her, as ten-year-old boys will do!). There's something in how they relate to each other that's fundamentally different from how my son relates to his sister, and I attempted to capture the strength of that connection between Eden and Bryce.

What made you decide to end the novel with David's perspective?

I didn't! I was writing and writing, worried about how I was going to end the book. I knew that David would run away from

Eden again, but I had no idea how to find the natural finish of the story. I was a little panicky, to tell you the truth. And then, I wrote Eden's "final" chapter, and knew that the reader needed to see how David ended up, so I kept going. The idea of him going to get his painting of young Eden and bringing it back to the shelter just flew out of my fingers as I typed—it was one of those rare, wonderful writing moments when I'm not really in charge of what's ending up on the page; the story was telling itself. David made it very clear to me throughout the book how much he adored his daughter. For me, that was a perfect note to end the book. I wrote that last sentence, tears welled in my throat, and I knew I was done.

You do a wonderful job capturing the experience of mental illness. How challenging was it to do this?

I think the most difficult part of writing David's viewpoint was to keep the balance between lucidity and his illness. I've struggled with depression at certain points in my life, so I pulled from those feelings and amplified them for David. I know what it is to have thoughts spin in my head, so I just took that experience to an extreme. Some of his darker thoughts and behaviors were painful for me to write. I cared about David and was rooting for him along the way, but I also knew I wanted to remain true to who he was.

When is your favorite time to write? Do you have a favorite spot, as well?

The mean, nasty editor who questions the value of my writing lives in my rational brain, so if I can, I like to write first thing in the morning, when that side of my mind is still sleepy and incoherent. But with how crazy busy my life is, that's not always possible, so I've gotten much better at fitting writing into the corners of my day, like "dinner is in the oven, I've got forty-five minutes—let's see how much I can get done!"

My desk is in a main thoroughfare of our house, and most of the time, that's where I work. I would love a "room of my own" someday, but for now, this spot, along with noise-canceling headphones, is more than enough!

David seems to suggest that his mental illness is just a different kind of normal, a different way of living—yet his mental illness seems to also lead him to abuse alcohol. In your opinion, does this invalidate David's argument?

I think his argument is simply a way for David to rationalize his choice to live the way he does, and I certainly won't say that living day-to-day anesthetized by alcohol is "normal" for most of society. But in the end, I think his point that it's his right to make that choice is valid.

With his steadfast refusal to traditionally medicate himself, I was attempting to illustrate the point that when a person has help thrust upon them, rarely is it well received. Whether it's alcoholism or mental illness, if the person isn't on board with getting treatment, it won't succeed. David chooses to "manage" his illness with alcohol, because it still allows him enough lucidity to be himself. Is that the right choice? Maybe not. But right or wrong, healthy or not, ultimately, it's his decision.

What do you hope readers take away from *Outside the Lines*?

I think more than anything, I hope that readers will walk away from the story affected by both David's and Eden's emotional experiences. I think it's easy to feel empathy for Eden, maybe less so for David, but I hope that what I've written might encourage readers to see him in a different light.

People who suffer from mental illness are often defined by their disorder, and who they are as a person—the fact that they actually *are* a person—gets lost amid the diagnoses. Whether or not they agree with the decisions David made, I hope readers will be compassionate and understanding about his right to make them.

What are you working on next?

My next novel explores what happens when a woman who'd previously decided to remain childless falls in love with a divorced father and is suddenly thrust into a full-time motherhood role. Blended families are so common in our culture, and I wanted to delve into those complicated emotional dynamics, especially when one person isn't exactly sure she should be part of them.

I also have a few more ideas brewing in my subconscious, and I'm working on fleshing those out, too. I'm always a little frightened the concepts for novels will stop coming, but somehow, they crop up in a flash of thought, and I latch on, ready to go for the next ride!